The Omega Series
Run, Omega, Run

By: Pamela R. D'Addato

BLVNP

ISBN: 978-1-68030-985-0
© **Pamela R. D'Addato 2018**

Please feel free to send me an email. Just know that my publisher filters these emails. Good news is always welcome.

Pamela R. D'Addato - pamela_addato@awesomeauthors.org

Sign up for my blog for updates and freebies!
pamela-addato.awesomeauthors.org

Copyright © 2018 by Pamela R. D'Addato

All Rights reserved under International and Pan-American Copyright Conventions. By payment of required fees you have been granted the non-exclusive, non-transferable right to access and read the text of this book. No part of this text may be reproduced, transmitted, downloaded, decompiled, reverse-engineered or stored in or introduced into any information storage and retrieval system, in any form or by any means, whether electronic or mechanical, now known, hereinafter invented, without express written permission of BLVNP Inc. For more information contact BLVNP Inc. The publisher does not have any control over and does not assume any responsibility for author or third-party websites or their content. This book is a work of fiction. The characters, incidents and dialogue are drawn from the author's imagination and are not to be construed as real. While reference might be made to actual historical events or existing locations, the names, characters, places and incidents are either products of the author's imagination or are used fictitiously, and any resemblance to actual persons living or dead, business establishments, events or locales is entirely coincidental.

About the Publisher

BLVNP Incorporated, A Nevada Corporation, 340 S. Lemon #6200, Walnut CA 91789, info@blvnp.com / legal@blvnp.com

DISCLAIMER

This book is a work of FICTION. It is fiction and not to be confused with reality. Neither the author nor the publisher or its associates assume any responsibility for any loss, injury, death or legal consequences resulting from acting on the contents in this book. The author's opinions are not to be construed as the opinions of the publisher. The material in this book is for entertainment purposes ONLY. Cover image from Shutterstock com.

Table of Contents

Chapter 1 1

Chapter 2 12

Chapter 3 22

Chapter 4 40

Chapter 5 56

Chapter 6 70

Chapter 7 78

Chapter 8 86

Chapter 9 92

Chapter 10 103

Chapter 11 114

Chapter 12 121

Chapter 13 131

Chapter 14 138

Chapter 15 150

Chapter 16 155

Chapter 17 163

Chapter 18 170

Chapter 19 181

Chapter 20 190

Chapter 21 201

Chapter 22 219

Chapter 23 230

Chapter 24 250

Chapter 25 263

Chapter 26 270

Chapter 27 278

Chapter 28 289

Chapter 29 296

Chapter 30 307

Chapter 31 315

Chapter 32 324

Chapter 33 331

Chapter 34 342

Epilogue 349

To Aunt Carol for inspiring me to write.

FREE DOWNLOAD

 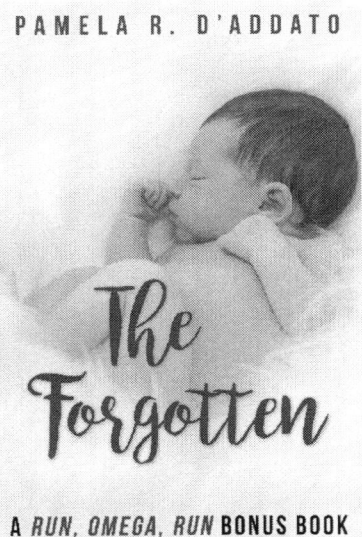

Get these freebies and MORE when you sign up for the author's mailing list!

pamela-addato.awesomeauthors.org

Chapter 1

Celia

My lungs burned, and tears spilled down my face like a waterfall. Crying while running was difficult, and I could hardly see where I was going, but I had no other choice. Would I rather suffer a penalty worse than death or run from all the pain in the world? The only option I had was to run away from the life I had back in my old home, my old pack. My heart raced, and my hands began to sweat even in the freezing temperature I was enduring.

It was almost impossible to run in torn leggings that were two sizes too small, but they were the only clothes I owned. The brown shirt that had once been white as snow stuck to my body like a second skin. It was only a tank top, and it was at least twenty degrees below freezing. My feet were cold, with just a completely torn sock on my right foot. The five-inch snow instantly froze my blood-covered feet.

Trying to wipe off the blood on my hands onto my shirt only seemed to make it worse. The scent caused me to wrinkle my nose in disgust, but I had to keep running. There was no turning back now. My chattering teeth and the hairs on my arms sticking up would easily draw attention I didn't want. The tears leaking from my eyes stuck and dried up with the speed I was going. Werewolves were naturally fast and could smell within miles away like bloodhounds. If I were to walk in the wrong direction with the wind, I could have been easily be discovered.

My hair whipping annoyingly across my body suddenly caught a tree branch, and I screamed in pain. I clutched the caught locks and tugged it out of the pine to relieve the pain. The sap stuck in my hair, but I tried not to mind how annoying it was. As a lower class pack member, I was used to being dirty. Rubbing my scalp, I paused when I heard a chorus of howls in the distance behind me.

It didn't take long for me to figure out that the pack noticed I left. Turning around again, I sprinted off to avoid being caught and most likely killed for my assumed crime. My bare feet began to ache from the coldness of the ground. I could hardly tell how long I had been running.

Trees turned into a blur the more I ran. Howls and snarls grew louder, and the pounding of someone's paws grew nearer. My throbbing heart felt like it was about to jump out of my chest with fear.

How could I outrun an entire pack?

Making lefts and rights, hoping to throw them off my trail, did not work to confuse them. They were smarter than me, and I should have known that. I was about to give up when I felt a change in the wind. Sniffing, I suddenly realized something that made my heart ache in joy. I was in no man's land and out of Blood Moon Pack territory. I was safe from my pack, but there were other dangers outside of it.

Since it was not smart to travel on foot with my shivering human body, I began to shift into my wolf form. My hands became claws before shifting completely into those of a wolf's paws. I collapsed on all fours and heard the cracking of bones.

They rearranged smoothly, and soon, I was looking cross-eyed at my own snout. Fluffing out my fur by shaking my body, I lifted up my ears and tried to listen for any signs of a rogue wolf. They were the most dangerous since they were men and women who left their packs because of either crime or treason.

Opening my eyes wide in realization when I smelled something smelling of urine and death, I moved my head swiftly from side to side. Without any warning, my head was pushed into the white snow, and I grunted in mild pain. A menacing growl vibrated above me, and I froze in my spot. The growl seemed dangerous and full of power.

Before I could struggle or comprehend who tackled me, a pair of sharp teeth tore through the skin in my shoulder. I cried out in pain, my wolf form whimpering, and I struggled underneath the wolf's grasp. Beginning to shake with fear, I felt the teeth sink into my skin again, this time, ripping off a chunk of skin from my forearm. Tears threatened to leak from my wolf being, but I tried to stay strong. I could die here, and I would for sure be alone.

Werewolves were prideful beings. We did not cower from threats. However, I was more of the submissive kind. It wasn't entirely my fault I was an omega. An omega was a lower rank servant in a pack and had little to no food or clothing. They had no rights and could be instructed to do anything without objecting.

The wolf above me growled again and bit my ear hard. Crying at the pain again, I kicked my legs back. Wiggling awkwardly at the dangerous beast, I managed to push him off my body. Gasping in air, I shakily stood up. I needed to stay on guard or I could die in an instant.

I was injured on my left arm from the shoulder down. The wound throbbed and stung every time a snowflake would melt on it. Slowly and cautiously, I placed my paw down, darting my eyes back and forth. The wolf that had attacked me was currently circling my weakened body. Blood was pouring out of my scrapes and gashes, dropping on the pearly white snow. They were sizing me up, figuring out where my weakest point was.

The wolf snarled and lunged at me again, but I dodged him with intense struggle. Taking the chance I had, I scrapped my claws against the passing side. He growled in pain and skid to a stop on my right. I injured him, and that was enough for me to defend myself.

I sniffed the wolf's scent again, and I knew instantly who he was. The wolf was an alpha but not just any leader I had ever encountered before. He was the alpha of one of the only rogue packs. He was known for being vicious and untamed, but I had never seen him this close before. The strange thing was he was never a threat to my old pack. Why was he attacking me? The only possibility was that he discovered who I was.

Whimpering in fear, I slashed his eye when he got close enough and fled. I knew the amount of pressure I put into that attack would leave a scar. It would definitely trail from his eyebrow all the way down to the end of his chin. That would be nasty to look at from its diagonal pose, but it was my life against his.

That's why I ran as fast as my small and injured legs could take me. Trees blurred, and so did every other shrub. My breath came in short pants, and I couldn't take the lack of air my lungs were receiving. The blood coming from my gashes stuck to my fur and matted it to my skin. It would take hours to get it to shine again. Dripping down from my paw to the ground, the blood left a trail. There was no way I could let Blood Moon Pack track the prints and find me. Trying as best as I could, I covered the blood with clean snow, but this slowed me down.

I must've been running for at least an hour or so. I couldn't hear the pounding of a heart or feet along the snow, so that was a good sign. However, my wounds were beginning to take a toll on me, including the blood loss. Clumsily running into trees or bushes slowed me down even more. I tripped over a log once or twice, and even over my own feet. My head was aching, and my feet were growing weaker. I could hear how slow and tired my heartbeats had been getting. It was only a matter of time before I either froze to death or died of blood loss.

There was no hope for my survival.

That was until I heard the strength of two pounding hearts. I began to whimper and yap for any possible help. Running into another tree, I soon collapsed to the snowy floor. Being so dehydrated caused me to do the wildest thing such as eating the snow. It didn't taste at all satisfying the more I gobbled it up. I was weak and dying; I would do anything to stay alive.

I whined again for help, and that was at the same moment I heard growling and snarling. Looking through half-closed eyes, I felt the presence of two strong wolves. They snarled at me again, and I tried to lift my head as best as I could. My vision was foggy, and it was difficult to fight through death.

At that moment, I saw the two figures. They were two silver wolves whose fur blended well with the snowy floor. Unlike my pack's wolves that looked exactly like the Ethiopian wolf with their red and black features; these looked beautifully calm and relaxed. Although, the moment I looked into the wolves' eyes, all I saw were bloodthirsty animals.

I panted loudly and showed them my neck in a submissive way. *I'm not here to fight. Either end my misery or help me.* I begged in my head. All they did was stare at me dangerously and angrily. That was then that I noticed something. I was in their territory, and in enemy territory at that.

Suddenly, the larger and slightly more muscular wolf transformed into a human. If I weren't in wolf form, I probably would've blushed when the man stood stark naked in front of me.

I tried to avert my eyes from his lower abdomen at all costs. My breaths came out in pants until finally, the man spoke.

"Rogue, you are trespassing into Ice Moon territory. Shift now." It wasn't an order, but I knew better than to disobey when someone asked for something. However, before I could shift, he spoke again, "A woman?" He sniffed the air and growled.

I shrunk back, wobbling up to my feet by using the tree for support. There was only one thing to do if I wanted to survive. I had to attack him. Taking one step towards him, I began to sway back and forth. I probably looked drunk to him. Suddenly, I heard a loud crack and cried out in pain. My forearm just snapped like a toothpick. Surely, it was broken.

Collapsing to the ground only a few feet away from him, I began to whimper for mercy. I could feel my body shutting down with every movement I tried to make. My breathing turned into short quick pants, and I looked up at the now two naked men in front of me.

Their faces began to blur but then became clear, then went back to blurry. This repeated for a while until I felt myself being lifted up. I whined in pain and tried to thrash as best I could. With little success, I lay limp in the man's arms.

"She's pretty bad, huh?" the man carrying me stated more to himself than me.

"The alpha won't be happy about this, Adam," the other man said, and I could just make out him shaking his head.

"It doesn't matter. Injuring a woman is bad enough, but leaving her to die is going against how we were brought up. Besides"—I felt Adam's eyes flicker back to my panting and weakening form—"she could have a mate here. There is no mark on her, so she is obviously unmated."

"You better hope her mate is here or the alpha will lock her up and slowly kill her."

"I know."

I let out a loud howl of pain and looked at my body to see I was drenching Adam with my blood. It was pouring from everywhere, from my arm to my waist and further to my hind legs. There wasn't a single spot that was unharmed. His strong arms held my delicate frame close, and I could feel my wolf not enjoying the touch.

Eyelids growing heavy and heartbeat growing weaker, I knew I had to do something. However, I couldn't because my body went limp and I was engulfed in darkness. I could no longer hear, and I could no longer see. It was hard to say if I was dead or not.

***

Cooper

I groaned in pain when Sage's knee made perfect contact with my lower region. Obviously, she didn't notice how bad that hurt because she continued to climb my tall, built body. Traveling up my body, she wrapped her legs around my waist and clung onto me. Seconds later, she kissed my cheek, waking me up fully.

"Wake up, Cooper!" My six-year-old sister tried desperately to wake me up. It was around two in the morning, so there must be a reason why she was also up. She should still be in bed by now. Only seconds later, my bedroom door opened, revealing my other sister who crossed her arms over her chest.

"What is it, Paige?" I could tell how frustrated she was, but I was exhausted as well. It was only an hour ago that I managed to get to sleep.

"Sorry to interrupt your decade sisterly bonding, but there's a problem." I hated when she brought up the relationship between Sage and me. It always made me feel bad for hardly spending time with her. Being an alpha to such a large pack took a large portion of my time, and this included my capability to bond with my family.

It was difficult being a son, a loving brother, and a tough alpha every day. It was unfair to my loved ones, but I had to sacrifice for the pack. That's just what alphas were born to do. Then I noticed the second part of her sentence.

"What do you mean there's a problem?" I slowly picked Sage's now sleeping form and let her rest her head in the crook of my neck.

"The rogue you wanted Adam to eliminate that crossed into the territory. Well, he let it live."

I growled in annoyance and placed Sage on the couch before taking Paige's forearm. Leading her into my office next door, I slammed the door shut and exploded. "What do you mean he let him live? I specifically told your mate to kill him!"

My best friend and beta, Adam, was my little sister's mate. They were destined to be together, so I couldn't prevent from being together. Still, my beta was my second in command, and he needed to be there for me and not her at times. I hated it with passion, but I couldn't go against fate. There was no way I could keep them apart. I had tried in the past. However, it led to consequences that still bothered me to this day.

"That's the thing, you blabbering idiot!" she snapped, and I growled at her rudeness to her alpha. "It's a woman!"

"What do you mean a woman?" I snapped, slamming my fist against the dark cherry red desk.

"The rogue! Yeah? It's a girl." Paige explained, thrashing her arms around her. It had always been a habit of hers. "A female."

I raised my eyebrows in surprise but quickly covered it up.

Female rogues were extremely rare. It was frowned upon to kick a female out of a pack, no matter what she did. She could go to a cell, but it was dangerous to put a female in the wild. Execution was more approved than exile for them. Females were easier prey to rogues, and that's why they needed mates for protection.

"Where is she?" I seethed, pushing past my sister and out of the office. "Where the hell is that rogue?"

I got several mind-chats from different pack members telling me she was in the sitting room closest to the kitchen.

As a pack, we shared one mind. We were also able to connect to each other through our minds by speaking and sharing feelings. It was hardly used in our everyday life, but we used it for emergencies like this.

I made my way towards my objective. My claws were slowly coming out from the tip of my short nails. I could feel my eyes growing dark with rage. I hated rogues with a burning passion. Male or female, they could be dangerous. A single rogue could potentially wipe out an entire pack. I needed to be careful. The females were generally the more manipulative ones.

"Wait, Cooper, you have to understand she's really hur—" I cut my persistently annoying sister, who believed she had the right to command me just because she was my beta's mate.

"Don't speak to me until I am calm enough to speak to you." I snarled before turning back around and walking fast to the sitting room.

The smell of blood hit my nose like a brick, and I tried to stop from scrunching up in disgust. What the hell? The smell was intriguing and quite riveting. My wolf that was like my conscience began to send me emotions I couldn't quite understand. It smelled metallic yet sweet like freshly baked brownies, but death lingered in the air. The moment I stepped into the bright room, I stopped dead in my tracks.

There, on my favorite coffee table, was one of the smallest wolves I had ever seen. Female wolves were relatively small, but she couldn't be larger than a full grown husky. Blood was stuck to her gorgeous black coat that matted to her skin. Her paws looked raw and full of blisters. What disgusted me the most was her broken arm that looked like a snapped twig.

I could see the bone poking through her skin. Before bile could rise in my throat at her condition, I felt my wolf stir inside of me.

He howled and screamed in happiness the one word I thought he would never say. "Mate!"

I was twenty-two years old, and most werewolves found their mates between the age of sixteen to twenty. I thought it would never happen. If you couldn't find your mate before or after you turned twenty, he or she could either be dead or lived all the way across the world. Finding out that my mate was here instantly made me feel overjoyed. I didn't even know I was capable of this emotion. I was always feeling the opposite of happiness or euphoria. I guess it came with my job.

Reality set in as I took in the state of my mate. Looking around, I spotted the pack doctor and instantly began barking orders. "What are you waiting for? Go get your stuff and meet me in my bedroom."

Sheila gave me a questioning look but left to retrieve her equipment. Meanwhile, I ran over to my mate and listened intently to her heartbeat to make sure she was at least breathing. It was wheezy and short, which worried me. Her heartbeat was irregular. She looked like she was dying, and I could do nothing about it.

Without a second thought, I carefully scooped her up in my arms, not before noticing the stain her blood had left on the table and on the floor. Requesting someone to clean it up, I carefully carried her wolf form up the stairs. Sheila wasn't far behind me when I walked up the long spiral staircase. The consequence of living in a four-story house when your bedroom was on the top floor was coming to light.

"Is she your mate?" Sheila asked, and I spared her a small glance before training my eyes on the black wolf I was carrying.

"Yes, but I need to know where she came from and who had the spine to harm her." I explained and ordered the closest pack member to form a running party.

"Yes, Alpha." The young girl nodded before going down the stairs behind me. She couldn't have been older than sixteen unlike my sister Paige who was seventeen. She looked so thin and frail, most definitely smaller than my sister. She almost looked sickly.

When we reached my room, Sheila opened the door to allow me to enter. Nodding in thanks, I walked in and placed my mate on the navy blue mattress before standing up straight. Turning my attention to Sheila for a split-second, I told her to do everything she could to save my mate. She didn't argue and sat on the corner of the bed.

Letting her do her job, I began to form a plan. Whoever hurt my mate better be prepared to die a painful death. No matter the consequence, I would make the person suffer, wolf or human.

Chapter 2

Celia

Groaning softly, I slowly opened my eyes. My surroundings blurred a bit, but the more I blinked, the clearer it got. That was when I was greeted with an unfamiliar. My eyes opened wide in fright, and I looked around the room, memorizing every detail to figure out if I was kidnapped.

I was placed gently under the covers of a navy blue bed, perfectly tucked in. The walls were a soft grey color, and the door in front of me was black. I'd never seen a room with this much furniture: dressers, desks, nightstands, and even a huge TV. Pictures around the room showed a stage of someone's childhood to present day. There was even one of a hockey player holding up some big trophy. Then there was a picture of a man carrying a little girl on his shoulders and a girl a little younger than him by his side. He was smiling in some of the pictures, while most showed him with a straight face and not even looking at the camera.

I heard movement in the room and looked around to see a figure facing away from me behind a desk. He was mumbling some words that I couldn't make out clearly, but I could tell he was annoyed about something. Papers were spread out around the large desk, and he would constantly move them around into different piles. The man let out a growl of annoyance, and at first, I thought he knew that I was awake, but then I heard him toss a crumpled paper in the garbage and take out a laptop.

Carefully, I threw the blankets covering me and shifted to the side farthest from him. Since he was on the right side of the room, I moved to the left. The moment my feet touched the wooden floor, I saw his ears perk up, and his head moved a bit. I stayed still, and he soon shrugged it off and resumed his tense position.

When I stood up, I instantly regretted it. My muscles screamed at me to sit back down and relax, but I wouldn't let that happen. I was dressed in a silk nightgown that went just below my knees and was surprisingly comfortable. Looking at my body, I realized that almost all the scratches were healed and were now just a faint mark. Disappointingly, my left arm was in a cast and hanging in a sling, while my shoulder had a large gauze pad taped on it.

With one last look at the man who was so occupied with what he was doing, I quietly made my way to the door. His back was still on me, and when I was at least a foot away from the door, I turned one last time. My eyes widened in fear when he was no longer in his chair, behind the desk. Taking my chances, I grabbed the doorknob and prepared to run out the door when a figure stopped me.

The man stood between the door and myself. His form was tense and a little confused when I stepped away. My heart was pounding a million miles a minute, but that didn't stop my overwhelmed mind. There was a gap in my memory, and I found it hard to understand where I was and how I got to where I was. I wouldn't be surprised if he heard it loud and clear. His expression was seemingly emotionless yet stern. He must've been important with his large muscles and frame. Even if I hadn't noticed his body type, the way he stood looking proud and powerful told me he was no ordinary member of the pack.

"Rest or you'll hurt yourself." He commanded, and I shivered at his voice. A smug look crossed his face when he noticed. "Your body is already reacting to me. Good."

"What do you want from me?" I trembled, taking a step back, which resulted in him taking a step forward. "I won't t-tell anyone I was here. You can let me go."

Confusion crossed his face, and I faintly heard him say, "What did Sheila do to you?" However, before I could ask anything, his face became firm, and he spoke again, "Rest. I'll come for you in a bit. I have things to do first."

I didn't move, and he soon became irritated. When I saw this, I walked back to the warm bed and sat in the middle. He nodded in a small thanks and left the room, carrying a few papers in his hand. Crossing my ankles, I hugged my knees close to my chest. The last thing I remembered was me being carried off. Where was I? What would he do to me?

Feeling very alone, I tried to contact my wolf, but she didn't answer. In this circumstance, I needed my her opinion. I tried again and scrunched my eyebrows in confusion when all there was was silence. Why wasn't she answering me? Reaching for her one more time, a wave of fatigue hit me, and I had to lay down.

Moments later, the door was swung open. I lifted my head tiredly to see who it was. It was a woman who must have been in her mid-thirties. She was carrying a large bowl of something with a delicious scent. She gingerly placed it on the nightstand and sat on the corner of the bed with a soft smile.

"My name is Felicity, the pack chef. You are?" she asked kindly. Her body language told me that she was a lower pack member.

"Um…I'm sorry it's just that—" I spoke, but she instantly cut me off.

"Right, my apologies. I shouldn't have been so straightforward." She chuckled a bit before sobering up. "The alpha asked me to bring you something to eat."

I looked at the steaming liquid inside the bowl beside me. Looking at it with uncertainty, I turned back to Felicity and asked, "What is it?"

She looked at me with confusion as if I were some alien. "Why, it's roasted chestnut soup with thyme cream. It's very healthy for you. Believe me, it's delicious." Reaching over, she placed the bowl on my lap. "Eat."

Smiling kindly at her, I dug into the creamy orange soup. A burst of flavor hit my dry mouth, and I held back a moan. Never in my life had I tasted something as good as this. Stirring the soup, I couldn't help but wish I knew how to make this. It went down my throat like silk and warmed my belly immediately. With the rank of an omega, I never got such pleasures in my life.

Disappointingly, I was halfway done with it when I felt very full. Putting in one last spoonful into my mouth, I thanked her and left it on my lap. When I looked back at her, she had worry lines all along her forehead.

"That was barely a cup that you ate, and you're already full." She seemed to be thinking hard about something. "How much food did you intake on a daily basis?"

I thought for a moment about how many days I would have a single non-filling meal. Coming up with the right time, I told her. "I would eat possibly every other three days with a small portion of leftover bread from the feast the alpha would throw every week."

She took an intake of breath, and her eyes seemed to darken. Slowly, she got up from the bed and left the room with my half-eaten bowl of soup. Shrugging it off, I lied back down and went under the covers to relax. Whatever was in the soup sure made me drowsy.

Closing my eyes, I welcomed the tiredness easily and quickly. That was when, for the first time in a while, I had a dreamless and nightmare-free sleep.

**

I was woken up by a large growl from downstairs and the stomping of feet traveling upwards. Trying to ignore the noise, I snuggled closer to the nice smelling pillow. But my brief rest was soon interrupted by the bedroom door slamming open. Almost immediately, I then heard it close with a loud bang. My eyes slowly opened, and I turned my head towards the noise to see who entered the room.

"What pack were you from?" He boomed, and I jumped in surprise and fear, shrinking back closer to the pillows.

He sighed at my terrified form and sat at the corner of the bed. Speaking in a gentler voice, he spoke again, "What pack were you from?" I soon noticed he was the man from before. He was the same man I had spoken to not too long ago.

"I'm not exactly…" I stuttered, trying to sort out the words to say. "I can't say that I am."

"Were you from Midnight?"

I shook my head.

"Eclipse?"

Once again, I shook my head.

"Dark Moon?"

I did the same.

"Were you from a pack?"

This time, I nodded.

Sighing, he stood up and walked over to the windows. He began opening the curtains, letting the light in. Doing the same thing to the other window, he positioned himself on the window sill. His body was very tense, and I felt bad for him for the amount of stress he must take up every day. I was around my alpha often back in my old pack. I could recognize one anywhere. He most definitely was one, and now I could clearly tell.

"Your wolf won't recognize me until tomorrow. I had the pack doctor put her to sleep so you could shift back to human form. You would've died from your wounds if it wasn't done," he explained. "She'll be back, I promise."

If my body was forced to shift back into human form, then that could only mean one thing—someone saw me naked. Regardless of whether it was him or not, it upset me. No one was allowed to see me like that but my mate, and since I hadn't found mine, this embarrassed me completely.

"You saw me?" I hissed. "What is wrong with you?"

"Listen. I—"

"All you alphas are just disgusting jackasses! You're all the same!"

Anger flickered in his eyes, and I instantly regretted what I said. Placing a hand over my mouth and keeping it there, I felt fear rise inside me, and a sob threatened to break out. Never in my life had I lashed out at an alpha. They'd been known to have short tempers, and purposely getting one riled up was suicide.

"Speak to me again like that, and you will regret it," he said in a deadly tone. "Do you hear me?"

"Yes." I whimpered, and he seemed to relax a bit.

"Good, then I suggest it's time for you to answer my questions."

Looking down at my hands, I nodded slowly. He rested his hands on his knees and leaned a bit towards me, which made me feel something I didn't know existed. Lust? Comfort? It confused me, so I just pushed the feeling to the side. I didn't know him. I shouldn't feel these things. Alphas weren't meant to give any emotions but fear to people.

"My name is Cooper Pierce, Alpha of the Ice Moon Pack. Can I have your rank, name, and pack name?"

I complied to his request and spoke, "My name is Celia, and I am an omega of the Blood Moon Pack."

It grew quiet instantly. All you could hear was my weak breathing and his strong heart pounding proudly in his chest. Alpha Cooper was silent and seemed to be thinking through something. Remaining where I was seated, I began to take in his appearance, which I didn't bother myself with before. The blessing of being an alpha was to be godly attractive yet intimidating.

Alpha Cooper must be around six foot four, an average height for an alpha. Wearing black jeans that clung to his legs made him very intimidating. The tight black shirt hugged his upper body, and I could see his muscles clinging onto him like another skin. The bumps and grooves from his eight-pack could be seen through his shirt. His biceps were perfectly chiseled, and it looked like the gods created the most amazing werewolf in the universe. He was very attractive.

Alpha Cooper's face was the epitome of perfection. It was perfectly sculpted with a strong jawline like most werewolves, but his outdid any man I had ever seen. His hair was a little longer than a crew cut, and I couldn't help but imagine how it would feel to touch. It was a copper color but looked brown with streaks of red. It was definitely a unique hair color. With full red lips that gave a peak of his pearly white teeth, I had the sudden wonder of how it would feel to kiss those lips. Those eyes were what brought me in, and I could stare into them all day if I had the opportunity to. It was the most beautiful blue color I'd ever seen—like aquamarine.

His nose looked like it'd been broken at least once but healed relatively fine. The Moon Goddess herself must have touched his face and sculpted his entire body.

"Your name is very pretty." He choked, but I could tell he was still bothered by the the pack where I was from.

Blood Moon had always been enemies with Ice Moon for as long as anyone could remember. Alpha Cooper had always been trying to agree to some term or treaty, but Alpha Zaire disagreed. Alpha Zaire had been my alpha and scared me to pieces. Blood Moon was filled with more dangerous criminals than all human prisons combined. On the other hand, Alpha Cooper could've picked some pretty cruel treaties. The man in front of me could be worse than Alpha Zaire.

I didn't say anything anymore to Alpha Cooper. I, instead, looked down at my long nails.

"I think you should rest some more. Your wound isn't entirely healed." Standing up from his position, he walked over to the door. "I'll be back when your wolf wakes up." He left without another word and closed the door behind him softly.

Now that I was alone, I tried to pass the time by letting the tears I had held in fall freely. The past couple of days had been frantic and full of heartbreak and loss. My chest ached, and I clutched it as if in fear of it being crushed. Sobs echoed inside the room, and I could only imagine Alpha Cooper could hear me.

I must've cried for at least six hours because when I gazed around the large room again, I noticed the moon had risen. Besides the lamp that rested on Alpha Cooper's desk, it was the only thing providing light in the room. Another wave of grief passed through my body, and I let the tears go down again. The fear of receiving the same treatment I got in my old pack caused more sadness to wash over me. Everything that had happened was like a bucket of cold water dumped over my body. I wanted to forget it all, but I knew that was impossible. What I saw would haunt me until the day I die.

A few minutes later, Felicity came in with a bowl of what she called vichyssoise. It looked good, and she told me it was basically a potato cream soup. Keeping my head down so she wouldn't see my tear-stained cheeks and red eyes, I thanked her and allowed her to leave. With that, I ate the soup in peace.

When I finished, I found it difficult to determine what I could and could not do. Making up my mind, I snuggled under the sheets and waited for sleep to come. Right when I was about to doze off, I heard the door open quietly and gently closed right after. The bed dipped for a bit, but the weight coming from the figure left as quickly as it came. A shuffle around Alpha Cooper's desk echoed throughout the dark room including the sound of the light flickering off. I could see through my eyelids that the light had gone off and heard the sound of leather coming in contact with a body followed by a loud grunt. I opened my eye slightly to see what was occurring. A figure was in the room, but I could hardly make out the figure before it relaxed in what must be a leather couch.

"Goodnight, Celia," the voice whispered softly before I dozed off entirely.

***

Sunlight leaked through the white curtains hanging from the windows beside me. Long streaks of light reflected on the dark wood floor below. The world was foggy around me, but it suddenly became clear when I heard the strangest noise. Someone was snoring, and to my slight amusement, it was loud.

Turning my head to the side, I was suddenly greeted with the one thing I'd been missing for the past twenty-four hours or more. My wolf. She was feeling on the edge, which told me I should be feeling that as well. Since she was my talking conscience, she had the ability to speak to me, though she didn't do it often.

What's going on? I asked, getting worried that she noticed something that I didn't.

Something's not right. She growled, and I instantly began to worry. If she thought something was wrong, she was always the first to know.

What's wrong? I questioned her, growing more and more worried.

The scent, I recognize it. It's...it's one of the most delicious scents I've ever smelled, she explained. I listened to her and took in a big whiff of the air.

She was right. The smell was mouthwatering. I absolutely craved it.

What do you think it is? I asked her.

Taking a big whiff, I could tell she was pleased with herself.

It smells like our mate.

Chapter 3

Frantically looking around the room, my eyes landed on a sleeping Alpha Cooper. He was snoring, and his long lashes were long enough that it almost brushed his cheeks. His entire body was sprawled across the leather sofa, his feet dangling off the side. *That's our mate.* My wolf smiled proudly, and I couldn't help but feel the same. Alpha Cooper was very handsome and attractive, and it would've been weird if I said I wasn't attracted to him.

Trying to sit up, I let out a whimper when my back collided with the backrest. With my hiss of pain, I knew he would've woken up from the noise. My thoughts were correct when he stirred in his sleep and opened his aquamarine eyes. When our eyes connected, he grinned as he sat up.

"Celia…"

"Are you…" I paused to collect my thoughts. "Are you my…"

"Mate?" He finished for me and nodded his head. "Yes."

Fear welled up in my body, and I felt my wolf worry the same thing. We were from rival packs, and I was an omega. I was weak and fragile, and with an alpha as a mate, he could easily hurt me without even trying to. What better way to avoid getting hurt than to do the unthinkable.

"Are you going to reject me?" I asked hesitantly. Alpha Cooper's eyes instantly went black, and he growled.

"No!" He barked, making me jump. "Why would you think I would do such a thing?"

Only a male werewolf could reject his other half. A man could tell his mate he was rejecting her and the reason why. This then would result in the bond being split and the two remaining mate-less for life. They could never reconnect the ties once they'd been broken. Many packs didn't allow the act to be committed, but not with my old pack, of course.

I tried to piece my words together, but I didn't get to speak when he moved to sit not far from me in a millisecond. He was seated on the bed now, only two feet away from me. Before I could ask, he took my small, cold hand in his large, warm one. Sparks erupted along my skin, making me shiver in pleasure. My wolf yipped in happiness and began calling out for me to mate him. Ignoring the urge to seek comfort from him, I pulled my hand away quickly.

Alpha Cooper showed no emotion, but I could tell that action hurt him. I knew he was curious as to why I moved away from him, but I didn't know what else to do. I was brought up differently than him and slightly feared him. The main reason was he was an alpha and I had bad experiences with them.

"I'm sorry. I just—"

"How old are you?" he asked out of the blue, and I looked directly into his inviting eyes.

"What?"

He rolled his eyes at me. That little gesture for some strange reason got me mad. "How old are you, Celia?" When my name flew off his tongue, I couldn't help but shiver at the way he said it. My name sounded so much better coming from his inviting lips.

Realizing he was waiting for an answer, I snapped out of my little ogling and answered, "Nineteen."

Alpha Cooper paused before speaking, "Twenty-two." I guess that was his age since he didn't exactly clarify it. "You should wash up. I can send up my mother to help you. Unless you want me to…"

A blush tried to creep up on my face, but I tried to hide it. "Um…your mother would be nice, but I think I'll be fine on my own."

He paused, and I could only guess he was mind-chatting with his mother. "She'll be here soon. Let me know if you need anything."

Standing up from the bed, he swiftly left the room.

"But—" Before I could dispute, the door closed behind him, and not a second later, a woman around five foot six walked in.

The woman was carrying a bundle of clothing in one arm and placed it on the bed. She had long curly blond hair that went down to her mid-back and a half fringe on her face. It covered one of her eyes, so I could only see one bright blue eye. The heels she was wearing were intense, and I couldn't see myself wearing a pair, even for my short height.

"Good morning, Celia," she greeted. "I'm Cooper's mother, Emilia."

"Hello." I didn't know how to address the former luna, so I hoped that was appropriate.

A luna was the alpha's mate, just like how a queen was to a king. She had the opportunity to make decisions and offer treaties. She was respected by everyone, and if she was disrespected, it was as if they were disrespecting the alpha. The luna was loved by everyone, even if the alpha was not.

Emilia chuckled and slowly slid down the covers I was holding. "That's exactly what I said when I met my mate's mother." Taking the warm covers away, she helped me out of bed, which I really didn't need. "Come on, hun. I won't bite."

Gaining my balance, I followed her out of Cooper's room for the first time. It was a very modern house. The flooring was covered with dark wood, and the ceilings were white with different black fine art. There were some mirrors here and there, but the place was mostly covered with black, white, silver, and some brown decor.

The hallway was wide and seemed to go on forever until Emilia turned right and pushed a door open. Gesturing for me to enter before her, I obliged and gazed at the room. It was beautiful like the rest of the house but was very small, strangely. It was clean and polished, and there were candles everywhere. Fairy lights gave the room some romantic ambiance.

"This is one of our private bathrooms." She chuckled at some memory. "A lot of mating took place here." Shuddering in disgust, she let out a very unattractive snort. "Don't worry. It's been sanitized more times than a baby's bottom."

Taking her word for it, I watched her turn on the water and helped me get out of the nightgown. She didn't seem to mind since she easily got me through it, and I was now standing completely naked in front of her. I tried desperately to cover myself, but she only smiled and checked the water.

"Since I'm a former luna, it's my job to take care of the young and old." She explained. "I've seen more things than I would want to see."

I was still a little bothered, but when the bath in the middle was filled completely, she turned the tap off and waited for me to go in. She carefully slipped the sling off my arm and pulled the gauze pad off my shoulder. I hissed in pain when the cold air touched the burning skin. It would tend to be over a hundred degrees when healing. A rising temperature was normal for a werewolf. It meant that the wound was being taken care of.

Emilia guided me into the tub, and I was welcomed with a sense of warmth. Sighing in content, I heard her squirt some shampoo and began washing my now wet hair. The minutes went by quickly, and she was now cleaning my back very carefully. It felt strange having someone wash me, but there was no way I was going to lift my broken arm and wounded shoulder.

"What's this?" She softly touched the large scar on the lower left of my back. Hissing in pain, I turned around to face her and covered it up.

"It's nothing."

"Does Cooper know about it?"

"No, and he doesn't need to worry about me."

She looked at me strangely but nodded her head. I knew she was going to ask something, but the door flew open unexpectedly. We both jumped, and I tried desperately to cover myself. Emilia thought fast enough and pulled a warm washcloth over my most private parts.

"What is it?" She barked, and I jumped at her tone.

Someone cleared their throat, and I turned at the noise. There stood a male no more than eighty years old. He was scratching the back of his neck that was slowly growing red. When he opened his mouth to speak, nothing came out.

"Um...I'm sorry." He looked very uncomfortable. "I'll be leaving." I shivered when I caught the sight of him grabbing the hand of a woman around his age. The old man guided her away from the door before leaving himself.

The rest of the bath was filled with no more interruptions. Emilia pulled me out the moment I turned into a raisin and helped me with the towel. She took very good care of me while drying me up, mindful of the bruises and wounds on my body. As soon as we were done, she made me follow her back to Cooper's room.

As one would expect, his room was neat and tidy when we entered. Emilia shut the door and this time, locked it securely. That was when she helped me get dressed into something more comfortable. Never in my life had I ever worn something so warm and soft on my body. It was loose on my skin but remained fuzzy and soothing.

"There you are." She beamed before pulling out a comb in her back pocket and sat me on the bed. "Now what are we going to do with your beautiful long hair?"

It's true that my hair had never been cut ever in my life. Sometimes I would tear at it, causing split ends but nothing major. That's probably the reason why it was down to my knees and still continued to grow. However, I liked it long, but it could get in the way. I never knew what to do with it, and cutting it scared me.

Answering her own question, Emilia began to brush it and let the end rest on the bed. Since I was facing away from the door, I didn't know who had entered when it opened. Ignoring it, I allowed her to continue brushing. The feeling of the brush stroking my scalp down to my back and the way she softly pulled the end of my hair on the bed was very relaxing. She stopped suddenly, and I was about to ask her why until I felt her setting the strands into sections.

She must have split my hair into five sections before she began to braid at the side of my head. Weaving quickly, she finished soon and tied the ends together. Her hands moved lightly, pulling my braids over my right shoulder. I looked down at the braids, and I had to admit, despite its ugly color, it looked really beautiful.

My hair was snow white. It was perfectly straight with not even a single natural wave. To be honest, I hated the color and wished it had more curls like the former luna. The part was crooked at the top of my head, but I didn't mind. It just added to all the flaws my body had. I had been very insecure after receiving negative comments about my looks.

"Thank you, Emilia," I gratefully said.

Emilia stood up from the bed, and her blond curls bounced happily as she exited the room. With her confident strides, coupled with a nice pair of heels, she could, no doubt, pass as a runway supermodel.

I began to slowly trace the braid on my shoulder. This was the first time someone had braided my hair, and it came out beautiful. The girls back in my pack sometimes braided each other's long chocolate or red curls. I had tried to do it by myself since no one offered to braid mine, but it always came out tangled and uneven. I wish things could've been different back then.

"Your hair looks nice."

I looked up at the voice only to see a back turned towards me. He was facing the desk, as usual, and sorting papers. The laptop was glowing brightly, and I could see he had typed out something. There was a portfolio in front of him, and I could just make out the face that he was examining. After staring intensely at it, he set it down and shuffled more papers.

Why does he always have to be so busy?

"Alpha Cooper." I greeted him, and to my surprise, he looked up from his desk and turned towards me. His usual bright eyes were now pitch black and terrifying. I couldn't help but feel sudden waves of fear run through me.

"Don't call me that," he stated, and I was about to question what he meant, but he opened his mouth again. "We are mates. We don't have to use formal words to each other."

"But—"

"Just don't." Cooper turned his head away from me and began to type quickly. He let out a sigh and flipped through some of his pages that were scattered in front of him. His fingers danced on the keyboard, but his eyes casually looked my way a few times. For the most part, his face remained solemn.

I wanted to get to know him more, but he was being very distant. And the only times I saw him alone was when he was staring at a screen or scanning through his towering stack of paper. I wanted desperately to know what's on his mind, but he wouldn't let me in. Perhaps he hated me for being a member of a rival pack and had no idea what to do with an enemy as a mate. That should be it, and he was probably disgusted with me.

Don't say that! My wolf howled, but I instantly pushed her to the back of my mind. Usually, I would listen to what she had to say, but she had been very annoying lately. My guess would be that Cooper was starting to bring out her more energetic side. In other words, the bond between her and Cooper's wolf was getting stronger.

Wasn't a mate supposed to be loving and always there for you? He hadn't even asked me if I was okay or how I got hurt. It's like he didn't want to get to know me for fear of me lashing out like I had done before. Maybe that's the reason he wouldn't talk to me—because I snapped. Was everything my fault? Or was it actually his?

"Stop." I heard him growl, snapping me out of my anger-filled moment. "I can sense that you're angry. I need to focus on this."

It hurt me for him to say that. I was his mate, and yet I wasn't being treated like his equal. It saddened me that it had to happen. In fact, it angered me that he was acting the way he was. He needed to be kinder to me if he wanted to show me that he respected me.

"Celia!" Cooper growled, turning his head towards me. I jumped at his tone and shrunk back a little in his bed. He sighed. "We'll talk soon. I promise…Just let me finish this, and then I'm all yours." A shiver went down my back when he said he would be mine.

That was when I started to wait. Time ticked by, and soon, the bright sunny day outside turned to black. Felicity came into our room with two bowls of what looked like a brown ground meat covered in a reddish brown sauce. She called it chili.

The food had a hint of spice in it and tasted very good. I looked over at Cooper and saw that he hadn't touched his bowl.

At around eleven o'clock, my eyes began to feel very heavy. Looking over at Cooper again, I noticed that he was still wrapped up in his work like how he had been all day. After one last glance at him, I closed my eyes and fell asleep.

***

I sprinted as fast as I could up the stairs and swung the door open. My heart was pounding hard against my chest in fear. He had stopped mind-chatting with me. Why would he block me?

I ran down the hall until the sickly smell of blood filled my nose. Stopping in my tracks, I came upon a large room, much like a ballroom. Allowing my senses to guide me, my bare feet suddenly touched something warm and wet. I looked down. What a mistake that was. It was everywhere around the floor—smeared into paw prints and later, hands. Puddles surrounded the floor and grew bigger the further I walked. It felt disgusting on my toes. It looked like someone had painted the entire room with blood.

I stopped when I saw exactly what I feared. In the center of the room was a naked body. Tears welled in my eyes as soon as I recognized the man. I ran over to him. His chest was covered in slashes and claw marks. Blood was still pouring out of his wounds, making me whimper as my stomach started to churn.

"No, no, no, you can't leave me." I begged, brushing his platinum blond hair out of his eyes. Fear was evident in them. "Please don't."

Touching his eyelids, I slowly brushed them close and cried. I tried to put pressure on his already dead body, begging for him to wake up. I apologized to him for letting this happen to him. I should've kept an eye on him. This never would've happened if he didn't find out. I was so stupid. Blood still seeped from his slit throat while bile threatened to spill.

My hands were soon coated with his sticky blood, sticking under my dirty nails and spreading onto my shins like another skin. The blood was smeared all over what was once a strong and young body. I couldn't take it. Although he wasn't my mate, he was the only person who could have helped me, saved me someday, and gave me true happiness.

"Please, I need you." I sobbed. "You can't…you can't be dead."

Hearing a growl, I looked up and saw a red and black wolf stalking closer to me. Blood was smeared on her muzzle and paws. My reflection showed through her raging black eyes. I clutched onto his body for dear life despite knowing he could no longer help me.

Lunging at me, I toppled over and cried when she bit into my wrist. Small scratches came after, and I felt her slowly tearing my body apart. I was crying out for help, for anyone to save me. The pain was unbearable, and I began to beg for death. It didn't matter if I died. I knew my real mate would find a better woman someday—a human maybe. Losing the one person I needed made me shatter into a million pieces. I didn't deserve to live a good life after all my mistakes.

"*Someone help! Please!*" I cried, trying to push the beast off me, but it was no use.

Then a voice came, and it felt like a sudden earthquake had occurred around me. "*Celia! Celia!*"

***

I opened my eyes and sat up quickly, causing me whiplash. I tried to ignore it as I became aware of my surroundings. My body was hot and coated with slimy sweat. A few strands of hair stuck to my neck and forehead, making it itch. The warm shirt I was wearing was drenched.

"I can't," I whispered, feeling the tears fall, and I quickly covered my face. "I can't! I can't! I can't take it." Curling myself into a fetal position, I tucked my head so no one around me could see.

Warm yet rough arms engulfed me in an embrace, and I tried desperately to fight it. I wiggled and squirmed, but the tight grip was too strong for me. Soon, I leaned into the figure's chest and cried my eyes out like a baby. He whispered soothing words to me, but none of them made me feel any better.

When I had finished crying, he slowly laid me back down on the mattress and began drawing patterns on my uninjured forearm. My body was facing the ceiling, but I was focused on half of the body that was hovering over me. I could tell he was tired, and I knew I must've woken him up.

"I'm sorry," I whispered, but he only hushed me and continued to trace something on my arm. "You can go to sleep now. I'm fine."

"No, you're not." Cooper argued in a hushed tone. "I'll stay up until you fall asleep again."

"But I woke you up. It's not fair of me not to let you rest."

"But that's what mates do."

***

The next morning, I felt physically and emotionally drained. When I opened my eyes, I came upon an empty room and bed. Growling in annoyance, I slid the bed sheets off me and slithered out of the empty bed. With a slight pain, I walked into Cooper's bathroom and looked at myself in the mirror.

My braid was messy and unkempt, so I slowly undid my braids and untangled it. When it was loose, I was surprised when it came out effortlessly and impeccably wavy. I ran my hand through it a few times, feeling the soft wave. It was amazing to finally have something so beautiful about me for the first time.

Placing the hair tie on the counter, I moved my hair out of the way to see my gauze-covered shoulder. Slowly, I peeled the tape away to look at the wound. I was kind of worried about what it would look like but pulled the rest away anyway while closing my eyes.

When I opened them, I saw to two surprises. One, the bite had mostly healed and was just a slowly fading scar on my shoulder. Two, Cooper had somehow appeared behind me, and his eyes were trained on the faint bite mark. I jumped a bit when I saw him but relaxed a little when he came up behind me and kissed the back of my head.

It felt nice for him to touch me, and when he hesitantly placed his large hands on my slim waste, I leaned into him. He breathed in the scent near my neck and planted a kiss behind my ear. This made my body shiver without me wanting to. It was pleasurable, and I wanted it.

With him still behind me, slowly traveling his hands up my body, he gently rested them on the lower part of my back. I sighed with contentment until he spoke, "The next time you get bitten here"—he touched the most fragile part of my neck—"it'll be when I finally mark you."

A mark was a claim that a mate generally placed on a person's neck. It let the others know that they were with their mate, and they were off-limits. I heard it could be painful, but it was one of the nicest things to happen to anyone. A mark also protected women when they traveled alone so no one could hurt them without facing another man's wrath.

Kissing the back of my head once more, Cooper swiftly left the room without another word. Breathing in annoyance, I grabbed the elastic and tied my hair up before walking back to his room. However, when I entered, I collided with a wall. Strangely, this wall caused sparks to erupt in my body. Rubbing my head, I looked up to see a very tattooed back. It was Cooper, and when he turned around, I noticed just how shirtless he was.

He had a perfect eight-pack and a well-sculpted V on his hip bones that would make any girl go crazy. His chest was hairless and looked as smooth as a baby's bottom. Muscles coated his entire upper body. What confused me the most was the tattoo on his back.

"What's that?"

He walked past me, and now his back was facing me again. The tattoo was full-on display, which allowed me to examine it. I'd seen a lot of tattoos, and most alphas had them to express power. Alpha Zaire had a few wolf tattoos across his shoulders and forearms. Cooper's, however, was very tribal and had solid geometric designs across his back. His hot muscles made it seem like the tattoo moved whenever he did.

My ogling was cut short because he reached into his dresser and pulled on a short white shirt over his body. He ducked under and pulled on one of his zip-up sweatshirts, only zipping it a fourth up his body, and then he made his way over to his bed and sat on it. I watched him pull out a very expensive looking watch, and he slipped it on also.

"It's a tattoo I got...maybe four or five years ago." Cooper explained, taking a pair of black boots and tying them on. "But I was drunk when I got it."

"I thought we can't get drunk."

He chuckled. "So did I."

Standing up again, he walked over to me and stood in front of me. Gently placing his hands on my hips, he pulled me so we were chest to chest. Although, I would rather call it head to chest because of my short body. It felt comforting for him to be touching me this way. Since we were meant to stay together forever, I would gladly welcome his touch any day.

"Turns out, I went to a bar to celebrate my eighteenth birthday and pretended to be an important celebrity." A giggle escaped me much to my surprise, and a big grin showed on his face. "I'm glad I'm the first one to make you laugh." His smile didn't disappear until I stopped laughing. "I know we need to talk, and we will, but—"

"You have your duties. I'll stay here." Regret crossed his eyes after I spoke, and he nodded slowly. After promising me he'd try to finish quickly, he kissed my forehead and left.

Alone for another time, I collapsed on the bed and tried to relax. Never in my life had I really relaxed. My life was filled with fear of so many things, and I never got the chance to unwind. All my life I lived in a state of dread and sorrow. I think it was time to finally slack a little since being an omega did take a toll.

Since I was an omega, there was only so much of what our body could take. Healing was a bit slower, and it would usually take weeks for a broken bone to fully heal and work again. I had jobs to do. One of them was taking care of the pups. This meant washing, cleaning, and changing, and nurturing each one. Though they were a pain, I did enjoy it.

Another job was cooking for the pack meals. Blood Moon had one large pack house, so cooking breakfast, lunch, and dinner was exhausting. Then there were those who wanted desserts, so I usually made ice cream, baked pies, cakes, and any sugary pastry on the planet. I was never told what I was making. I was only given the recipe. I recognized some of the dishes Felicity gave me but not all of them.

I had also been the maid in the pack which made me want to rip my hair out. Teenagers would always leave a mess with the dishes and junk food littering the floor. There had once been a food fight, and I spent all night cleaning the large dining room. Another time, a baby threw his food across the room, not liking the taste. I also made everyone's bed. And it had taken me forever to make 1,552 beds. Dust covered half the rooms that were never used in the pack house, but Alpha Zaire still wanted them clean in case a traveler would arrive.

Finally, I was also the butler, waitress, or chauffeur for any big event. This was during the night or whenever Alpha Zaire would throw a party for other packs. I remember taking each key from every person's car and later giving thousands of people their meals. Making drinks for any person who wanted one kept me up until three in the morning once. I wasn't the only person doing this. It was the job of all the omegas in the pack. We would help each other as best as we could, but everyone feared Alpha Zaire. If anyone offered to help and he would see, they would meet his anger and fist.

Maybe having a mate would make life easy.

My thoughts were interrupted when a soft knock echoed from outside the door. Before I could get up or speak, it was swung open, revealing a cute little girl. Two blonde curly pigtails hung from her adorable little head. Blue orbs, like Cooper's, shone on her chubby face that was lightly dusted with freckles. A grin was plastered on her face the minute she saw me.

"Hi!" She beamed, running over to me and jumping on the bed so she sat in front of me. "I'm Sage."

"Hi." I cooed, smiling when I noticed her deep dimples. "I'm Celia."

"Yeah, I know who you are." She chuckled, squatting. "You're Cooper's mate."

"Is he your brother?" I had to ask. She had his eyes, and I noticed that not everyone in the house had the same color as his eyes. The curls and color of her hair obviously came from Emilia.

"Yep!" Her smile seemed to grow the more she talked to me. "Why are you alone in here?" She cocked her head to the side in a state of confusion.

"Well, I want to be," I stated, reaching out to her face and brushing a curl away. "But you can stay with me if you want."

"We'll be best friends, right?"

"Of course."

We spent the rest of the morning talking about mindless things. Sage spoke the most, and I could imagine that her happy personality came from Emilia. The girl wouldn't stop talking about what she wanted for Christmas and that Thanksgiving was only a few weeks away. She wanted the latest Barbie doll and a new dollhouse. She even went as far as wanting a baby brother, which I had to laugh at.

Later on, Felicity came in with two plates of egg sandwiches. It was more like brunch, but it did make my taste buds tingle. There was no way I would get used to living with Cooper and his cute family. I'd only met his mother and younger sister, Sage, and I already felt at home. The girl wouldn't stop talking about how amazing her older sister, Paige, was. I had yet to meet both Paige and the former alpha.

I zoned out a few times when she told me about her friends. It was difficult to keep up with her mouth always moving. Whenever she'd ask me a question, I'd just nod my head and say, "Sure".

We ate our food quickly, but even when her mouth was full, that didn't stop her from talking.

Around three o'clock, Sage told me she had nap time but explained that she didn't want to leave me. This resulted with her lying on my right side, snuggled close to me. Her breathing was even and deep all throughout the time. I even think I dozed off once or twice because of how quiet it was in the house.

Suddenly, I heard a pair of loud footsteps walking closer to the bedroom, but I didn't mind since I knew it was Cooper. He opened the door softly and closed it behind him. Immediately, he froze and spun around in his supernatural speed. His face showed alarm and concern, probably wondering who was in the room with me. When he saw his sister, he relaxed and gave a small smile.

"Hey," he greeted, tossing what looked to be his sweatshirt onto the dresser. "Is she—"

"Asleep?" I finished for him in a whisper. "Yeah."

Slowly, Cooper sat on the bed next to me where my arm was still cradled in a sling. When I looked up at him, I noticed the large bags under his eyes. He looked extremely exhausted. Instantly, I felt guilty for waking him up last night and having him stay up. I reached out my hand and traced the dark circles with my thumb. I could tell that he was holding back a yawn with the way his jaw was clenched. The bags were a little puffy and tender from the cold outside.

"You should rest too…"

Sage shifted in her sleep from my slightly loud voice. She let out a huff of air before her body relaxed again. Once I made sure she wouldn't wake up, I looked back at Cooper who was shaking his head.

"I can go weeks without sleep. I'm fine." He assured me, but I could tell he was only trying to put my mind at rest. I removed my hand from his slightly bristly face.

"That's a total lie, Cooper. You're tired. I can tell by the bags under your eyes and how colorful they are. I want you to be strong all the time, not when you're three seconds from collapsing from stress." I explained, getting a bit annoyed with him. Why was it so hard to let him take a nap alongside his sister?

"You really want me to sleep that badly?" He chuckled, shaking his head with amusement. I didn't laugh with him. "I will tonight. I promise."

"You're making a lot of promises you aren't keeping."

That quieted him instantly. He knew I was right. He hadn't made any of his promises. We hadn't really talked and gotten to know each other like most mates would. I only saw him in the morning when he was getting ready to leave. When I went to sleep, he was usually at his desk, not even facing me, which bothered me sometimes. Every day, I could actually see his face for only a few minutes.

"I've been busy lately."

Of course, that would be his only answer. That had been his excuse for the past few days ever since I woke up. Like I said before, he never asked if I was okay. He never wondered why I left the pack or why I was injured. His behavior didn't make sense. Even Alpha Zaire wasn't this moody when I lived with him.

"Clearly."

Chapter 4

It had been about a week since I got here, and my relationship with Cooper had not improved. I rarely left his room other than to use the bathroom or wash up. Felicity regularly brought me food and cleared the plates after, but nothing significant had happened. Sage would run into the room with her princess backpack and asked me to help her with her math the minute she got home from school. Once we were done with her homework, she would tell me about her day and then leave at around five-thirty to eat dinner with the pack. Subsequently, she would be rubbing her eyes and telling me goodnight the next time I saw her.

Of course, once again I was sitting alone watching the sun slowly rise.

That left me in the bedroom most of the time, alone and reading different books Cooper had on his shelves. Most were about the pack's history. That was okay. I never took him as a reader anyway. Although, some were recently published books that were actually pretty good. He put some new ones in when he saw me reading an encyclopedia when he walked in about two days ago. The books were the only distractions I had so I could avoid what happened a week ago when I had arrived here and later lashed out.

My thoughts were cut short when Cooper's bathroom door swung open and out came my one and only mate. I looked up from the book I was reading on the windowsill. I particulary loved that corner of the room because it gave me a perfect view of the snowy mountains and the vast forest outside.

Cooper dried his hair with a towel. His luscious mane was slightly longer than the first time I met him. The five o'clock shadow he had before disappeared, revealing a strong jawline and slightly rough skin.

"You've been here for a week, Celia, and I think it's best if—"

"If what?" I cut him off before he could finish. "That I leave and then what? Get hurt injured again? My arm has fully healed, and now you want me to go out there and get exposed to more dangers?" I know I was being a little over dramatic, but alphas couldn't be trusted, and they could be cruel to their mates. I had seen their violence first hand.

"Three things. One, don't interrupt me when I'm speaking." Cooper's eyes had darkened a bit but soon went back to their normal blue color. "Two, you're wolf hasn't been let out in a week, which is unhealthy. Finally, three, I think it's best if you get introduced to my pack, including the rest of my family."

An awkward silence filled the room almost immediately. He was now *my* alpha, and I shouldn't have acted like that, even if he was my mate. And the only reason I could think of to justify my behavior would be because my wolf was getting desperate for Cooper to mate with us even though I wasn't ready. It was still pretty confusing why he was resisting the bond.

Why won't he mate us? My wolf whined, adding a small whimper at the end.

It's like he doesn't want us, I answered for her, which only earned a growl from her.

No! I can sense his wolf. He wants us just as badly as we want him.

After realizing that Cooper was waiting for an answer, I opened my mouth. "Oh..."

I looked at my hands and then back out the window. The snow was falling down softly, and I could only imagine how cold it was outside. There was no way I was leaving this room.

"What if I promised a date? In return for you to meet my family. Perhaps we can finally get to know each other." He compromised, his eyes hopeful.

This caught my attention, and my wolf instantly screamed yes. My answer wasn't far from it, and he gave a small half smile once I spoke. I couldn't help but look forward to our date, but I dreaded meeting his family. His sister and mother were very loving, but he must've gotten his habit of ignoring people from his father. Let's just hope he wasn't worse.

"Good, my sister bought you this morning." He pulled out a large shopping bag behind him and cautiously placed it on the bed and went through it.

I didn't waste any time and surveyed the outfit curiously. Never in the world had I ever seen the girls in my pack wear one, let alone had one. They all wore belly shirts and booty shorts to make all the boys whistle at them. This, however, was beautiful. It was a cute winter dress that looked perfect for a winter dance that I never got to go to. The sleeves were long but didn't look itchy like a sweater would. Its length just went below my butt, but before I could ask, Cooper pulled out some black leggings.

Since I was perfectly healed, I was able to extend my arm, and I took the dress when he offered it to me. I then decided it was best to take a shower first. Baths were great, but taking one every day for a week made me feel waterlogged. Cooper handed me the rest of the bag that contained my undergarments and left to get dressed in something fancier. Looking down at the clothes one last time, I turned on my heel and entered his bathroom. Placing the bag on the counter, I leaped into the shower to clean my morning gunk off.

Cooper was right. My wolf needed to be let out soon. My skin was on fire from the need and was constantly itchy and had bothered me in the most uncomfortable places. This usually happened to werewolves if they couldn't shift in about a week, but I had gotten used to how uncomfortable this was. I had gone on months without shifting when I was little, and it felt like hell was being dumped on me from a bucket.

I must've been in the shower for a really long time because it started to get cold, forcing me to get out. The cool air inside nipped my bare skin, and yet I still had the urge to jump in the water one last time. Ignoring it, I grabbed a navy blue towel on the racks and began to dry myself.

Getting dressed was a little complicated because the muscles in my arm were still sore and were no longer used to movements like putting on clothes. My bra was the most challenging part since I had to reach my back and twist my wrist in order to clasp it. I was getting really annoyed when I couldn't hook it and even went as far as growling. Leaving that as the last to put on, I pulled my panties on before tugging the skintight leggings onto my legs.

After many failed attempts at fastening the bra from the back, I heard a soft knock on the door. "Celia, are you okay in there?" Cooper asked.

"Yeah, just—" Reaching over a little too quickly, I growled in pain and missed the clasp. "Damn it!"

"Need help?" I could hear a hint of amusement in his voice, but I chose to ignore his comment. I was sure he just wanted to touch my already heated skin. Cooper chuckled before speaking again. "C'mon. I know you need help."

"It's nothing, okay?" I growled and whined. "Can you get Emilia in here?"

"What's so bad about me helping?"

I looked at the disgusting scar on my waist not far from my hip bone. If he saw see this, there was no way he would remain calm. Surely, he would go all crazy-possessive-alpha on me. Thinking quickly, I grabbed my leggings and pulled them up, covering my entire belly button. In just a split-second, Cooper opened the door. My back was to him, but I turned my head to look at him. His eyes were pitch-black as he examined my half-naked body without any shame. I waited patiently for him snap out of his trance but became impatient when his eyes traveled lower, down to my bottom and legs.

"Cooper."

His eyes snapped to mine, which held a glint of lust but also compassion.

Slowly, he walked over to me and grabbed my shoulders, forcing me to look into the mirror in front of me. His touch was like fire on my blazing skin, but he didn't seem to mind it. I was clutching the bra tightly to cover my breasts. This felt so dirty. I couldn't quite comprehend what was happening.

As Cooper rubbed my shoulder blades with his thumbs, I slowly relaxed and leaned into his touch. Gliding his hands down my body, he left a trail of tingling sensation on my bare skin. When he reached the clasp, he moved his hands closer to my chest where the metal that held everything was. Grabbing the thin fabric, he guided his thumbs towards the center of my small back. He was making sure it wasn't twisted. The closer he got to my back, the hotter I began to get. My hands grew clammy, and I had to wipe them in my wet hair to make it seem like I just got it from the water from my hair.

"Which one?" Cooper asked, waiting for me to tell him which hook should he use to fasten the bra.

"Just the middle one." When I heard a faint snip, I knew he did the job. "Thank you."

"Don't forget," he whispered seductively in my ear, "the next time your bra and I meet, it'll be when I'm taking it off you."

His words made me shiver in pleasure but also in excitement. I couldn't believe he told me that!

With that being said, he kissed the back of my head and walked out of the door to the bedroom. The blue plaid shirt he was wearing was rolled up to his elbows, making his arms look more muscular. The black jeans he wore was held up by a matching belt. His feet were covered by nice dress shoes. He looked absolutely incredible.

Shaking my head, I slipped the dress from my feet up and examined my body. It was the most beautiful casual dress I'd ever seen. The sequins were a champagne color and seemed to sparkle even with the dim lighting. I looked at my body a few times and turned when Cooper came back in.

"You look beautiful," he stated as if it was nothing, but it meant something important to me. No one had ever called me *beautiful*.

Tears threatened my eyes, but he instantly appeared in front of me. I bit my lip to hold back a sob. He gently placed his hands on my cheeks and looked at me with confusion. A tear slipped from my eyes, but he quickly brushed it away with his rough thumb.

"Celia?"

"No…one has ever said that to me before." I trembled, and I could feel my lip quivering uncontrollably.

He let out a big puff of air before engulfing me in a large hug. Over and over again, he told me how beautiful I was and that he couldn't ask for a better mate. Explaining every detail about me in perfection, he placed his large hand on the back of my head and deepened the hug. I remained silent while he kept going on about everything that he loved about me.

"And damn those violet eyes of yours..." He shook his head. "Those are the most beautiful and unique accessories on your wonderful body that I will always cherish."

And Cooper had to bring up my eyes. The glowing orbs that stuck out against my pale skin were the worst thing on my face. Calling them beautiful was crazy to say the least. Who would find violet eyes on a girl with white hair and milky skin beautiful? It looked terrible on me.

We spent the next few hours waiting for the big event of the meeting, but I learned a lot from them. Cooper finally kept his promise and told me about his pack. Cooper's pack was a lot more protective over each member. They treated each other like family, and they held a lot of pack events. He told me the best ones were the New Year's Eve party and the Christmas celebration. Also, during the summer, he would take the pups to the United States for a long and fun road trip. He had Adam, their beta, take the alpha role during the summer, but only every other year. He had his father and him switch so Adam could enjoy his summers too. There's also a large hockey game around February, and the pack usually played on the lake not far from the pack house. My old pack never did any of those things.

Looking around the room, I soon realized what all the hockey pictures were about. "You play hockey?"

He smiled with admiration when he looked at the picture hanging from the wall near his desk. It was like he was lost in a memory before nodding his head and speaking, "*Played*. I haven't had time since I graduated from high school and took the title as alpha. I would love to reunite with the players on the team and catch up, but most were humans, and they have moved away."

"Were you any good?" I questioned, shifting on the bed for a better position. We had moved to the bed to relax and lay back while we waited for the event.

"People told me I was the best on the team." Cooper chuckled. "Hell, I scored a goal from the other side of the rink."

I wasn't really athletically inclined, so I barely understood what a rink was. It probably meant something, like the other side of the field in a soccer game. So I guess that's good. The only time I watched sports was when the boys in the TV room screamed when the 'puck hit the post.' It made me feel ignorant.

"That's great." I smiled at him kindly and remained looking at the pictures around the room. My eyes landed on the picture of hundreds of people grouped together. "Your pack is enormous."

"Our pack." He corrected me, and I looked at him in confusion. "You're my mate. Soon, you will take up the role as luna. It may be in a month, or even a year, but you will be mine."

When he finished that sentence, a welcoming chill ran down my spine. The thought of him mating us, my wolf and I, was a wonderful and exciting thought. Smiling at the imagery, I closed my eyes and let out a breath of air, soothing my wolf a bit. She was really awake after what he said that.

A very loud high-pitched bell rang and Cooper jumped out of the bed automatically. I mirrored his movements and soon followed him out the door. Knowing it was time, I felt my hands grow clammy.

That was when I realized I never really took in his house. It was beautiful and modern looking, almost Asian styled. Just like the first time I got to see the house, I still couldn't help but feel in awe at how beautiful it was. The flooring that my ballet flats were tapping on was dark red. The railing to the long staircase was glass, and you could just make out some figures on different levels of the house. White paint covered the wall and ceiling perfectly, and it was obvious that a professional home decorator decorated this house.

While walking down the stairs, I noticed several pictures that were black and white. Others were paintings that were beautifully colored. Each man in the pictures didn't smile, and each had a smiling woman on his shoulder. Every person was more attractive than the last in the paintings. To my surprise, some women were dressed in long fluffy dresses that looked extremely old. There were also women who wore tight lace shirts that hugged their breasts tightly and the most interesting makeup. Men wore fine clothing with different designs that clearly were not from this century. When we reached the second floor, many of the paintings were turned into photographs. These people looked to be familiar, and I soon realized it was Cooper's family.

What I noticed among the women was the same wedding ring that Emilia wore. It was beautiful with diamonds outlining the silver band. A large heart-shaped diamond was in the center and sparkled on each painting or picture.

"Those are the past lunas with their alphas," Cooper whispered in my ear, nodding his head in the direction of the painting we recently passed by.

"The lunas are always wearing the same ring as Emilia's." I paused and looked into Cooper's orbs. "Why?"

He shrugged with a smile and said, "I can't tell. It's a secret."

"But Emilia wears it. Is it a family heirloom or something?"

"To be honest, my parents won't tell me." Cooper chuckled with a little meaning. "Not until I decide to ask my mate for her hand."

It was strange that his parents kept that a secret.

He cleared his throat before stopping in front of a door. "This is it." He placed his hand on the doorknob. "You ready?"

I nodded my head and allowed him to open the door. My hands were growing extremely clammy, and I tried desperately to get the sweat off it. I'd been nervous many times, but never like this. Probably because I was meeting my mate's family and they soon would become *my* family. It's best if we got to know each other before Cooper marked me.

When the door reached the wall behind it, it made a soft tap. That was all it took for the room, which had once been filled with chatter, to become silent. The floor had a velvet rug that held a long wooden dining table. The wood was just like the rest of the furniture, a dark cherry red. The walls are covered with a light gold color. I was amazed that this was where the higher ranks would dine. It was absolutely stunning, and it took my breath away.

"Celia, darling!" Emilia, Cooper's mother, squealed as she stood up from her seat at the table, placing the silk napkin beside her plate. I was surprised at how fancy she looked in her zebra print cocktail dress, and my eyes widened at the four-inch black heels she was wearing. "Oh, sweetie, I'm so glad to see you finally up and about!"

I only nodded and moved closer to Cooper for some comfort. "Yeah, she's doing much better," Cooper answered for me, looking down at my small frame.

"Well, I guess it's time to introduce you to the Pierce family!" Emilia spoke cheerfully. As she nodded at the people sitting around the table, they all stood up at once. "Why not start with my mate, Patrick?"

A man, looking like the older version of Cooper, walked over to me with his hand held out to me. I took it cautiously but soon pulled away when I noticed how strong and rough his handshake was. When I placed my hand on Cooper's chest for safety, he let out a low growl that only I seemed to hear. Patrick seemed confused by how much I shrank away, but he seemed to intimidate me just by the power he radiated.

"Dad…she's just recovered from an injury. Don't touch her." I knew he meant that he didn't want any other male touching me, and Patrick seemed to understand.

"My apologies, Celia."

"It's alri—"

"Cici!" a high-pitched voice screamed, and I looked down to see Sage smiling brightly at me. Her curly blonde hair was in two French braids that made her eyes stand out. I could imagine her being very beautiful in the future with all the guys chasing her.

"Hi, Sage." I bent down so we were eye level and allowed her to kiss my cheek.

"We're going to be sisters!" she cheered, and I smiled at her excitement with a nod.

"And I am feeling pretty loved right now," a new voice said that I couldn't help but noticed the sarcasm laced around every word. "To think we would be inseparable best friends hurts my ego."

Standing up with Cooper, looking at me with an unknown expression, I turned to see someone completely different. She had the family's blue eyes, but her hair was a reddish brown, much like Cooper's. I could tell she had put a lot of effort into her hair to curl it.

"Stop, Paige," Cooper snapped. I could tell that his slightly younger sister annoyed him a lot.

Paige looked like she had some bug up her butt with her arms crossed and annoyed expression. She was wearing a sweater dress, much like mine, but showed a lot more skin. You could see her black lacy bra underneath, which made my nose unknowingly wrinkle in disgust.

My thoughts, however, were soon cut off when a man, the same age as Cooper, latched his hand around her waist. She physically relaxed, and a small smile showed on her face. My guess was he was her mate, and they had been bonded for a while.

"Now, now, Paige." He chuckled, flicking his finger on her nose like a child. For some reason, this made her giggle. When he noticed I was examining their mate-to-mate contact, he let a big grin make its way on his face. "Well, Celia, you are looking much better than the day I found you. My name is Adam Desmond, beta of the Ice Moon Pack."

I gave him a confused look before looking up at Cooper, then back at the Adam. "Found me?" I was beginning to like this Adam guy.

"Yeah, my cousin Chris and I found you when you had wandered into our territory," he stated. He soon gave me a curious yet suspicious look. "What were you doing there anyway, and, of all the pack territories, why did you wander here? I mean, we are your pack's enemy."

My eyes went wide along with my mouth, and I knew I spoke way too soon. With my jaw dropped to the ground, I subconsciously began to stutter. There was no way I would be able to explain to them what happened without breaking into tears.

"This isn't exactly dinner conversation." Emilia interrupted us, giving Adam a very dangerous look although it went away as fast as it came. She looked at me and motioned for me to sit somewhere. "Come, darling. You must be hungry."

Cooper gave Adam a nasty look, just like his mother, and guided me into a seat. When we both turned away from them, I heard a loud *whack*, and I could only imagine Paige had knocked some sense into him. Adam gave a soft grumble but didn't do anything else. Only females were allowed to physically hurt their mate to show them when they did something wrong. However, women hardly harmed their mates since they had a calmer wolf in them.

"Celia, sit next to me!" Sage begged, and I couldn't help but scoot out of Cooper's hold to sit next to the bundle of giggles. "Celia loves me the most!"

"Not for long." Cooper snorted, taking the seat beside me and giving me a wink. This made Sage giggle uncontrollably and shake her head.

Everyone went back to their seats and began to talk mindlessly. No one asked me anything about my pack because they knew it was a sour subject. They must've had an idea that I had left and had gotten hurt along the way. Cooper, obviously, wasn't happy about the blunt answer, but that was all he was getting.

The past was the past. We couldn't fix it.

While Emilia was talking about some new furniture they were thinking about ordering and Cooper was talking to Adam about hockey, Paige suddenly stood up.

The room went silent as we all noticed how pale she looked. She ran out of the room as fast as she could. Emilia instantly shot out of her seat but was stopped when Patrick placed his hand on hers. He shook his head and sighed before looking at me. All eyes went to me since it was so silent.

"Celia, can you go see if she's okay?" he asked kindly, and I felt a pang of guilt when I knew I couldn't argue.

"It's probably just the food." Sage shrugged, looking at the food a bit strangely. I was happy she was able to save me from leaving without Cooper with me. I was relieved I didn't have to go after Paige and could finish my dinner. "It does have a strange taste to it, and the meat is a little raw."

"Felicity probably undercooked it. She's been doing that a lot lately." The former alpha added, looking at the steak a little longer than necessary.

"Yeah, Gabriel got sick yesterday." Emilia pointed out, nodding her head in understanding. "He's fine now."

The rest of the meal went by slowly and uneventfully. Sage would talk about her good grades in school, and Adam would talk about different people requesting to become part of the pack. Emilia laughed with Patrick whenever he would make a flirtatious comment. I was the only one who didn't speak.

However, it soon ended when Emilia asked me a question that really hit me. "So, Celia, do you think your parents back home are worried about you? I mean, you have been gone for a week now."

I looked down at my half eaten steak and pushed a piece of broccoli around the plate. All conversations stopped, and I could feel everyone staring at me. Biting my lip, I placed the knife and fork on the table, making a loud *clank* echo throughout the room. After springing my chair back, I stood up and bolted out the room like everything was on fire.

"Shit," I heard Cooper whisper under his breath. "Nice, Mom."

"I didn't know her parents were problematic. First, it's her pack, and now it's her parents!" she bellowed, but I was too far from earshot to listen anymore.

My ballet flats tapped lightly while I sprinted up the stairs, brushing past a few people walking down. I followed the same way Cooper and I walked before. My heart in my chest was pounding loudly, and I could only imagine how loud it was for Cooper since he was an alpha with heightened senses.

By the time I reached his room, I slammed the door shut and locked the door. Growling in annoyance, I entered Cooper's bathroom and began slipping off the jewelry I had put on earlier. Tears were falling quickly out of my eyes, and I howled when the bracelet wouldn't come off. The water coming from my eyes fell down into the sink and on the countertop.

A knock on Cooper's bedroom door interrupted my slowly oncoming breakdown. "Celia? I know you're in there. I can hear your heartbeat." I didn't answer him. "Unlock the door, or I swear I'll break it down."

"I-I don't want to talk about it." I snapped at him. I wiped the tears away quickly off my cheeks when the doorknob rattled a bit.

I was in the middle of taking off my earrings and setting it on the dresser when the door was kicked open. My mate strutted over to me and hugged me from behind. With my hands in midair, I didn't have any way of hugging him back, so I just stood there with my fingers clutching my earrings. He inhaled my scent like it was a drug and sighed loudly.

"My mother shouldn't have asked you something so personal." Cooper turned me around briskly so I was facing him. I would've been terrified of that sudden movement from an alpha, but I knew he wouldn't hurt me.

I shook my head at his statement and spoke, "No, it's what most parents would ask first. She was just trying to get to know and probably to get me to talk more. I should've tried a little more." I looked down at the floor, slightly ashamed of my action earlier.

"Hey..." He soothed me, and I felt a finger brush under my chin and lift my head up. Our eyes met, and all I could see was pure compassion plus a little of something else. "You were in a room full of high-ranked wolves. You may be an omega, but you are not used to it, and I could feel how uneasy your wolf was, and we haven't even bonded yet. It was a natural reaction from you."

I bit my bottom lip softly and gave it a little nibble before looking back into Cooper's eyes. They instantly darkened for some strange reason but I instantly realized why. When I bit my lip, it caught his wolf's attention, and he wanted to bite it also. A low growl echoed deep in his throat, and I held back a purr from my own wolf.

Suddenly, his touch felt like fire on my skin. Shivers ran up and down my spine, and I unintentionally trembled a bit, but it went away as quickly as it came. Cooper noticed this, which meant that we just took another step in the mating process.

Cooper seemed pleased at my response because a big grin was plastered on his face, showing his straight white teeth. Slowly, he leaned in and placed a gentle kiss on my chin, making me shiver in pleasure. He was being sweet to me, and it made me happier than ever.

When he looked back at my eyes, he growled again and grabbed my face. "Have you been crying?"

"I mean..." I shoved him away gently and covered my stinging cheeks that had been caused by my salty tears.

"You should never cry again for any reason," he said before reaching out to me and hugging me tightly to his chest. "You're my mate. I hate to see you upset. I don't like to see any tears come from your eyes."

It felt amazing to actually have someone who cared that wasn't a family member or a close friend. My heart raced at his words, giving me a fuzzy and tingling feeling as tears threatened to spill from my eyes. I felt appreciated and understood by him. He made me feel safe in a treacherous world.

Slowly, I planted my cheek against Cooper's strong chest and listened to the loud thumping of his heart. Even his heart radiated power and strength, causing my mind to flood with impure thoughts. He bent down a bit to kiss the top of my head and snuggled me closer to him. Heat radiated from him, making my chilly fingertips warmer.

"You want to sleep?" he asked. "I promised, didn't I?"

"Sure," I answered him and released my iron grip on him.

Chapter 5

It had been two weeks now since I first arrived at Cooper's pack house, and it had also been weeks that I had remained cooped up in my mate's room since Emilia asked me about my parents. She apologized the next day, and I couldn't help but forgive her. Paige came in the day after that, and she explained to me that she hadn't been feeling well the past few days. I nodded with an understanding that even werewolves could get sick sometimes. I had been many times in the past.

About five days ago, Cooper came into his room utterly annoyed. When I asked him what was wrong, he told me he was handling it and that Adam wouldn't be back for three weeks. When I spoke to Felicity about it, she told me it was just a situation with the rogues that they normally dealt with and I shouldn't worry so much. She also explained that Cooper had been stressed out lately because of some issues with the pack treaties going wrong and people from other packs had suddenly expressed their interest in joining our pack.

I woke up this morning to an empty bed, like always, and I sighed in annoyance at the realization that I hadn't really woken up with Cooper beside me ever since. However, I knew he had a tight schedule since he was the alpha, and I never really got worried because he left me a note every morning which usually would be like this:

> *Celia,*
>
> *I'm sorry I couldn't be the first face you saw this morning, but it warmed my heart when I saw yours. Since it's Monday, I'm the busiest with my duties. For some odd reason, everyone needs an alpha's help more frequently on this day. But on the bright side, most of the members have gone to work today, so I'll have plenty of people to help speed up the process of the day. Please don't leave the house until I get back.*
>
> *~Cooper*

Aside from the note, he would leave a flower or a pair of earrings on the bedside, although I didn't want jewelry or roses. What I really wanted was my mate. Why couldn't he see that I wanted to spend time with him? There's only so much I could do by looking out the snowy landscape or reading his ancient books. I couldn't forget about the date he promised me that he hadn't taken me on yet.

As much as I wanted him to spend more time with me, I didn't want to be that mate who craved attention twenty-four/seven, so I didn't complain. Obviously, Emilia and Patrick, Cooper's parents, didn't really talk much. I met Patrick the week after I met his mate, Emilia, so that proved that life as a luna and an alpha could be lonely. Though I was confused slightly. He was a retired alpha anyway, shouldn't he have a lot of free time?

I slipped into Cooper's green sweatshirt and grey sweatpants, rolling them up so they would fit me. Next was a pair of warm socks and then a grey beanie that matched the pants I was wearing. Drowsily, I walked into Cooper's bathroom and began to wash my face. I picked up a hairbrush from the bathroom vanity and began to run it from the top of my head down to my knees. My hair was way too long for me to enjoy brushing it. About twenty minutes later, I had brushed my hair and braided it.

With one brave breath, I pushed Cooper's door open and entered the hallway. It was extremely quiet that it was almost disturbing. Using my heightened sense of hearing, I listened to my surroundings. The only sound I heard was a shower running, about a story below the floor I was on.

Shutting Cooper's door, I made my way down the hall and to the stairs, slowly and quietly, taking the staircases one at a time. I soon arrived at the bottom, and it took me a while to find the kitchen, but I did, and what a beautiful kitchen they had.

The flooring was just like the rest of the house, and it had an island counter in the center. Dozens of counters outlined the kitchen with different food processors and blenders. Coffee makers were in the center: one that made decaf and one that didn't. A microwave was above the large black stove, completing the entire room. There was a toaster plugged into an outlet and even a waffle maker. It was a chef's heaven. No wonder Felicity spent so much time cooking. She obviously loved spending most of her time out here.

I took one of the pans that was hanging from the racks and placed it on the stove. Since no one was around, I might as well cook for myself. I turned the stove on and walked to the elephant-sized refrigerator.

If the kitchen was full of so many things, the refrigerator beat it. Every single item was organized into different categories like dairy products, meats, and vegetables.

Taking out the ingredients that I needed like an excellent piece of meat, spinach, peppers, olives, and some mushrooms, I placed them on a free counter and began to prepare them. Rows of knives were loaded in a single drawer beside me. After pulling out the items I would be using and cutting the vegetables and dicing the meat, I cracked the eggs into a bowl and stirred with a whisk and carefully dumped it into the pan. I decided an omelet would be a good thing to eat. It's both healthy and light.

With the remaining time I had, I went back to the fridge and pulled out two kinds of cheese, mozzarella and cheddar. It took a while to grate both, but soon, it was perfectly shredded. I dumped my dairy, vegetables, and diced meat onto the eggs and flipped it over. Allowing it to cook, I cleaned each utensil and bowl I used and placed it back to where I had found it. Cooking was what made me feel better, especially if I was cooking for myself.

"Damn that smells good." My head snapped to its direction. In the blink of an eye, I had fled to the other side of the kitchen and hid myself behind a wall. Looking around, I noticed I was in some kind of a lounge area. I heard the man sigh. "I can smell you and hear you. Come out, Omega."

My heartbeat increased, and I knew he could hear it. With a sudden gust of bravery, I revealed myself to him only to stop dead in my tracks. The guy in front of me was my age, perhaps even younger. I couldn't see his eyes since they were covered by his dark hair, but I knew he wasn't any danger. My wolf instantly told me his rank. He was an omega too. It was easy to tell with his slim figure.

He sniffed and inhaled deeply before cursing loudly. "You're the alpha's mate. Damn it." I could just make out his eyes and noticed how greyish they looked that they were it was almost white. Whenever he spoke, the piercings on his bottom lips trembled.

"Yeah, and she'll always be mine," a new voice barked, and I looked behind him to find Cooper's strong figure. "Scram, Jeremy."

"Yes, Alpha," he whimpered, and I instantly felt bad for him. Jeremy was just like me. I could relate to him more than anyone knew.

I crossed my arms over my chest when Jeremy left, and Cooper walked up to me. Slowly, he placed his hands on the top of my shoulders and began to rub them soothingly. My tense muscles instantly relaxed at his touch, and I looked down at the floor.

"You okay?" Cooper murmured, caressing my cheek.

I nodded. "Yeah, I just don't like seeing people like me get bossed around just like I had once been." My tone came out a little aggressive, but I could feel how agitated my wolf was.

Cooper's eyes softened, and regret filled them. "I'm sorry. I just don't like males flirting with what's mine." Cautiously, he moved his face so it was in the crook of my neck. He inhaled. "You smell so good."

I pushed him away lightly and took the omelet off the pan. Turning off the stove, I reached for a plate and placed my breakfast on it. Sparing a glance at Cooper, I noticed how his eyes were trained on me.

"What?" I questioned, taking a fork and walking to the island counter to take a seat.

"Do you mind me asking what you did as an omega?" I instantly froze and looked at him with wide eyes. "My apologies. I shouldn't have—"

"Caretaker." I interrupted him, and his eyes snapped to mine.

"What?"

"I was a caretaker," I stated but soon explained. "I took care of the house and children most of the time, but I also cooked and served the meals to the alpha."

My mate seemed surprised at my sudden option to open up to him. I could tell he was stunned by my answer but also annoyed. He didn't want me to do that kind of labor, but I did. Cooper reached his arms out to me.

"Come here."

Wiping my mouth with a napkin, I stood up and stood in front of him.

Wrapping his arms around my waist, he looked at me dead in the eye and spoke again, "Let's go for a run. I miraculously finished my duties early, and you need to let your wolf out."

I gave him a nod of understanding and went back to finish my breakfast. He was right; my wolf was pacing and begging to be let out. She even tried to make me shift without wanting, but I pushed her away with. I was also excited to finally see his wolf. I wondered what he looked like. Did he have black fur? Or did it match his hair color? Was he silver like the rest of his pack members? Would his eyes remain bright blue or would they darken once she shifted? More questions flooded my mind with every passing second.

The omelet was delicious, and I stood up to clean it only for it to be taken out of my grasp. Cooper placed the dish in a nearby sink and took my hand. I knew he didn't want me working, but washing a plate wasn't a difficult task.

Huffing in annoyance, I let him guide me out the door where the cold breeze hit my face. I could feel my cheeks getting rosy from the wind pelting down on us. My mate wrapped his arm around me to keep me warm, and I could feel my socks getting wet from the snow. I stopped a bit to take them off and mindlessly threw them somewhere in the snow.

Cooper kicked off his shoes and placed them deep in the woods against a large tree. He tugged off his grey t-shirt and was now showing off his eight-pack and sculpted chest. I tried desperately to look away, but my wolf began to claw at the surface. Then he began to unbuckle his belt and suddenly stopped.

My face snapped up to meet his smirking face. "Like what you see?"

"Well, yeah…I guess." I stuttered, moving my eyes around the snowy landscape, trying to distract myself.

"Of course, you do. You're my mate." He winked at me. "Plus, I can smell your…interest."

At that, I blushed darker than a cherry red tomato. Damn, his heightened senses would be the embarrassment, and ultimately, the death of me. I placed my hands over my heated cheeks, but it only seemed to amuse him. I tried everything from looking at the ground to pretending to cough in my sleeve.

"Don't hide your blush." He smirked, which only made me shiver a little. "You look pretty when you do."

I chomped on my lip again and searched for a tree to hide behind. When I found a large pine, I stood behind it and shed the clothes off me. Closing my eyes, I took in every sound—from the falling snow to the morning birds chirping above. Taking deep breaths, I allowed my wolf to begin the shift.

My skin started to stretch along with my bones and muscles. I could feel my skin growing hotter and hotter with every passing second. The ears on my head grew into wolf ears, and my nose and mouth stretched out to become a snout. Paws and claws erupted on my hands and feet, forcing them to look like my black wolf form. Fur seeped through my pores and began to grow thick. My spine curled, forcing me to go on all fours. My wolf head had formed successfully, and now I stood proudly in my complete wolf form. Shaking my black fur one last time, I rounded the large tree and searched the snowy landscape for Cooper.

What I found made excitement build up in my body. There stood a large pure white wolf with black dust coating his long coat. A white wolf usually showed innocence, but the black dust along the tips of his fur made it seem like he had been through a fire. As he stood proudly, his coat expressed bravery, and not only did it look amazing, but his large wolf frame was twenty times the size of mine. The aquamarine eyes he possessed seemed to glow the more he examined the territory. His head snapped to mine when he heard me approach him.

Meeting me half way, we both examined each other's wolf's body. Unexpectedly, he licked my jaw, making my wolf figure tremble from his touch. Guiding his large head along the side of my body, I felt him slowly trail downwards. Cooper's massive head trailed down my tiny frame until he reached my tail. He blew on it teasingly, and I instantly curled it, so it was between my legs. I growled playfully, which he only returned with a wolfish grin.

Motioning for me to follow him, he began to walk. It didn't take me long to follow, but at his pace, I needed to fast walk. When he noticed I was slowly falling behind, he walked a little slower and turned to look at me looking a little impatient. Trying my best to keep up with him, I soon realized that maybe he wanted to chase me. From what I had observed, mates usually found it very entertaining to chase their mates. Deciding it was worth a shot, I began quickening my pace until I was ahead of him. I heard Cooper let out a playful growl, which I returned.

I tried to push my tiny legs faster, and I could hear him catching up to me. I jumped in surprise when I felt a playful nip on my tail. Trying to throw him off, I took a left, but that didn't slow him down one bit. This time, I really began to push myself, but when I turned around, all I saw was him trotting behind me. He didn't even look like he was out of breath. I growled in annoyance that he didn't have to put a lot of effort into chasing me. Soon enough, he was right beside me.

I like this, my wolf said excitedly, and I could tell she was trying to help me run a little faster. *I love it when he gives us his full attention.*

I had to agree with her on that one. *Me too.*

I was really growing out of breath, so I slowed down instantly. Cooper stopped a little in front of me and watched me pant. Deciding it was best to lie down, I let my legs collapse slowly underneath me and rested my head on my front legs. He soon joined me and lay down beside me. I must looked like a small pup next to him.

Then I felt a nudge on my shoulder. I looked up to see Cooper standing up. I soon followed him and watched as he turned around and began walking. Thinking he wanted me to follow, I obliged, examining his long flowing tail from behind. His pace picked up, and I let out a little yip so he would know I was falling behind. He turned around to look at me and noticed how much trouble I was having in the deep snow. Sighing, he walked over to me and gently picked me up by the extra skin on the back of my neck as if I were a puppy.

With that, he took off fast like a bolt of lightning. I could only see a small image of a tree before it disappeared from my sight. He was running so fast it would look like it wasn't even a werewolf but a blur that no one could keep their eyes on long. Soon, we were in front of my pile of clothes. They were drenched, but Cooper just dropped me in the snow. I whimpered a bit when I landed awkwardly, but I heard him run back over to his pile of clothes.

I called my human side back and shifted quickly. It didn't take long for my spine to rearrange and for my fur to go back into my pores and the regular hair to come out. Tugging my wet clothes on, I reappeared from behind the tree and searched for Cooper. He seemed to be waiting for me because he grabbed my arm roughly and dragged me back to the pack house, not literally of course. His movements startled me, and I instantly spoke.

"Cooper, what's wrong?" I asked, a little frightened. Why was he being like this? We had just enjoyed chasing each other only minutes ago.

"Someone trespassed into our territory. A scout said that it's a rogue. He told me he got him." He explained and quickly led me into the house. "He's kept for questioning. I need to find out why they've recently been coming."

I stayed silent and prayed it wasn't anyone from my old pack. What if Alpha Zaire sent him? What if Blood Moon was going to attack Ice Moon? A war could start because of me. The deaths of hundreds would be on my hands. Cooper's pack probably never would've been in danger if I hadn't trespassed. The thought made me wonder if I should leave when I still could.

Cooper and I entered the lower ground hallway, and I could see all the pack members had been waiting patiently for his arrival. All of them bowed their heads in respect to him, but he didn't pay attention to them. He held my hand tightly when we passed his family members. He turned to look at Paige for a moment.

"Take her upstairs. Bring Sage with you." He ordered. "Keep her in your room and stay with her no matter what. I will go back upstairs as soon as I'm done with the interrogation."

"But I want to stay with you," I whispered, and his eyes snapped to mine. His eyes softened a little, and I knew he regretted leaving me along.

"I'll be back soon." He coaxed before looking back at Paige. "Take her upstairs now."

Paige jumped at his tone and took my hand along with Sage's. It felt strange to hold someone else's hand that wasn't my mate's, but I had to ignore to the uneasiness. I knew Paige felt the same because her hand was tense and stiff, but it could also be from the order Cooper gave her. Sage was shaking like a little puppy, and I felt sorry for her. She was really young and didn't deserve to be really scared right now.

We arrived on the fourth floor and entered a light grey room. It was simple, and I could tell Paige designed it because most of her things were scattered around the room. There were a few of Adam's shirts in an empty dresser. Adam must've left in a hurry. Paige picked up her little sister and placed her on the bed. We both tried desperately to stop her from shaking. I even tried to lull her to sleep, which didn't work at all. It must've taken us about an hour to have Sage finally take her nap. Paige and I decided to talk since we could both use some girl-to-girl bonding time.

"It's funny when both of our mates are like that." She chuckled, and I gave her a confused look. "When I as in heat like two weeks ago, Adam locked me in this room for five days. Why do you think you didn't see me when you first got here? The day you came was also the day I was in heat."

"But I'm not in heat," I stated, feeling my skin for any symptoms. I wasn't sweating, and my skin wasn't on fire at all. What was she talking about?

Heat was the time when a female werewolf was most fertile, and the male could normally feel it. It was usually a way for a female to produce an heir for her mate, but that was created during the times when werewolves' population was decreasing several hundred years ago. Based on history, a great war had nearly wiped out the race. But that was then. Now, the heat was just a mere excuse for mates to be intimate with each other.

"Oh, well, I guess alphas are really overprotective." She chuckled. "My brother is so infatuated by you."

I chuckled at her words and looked at Sage. A question had been bothering me for a while, so I had to ask. "Why is there such a huge age difference between you and your sister?"

Paige turned to look at her sleeping sister. "Mom and Dad have always been terrible at planning. I knew Mom went into heat one time and Dad relieved her without protection." She shivered in disgust. "Bad image."

I chuckled at her uncomfortable state.

"How about you? Don't...don't you have any parents?"

My eyes widened in surprise, and I looked into her eyes and debated whether to tell her or not. It didn't feel right to tell her, but I knew my silence had already answered her question. She nodded in understanding even though she probably didn't know how much it actually bothered me. I never enjoyed people who thought they could relate to me when they really couldn't. Even Cooper hadn't even figured it out.

"No, I don't have any parents," I told her truthfully, and she smiled sadly at me. "I never really knew them."

"Wow. That must've been difficult for you."

"You can't tell Cooper! I'll tell him. Just not now."

She nodded in understanding after I said that.

"Thank you."

We spent the rest of our time talking about mindless things. Paige told me she hadn't been feeling well and had been thinking about seeing Sheila, their pack doctor, ever since she threw up. I told her I had the same virus she probably had a few months ago. It was awful. I also found out that Thanksgiving just happened to be tomorrow and she was really looking forward to eating the turkey. I laughed at her and nodded in agreement. I remembered cooking the turkey at my old pack a few times and stealing a few bites. While I was explaining how to prepare a turkey, she stood up and ran into the bathroom. I could hear her throwing up and crying a bit into the toilet. I waited for her to come out.

A few minutes later, she came back with freshly brushed teeth and a small smile on her face. I knew she wasn't feeling good, but I knew her sickness would go away soon. It would all depend on how fast her wolf would fight the virus. She collapsed on the bed next to Sage and closed her eyes. I knew she was tired, so I moved off the bed and sat on an armchair that faced a fireplace. I lit it and watched the fire dance on the log.

I could feel my eyes growing heavy, but I fought hard to keep them open. Time flew by, and I couldn't help feeling really annoyed with Cooper. I stood up and decided it was time to be brave and see this rogue. If Cooper wasn't done with the rogue, then what else had he been doing aside from questioning it? Was he killing it? Torturing the poor man? There was no way it would take him this long to interrogate one person.

Sucking in all my strength, I stood up and walked out of Paige's room. The house was silent that it seemed to really freak me out. Did all the pack members leave? I gently walked down the stairs. Any quick movements could be heard by Cooper if he was down the stairs. It took me ten minutes to finally reach the first floor, and I could hear Cooper yelling faintly. Following his voice, I stopped at a room that I knew must have soundproof walls. Breathing in deeply, I reached for the doorknob and turned it. There's no way Cooper would be happy about this, but I had to do it. Exhaling, I pushed the door open and looked inside. What I saw was a total shock.

Cooper was leaning over someone who was tied to what appeared to be like a silver chair.

Silver had always been a werewolf's weakness. Just the touch of it could burn the skin, and to have it flowing in a werewolf's bloodstream could kill even the strongest one. Even silver could kill an alpha, which was really frightening to think about. I had a lot of experiences with silver; I should know.

"Who are you looking for? Answer me and I will make your death fast!" This was Cooper. His voice was menacing and with so much authority, even I felt affected.

Cooper's head snapped to my direction, and he growled. "What are you doing here? Go back upstairs where it's safe." He ordered me.

He ordered his own mate to get away from him. My wolf whimpered, and even I let one escape my lips. However, this didn't seem to bother him at all. "Go back upstairs now!"

I didn't move, so Cooper walked over to me. He roughly grabbed my arm, but before he could explode again, a new voice spoke, "Celia."

Both our heads snapped at the direction of the voice, and my eyes widened in fright. I could feel fear growing in my chest, and my heart skipped a beat. My body shook, and I felt Cooper trying to make me move, but I was frozen. My eyes must have looked like saucers and probably looked funny to anyone who passed by. However, this wasn't in any way a joking matter because the man in front of me strapped to the silver chair was related to the Blood Moon's beta. In fact, he was his son.

Chapter 6

I stood there, frozen like an ice cube. My legs couldn't move. They were glued to the floor. Cooper looked the most confused but soon snapped out of it and pushed me behind him instantly. He let out a menacing growl to the Beta's son, which the latter only returned.

"Malcolm?" I asked, finally regaining my voice. "How are you alive?"

How is this possible?

He smirked before letting out a chuckle. "What a great way to greet an old friend, eh, Cici?"

"Don't talk to her, Rogue." Cooper seethed, pushing me further behind him so I couldn't see Malcolm's beaten face. "Answer me. Who are you looking for?"

It was as if Cooper didn't care that I had just identified the rogue he was holding captive. What was wrong with him? He was never like this around me. Maybe it was his possessive side seeping out. Or maybe he was just furious at me.

Malcolm chuckled at Cooper's attempt to intimidate him. Since he's a beta's son, he wouldn't be as submissive as I would. He's almost as powerful as my mate standing before him, but even he could hold against an alpha trying to intimidate him. "I was out looking for my pack's little runaway. News travel fast from Zaire, and half of the Canadian packs know about her disappearance. He wants her back for what she did. Well, I think I should pay dear old dad a visit, don't you think? Oh wait. I can still mind-chat him."

"You're covered in silver. There's no possible way you can mind-chat with the amount on you." Cooper growled, pushing me back further so my back was now pressed against the door, closing it in the process.

Malcolm only chuckled. "Don't worry, a mate's connection is stronger. Good thing she's in my pack. I'll contact my mate, and she'll go running to my father." He closed his eyes, and a minute later, he opened them. "Enjoy hell as it comes up from below your feet. She got my message, and although she knows I can take care of myself, Alpha Zaire will be sending people after me and Celia."

This time, I followed Cooper's order which he had repeated many times. I opened the door and ran out as fast as I could. Taking the steps two at a time, I finally arrived on the fourth floor and out of breath. What if Malcolm told my mate something? What if he told him what happened? Cooper would never look at me in the same way. My own supposed loving mate would reject me. Cooper hadn't taken any significant steps such as kissing, marking, or mating me. He still had the power to reject me.

I passed all the former alphas' and lunas' portraits and soon made it safely to Cooper's room. I closed the door way too fast, causing it to slam. I locked it quickly. Pressing my back against the door, I slowly slid down and covered my face with my hands while my tears spilled. Malcolm had relayed the information about me to his pack, and I was pretty sure they would soon be coming over after me, and there was nothing I could do.

This couldn't be happening to me. I needed more time to tell Cooper even though I never planned on it. How could I possibly be able to tell Cooper what had happened? He'd be disgusted with me. He wouldn't want to be with me as soon as he found out the truth.

A soft knock on my door intruded my thoughts. I pushed myself up with a little difficulty. Taking the knob, I twisted it and pulled the door open.

Cooper and I both stood there, looking at each other and not knowing what to say. I was the first to look away and sighed loudly. He knew I was crying, and I still was, but that didn't stop him from speaking.

"Get inside. I need to speak with you."

I nodded. He closed the door softly, and I sat on the corner of the bed. I braced myself for what he was going to say.

"Why did you disobey me? I told you to stay upstairs, but you came down anyway. You could've been hurt. He would've—" He paused. "Look at yourself. I should kill him for making you feel this way."

His voice was somehow calm, but I knew he was holding in his anger as best as he could. I opened my mouth and decided it was best if I spoke. "I was worried about you. You were in there for a long time, and I thought something had happened. I didn't know Malcolm was there. I didn't know he was the rogue."

Cooper growled. "How do you know him? What is his rank if his father is a beta?"

He was really starting to scare me now that his voice had risen. Not only had he never spoken to me this loud, but he had never been this angry with me. I didn't want him to be mad at me, but he needed to understand I was just as worried as him. Standing there so close to Malcolm, he could've easily dug his canines into Cooper's jugular.

"We had talked when we were younger. Maybe when we were eight years old. I would always make him his favorite dish when he asked me politely. Both of us had gotten along like siblings." I explained to him, but Cooper just raised his eyebrow, waiting for me to continue. "He's the beta's son from Blood Moon Pack. Everyone thought he had died when a group of rogues attacked the pack a few years ago. I never would've thought he would turn into a rogue himself because no one knew him better than I did. When he turned, Malcolm really changed. He used to be very kind and never mocked or threatened anyone."

"Then why in the hell was he looking for you, Celia?" Cooper barked and I jumped, but he didn't seem to care since he kept talking. "What did *you* do?"

I stayed silent and pursed my lips. Why did he have to be this aggressive ? Why couldn't my mate understand that I didn't want to talk about it nor did I want to think about it? It's like he didn't care that I was hurting on the inside. He probably really didn't with the way he was reacting. I wanted him to understand, but would he?

"Goddamn it, Cooper, why can't you understand that it hurts!" I cried, tears falling down my face as I stood up. "You never stop and think how much your words could hurt me! Do you think I want to talk about this? My old pack was like a living hell! I don't want to relive everything I have been through and tell you what my life has been like. You might as well find another mate if you can't handle wondering who I am. You know my name, and that's all you'll ever get to know!"

"I want to help you, Celia, and understand you!" Cooper bellowed, taking a dangerous step towards me. I stepped back, hitting the bed with my legs. "Can't you see that? Or are you really that damn blind?"

"You're such an asshole!" I shouted, pushing his chest roughly. His blow really hit me hard. "All you care about is this stupid pack when you never paid attention to me—your mate. You keep drilling me with questions that I'll never answer."

"Don't you dare insult *my* pack!" He seethed. "Do you think I need you? I don't! I can get any unmated female I want!"

My jaw dropped at his words. Was that classified as a rejection? How could he say such hurtful words to me? My wolf whimpered and began to cry loudly in my head. My heart shattered instantly, and the tears fell down faster than a waterfall. That's when I did the one thing I never thought I would never do in my life. I slapped him. The impact of my palm connecting with his cheek made a loud snap. Cooper's cheek turned red. He didn't bother to look at me after.

"Go to hell!" With my final words, I pushed him roughly on his chest and ran out.

I needed to get out of here. I couldn't stay. After what just happened, why would I stay? After he just said, why would I stay for my mate when, clearly, he would rather settle down with another woman? He didn't really care about me, and he made that perfectly clear.

My legs carried me down the stairs. I couldn't believe how fast I was running because I had managed to get out easily. I swung the door open and was greeted with a dark sky with heavy snow flurries coming down fast.

It was a blizzard, and it was coming on hard. Sucking in a breath, I shed my clothes and shifted quickly into my wolf. I didn't care if anyone saw my naked body that I had once only wanted my mate to see. Well, it didn't matter to me anymore. He didn't even want to see *it*, so why should it matter?

Lifting my head up, I gave Cooper a howl goodbye before sprinting off into the dark woods. Thank god for night vision because I would be lost without it.

I passed about a dozen unwary guards without any problem, and soon, I was leaving Cooper's territory and running into no man's land. I was finally free from my persistent mate who didn't care about my feelings or anyone else's. Why would I, for even a second, think about going back to him? If he didn't need me, then I guess I didn't need him.

He didn't mean it. My wolf whimpered, but I just ignored her pleas to go back. He should've thought what he was about to say to me before he spoke. He was being stupid and selfish. I couldn't believe he was my mate.

Stop it! I love him and his wolf! He loves us too. I can feel it in my gut!

Oh, yeah? Did your gut tell you that he was okay to mate with another woman? Whomever she may be? Stop being so naïve and get over it. I snapped at her stupid choice of words. Cooper? Love me? There's no way he was capable of such emotion.

Ignoring my wolf's constant pleas and cries, I ran as far as I could in the night. Pure adrenaline was pumping through my veins, fighting off any fatigue that came my way. I couldn't stop. Cooper was a great runner, and he proved that today. If he were to run after me, he'd be able to catch up to me in no time and could possibly mark me by force. If he did that, I would hate him forever.

I knew my wolf was trying to prove a point by crying, but I didn't want to give in to her sadness, although a part of my heart ached for Cooper and I couldn't stop crying too. But his words hurt me. He hurt me in a way I never imagined he would.

Rolling in the thick snow for a little, I sniffed a few times, trying to hide my scent. My so-called mate couldn't find me. I didn't want him to. If he couldn't find my scent, then I would be a free rogue. I'd be able to do whatever I wanted when I wanted. It didn't matter if Cooper wanted me back. His words were hurtful. I would never willingly go back to him

I stopped dead in my tracks when I heard a nearby shrub shake. Growling menacingly, I snarled when I saw who it was. Getting into a defensive stance, I prepared to charge when necessary. The wolf chuckled and trotted over to me with ease. He soon shifted and pulled on a pair of jeans to hide his most private parts.

"You're the one they're looking for." The rogue chuckled. His voice was rough and dry, and I was curious about how he found me. "I could use you as a part of my rebellion. Care to join us?"

I shook my head at him and turned around to walk away. However, he soon appeared in front of me and crossed his arms at me. Like I really needed to deal with him right now. Why not kill me like normal rogues would do?

"Come on, darling. You'll be my beta."

Now that got my attention.

He was an alpha, or at least an alpha rogue. I didn't know those even existed, but it made sense. Some werewolves were exiled from their packs sometimes for no apparent reason. It made sense for those people to look for a pack to be a part of. Of course, it wouldn't really be recognized as a real pack since rogues would be controlling it.

Before I could nod my head, I heard a voice in the distance. "Celia! No!"

I turned my head.

I growled at his voice and nodded my head at the alpha rogue. He smiled happily and nodded his head for me to follow. My paw moved, and soon, I was following him, someone I didn't even know. I trotted only a few steps behind the shirtless man and wagged my tail a little in happiness. I could be a beta. My life would finally change, and I would be able to roam around the world in safety. Since I would constantly be moving, I would be safe from my old pack as well. Blood Moon would never find me, and they could never hurt me. If Cooper wasn't going to have me as his luna, I would be something else. I couldn't wait.

Chapter 7

Cooper

    I sat in the armchair absolutely wiped out. How could she? How could my very own mate leave me and join a rogue? He offered to make her beta, but I knew it was a complete lie. They had run off before I could reach them, since my knees had collapsed at my mate's betrayal and I came crumbling to the ground. My pack members had suggested we regroup and formulate a plan to go after Celia. However, as I sat, my mind continued to formulate questions. Why did he even want her? She was an omega. What use could she be to him? Celia was incapable of killing or hurting someone. What was it about her that made him interested in her?

    Hearing the stomping of a pair of very loud heels, I soon dreaded what I was about to hear. Please, dear Moon Goddess, help me. There was nothing worse than an alpha getting scolded by his own mother, and I couldn't yell back at her because she'd get my dad in here. That would be a quite a sight. I wouldn't be able to talk back to my dad because he could easily take away the alpha title from me and give it to Adam. I wouldn't want that. He may be my best friend, but I didn't want him to come anywhere near my title. He was lucky enough to be a beta.

I looked up, and there stood my worst nightmare—my mother, my father, and Paige. All had their hands on their hips and were waiting for me to say something. Looking behind my sister, I could just see Sage glaring also at me.

"What the hell did you do?" Paige snapped angrily, but I only glared at her. "How in the holy hell did you get the strength to even tell your mate you wanted another female? Your temper will cause you to lose any possibility of love."

Now my mother would've yelled at my sister for her language, but soon she joined in. "When she gets back, you will be kissing her feet. How can I call you my son after that idiotic stunt you just pulled?"

"Dad, do you have anything to say?" I asked, sending him a look, which he only returned with disapproval.

"You, my son, are a total ass." For an alpha, he didn't even give out a speech and was entirely blunt with me, which he never did before.

"You're a meanie, Cooper." Sage pouted, crossing her arms and looking at me angrily. "I miss, Celia, too."

I looked at my hands and sighed. How could I possibly tell them this? They would never think about Celia in the same way again if I told them that she left for the rogues. I still couldn't believe my mate had done something so reckless, but as they always say, 'A broken heart can make you do crazy things.'

"Celia was recruited by a rogue and has decided to join the Rebellion of Rogues."

Loud gasps echoed from my family.

"She accepted the offer and went with Warner. I got there just in time to see her accept his offer. He promised to make her beta, which made her ecstatic. We need to find her before she gets hurt, or worse."

"We don't know where the Rebellion of Rogues camp is. No one does," my father said, and I growled in annoyance.

"Call all of our warriors for a meeting. I have something to announce to them."

"Right now?"

"Yes now, Dad!"

He nodded and took hurried steps out the door. My mother soon followed him, but my sister remained. I couldn't deal with any of them right now. Without any warning, Paige walked up to me and slapped me in the exact spot where Celia had. However, Paige's slap was harder and made my jaw ache a lot more. She must've put some extra force into it.

"I'm mind-chatting Adam right now to come back. You may need him. Although he knows that I need him too because I'm still sick, and I know him leaving while I'm still in this condition would be hard for him."

"He can come home," I told her before standing up and exiting the lounge room. My sister deserved to be happy. Why couldn't I do anything right when it came to Celia? I wanted to make her happy, but I didn't know what pleased her.

Sighing, I walked out of the room and to the front door where my mate had run out of only hours ago. I was so stupid. I should not have said what I said. I swear on my life I didn't mean those words, but I was getting tired of all the secrecy. A relationship had to be based on trust, and I'm disappointed to say that I didn't trust my mate one bit. My words may had been harsh, but it probably woke her up from her strange trance. I'd noticed that she spaced out a lot and didn't talk much when around people, even with me. I knew my alpha duties kept me busy, but at night I would enter my bedroom to see her looking out the window or staring at her hands. Either a lot must have been on her mind, or there was more to my mate than I believed.

When I was ready to speak to my people, I swung the front door open. I was greeted with at least fifty yards full of my fighters. Most of them looked very tired because it was very late, and some were even still in their boxers. I assumed I had woken them up in the dead of sleep, and not wanting to anger me more than I already was, they hurried quickly to my meeting. They were rubbing their eyes and stretching, but when I came into view, they straightened up and looked up.

Placing my hands on the railing, I leaned over and spoke, "Rise and shine, gentlemen. Today I have something very important to tell you, and I want you to take in every word." I paused and began to explain everything that was going on. "Your soon to be luna has been deceived and has been sucked into Warner's lies. We must find where they camp and bring her home. I will be in your debt if you find my mate and bring her back. I want groups of five scanning the perimeter and groups of ten exploring outside our territory. No one's sleeping tonight. We're finding her today."

***

Celia

I opened my eyes and woke up to a dull room. The shades hiding the sunlight were closed. My muscles stretched when I sat up in the bed. I gave a little smile when it felt relaxing. I turned to my left, expecting Cooper, but came up with an empty bed. I was about to question it before I was hit with a sudden realization: Cooper and I had a fight over Malcolm and my past; I ran away and opted to leave Cooper's pack for good. Everything that had recently happened quickly flooded my mind.

Sighing in sadness, I threw the sheets off and walked out of the room. I needed to speak with the rogue alpha. We needed to talk about my tasks as her beta. I was a *beta*. My new rank felt like music to my ears. Who would've thought an omega like me would go up the ranks. It felt incredible to feel such power and authority over things. It was felt overwhelmingly really good.

When I entered the living room, I found the rogue reading a newspaper and smoking a cigar. I cringed at the smell and sat a few chairs away from him. The scar on his face was extremely noticeable. It was red like a fresh wound. I knew I gave that to him. He had attacked me when I first came in contact with him. He had tried to kill me right before I ran into Cooper's pack, but here he was helping me.

He was on the far side of the leather couch, but when I sat down, he looked up immediately. Chuckling, he looked at the rusty watch on his left wrist and gave a loud, unattractive snort. Giving him a confused stare, he began to explain why he had done that.

"You've been out for fourteen hours. It's one in the afternoon." My eyes went wide when he finished his sentence, but he only seemed to laugh more. "I completely forgot to introduce myself. I'm Warner."

"Warner?" I asked, stunned. With his tall frame and bulky muscles, I never would've passed him for his name. "Well, I'm Celia."

"Yeah, I know who you are, doll. You've gotten pretty famous over the past few weeks. More than half of the packs in Canada are looking for you to bring you back to Blood Moon."

I wrinkled my nose in disgust at the name. It sounded like poison coming from his tongue. "I'm never going back to that vile place. I'd rather chew my own foot off than spend another torturous day there. I can't go back to my old pack, not after what I ran from. Not after…"

"I couldn't agree more with that horrid pack. The only good thing that came out of that pack was my mate." Warner snorted before his face dropped for a second.

"I have a question," I said, shifting on the couch a bit as I settled for a comfortable spot. I remembered his eyes, and the mark I had left on his face had questions swirling through my mind. "Why did you attack me a couple weeks ago?"

"Call it boredom." He shrugged. "Plus, anyone who can survive an alpha's attack is born to be mated to one. I let you go because I didn't want to piss off another alpha in the future. Goddess only knows what he'd do to me."

I rolled my eyes and lay back a bit. Cooper would never spend, even a second to try and avenge me. If I died, I doubt he'd care. I was just a worthless mate to him that never bothered to talk to him. This was his fault too. I never would've left if he hadn't spoken out of line. He had gotten me really angry and said worse things to me. I may never forgive him.

My thoughts were interrupted when a young teenager ran towards us, looking hot and sweaty. He panted and began to talk. "Someone has entered our borders. He's coming in strong, and I can sense it's a powerful alpha. He has an army with him."

Cooper. It had to be him.

"Well, I think he and I should have a chat. Guide him to the back gate. I'll meet him there." The boy nodded and walked off. "Ready to have your first negotiation?"

I agreed and stood up.

It didn't take long for Cooper to arrive at the house, and when I got there, he growled at Warner angrily. I couldn't believe the possessiveness he was showing. He must be an excellent actor. We were a good five yards in front of each other, and I could see his eyes had turned black.

"What're you doing here, Cooper? We had an agreement. I stayed between you and Blood Moon's territory to prevent you guys from starting a war. This, this is a violation of our deal." Warner scolded like he would to a five-year-old.

"Give her back." Shaking his head, Cooper took a step forward.

"I'm afraid I can't do that, son. She isn't allowed to leave unless I say so."

Cooper growled at his unwise answer and took another dangerous step forward.

"She's my mate. So unless you want to go against fate and the Moon Goddess, I suggest you give her to me before I remove your head from your neck." His voice was laced with so much venom that even I shrunk back at his tone. My mate was furious.

Warner let out an angry sigh. "Take her then. I don't want to go against fate. It would be wrong of me to forbid a man his mate when some are unable such privileges." He nodded his head a look of pain on his face. I was roughly pushed into Cooper's direction.

He caught me just in time, and I was greeted with immense sparks and tingling sensation. I struggled against Cooper's hold, but he wouldn't budge. Nodding his head in thanks, he picked me up and threw me over his shoulder. I pounded on his back and began yelling curses at him. I hated him, but why did he have to make me feel this way? The slaps and kicks I gave him didn't seem to be enough to affect him, and I soon gave up instantly.

"Put. Me. Down!" I cried, getting angry with him. "I hate you! I hate you so much. Why can't you get that into your selfish head?"

That's how it went for at least two hours. I couldn't get my idiotic mate to let go of me. Now, I lay limp on his back, completely wiped out from my little scruffle.

Cooper didn't bother talking to me because I knew he was still very mad, but so was I. All the blood in my body was going to my head, and I was slowly getting dizzy from Cooper's sway while holding me. It felt like I was being spun around so many times. Whenever I tried looking over his shoulder, he would grab the back of my head and push it away. Sometimes he would even smack my butt, and that got a reaction from my wolf.

Reality finally set in, and I realized how much trouble I was really in here. Mates never, ever left each other for any reason. Usually, the couple would sort it out and try to figure out a way around what they had either said or done. What would Cooper do to me? Would he lock me in his room for life and never let my wolf out ever again? That got my wolf annoyed, but she then started thinking of dirty thoughts that involved my evil mate.

Being an omega had really affected my sense of judgment. I never should've run away. But that was my nature. If I feel threatened or endangered, I would flee and hope for the best, no matter who I was leaving behind. Sage. That sweetheart must be heartbroken that I left. Then there's Paige. I told her one of my many secrets, and she didn't even let it slip to Cooper. How could I be so selfish to leave people who actually cared for me when the only reason I left was because of their brother? Emilia showed kindness to me and treated me like her own daughter. It was what I'd always wanted, but I blew it off and followed my impulsive nature.

Cooper was not the only one to blame. I hid secrets from him, and he got annoyed, which was common in most alphas. They had short tempers, and they would attack anyone verbally or physically if provoked. His family would probably laugh at me for being the self-centered girl I was.

Chapter 8

I heard the sounds of feet walking on wood, and I snapped my eyes open to look at the dark wood I'd always seemed to like. Bracing myself for the unwelcoming argument we would be having have again, I felt Cooper placing me on the ground gently. There's nothing I could possibly say to him that wouldn't make him hate me more.

About to open my mouth, as I stood up, I was soon greeted by a loud squeal, and I felt something hugging my hips tightly. "Celia, I missed you so much! My brother is a meanie for saying those rude things to you. Can you please forgive him? I don't want you to leave again!" Sage's adorable voice cried. I turned around to see tears leaking out of her eyes.

Bending down, so we were eye level, I hugged her and whispered, "I can't promise you anything. Your brother is the one that needs to make up a damn good apology."

The little girl sighed and kissed me on the cheek real quick before leaving. I stood up and ran down the hall. My feet carried me down the hallway and up the stairs. Next thing I knew I was in Cooper's room, looking for something to wear. Deciding it was best to wear something that wasn't my mate's, I exited the room and decided to go to Paige's. She was a girl with a sense of fashion. I could just borrow her clothes for the time being. Surely, she wouldn't mind.

I stopped at her door and knocked once. It was swung open, and I was pulled inside in a matter of seconds. A rush of whiplash hit me, and before I could complain, I was engulfed in the biggest hug in history. Hugging Paige back, I let her strangely cry on my shoulder. Why was she even crying?

When she released me, and that was when she exploded. "You left without even saying goodbye to me!" Paige hugged me again and sobbed. "You're my sister now. You can't just leave like that. Promise me no matter how stupid my brother is or what he says, you'll punch him in the face instead of running away."

"Paige, you have no idea how much his words hurt me," I whispered, feeling my throat get tight.

"You have to understand Cooper, Celia!" she bellowed, releasing me and throwing her hands up in the air. "He doesn't know how to express his feelings. My brother doesn't know how to tell someone he loves them. Never in my life has he told me once that he loves me, or even Sage. Cooper can't show people his feelings because he thinks it would give his enemies an idea that he's weak."

My mouth instantly dropped, and my eyes went wide. Was that what Cooper really thought? He thought that showing your feelings was a sign of weakness? Love had always been a sign of strength.

I remained silent, not knowing what to say about Cooper. Maybe it's just how Cooper was programmed; he couldn't direct his feelings towards anyone. My mate may never be able to love me the way I would want him to. When I thought of him, I thought of someone who would love me no matter how different or complicated I could be.

"By the way, your 'one and only' didn't even let my mate visit me when he went looking for you. We've been mind-chatting a lot, but that's it." Paige added with a long sigh. "Adam was forced to go back to hunt for rogues and to bring back anyone who may have information about you."

"They're trying to find why I had left my old pack?" I asked, flabbergasted and a little worried. If Adam found out, there was no way he wouldn't tell Cooper. My secret was doomed along with any hope I had of being truly happy.

"That's how Cooper is. If you won't tell him, he'll find it out himself. My brother has the knack for finding things and doing everything when necessary just to get results. Watch your back at all costs, Celia." Paige warned, shaking her finger at me. "Who knows what he will find."

I pinched the bridge of my nose and mumbled, "What do I do?"

"I think it's time for you guys to have a talk." Paige encouraged, patting me on the shoulder and roughly pushing me towards the door. She opened it and threw me into the hallway and closed the door behind her with a loud slam. "Good talk! Good luck!"

Bracing myself, I walked back the hallway and to Cooper's room. I was beginning to sweat just thinking about it. My heart was racing, and I was terrified. This may mean life or death for me. Any revelation could get me killed if the information was misunderstood. Sucking a brave breath, I opened Cooper's bedroom door and walked inside.

There he was, looking at the ceiling while lying on the bed. I walked in slowly and closed the door behind me. Leaning against it, I watched him scrunch his eyebrows in deep thought. I wondered what's going on inside that pretty little head of his. His eyes were trained profoundly on the white ceiling, blinking only a few times. Then he let out a big gust of air and sat up to face me. Shockingly, his eyes were filled with regret.

"I didn't mean what I said before. It was wrong and childish to say something as stupid as that." I couldn't believe an alpha actually had admitted he was wrong about what he thought or did. "Please forgive me. I think about you and only you when it comes to something serious…like the mating process."

I didn't speak but just stared at him emotionlessly. Quickly, he sprang up and cautiously walked up to me. Ever so gently, he placed his forehead against mine and breathed in my scent. My eyes fluttered close from his close proximity, seeing how close his lips were to mine. Every single part of my body turned to goo at his next words.

"You're mine and only mine—" he paused, swallowing hard that his Adam's apple bobbed "—forever."

My heart melted immediately without me wanting it to, and it really got me annoyed. He couldn't just say I was his and thought it would mean something to me. Sure, it made me feel somewhat wanted, but that still didn't make up for the mean things he said. Cooper needed to earn my forgiveness, not just ask for it casually.

I gave my mate a blank expression before speaking, "Is that supposed to mean something to me? Or do you really think calling me yours will make me forgive you? You have to understand that what you said hurt me. Go think about ways to earn my forgiveness because right now, I really don't want to see you or even talk to you."

Cooper's eyes went wide, and his jaw clenched angrily. My insides began to throb with fear, and I pressed my back harder against the door if that was even possible. He moved his head closer to me, and my breath hitched in my throat.

I shrunk back in fear, but instead of hurting me or saying something that would make me cry, he whispered in my ear, "Then I guess I have to do the one thing I've wanted to do ever since I saw your beautiful face." He moved his head only a centimeter away from me.

Before I could say no to him and what he's about to do, he did the one thing I never thought he would do. He swooped his head down and crashed his lips to mine. Sparks exploded all around me, and I closed my eyes from the pleasure. It felt amazing to finally kiss him for the first time. There wasn't anything I wanted more than to kiss his lips for the next hundred years.

Our lips moved in perfect sync, but Cooper didn't try to deepen the kiss. Occasionally, he would brush his tongue against my lips. He rested his hands on my hips to hold me in place against the door.

I was kissing my mate. Or more notably, he was kissing me. With his rough hand, he began to slowly draw small circles on my cheek while still kissing me.

When Cooper pulled away, I could still feel the taste of the kiss lingering and tingling on my lips. Slowly, he pulled his hands away and rested his head against my forehead again. I was panting, and I could see that he was a little out of breath too. My eyes fluttered open, and I looked up to meet his beautiful blue eyes. The pair stared intently into my violet ones.

"Now, am I forgiven?" His voice was hoarse and husky, creating a sexy and hot shiver down my small, cold body.

"Not quite," I whispered before taking his face in my hands and bringing his lips back to mine. Already, I missed the feeling of them, and I welcomed them back with a smile.

Cooper chuckled in the kiss before slowly moving his lips with mine. I didn't know what to do since I was inexperienced, so I let my mate take the lead. The kiss grew more passionate by the second, making my knees buckle. Luckily, Cooper was able to catch me, and lifted me up without leaving my desperate lips. Within a second, I had my legs around his hips.

To my disappointment, he removed his lips from mine and began to pepper light kisses along my jaw. I was in complete shock when I let out a purr after he kissed my soft spot. Soon, he was kissing my neck, biting softly and licking the skin, driving me crazy. I dug my nails into his soft hair when he began to suck a certain spot that caused chills to run up and down my spine. I moaned softly in his ear.

"Am I forgiven yet?" Cooper grinned, looking proudly at me.

"Are you seriously asking me this?" I asked in shock over the intense kiss.

"Well, yeah, I mean you seemed to be really enjoying this." Leaning down at me, he gave me one long fiery kiss on my lips. A moan escaped from my slightly opened mouth. "Am I forgiven? Or do we have to have a more intense make-out session that involves less clothes?"

"Yes!" I shouted, covering my blushing face. Thinking about him with less clothes made my wolf stir with excitement. "Yes, you're forgiven."

Chapter 9

The next morning, I open my eyes, and they widened at the sight next to me. Cooper was beside me in bed and sleeping like a baby. His copper hair was in his eyes, but I could still see how long his eyelashes were. Not only this, but his mouth was open just a little for a husky breath to escape. With his chest on full display, I couldn't help but enjoy watching him sleep. I may never get over how perfect he looked. It's amazing how peaceful he looked right now.

I tried to shift a little but soon realized that my mate's arm was pinning me down to the comfortable mattress. However, my main concern was going it to the bathroom. Now, under any other circumstance, I would be very happy to have Cooper hold me like this, but I felt very uncomfortable.

I couldn't hold my bladder for another second, so I lifted the layers of sheets off me. One by one, the warmth I had been under was now disappearing, and I was now only warmed up by Cooper's body heat. Deciding whether to just throw his arm off me or gently lift it, I was interrupted by a loud ring from a phone.

Cooper jumped up on his sleep and shoved the sheets off quickly as if not realizing I was awake. My mate ran over to the phone on his desk and answered it in a soft whisper. Rolling my eyes, I got up as well and walked past him to use the bathroom. A shower seemed like a good idea, seeing as I hadn't taken one in almost two days. I felt disgusted. How did Cooper manage to sleep in the same bed as me when I was like this?

Opening the bathroom door, I turned one last time to look at my mate. He was still shirtless, showing his lovely eight-pack that I could never get over. When he finally saw me, he shockingly gave me a small smile and continued his conversation with someone on the phone. I entered the bathroom with a huge grin on my face. I was glad Cooper and I could finally look at each other without me being so terrified of him. We both had accepted each other.

Sighing in blissfulness, I peeled the my clothes from my body and dropped them on the floor. Flicking the water on, I tugged my hair out of its bun and fluffed it up. When I was sure that the water from the shower was warm enough, I jumped in and began to wash myself. Putting the shampoo in my hair, I began to massage the shampoo to remove the dirt. Rinsing the suds off, I scanned the shower for any razors. My face brightened when I found a bright pink one resting next to Cooper's.

When I was done cleaning and shaving, I got out of the steamy shower and dried my body off. Water annoyingly started to drip from my hair. Thinking fast, I grabbed a hair tie and made a large bun at the top of my head. With the towel I had used to dry off, I wrapped it around myself and walked out of the bathroom.

A blast of cold air hit my exposed skin, and when I entered Cooper's bedroom, I noticed he was already getting dressed and ready for his alpha duties. He was buckling his pants with a belt when he looked up at me. Immediately, he gave me a small greeting before walking to the nightstand for something. I waited patiently for him to put on his favorite watch while I sat on the leather couch. My mate was still shirtless, but my ogling was ended when he pulled a navy blue wifebeater on. But it didn't help in any way to hide his eight-pack when he turned to look at me.

"I'll be back by seven. If there's any problem, we have guards posted in every exit." He explained.

"What? You ordered men to guard me?" I snapped, clutching the towel tightly in anger. "Why would you do that?"

Cooper pulled on a grey hat over his head and looked at me without showing any emotion. "Do you think it didn't cross my mind that you would run away from me again?" my mate stated simply before tugging on a pair of boots. "It's the most logical thing to do, Celia."

Making his way across the room, he picked up his laptop and walked to the door.

"Are you kidding me?" I shouted, walking up to him. "What am I supposed to do all day?"

"Well, my sisters are at school. My parents are out, and everyone else is gone but Jeremy. I don't know. Think of something." My mate shrugged before walking out the door and shutting it behind him.

I stared at the door in complete shock. What was I supposed to do with Jeremy? I didn't know the guy. Paige wasn't around for me to take care of; Sage was at school. Emilia and Patrick were both currently unavailable and were off to somewhere. How was I supposed to keep myself busy and entertained? Just when I thought my mate had finally trusted me, he had guards to watch my every move.

I got dressed quickly into Cooper's clothes since I Paige was gone and I didn't want to rummage through her stuff without her permission.

Like always, Cooper's clothes smelled just like him, and I took in a big whiff of it. His scent was so masculine yet sweet like apples. It was almost like a drug. My scent was probably close to his scent since I'd been around him so much and bathing in the products he used.

Walking around in my mate's big socks, I exited Cooper's room and went down the stairs to the kitchen. I finally decided to cook something delicious. I could make pancakes and fill it with fruits or candies. I couldn't really remember what it was called, but it tasted delicious and sweet. Entering the beautiful kitchen, I thought I would never get over how amazing this kitchen was. It always looked brand new to me.

Just when I thought I was alone, Felicity appeared from under the cabinet, holding what appeared to be a wrench. She was grumbling angrily something under her breath and tossed the wrench aside. The poor woman was covered in grease. I had to hold my nose from the awful smell that was radiating off her flawlessly tanned skin.

When she looked up at me, she got up at once and she plastered a fake grin on her face. "Oh, Celia dear, I'm glad to see you." Her smile was forced on her face, which made me a little suspicious. "Would you like something to eat? Breakfast perhaps?"

Eyeing her dirty hands, I shook my head at her. "I know how to cook. Why don't you get washed up? I love to cook, and I'd love to prepare my own breakfast from now on," I told her.

She happily agreed. Hurriedly, she ran out of the kitchen to wash the grease off her petite body frame.

Once I was alone, I began preparing the ingredients for my breakfast. I was still trying to remember what the food was called, but I knew it would come to me eventually. Taking the pan that was on the stove, I cleaned it and placed it back where I had found it. Remembering the recipe by heart, I quickly got the ingredients: one cup of flour, a pinch of salt, an egg, a cup of milk, and a tablespoon of butter.

I got all the ingredients from the food pantry and the huge refrigerator and placed them all on the counter. Whipping the batter quickly, I poured a large circle in the center of the pan and moved the batter around by turning the handle. While the batter was melting in the pan, I decided to slice some bananas, and then after that, I flipped the dough over and let it cook on the burner.

Letting my breakfast to cook, I walked back to the fridge and pulled out a spray can of whipped cream. Placing the sugary goodness on the island, I took a little pancake on a plate and placed it on the island. The moment I tossed my banana on my breakfast, a familiar voice echoed from the stairs.

"Do I smell crepes?" I heard from down the hall. "Hey, Felicity, why are you cooking so late?"

The next thing I knew, a guy walked in with messy hair and a pair of sweatpants with a matching t-shirt. When he saw me about to spray some whipped cream on my food, he let out a low chuckle.

"Long time no see, eh, love?" He chuckled, and I soon noticed his accent. It was hidden, but I could point it out with ease. "What is it that you did again? Oh, right, you ran away from your only chance of having a soul mate." He paused, leaning against the door frame and examining me. I glared at him for his blunt comment. "Oh, right, I forgot to introduce myself. I'm Jeremy."

Giving him a halfhearted smile, I responded, "I'm Celia, Cooper's mate."

"I've noticed. His scent is all over you." He explained, entering the kitchen. He snatched an apple from the counter. Biting into the fruit with a crunch, he spoke with his mouth full, "I don't have a mate. Don't want one really. I mean, why would they want to mate with a weak, pathetic wolf such as myself when there are stronger, unmated ones out there? I'm an omega, the pack's servant as some may call me."

"Don't doubt yourself, Jeremy." I scolded him. "I'm an omega just like you and my mate didn't reject me."

Slamming his fist down the countertop, he growled in frustration. "That's because he's an alpha. And he needs a luna to keep this pack in order. I mean, you could be doing half the things he wastes his time doing."

"I just got here only a couple weeks ago," I stated, getting really annoyed with this kid. "I need to settle in and such. He does what he does, and I'll do what I—"

"Do you know that your very own mate is investigating you and looking for any record of you on file? Hell, he ordered hackers to get into Blood Moon's database."

With that, I almost choked on my own food, but luckily, he handed me a glass of water. Cooper was hacking into Blood Moon's systems just to find out who I was and why I ran away? What if he found the records Alpha Zaire had in his personal files? I could be interrogated because of it. I would never be able to handle an interrogation after seeing what Cooper did to Malcolm.

I opened my mouth to speak, but no words came out. Clearing my breath and sucking a big gulp of air, I tried again. "How long has he been doing this?"

"A little over a week," Jeremy answered, looking worriedly at me. "What are you going to do?"

"What mates are supposed to do—straighten things out with him."

***

I was pacing in Cooper's room for at least a hundred times, maybe more. I was really getting anxious. My mate wasn't back yet. He was really in for a big surprise that would either hurt our relationship or strengthen it. I didn't like it when he kept secrets from me—like going through my files. I may not be the definition of the perfect mate, but doing something as rude and selfish as investigating me behind my back was just too upsetting for me.

When the door finally opened, I took a deep breath. Cooper walked in looking tired than ever before. Bags had formed under his eyes, and his tight skin and clean shaven face was loose and rough.

His eyes snapped to mine when I had stopped my pacing. I was now glaring at him.

"You okay, Celia?"

"I don't know. You tell me. You're the one who's ordering people to investigate me." My voice was sharp as a knife, and I knew it cut pretty deep.

"What're you talking about?" he questioned.

"Stop lying!" I bellowed, angrily tossing my hands in the air. "Just for once, tell me the truth."

I knew he was confused until I saw recognition on his face and then regret. Jeremy was right; my mate was doing things behind my back. I was beyond angry with him. I noticed his shoulders sag, and he walked further into the room. He placed his laptop on his desk and turned it on. While he was waiting for it, he let out a long sigh.

"Who told you?" Not answering his question, I remained silent. "I ordered anyone who was on it not to say anything about it. Who told you?" His voice was rough with exhaustion, but I wasn't going to rest until he told me what he had found.

"That's none of your business. And my business is you going through my files without asking me. Cooper, you even ordered your people to hack into Blood Moon's database!" I cried and looked away from him.

"For what it's worth, I didn't find anything but your name and rank," Cooper whispered while he walked over to me and gripped my waist. I was still upset with him, so I tried to escape his grasp, but he wasn't having any of that. "I'll end what I'm doing if it makes you happy."

"Yes, delete anything that you found. When you do, you can go to sleep," I spoke and turned my back to him so he could do his work.

Cooper went back into his desk and began to scan the computer but soon stopped and looked back at me. I tried to turn my back on him but stopped when he said something.

"You never told me that they found you on Zaire's steps, that he had adopted you and that you never knew your real parents."

My entire body froze as my breathing began to pick up. My chest was aching, and I tried everything to calm myself down. The thought of going back to the old pack was something I could never deal with.

"Yes, he did adopt me, but I never saw him as a father," I stated and finally gained control of my limps. Walking slowly to the bed, I soon realized that there was no way I was going to sleep. "I am going to go for a walk."

"Alright, just stay on this floor." He informed me and then looked up at me, smiling. "I don't want you getting lost on any other floor."

Nodding my head, I exited Cooper's room and ran my hand through my hair. Cooper's words probably didn't seem like it meant something, but it did to me. It brought back all the memories, the times when I had been so afraid of my own shadow. Hot tears threatened to fall down, but I pushed them away as I rounded a corner. I didn't know where I was going, but I needed to process what he had found out about me. If he found out more about my past, he'd start asking questions that I knew I would never have the guts to answer.

While walking aimlessly, unaware of my surrounding, I suddenly rammed right into a black hooded figure. Apologizing right away, I kept walking. I walked a little further. I then turned another corner but came face to face with something I had seen not so long ago.

Blood.

A large pool of the red liquid littered the floor. I covered my mouth to stop myself from screaming out in horror. Tears leaked from my eyes and I tried to scream for help, but I suddenly lost my voice. I just stood there like a fish out of water, trying so hard to yell.

Rounding a corner, I slowly walked and traced some human flesh as I walked a little further ahead. The tears were now streaming down my face. As I walked closer, I saw organs spread across the floor, and when I looked up, I was already facing a dead end. And that's when I was finally able to scream.

In front of me was a male's naked body nailed to the ceiling—with a slit on his throat and a large gaping hole in his chest. His sandy hair was covered in dirt while his body had chunks of his skin missing.

I looked around for help. I looked down at the floor to see a large chunk of meat. Looking closer, I screamed a murderous wail when I noticed what it was.

It was a heart, and it obviously from the dead body.

"Cooper ..." I whispered and turned to the only exit I found before shouting. "Cooper!"

I backed away from the dead body, but soon my back was pressed against a warm body. It wasn't comforting like Cooper's, and right away I knew it wasn't him. I spun around and saw the hooded man I bumped into earlier. The hood was still up so I couldn't see his face, but what I saw was a bloodied knife in his hand.

"Cooper! Help! Cooper!" I screamed, but the man placed his hand over my mouth to shut me up. I cried for help from anyone, but my voice was muffled.

"Hush, this will only take a minute," the man's creepy voice whispered, and he grabbed my right arm and rolled my sleeve up.

I tried shaking away from him while he drew the knife closer to my fragile skin. Thrashing and crying, he soon had to remove his hand from my mouth after I bit his leather glove. Once I was able to speak again, I cried out, but the cry for help soon turned into a cry of pain after a painful sting erupted on my forearm. The hooded man began to carve something into my skin, but I closed my eyes in pain. I screamed in pain as he trailed the knife further down my arm and closer to my wrist.

Once again, he tugged the knife into my skin with a lot of force, and I cried out again. The pain was excruciating. I begged to stop. My own blood mixed with the blood on the floor caused a sickly smell to waft in the air.

"Cooper! Please!" I bellowed, tugging for my arm to be released, but it only made the knife dig deeper. "Stop! Please! Cooper!"

Suddenly, my shoulder was touched, and I was spun around. The grip the man had on me was gone, and I wrapped my arms around Cooper's warm frame. I cried onto his chest, and he whispered soothing words.

Why isn't he attacking the hooded man?

Looking up, I faced his confused face. "Celia, what's wrong? Who hurt you?" He was rubbing my shoulders comfortingly.

Pushing myself out of his grasp, I pointed to the scene on the floor "There! There's blood everywhere and even a dead body!" I looked around and then stopped.

The dead body was no longer there, and even the man who had killed him was nowhere to be found. The blood on the floor was gone—even the organs and the heart. The nails that had held the dead body was now holding a large mirror.

Where did everything go?

Looking down at my feet, I noticed that there was blood dripping down my arm. Before I could roll the sleeve up, Cooper was already doing that for me, examining my wound.

"Celia, why did you do this to yourself?" Cooper asked, looking at the wound in horror.

Confused by his words, I was about to tell him it wasn't me but stopped when I saw a knife in my left hand. My eyes bulged out of their sockets in shock. I dropped the knife as if it had burned me. My left hand was covered with my own blood from the cut that I myself had made. The tears in my eyes didn't stop from falling.

Looking down at my rolled sleeve, I scanned my bleeding forearm. I leapt in horror as I gently touched the symbol. I'd seen one person doing it on someone's flesh—Alpha Zaire. It was a red circle, much like the moon, with two stars in the top right corner. He had told me it was his symbol—a sign which meant to tell who he was. If he had caught a rogue in his territory, he would carve the symbol on his or her forearm and release them and then hunt them down. It was like a game of cat and mouse to him.

"Celia, why did you do that?" Cooper asked, shaking my shoulders in order to gain my attention. I removed my eyes from the bleeding symbol and looked up at him.

"I don't know."

Chapter 10

Cooper swiftly placed me on a medical table that I'd been all too familiar with in my life. The metallic surface was cold on my hands after I placed them on it. My blood's scent was still heavy in the air, and I noticed Cooper look at it one last time before looking up into my violet eyes. I knew I was pale from blood loss and my skin was growing hot from trying to heal itself. My mate touched my sweating palm, not minding at all even though I probably looked disgusting.

I couldn't stop shaking with fear and paranoia. The thought of the hooded man appearing again terrified me to no end. My eyes racked the medical room, worried that something would jump out at me. Beads of sweat formed on my brow, making it shine from the bright lights above me. This was becoming too much to handle, and I couldn't find any way to calm my nerves down. Not even the presence of my own mate helped me.

"We'll find out what's been going on with you. I promise," Cooper whispered comfortingly, trying to stop my body from shaking terribly. He ran his large callused hands over my shoulders affectionately, but I just took them and pushed them away, my blood dripping onto the floor in the process.

The door was swung open, and in came a woman with a clipboard and a huge smile on her beautiful tanned face. Her green eyes seemed to sparkle when she saw me, but it soon disappeared when Cooper walked in front of me. He growled warningly at her. She just rolled her eyes and placed the clipboard beside me. My mate unwillingly moved slightly away from me. A whimper escaped my lips when he removed his hand, and he instantly moved closer to me so he could take it once again.

"Well, Celia, it's very nice to officially meet you. My name is Sheila. I'm the pack doctor." She introduced herself. "How have you been feeling?"

I looked at Cooper for help, not wanting to speak to Sheila. I was still in shock from what had just happened and the blood was making my insides squirm. My mouth wouldn't form words, so I just kept quiet. I wanted to speak, but for some odd reason, I couldn't form the proper words.

"She did this," Cooper answered for her and rolled up my sleeve, so it was almost to my shoulder. "Without her even realizing she was doing it."

I looked at the wound fully now and couldn't help but feel the bile rising in my throat. I knew I was going to be sick if I didn't look away, but I couldn't. The wound was raw, and blood was dripping out of it. Bits of skin stuck out from the surface, making it look almost like rubber. How could I do so much damage to myself?

"I didn't do this to myself." I argued, looking Sheila in the eye. "The man did it. He killed the teenager and did this to me. He had a hood on so I couldn't see him, but I know he killed the boy."

I was telling the truth, but something inside me told me they didn't believe me. It was true though. Someone must've removed the body and cleaned up the blood on the floor just in time so Cooper wouldn't see it. It made perfect sense.

"She's been saying this to me over and over again. I sent some people to look for a dead body, but they didn't find anything. There was no other scent when they checked the place. And no one ever goes to that part of the house." Cooper explained, looking at me worriedly before turning back to Sheila. "I don't understand why she keeps telling me this."

My heart literally shattered at his word. How could he? Was he indirectly accusing me of lying? I was his mate. I would never lie to him about something as serious as a dead body.

Sheila pulled out a penlight from her pocket and pointed her finger at the wall. I watched the finger while she moved the small light into my eye from side to side. "Well...it seems that in her mind it was real when in reality, it never truly occurred."

"What does that mean?" Cooper growled, tightening his hand on me, almost close to crushing it. I squirmed from his grip, but he didn't slacken it one bit.

Sheila took a step away from me once she had turned the annoying light off. "It means she was hallucinating." She began to touch different parts of my body. "Is she taking any medication?"

She touched my shoulder, making me hiss in pain from an old wound. It was still raw and tender, but I didn't want Cooper to worry about that right now. I wanted him to understand what was going on with me, but I didn't want him to know about my past. It was too complicated for him to comprehend. I didn't want to share that part of my life with anyone.

Cooper shook his head. "Celia doesn't even know where the medicine cabinet is, so no."

"Cooper, make her stop touching me." I begged, trying to move Sheila away from me. "I don't want her touching me."

Regret flashed in his aquamarine eyes, but he didn't say anything. I was looking at him with desperation written on my face. It hurt to see him feel guilty even though none of this was even his fault. He shouldn't blame himself for something what had happened to me.

Ignoring my pleas, Sheila took my face in her hand and examined me. "Dear, have you been through any traumatic events?"

Every single place she touched me began to trigger different memories. I wriggled for her to release me and even went as far as kicking her in the gut, which made her lose her balance. Thankful that she released me, I relaxed. "I'll take that as a yes," Cooper mumbled, helping Sheila regain her balance. "You, okay?"

"Yes, and I think I know what's actually wrong with your mate," she stated, rubbing her stomach that I had previously kicked. "She has a major case of PTSD." *What the hell is that?* "Post-traumatic stress disorder."

I gave her a confused look. There was no way I even had a disorder. It made absolutely no sense to me. I may still be in shock from the events that happened to me before, but they couldn't do anything to me. I tried my best to believe that the past was in the past, but I couldn't.

"How do you know for sure?" Cooper asked, placing his hand on my waist for comfort. My body relaxed a little, and I leaned into his touch.

"Well, the symptoms include auditory hallucinations, intruding dreams, numbing, and avoidance." Sheila explained. "Frankly, she's being escorted into her past multiple times that have involved some terrifying event. Her mind is taking her to the exact time and place of some disaster. This could explain how she reacted upstairs. She was reliving that moment."

Cooper scrunched his eyebrows in confusion and thought for a moment. *Please don't say it. Please don't.* I mentally crossed my fingers and waited. I knew he was thinking hard about his answer, and the wait was killing me. I could feel my heart beating in my throat, almost giving me a borderline panic attack.

Finally, Cooper answered, "Well, she cried for someone in her sleep saying he was all she had left, and most of the time, she cried out in pain even though she wasn't really hurt. This hallucination involved a dead man and a hooded man who, in her dreams, probably killed the guy." My mate slowly turned to me. "Celia, did...did you witness a murder?"

I remained silent and looked at him with my eyes, pleading for him to let this go. My insides were burning with fear, and my wolf was pacing, trying to figure out how to answer him. Biting the inside of my mouth, I tried desperately not to cave in and tell him the entire story. He would see it as a joke or roll his eyes and ask for the truth. With that, I kept my mouth shut and did not answer Cooper.

Thankfully, Sheila interrupted our staring contest. "There isn't much I can do for her. However, having support from others can provide some relief."

"Thank you, Sheila. You may go."

"Have a good night." She spared me one last glance before she left the room.

Cooper nodded his head, not bothering to remove his eyes from mine. Carefully, I peeled his hands off my body and leaped off the medical table. My legs felt wobbly, but I regained my balance and walked away from them. Sheila's and Cooper's eyes burned on the back of my body when I left the room. My heart was hammering, and I tried to let the new information I had learned process in my head. I couldn't even understand how to make my body function now that Cooper was close to figuring thing out. How in the world could I explain to him what had happened in the past? How could I explain my entire life to him?

Slowly taking the stairs, I didn't bother listening to the argument that had begun with Cooper and the pack doctor. I felt numb and scared. Cooper was going to figure everything out eventually, whether I liked it or not.

When I reached the bedroom, I rolled over on the bed and cradled myself. Only seconds later, I heard the door open but didn't bother to look over to see who came in. The tears were threatening to escape my eyes as I felt a presence behind me. I forced myself to shut my eyes, hoping to stop any chance of tears from falling.

"Celia?"

I sniffed as I heard Sage's angelic voice and turned around to see her hugging a teddy bear close to her chest. She was rubbing her eyes.

"What's wrong, Sage?" I asked, running my hand over her cheek.

"I had a bad dream." She sobbed, and her tears fell down from her eyes like a waterfall.

Scooping her up, I sat up and cradled her in my arms. She clung to me, and soon, I was doing the same to her. We cried on each other for different reasons: her for her nightmare, and me for what was happening to me.

"You won't leave me right?" Sage asked, and I almost sobbed loudly at her words.

"I will never leave you." I promised before I kissed the top of her head gently. "Never."

I remembered saying those exact words to the only person I cared about once—the only person I needed to survive back then. My promise was short-lived, and I knew it was best to forget, but how could I?

Holding Sage close, I lay down on the bed to let her rest her head on my chest. It was an uncomfortable position, but I wanted to make her happy—the same thing I wanted for him.

***

I blinked my eyes open, adjusting to the darkness that had still engulfed me. Trying to move my muscles, I was instead greeted by a head rested on it. My head snapped so fast that I thought it was going to break, but I relaxed once I saw Sage in a fetal position beside me. Her breathing was even and tickled the hairs on my arm. She was still fast asleep in my arms.

I looked around in search of Cooper but found him nowhere in sight. I sighed. We needed to talk. I wanted to know how he felt about all this. Having a mate with PTSD must be hard on him, especially since he was an alpha. I knew how much he wanted to protect me from others. Unfortunately, he couldn't protect me from my own mind.

Sage stirred a bit in her sleep, and I took the chance to lift her up on my lap. Sitting up, I stroked her soft hair and hauled her up. She rested her head on my shoulder, and I stood up slowly. Her legs wound around my waist, and her arms hung lazily. Shifting so she was more comfortable, I began to carry my mate's sister out of the room.

As I walked to Sage's room, I overheard a discussion downstairs but shrugged it off thinking it was nothing. After putting Sage in her bed and kissing her forehead, I wrapped the blankets around her small frame. A babyish snore came from her throat, and I couldn't help but smile at her innocence. I wondered if I would've been like that—at peace all the time.

Shutting the door behind me, I traveled my way back to the room. However, before I could reach for the door handle, a loud shout came from downstairs. I snapped my head in the direction where a soft stream of light was coming from. I scouted the hallway before making my way towards the stairs. A hushed whisper calmed the voice, and I instantly recognized the whisper as Emilia's. Why was she up so late?

My bare feet touched the glass staircase one at a time, and the further I went, the louder the voices became. They were coming from the second floor, two stories down from where I was. I'd never been in this part of the house and couldn't stop myself from exploring every inch. I heard another annoying voice, and I turned to the left where the light was leaking from a dark door.

I gripped the handle and pushed it open slowly, blinking rapidly from the light. When my eyes adjusted, my eyes shot up in surprise at the sight. There was Cooper, sitting on a small table, speaking to his mother. He was holding a half empty glass of amber liquid, and occasionally, he took a sip but remained his eyes on his mother.

"Talk to me, Cooper, please." She begged, gripping his hand, which he only pulled back. "I hate seeing you this way."

Cooper was silent and only knocked back the last of the drink before grabbing an almost empty glass bottle. He was drinking.

"Cooper!" Emilia growled, and he jumped slightly from her wolf. "I've been sitting here for three hours watching you drink your scotch glass after glass. You requested to talk to me."

"I only said I wanted to see you." He slurred, taking a large gulp from the crystal glass. "I didn't say I wanted to talk."

"You're drunk." She shook her head at him and slumped back in her seat. Judging by the dark circles under her eyes, she was tired. "This is the only way I could get some information from you, so talk."

My mate sighed before leaning forward, so he was basically in her face. She scrunched her nose in disgust from his breath. "It's Celia."

The former luna's eyes softened at my name, and she gave her son a confused look. "What's wrong?"

"It's the same thing Grandmother had," he whispered. He sounded vulnerable, which surprised me.

She let out a gasp and covered her mouth with her hand. "No." Tears welled in her eyes, and I couldn't help but be worried. "That poor girl."

"She won't tell me what happened, and it infuriates me." He growled, and I could sense through our faint mating bond that his wolf was threatening to escape. "I want her to understand that she can trust me."

"Well, maybe you shouldn't have pushed her away in the first place."

"You know I had to." Cooper snapped, chugging down the last of his drink. "If Celia found out I was seeing a human girl, she would've been heartbroken."

My jaw dropped, and I had to bite my tongue not to bark at him. A human? He dated a human? That's why he couldn't touch me or look at me. It was for some pathetic being! How dare he? To think he actually cared about me when we first met. He probably couldn't decide whether he wanted to be with me or with that human.

"I never even understood why you were with someone as pathetic as her." Emilia scoffed, making me completely agree with her.

"She was a hybrid. Dating her and hiding my own werewolf side was to determine if she had the spirit of a wolf inside of her." Cooper explained, seeming to sober up a bit. "She was half human, half werewolf. I had to know because as strong as our pack is, I need to add as many people to it as I can. I had no feelings for her."

"Which she didn't. She didn't get her mother's gene, so she is going to live her life as a normal and wolf-free human."

"And I dumped her days ago once she showed no werewolf traits. Why can't you see she's in the past?" He argued. "I'll never see her again anyway. Our secret is safe."

"But your mate doesn't know about that! Celia doesn't know you interacted with a female human for a week or two while she was around—even be intimate with her because you couldn't 'control you attraction to her.' You kept yourself away from Celia because even though she is your mate, you wanted to remain faithful to that human." Emilia slammed her palms on the table, and I watched as her eyes grew black. "And she doesn't deserve to have a mate who won't talk to her. You suggested that date with Celia only after you ended things with the human. The human's feelings shouldn't have mattered. Your mate goes above all else."

Cooper looked ashamed of himself as I shot daggers at his head. Suddenly, he sniffed the air, and his eyes snapped to where I was peeking through. His mouth fell open slightly, and he looked suddenly lost. I backed up, not able to look at how tired and stressed he seemed at my anger. Spinning on my heel, I hightailed out of there.

My feet pounded loudly on the floor as I ran, and I faintly heard the sound of a chair moving across a flat surface. With my heart pounding, I made it to Cooper's room before slamming it shut and probably waking up every person in the house. Tears blinded me and fell down freely, making me scowl at the thought of crying again.

Breathing was heard on the other side of the door, and I whimpered when I smelt Cooper. "Celia, you have to understand I had no intention of hurting you."

I turned away from the door and leaned against it. "But you did. You hurt me."

My mate growled, and a soft pound came from the other side. "How much did you hear?"

"You were with a human," I whispered.

There was a long pause that seemed to go on forever. "Yes. I was with a human." My heart shattered at his words, and I sniffled loudly. That was when he began explaining himself. "I never touched her when you came. I was only with her to find out if she had the wolf gene so I could add her to my pack. When I found nothing, I left her. I never loved her. I only wanted information about her. You're all that I think about."

"What about what's wrong with me?"

He didn't answer, and for a second I thought he left. I waited for him to say something, but he didn't, and that's what scared me.

"You should sleep, Celia." He ordered, and I could hear his retreating footsteps. "Goodnight."

Chapter 11

"Come here, Celia." Alpha Zaire commanded, and I scurried over to him. I had just been cleaning the pots in the kitchen, so it was strange that he wanted me when I was very busy. The beds needed to be made before everyone came home from school or work.

"Yes, Alpha." I gave a slight bow before looking up, not making eye contact.

"Go downstairs and wait for me."

I knew what was coming, and panic took over me. "Yes, Alpha." I trembled and swiftly walked out of his office.

I walked as fast as my little twelve-year-old legs could take me. I was weak compared to the many growing werewolves my age. Even a regular omega wouldn't be growing this slow, but I had theories as to why.

When I entered the cold room, I sat up on the metal desk and waited. My bare feet only made me shiver more. The thin night gown I was wearing didn't bring me any warmth.

The black barred door sprung open, and the man I feared entered. I flinched at the deadly look in his eyes and gripped the table tighter. I hoped for a quick and painless death, if that's what this was all about. At such a young age, there were so many things I could have still done in the future for this pack. But death? No, I didn't want this. I didn't deserve this.

Alpha Zaire pulled out a silver knife and pierced it into my midthigh. I howled in pain and bit my tongue, the metal taste of blood greeting my taste buds. He pulled it out and plunged it into my other thigh. Pain was all I felt. I felt dizzy and weak. My weakness had made him feel powerful and dominant.

The alpha pulled the burning blade away and placed it beside me. The knife was dripping with my own blood in front of my innocent eyes. He then grabbed a handful of my platinum blond hair and tugged it. I squeaked in pain.

Getting a better grip of my hair, he lifted me off the table. I cried and clawed at his bare hand with my short nails. I felt myself flying through the air and hit the wall. I My hip bone let out a painful crack. I cried in pain and lay defenseless on the floor. I clutched any body part that was throbbing in pain. I wanted to be free from this life, but I knew he would not give me the privilege. Alpha Zaire wouldn't allow me to just die; torture was what he craved for.

I cried in pain when my shoulder spun around and twisted in an awkward. My skin was burning, and black fur was slowly starting to cover it.

What was happening?

Then my ankle popped out, and I cried out on pain. I felt like I was on fire, and my body felt like it was being stretched. This was the worst pain I'd felt—far different from the beatings I received from Alpha Zaire.

I looked down at my hands and found paws instead. Confusion punched me in the gut at the sight. I was not supposed to shift until I turned sixteen. My mouth and nose began to ache, and I crossed my eyes to see a snout forming. On both sides of my head, my ears tugged and pulled. A pair of wolf ears had grown on each side. I felt extremely uncomfortable and in pain when a tail came out of my rear.

Then suddenly, the pain disappeared, and I lay limp on the cold ground. With a smug look on his face, Alpha Zaire watched my wolf body panting. Slowly, he approached me and knelt down, grabbing my muzzle so I wouldn't attack him at all.

"Now, I can use you to get my mate back." He growled standing up and leaving me to heal.

Suddenly, a calming voice echoed in my head. "Hello."

I jumped but instantly realized that the voice came from my own wolf. "It's alright. He can't treat us this way forever. We will find our mate, and I can already tell that he's quite powerful. I promise you that we will be free soon. I promise you that one day our mate will rescue us from Alpha Zaire's brutality and we will be free."

***

Another terrible dream.

I slowly opened my eyes and tried to calm down, hoping the dream that brought about a fright would wear off. Unfortunately, it didn't, and I groaned loudly in despair.

Zaire had done so many horrible things to me, a lot worse than what he did in the dream I just had. I didn't want to admit it, but shifting was one of the worst things that happened in my life.

Werewolves never shifted at the age of twelve because their body wasn't done developing, and neither was their wolf. That's why my wolf form was so small. She was never fully developed physically. I would have died that day if it wasn't for my wolf coming to my rescue. Since I was put in a position where I was in danger, the only way of protection was if my wolf came out to save me. If it wasn't for her, I would not be alive today. Unfortunately, my wolf would always be tinier than Cooper's massive height, but at least he radiated power in order to protect me.

Snapping out of my own thoughts, I looked to my left to find an untouched, empty bed. He obviously didn't want to see me, not after yesterday. I didn't want to face him either. Pulling off the covers with slight anger, I decided it would be a good idea to borrow Paige's clothes. I found Cooper's clothes to be more comfortable, but I didn't want his scent to distract me.

Getting up, I scurried out of the room and down the hall to Paige's room. I didn't think she'd mind since I'd been wearing her clothes for a while now. She was obviously at school, so I didn't even bother knocking. However, when I opened the door, she was inside, taking out some contents out of a bag. Her hands were shaking, and when the door softly hit the back of the wall, her head snapped to me, looking at me with fear.

"Celia." She sighed, relieved to see me. She tossed the empty bag to the floor. "I'm so happy you're here. I was about to get my mom, but I didn't want her to freak out like she usually does and be all—"

I interrupted her before she could continue. "Paige, what's this about? You're ditching school? This isn't like you. What's going on?"

She bended down and picked up a box before tossing it to me, which I look at curiously.

"I'm late!"

I looked at the pregnancy test in surprise. My head snapped to her with worry.

"I mean, I have all the symptoms, right? I've gained weight, and I've been getting sick!"

My mind began to process all that she said, and I started to believe that she may be right. She could be pregnant. However, she hadn't taken the test yet. She wouldn't be able to tell until she tested it out

"There's only one way to find out," I stated, handing the box back to her.

Paige nodded, but I could tell she was shaken up. I couldn't imagine me having kids right now. There was no way I would be able to handle that kind of responsibility. I turned around to give her some privacy and stared out the window, thinking again.

I imagined Cooper becoming an uncle—him carrying a tiny baby next to his large body. It would be quite a scene too; that's for sure.

I heard the toilet flush and out came a scared looking teenage girl. Paige kept running her hands through her straight hair as we watched the pregnancy test do its job. Forcing Paige to sit down on the bed so she wouldn't stress herself if she were pregnant, I tried to help her in any way. Tears were waiting to fall down her face. Whether it would be tears of joy or sadness, it was up to her. I was about to try and comfort her, but the beep of the test stopped me.

"You look first," she whispered, hugging her knees close to her. "I want you to know before I do." Shrugging, I stood up from the chair and walked over to the test that rested between the headboard of the bed and Paige.

I rested my back against the headboard and looked at the pregnancy test. I looked up at Paige's face, then at the test, and then to Paige's flat stomach. I finally spoke, "Positive."

"What?" she whispered, scooting over to me and snatching the little stick out of my hand. Tears began to fall down her face, and she threw the test across the room, causing it to shatter. "It's positive? No, I can't be a mother. I can barely take care of myself!" She placed her head in her hands and cried her eyes out.

"You'll figure it out." I tried to encourage her, continuously rubbing her shoulders for support.

I tried my best to comfort her, but I knew there was no way to make her feel any better. "I'm only seventeen, Celia. What will my family say?" She paused and looked at a picture of her and Adam smiling together in a photo. "What will Adam do?"

I shrugged and said, "Like most mates would do, he'll accept it."

"But Cooper warned Adam that we can't start a family until I was eighteen." She cried, tossing her hands up and letting out an earsplitting cry. "He'll hurt my mate because of something we both did. Cooper will make him go on a yearlong hunt party or something until the baby is born.

"I'll talk to him. He won't take your mate away from you or your child." I promised, resting my hand comfortably on hers. "No one deserves to be alone in times like this."

After helping Paige get through this hard time, she happily let me borrow her clothes so I would stop wearing Cooper's. I left the room and went down the stairs feeling fresh in soft and comfortable clothes. My wolf was itching to be let out, but I didn't want her to move around in an unfamiliar environment, not after what happened to us before. I wasn't going to ask Cooper either. After finding out about his betrayal, about the human girl, there was no way I'd be talking to him again.

It's disgusting to think he would be so close to something as uninteresting as a human. They hardly had manners and spent most of their free time sitting on the couch watching television. Many were lazy and didn't believe in the idea of a mate for life. I was supposed to find a mate who waited for me to come into his life, unlike Cooper. He found a woman to be intimate with before me.

Cooper and I were supposed to form an inseparable bond, but that's not the case between us. He was always too busy to be with me. I usually woke up alone in our bed. It had hurt me so much to think that he had better things to do than get to know me. It's unfair and utterly hurtful. Should I even try to talk to him about this? Would he care?

After walking into the sitting room, I rammed straight into a solid chest. I was about to step away and apologize until the welcoming sparks heated up my skin, and I looked up immediately. A scowl crossed my face when I saw *him*, giving me an overly concerned look. His eyes held something I couldn't entirely read.

"We need to talk," Cooper said, giving me a pleading look. I only shook my head at him.

"No." Crossing my arms over my chest, which caused his eyes to flicker downwards. I let a low growl escape my lips, which he only returned. "You should've told me you were with a human."

His body began to shake, and I could only imagine how difficult it was for him to control his inner wolf. I didn't bother touching him to help him relax. I just stared at him, showing no emotions. He was not going to win this argument. Everything he caused between us was because of him.

"Why can't you see that I want us to work? What you are doing is pushing me away, Celia!" The snarl that followed after caused the walls to shake and windows to almost shatter.

"I know I've messed up every chance at getting close to you, but I want to try." His voice was softer, but his shaking body didn't subside.

I looked around the room to see a few pack members scampering out of the room, obviously worried there that their alpha would lash out at them. In the center of the room was a few toddlers playing with dolls. Cooper's eyes were black the moment we locked eyes, and I sighed.

"I'll give us a chance, but you have to promise me something." He seemed hesitant to answer, but he caved in. "You have to guarantee that you won't get mad at Paige."

"It depends." His voice had oddly sounded deeper, and a small shiver went down my back.

"Just promise me you won't get mad at her." I took a step forward and rested my hands flat on his chest. A warning growl escaped his lips, which made me roll my eyes. That had become his usual reaction, and I was getting used to it.

"I promise." He let a small smile escape his lips.

Chapter 12

I lay painfully on Cooper's bed, aching terribly from my abdomen to my back. I cursed Mother Nature for forcing women to go through this every single month. I wished there were some magic that would take this pain away, but it was something I would have to always endure; every woman must.

Cooper's out and about doing god knows what around the territory—the only time when I needed to be distracted. Although his promise was made, it felt like he wasn't putting in his best effort. I understood that he was very focused on the pack and punishing those who would dare disobey his orders. Still, I wished he would take a day or two to help me in a time where I would appreciate his company to be a wonderful distraction. I wondered if he felt my pain. He deserved it anyway for not even talking to me ever since our agreement, which was five days ago.

Paige was doing perfectly fine and couldn't wait for Christmas since Adam would be back by then from hunting. She had somehow managed to keep her pregnancy from anyone. I knew Emilia would probably burst with joy if she found out. Adam was in for a big surprise too.

I buried my face in the pillow, ignoring the sound of the door when it opened.

"You look like a mess—" I heard someone chuckle "—love."

I looked up and saw Jeremy. "Very funny, Jeremy." I faked a laugh. "What are you doing here?"

"Cooper wanted to make sure you were okay. I heard you guys aren't on speaking terms, so I happily obliged."

That made me happy. My mate still cared.

"Tell him I'm dying and I'm currently in the worst pain in my entire life. Explain to my mate that I'm angry at him," I say before ramming my head back into the pillow and shifting into a fetal position.

"Your funeral." Jeremy shrugged and remained silent for about two minutes. "Well, I'm going to leave now. Cooper just wanted me to check up on you."

"Thank you, Jeremy," I stated before closing my eyes and letting out a loud growl of pain.

I heard the door close, and I relaxed once I was finally alone. Over the past few days, I had noticed how my PTSD had worsened. And I had started avoiding people because of this. This resulted in the avoidance of anyone I passed while venturing around the house. I was scared of getting a flash of something that would trigger me. For me, it was best to keep my head down and avoid any interaction with people.

I hadn't checked up on Paige for a while, and I hadn't spoken to Sage since I put her to sleep, the night I discovered my mate's betrayal. Emilia completely slipped my mind.

Jumping up from the bed, I accidentally landed on the floor when the door suddenly swung open. I pushed the upper half of my body up and looked up at the door. My eyebrows shot up in surprise, and I scrambled to put myself in a less embarrassing position.

Cooper stood smiling like an idiot, looking down at me. He surveyed my body before letting out a chuckle. I felt a pang of comfort hit my heart, happy that he had been concerned for my safety.

Narrowing my eyes at him, I spoke, "What are you doing here? I thought you had pack business to attend to, like always."

Not much to my surprise, he ignored my comment and helped me stand up. Just the simple touch from him brought me so much bliss, but I tried to ignore it as I waited for his answer.

"So it was true." He nodded his head and looked down at his shoes. "I know what's wrong with you." I raised an eyebrow and waved my hand for him to continue. "It's what all females go through when they're about to go into heat."

"Excuse me?" I asked, staring at him strangely as if he grew two heads.

"Between the time of your period and the following month, you will be going into heat." My mate explained, looking uncomfortable. He scratched the back of his neck that I knew was growing red. "It's the time when we have to mate."

"How do you know?" I asked, crossing my arms over my chest.

"Well, for one, you will become jumpy, irritable, and you will be experiencing uncomfortable cramps and backaches. That will be all the evidence of your heat, and I will be the only one to relieve the pain you would be going through. Believe me, I'm dreading that too since your wolf and mine would desperately want to mate." He coughed into his hand and ran his hand through his hair. I could feel my eyes instantly growing dark without me wanting it to.

"But you haven't been around me all that much," I whispered, but he only chuckled and walked closer to me.

"That can change," he said huskily before picking me up swiftly and pinning me to the wall.

My lips were instantly covered by Cooper's, and I kissed him back with just as much passion. The kiss was long and hot, and soon my mate trailed his tongue against my lip. Nervously, I opened my mouth, and his tongue entered my mouth slowly. Together, our tongues created a massive spark, making me moan loudly. He growled in satisfaction.

With our tongues dancing with each other, I could barely feel Cooper moving his hands around my pajama top. He lifted a bit of the shirt, so it was up to my belly bottom, and he rubbed soothing circles on my hip bone. With our tongues still dancing passionately, I barely noticed that he had lifted shirt up to my breasts. His hands were now rubbing my flat stomach, making my mind go fuzzy, and knees go weak. I could barely think straight.

Cooper removed his lips from mine and trailed his lips around my face and neck. I moaned loudly and wrapped my arms tightly around his neck in fear of him walking away. I had felt wanted again.

I jumped up when Cooper had placed his hands on my butt and wrapped my legs around his waist tightly. Giggling at the sudden movement, he removed his lips from the bottom of my ear and laughed lightly from my reaction. I snorted a little, and we just laughed harder. This moment was perfect, and I could not think of anything better.

"You're so beautiful," Cooper whispered in my ear, and I smiled like a lovestruck fool. "You're so perfect." I bit my lip to hide my smile, but Cooper didn't bother hiding his.

Leaning again, he pressed his lips to mine. This kiss was slow, and I knew this was what it felt to be loved. I felt butterflies in my belly. While he was kissing me, I jumped when I felt his hand unclasping my bra from my back. I was about to tell him off but decided not to when I felt him rubbing my upper back affectionately.

"Cooper!" I jumped when I felt him bite my lip, tugging it playfully. He released it just as fast as he had snatched it and kissed me again. We kissed for a few more minutes before he touched the one part of my body that I had been trying to hide from him. "Ow!"

He moved his hands away from me like he had burned me and looked at me furiously. I knew he didn't mean it because I knew he didn't even know it existed. I squirmed when he lowered me to the ground and turned me around, so my stomach was to the wall. He lifted my shirt up, and I shivered from the cold. I covered my chest that was revealed, though he wasn't looking at my breasts.

"Wait, Cooper—" I wanted to explain, but he wasn't going to let me speak.

"What the hell is this?" His voice was deadly. "Celia, what the hell is this on your back?"

"A permanent injury," I stated, trying to get out of his grasp. But I couldn't move as he held me tightly to the wall.

"I think now would be a very good time to tell me what happened to you and why you left your pack." He demanded.

This was going to be a long story to tell. There was no way I would be able to tell him every single detail that had happened without crying my heart out. I looked down and turned around slowly. He was already staring at me with such intensity. I bit my lips and tried to process any words.

"Okay," I whispered before brushing past him. I sat on the bed.

What was I supposed to do? If I declined, I knew he would get really mad at me and maybe ignore me again, which I wouldn't be able to handle. I needed him.

He walked over to me and sat on the bed. He waited for me to begin, but my heart was stopping me. I'd never actually told anyone my story, and it was scary for me to finally do it.

What if he'd just laugh at me? What if he wouldn't care I told him everything?

No, he's our mate. He'll care genuinely for us. My wolf urged me, making me feel a bit uneasy. *I want him to know about our past.*

Gaining enough courage, I finally spoke, "When I was born, my parents didn't want me, so they dropped me off at the nearest house they found. The house happened to be Alpha Zaire's. He found me, and a name tag, inside a basket on his doorstep. He took me in. He took care of me as if I were his own child—until I turned four. He found another baby on his front step. It was a boy, and just like me, the boy had nothing but a name tag inside the basket that had carried him. The baby boy was Logan. Zaire had a DNA test on both of us and found out that…" I stuttered, already feeling the tears threatening to fall. I swallowed hard before continuing. "Well, it turned out that Logan was my brother."

My throat was getting stuffy, but Cooper's caring face assured me that I had his full attention. That was when I knew I could continue and tell him my complete story. I knew right then that he would accept me for what I was and that he would love and respect me without judgement.

"Over the next year, I had grown close to my brother. I nurtured him and cared for him. Without Logan's knowledge, Alpha Zaire had been abusing me every day since he came. It was my secret that I had tried to keep from him. I didn't really know why he was hurting me until he had forced me to turn at age twelve."

"You turned at age twelve because of that sick bastard!" Cooper growled, and I knew he was trying to keep his wolf from surfacing.

I continued, ignoring his comment. "My wolf was the one that helped me go through all the beatings I had gotten from him." A small smile made its way to my lips, but Cooper looked mad as ever. "Zaire's mate had rejected him. She was still part of the pack and didn't really seem to care. After that, he had started trying to figure out how to get his mate to love him, to want him. And the moment I turned, that's when the experiments began. Every other day, Zaire would beat me, and in between those days, he would inject me with several different needles. Sometimes he would take different tissues and blood samples from my body, leaving me weak and useless."

The tears were now running down my cheeks in hot balls of water. I couldn't even control them because the memories were too painful.

"When I was thirteen, I tried to kill myself because I couldn't take the pain anymore and ended up getting punished for it. My fears grew, and I became too afraid of almost everything. Every time I came into the room I shared with Logan, he would ask me why I was limping or why I was bleeding. I lied to him every day, telling him I was too clumsy and tripped."

Images of my brother's worried face popped into my head, and the tears never stopped. Cooper was holding my hands now, trying to give me some help. He knew I could shift right here, right now if I continued with the story. It was only a matter of time.

I sighed loudly and wiped my tears.

"Turned out Alpha Zaire was searching for ways to find my wolf and take her out. I was so afraid that if he took her out, I would never find my mate—that I would never find you. That disgusting man was going to switch his mate's wolf with my wolf and make me his mate, forcing someone as weak as an omega to accept him." I explained with as much detail as I could.

"He never figured it out. He also experimented with the way I looked. He wanted to make me unique and whatever's beautiful in his eyes. My hair used to be golden blonde, and he changed it to white. My skin tone used to be tan, but now it's as pale as milk. My violet eyes—they used to be golden honey in color, and I missed them the most. He changed me into someone I'm not, Cooper. What you are seeing now isn't real. The person in front you now is a result of an experiment."

That was one of the most heartbreaking words that had slipped out of my mouth. I couldn't accept every compliment that Cooper had said to me. He was loving the beauty after the experiment.

Cooper stared at me in utter shock. He reached for my arm and rolled up the sleeves, looking at the tiny scars from the needles that Alpha Zaire had used on me.

"What about the wound on your back?" It was hardly a whisper, but I caught his soft words. I knew this was hurting him too.

Trying to smile weakly, I began. "It's the wound I got from different types of silver he had used to scare my wolf. Terrorizing my wolf was his evil way to get her. With the amount of silver he used on me, Zaire had almost killed me. Shockingly, I survived and somehow endured it. Silver doesn't hurt me anymore. But the wound didn't disappear. It has become a every evil thing that Zaire had done to me."

"Why didn't you tell me this?" my mate whispered, cupping my cheek.

"It's too painful to think and recall." I croaked. "And Logan started to suspect that something was going on. It didn't take him long to finally figured out everything. And one night, when I came to our room, looking totally beaten down, he asked me again and…he found out." I began to choke on tears.

"Baby, you don't have to tell me," Cooper whispered, but I shook my head.

"No, you have to know why I left. It was my fault," I stated, looking down at my clammy hands. He would never forgive me after I told him my darkest secret.

"You're my mate. No matter how big of a package your life is, I'm willing to stay with you through anything."

"Good," I whispered and placed my hand on Cooper's warm hand. "Because I'm the reason Logan's dead."

Cooper's eyes widened, and he moved his hand away. "You're lying."

Shaking my head at him, I tried to explain through the tears.

"After Logan found out, he went after Zaire. I tried to stop him. I tried contacting him through mind link, but my stubborn brother blocked me. I searched for him everywhere. And then…I found him in a large ballroom, soaked in his own blood. I cried, trying to wake his torn body. His heart was ripped out of his chest and was tossed on the other side of the room. When I heard a growl in front of me, I couldn't believe who it was." I could feel my throat tightening up at the memory. "It was Carly, Zaire's mate. She changed back into human form for a split-second yelling at me because I was the reason her mate never looked at her, never tried to go after her. She rejected him when he started experimenting on me, and not long after, he tried to make me his mate. No one knew about the experiments. She soon found out about his determination to switch our wolves and wanted me to know what it felt like to lose someone who was meant to be in your life for so long. That was the motive, Cooper, to make me feel her pain."

Tears were leaking down my face while I mourned over my brother's death again. I still couldn't believe he was dead because of me, that I had been with Zaire for a long time against my will trying to switch wolves so we could be together. It was wrong for him to use me, and now it's the cause of Logan's death.

I took a deep breath, looking at my hands that were shaking violently.

"Carly framed me. She accused me of killing my own brother in front of Zaire. We had a huge fight. I tried to attack her, but I had gotten bitten badly. I ran like a coward. Logan deserves retribution for what was done to him. For goddess's sake, he was only fourteen."

"That's how you ended up here, isn't it?" Cooper asked through gritted teeth, and I was surprised how much he was able to calm himself down.

"I was planning on heading for America where no one would know who I was if the word spread of the murder. Blood Moon isn't looking for me, Cooper. Alpha Zaire is. He wants to kill me. He believed Carly's lies, and now I have a bounty on my head," I said. My grief was turned into anger. "They want me dead, and they're willing to do everything, no matter the costs."

Cooper blinked at me a few times, obviously trying to process the information. It was a lot to take in, but he deserved to know. I had kept him in the dark for too long. I knew it would be painful to tell him everything, but it had to be done.

Mates don't lie, and mates don't keep secrets.

After he continuously just stared at me for a few minutes, he closed his eyes and let out a breath of air before leaning forward towards me and engulfing me in a hug. His embrace comforted me, and I relaxed after breathing in his scent. His muscular arms tightened their hold on me, crushing me closer to his chest. He kissed the top of my head, leaving his lips to latch on for a minute longer before pulling them away.

"You'll be safe here," he whispered, holding onto me for dear life as I did the same. "I promise they won't hurt you. They won't get anywhere near you."

I nodded and let out a long breath of air. This was all that I needed, a comfort from my other half. The small bumps in the road no longer mattered. We were going to stay strong together. It would just be him and me against the world, and nothing would ever separate us.

Chapter 13

It's amazing how I'd never realized how much people actually needed me. Paige was too scared to tell her family about the little bun in her oven, and Sage needed me to help her with her homework since her parents were busy. Jeremy didn't do his job as an omega. I was able to help with his mate problem, and he tried to look for her around the pack. Much to his disappointment, none of the women in the pack made his wolf go wild. Felicity needed me to taste her food before serving it since Jeremy won't bother doing it. So as a result, everyone had been coming to me for guidance.

Then there's Cooper, my mate. I had him tell me every single thing he did from the moment he got up to do his duties in the pack. It's not like I told him to do it. Emilia told him it was better that way, and this would also keep the bond between us strong. Cooper needed me to keep him sane and help him control his temper. I'd witnessed how he lost his temper.

Now, here I was helping Felicity cut the vegetables beside her, sending constant smiles her way. I had a fear of knives but was finally able to overcome it at the age of eleven. I knew it was stupid to fear things that could also protect me. Shaking off the small fear for a brief second, I scooped up chopped carrots and broccoli and tossed it into the large pie. Felicity decided now was a good time to bake a delicious chicken pot pie.

"Is this good, Felicity?" I asked, showing her the food.

"Yes, that's perfect, Celia." She nodded, slicing the last of the cooked chicken.

"The kids won't be able to take their paws off this delicious treat," I said.

"Or I won't be able to keep my paws off you." Before I could turn around at the voice, I was engulfed in a hug from behind. "Right, baby?"

I chuckled and spun around in his arms, smiling like a fool. Cooper looked down at me with a small smile that showed just how much he needed me in his life. His warm hands moved down to my hips. I tried desperately to push him away, but he wasn't having that. Instead of kissing me, he gently pinched my hips and released me.

"So irresistible. I just can't keep my hands off you."

I gasped and moved away from him to Felicity, keeping a playful smile on my face. He was about to run over to me until she interrupted. "Not in my kitchen. I really don't want to be cleaning up my kitchen after…" She raised her eyebrow, making me blush uncontrollably. My mate only seemed to enjoy my embarrassment.

"Well, I guess we have to go somewhere more private." I squeaked when Cooper snatched my waist once again and lifted me up before throwing me over my shoulder.

"Cooper!" I cried, but it was more of a playful screech.

I didn't know where he was taking me, but by the time I could ask, I was pushed against a wall gently. Cooper smiled at me, and it showed true happiness. I guessed our little confession day actually meant something to our bond, and I was overly satisfied. The smile that appeared on my face and the soft giggles were what

I had always wanted from my mate. For the first time in my life, I was finally carefree. There's nothing that could ruin this moment.

When Cooper's lips touched mine, I gave a little purr of blissfulness. I tangled my fingers into his hair, kissing him back with more passion. This was what mates did. People said that actions speak louder than words, and this was the only way for Cooper to express how he felt. My mate rested both his hands on the sides of my face and kissed me gently while I leaned against the wall.

"Cooper, I have something you may want to—" Sheila stopped.

Cooper instantly pulled away and took a step back, running his hand through his hair angrily.

"What is it?" He growled, glaring at her as his frustration suddenly grew.

"Well, I ran some tests on Celia when I took her blood to make sure she was fine, and something came up," she said, nodding her head towards her small office. I looked at Cooper, and he took my hand and guided me, following the pack doctor.

I was beginning to get worried since her expression was grave as we entered one of the rooms that held a checkup station. Cooper picked me up gently and placed me on one of the medical treatment tables. I took his hand in fear of hearing something that I knew would affect our lives. It was hard to believe that only a few seconds ago, I was so happy with my mate. Now here I was, anxious about my health.

Sheila looked at her clipboard and spoke, "Well, her wolf was a bit affected by what you had told me, Cooper. I want to see Celia regularly when she's in wolf form. The injury on her lower back will fade over time as long as she doesn't get touched by any silver. Her resistance to silver will soon start to fade too. Don't worry because her internal organs are okay."

We both sighed in relief.

"But..." The feeling of relief suddenly faded as soon as we heard her say. "There's something else you need to know..."

The thought of dying immediately filled my thoughts. Cooper noticed my fear and held me close to him, snaking his arm around my waist. My heart was beating fast, and I was starting to think it would fall out any second. He kissed my temple, and the sparks comforted me immediately.

"Celia, honey."

I looked into Sheila's eyes as she spoke.

"You and Cooper can never have a child."

My heart plummeted to my stomach.

I thought my heart had stopped beating as soon as she said those word. Having a baby boy or girl would had been perfect.

"Celia," Cooper whispered, trying to comfort me by rubbing my back. Sheila left to give us some time to think and talk things through.

"I..." I stuttered, looking down at my hands, trying to figure out how to process this new information. My lips trembled, and I didn't even have the strength to look at my mate.

"Celia, Celia, look at me." My mate hushed me and lifted my chin. I didn't have the energy to push his hand away. "Baby, please."

My eyes flickered to his, and I knew how much this was affecting him too. I knew this because all alphas wanted an heir to keep the bloodline. If the luna couldn't bear a child, the line would end and the title would be given to the beta.

"This won't change how I feel about you. This is just a bump in the road that we'll overcome," he said, looking at me with the same pained expression. Taking my hand in his, he spoke softly to me, "Because I want you to know that I lo—"

"Alpha! Alpha!" someone shouted, interrupting him. Cooper growled and stood up angrily. He swung the door open and looked out. I couldn't see much, but I saw a man, a lot shorter than him, panting. "Rogue...female...powerful person waiting."

"Calm down, pup. What happened? What rogue?" Cooper asked while I sat on the verge of an intense mental breakdown.

The teen gasped for breath, and I could tell he must've shifted because he was only wearing a pair of ripped up jeans. I knew he was mad for being called a pup, but when an alpha called you that, it was usually done to show that he's in power. It shouldn't really be an insult, but being called a dog was worse. Wolves aren't dogs. There's a big difference.

"A female rogue ran into our territory. We all know she's powerful because she was able to outrun me and my brother." He must be related to the third in command, who I hadn't met yet, I thought. "I've never smelled something like her scent. It was so strong. She must be from the US or even Mexico. She's waiting for you outside."

Cooper processed the boy's words and turned to me. I knew he wanted to stay with me, but he needed to take care of the rogue. I nodded and got up, knowing he would want me to stay with his sisters. Before I could slip past him, he took my forearm and pushed me close to him. I guess I was wrong.

"I want you here." I was beginning to feel wanted, so I took his hand. He tugged my hand, and I was forced to follow him. We followed the teen through the through the house.

How could rogues pass through the territory? Why couldn't Cooper put more of his people to scout the area? There must be a reason why he hadn't taken any major action. Was he waiting for something?

Cooper pushed the boy out of the way gently and went out the front door. The breeze made my loose hair flow around. I was a little cold, so I snuggled closer to him as we walked. When I turned to look at the landscape, I noticed a woman, maybe Paige's age, with her arms crossed, looking extremely serious. Men surrounded her, but none touched her.

The rogue was wearing a black dress that was tight on her and was just under her butt. Dark makeup covered her shining green eyes. Her lips were covered with black lipstick that showed off full lips. Her red hair was straight and tucked into a tight high bun, the neatness of it clear. Just the shine from her hair proved that she was healthy and strong.

"What are you doing in my territory?" Cooper questioned. "Tell me your name and rank."

"Don't let that temper get the best of you, Cooper." She chuckled, and I was surprised at how light her voice sounded. "My name is Trixie, and I was once the daughter of Alpha Leonardo from Blue Crescent."

My eyes widened, and everyone's jaws dropped, including mine. Even Cooper showed a bit of shock after hearing the fallen pack's name. Blue Crescent had suddenly vanished about nineteen years ago. Thousands and thousands of dead bodies had been seen sprawled across their open land. The alpha was dead in the center with the his luna by his side. The pack had been one of the strongest packs in Canada. They were involved with many victorious battles. After what happened, no one had heard anything from that pack again.

Cooper examined and sniffed the air, trying desperately to figure out if her words were true. Emilia and Patrick were listening from afar as well, trying to figure out whether the rogue was telling the truth. As I had read from one of the books in Cooper's bedroom, Blue Crescent and Ice Moon were allies once.

"I'm not here to pay your pack a visit. Though, it's nice to see an old friend after so long," Trixie proclaimed, letting a bit of her alpha power into her voice. She turned to look at me, eying me up and down. "I have seen my share of criminals, but have never seen one as innocent as you. You must be, Celia. Correct?"

I looked up at Cooper, but he just nodded his head and turned back to Trixie.

"Correct." I whimpered, clutching onto Cooper's sweater.

"Well, it seems that you've gotten the wrong alpha angry, honey." She waved her hand dismissively. "But I think it would be smart to tell you what has been going on around Canada. I'll make you a deal. Let me stay here for a little while, and in return, I will give you the information I have."

Cooper bit his lips in annoyance and looked over to a man, his third in command, and they were mind-chatting. I really wished I knew what was going on inside that gorgeous big head of his. He seemed concerned for a bit but soon turned back to Trixie.

"You can stay for a week, tops. Let us speak again tomorrow." That was his final word because he wrapped his arm tightly around me and guided my shivering body back inside.

My body still felt numb from the recent news about me, and now there was a stranger living in the pack house. This couldn't be happening. She was a rogue for goddess's sake! How could Cooper trust her? That would explain why he wasn't so surprised. He knew Trixie from somewhere.

I really didn't feel like talking, so I shrugged Cooper's arm off me and removed my hand from his once we were inside. He looked confused, but I didn't want to look at his expression. I ran up the stairs. My mate didn't grab me or chase after me, which I was thankful for. Obviously, he knew why I wanted to be alone.

Once I was inside our room, I slammed the door and locked it. My back pressed against the door, and I slid down, hugging my knees tightly to my chest. Life wasn't fair, and it never would be. I had wanted many children with Cooper, but that would never happen now.

It's all because of one man, Alpha Zaire, and I was willing to kill him for this.

Chapter 14

I lay on my side, hugging a pillow close to my chest. My legs were tangled in Cooper's bed sheets, and I knew there was no way I could possibly get out. I struggled to find any reason to get up and out of bed. My life was crumbling, and there was nothing I could do to stop it.

A knock on the door came from outside, and I didn't even bother to tell anyone who was on the other side to go away and never come back. Right now, I didn't even have the energy to move my mouth. I had no desire to interact with people. I was upset and heartbroken.

A groan came from the outside, but I didn't even bother moving when the door was slammed open, making the pictures on the wall rattle. The bed dipped from behind me, and I was engulfed in a comforting hug. I sighed and pulled the blankets closer to me. All I heard was a chuckle behind me. There was a long pause before the person spoke. A set of keys dangled from her fingers as she smiled triumphantly. I sighed and sat up. Her smile disappeared immediately.

"He told me," Paige mumbled, and I could hear a hint of sadness in her voice. "Cooper told me everything that happened to you. I know it wasn't his story to tell, but I threatened him."

I had been crying for the past six hours, and as soon Paige had reminded me of what the pack doctor said, the tears came streaming down my cheeks again They soaked Cooper's pillow again and left a large stain. Paige rubbed her hand up my arm. My wolf and I seemed to like it.

"I know this isn't fair to you. Hell, I'm complaining about my baby when, here you are, not even having the choice to have one or not. I'm so selfish to not want him." She soothed, but only one thing caught my ear.

Him? She knew it was a boy? Was it an intuition or did she have an ultrasound without Adam knowing?

"I know you're really hurting and stuff, but I think it's best for you to try to move on. We can go shopping if you'd like. I really need to get some food since I'm really craving some strange stuff." Paige was obviously trying to lighten my mood, but it really wasn't working.

I lost her after that and tuned her out. Paige was amazing, but her rambling really was giving me a headache. It really bothered me that Cooper had told her. Right now, I didn't want to talk to anybody.

"I mean, raw fish? Like I can't believe I actually ate that, but you know, my baby's weird." Paige continued, and I just continued ignoring her as best as I could. "I think it's a boy. What do you think?"

When she smacked my shoulder gently, I jumped a little but didn't look at her. I sniffled again and hugged my pillow tighter. My cheeks burned with every tear that fell. I didn't have the energy to even wipe them away. I must have looked pathetic, but I really didn't even care.

"Celia, are you even listening at me?" Paige snapped, and I felt her roughly shoving me. "Celia?"

She looked at me with a worried expression on her face. I glanced at her and stared at an empty space. Depression was slowly sinking into my body.

Paige sighed loudly. "That's it." She hissed under her breath before she stood up and left the room. I rolled my eyes at her weak attempt to get me to talk.

***

Cooper

My eyebrows remained raised at my huffing and puffing sister. Not only did she look exhausted from running down a flight of steps, but something seemed off about her. Although I really couldn't tell if it's just her worry over my mate. I honestly couldn't believe how Celia was able to stand Paige right now. I mean, my sister had become difficult.

Sucking in a breath of air, she spoke, "Celia is getting worse. She won't talk to me, look at me, or even acknowledge me. The inability to conceive a child has really taken a toll on her, and I think we're losing the part of her that's human."

"You didn't tell her I told our family about her past did you?" She shook her head, and I gave her a confused look. "Then what are you saying?"

"Gears are turning in your mate's head. I think she's thinking of something that's unholy in my book. Celia's vengeful, and she'll probably go after Zaire on a suicide mission." Tears filled Paige's eyes, and I was really starting to wonder if I should take her to Sheila. I had never seen my sister cry before. "Cooper, you have to do something."

I mumbled useless words under my breath and ran a hand through my hair. How was I supposed to deal with Celia when I knew she's close to running off the rails? This was obviously affecting our relationship. Thinking it through, I suddenly thought of a pretty good idea of how to comfort her. I may never get the chance to have a child with her, but our love for each other will last an eternity and will be worth it. But again, I could only hope.

"Get Celia dressed. Have her wear one of your dresses. Give her something warm. My mate and I are going on our first date."

***

Celia

I'm going to kill her. I'm going to kill Cooper.

Paige deserved to drown in the one foot–deep water I was currently bathing in. How in the world was she able to pick me up and throw me over her shoulder in a matter of seconds with her condition? She was a pregnant teen!

Paige was watching me like a hawk while she sat on the counter beside the sink, eating some strange food she made herself. My entire body was covered in thick layers of bubbles that were piled up to my chin. I could barely see through it.

"So, I was wondering," Paige said through a mouthful of her food. "Are you going to ask him to mark you? I mean, because alphas get way too possessive over their mates. He would feel more comfortable with you being out in public if you were marked. The mark prevents men from finding any interest in you. Plus, it is possible that his mark could fix you. Part of his DNA will flow through your veins, making you a luna, which would probably heal your body completely. And maybe then, you would be able to conceive. Alphas do need another heir, and there is no way my baby is running a pack."

Telling me to mate her brother easily made me uncomfortable. I certainly didn't want her to pressure me. I was already hurting that I couldn't produce children. Her remark about her own child hurt me.

I dropped my head back onto the water and kept scrubbing my body. The water splashed every time I moved. Life was getting difficult, and I needed to act soon. Alpha Zaire deserved to die after what he did to me. He would get the same treatment that he had given me. All I needed was a way to get to him without Cooper noticing. Logan deserved to be avenged. I would kill Alpha Zaire and his mate.

"Celia, for the love of the Moon Goddess, stop having that little glint in your eyes. It's really scaring me." I snapped out of my trance and looked back up at her. "I know exactly what you're thinking, and I really don't think it's a good idea."

I glared at her and she seemed taken aback by my actions. My eyes narrowed, and I looked back at the warm water, letting it flow through my fingers. It was calming me a bit, but I knew what I had to do. Paige couldn't tell Cooper what I had in mind. I needed to do it when my mate was distracted. It was the only way to get my revenge.

"Alright, time to get out before you look like a raisin." Paige smiled. She offered her hands to help me out. "Come on, let's get a move on. I have the prefect dress for you to wear."

Grumbling, I stood out of the bath a little wobbly, but I was soon able to compose myself. Walking past Paige totally naked, I grabbed a towel and wrapped it around me. The cool air kissed my warm skin, making the hairs on my arms stick up. Paige rolled her eyes and skipped into Cooper's room. I followed behind her and held the bath towel firmly around me. My bare feet stuck to the wood floor gallingly.

Once when we entered Cooper's room, I raised an eyebrow at the outfit that was resting on his bed in a neat pile.

There's no way I'm wearing that.

"Well, isn't it pretty?" She lifted the dress that compared to a giant coat. The leggings beside her looked comfortable, but my eyes widened at the piece of fabric beside her. I remembered all of our pack sluts wearing that. It was a thin lacy fabric that resembled an eye patch. What were they called? Beside the "eye patch" was a matching black lace bra.

I didn't speak but quickly slipped on the undergarments Paige was letting me borrow. It's strange that I had the same body type as her. I couldn't believe she hadn't put on some weight despite of her munching on something most of the time. She helped me put on the large dress, which I really didn't need, but she insisted. The leggings were simple to put on, and soon I was dressed in the outfit Paige was forcing me to wear.

"Now, I think your hair deserves a haircut. Don't worry, I do all the girls' hair around here and they're always happy about it." She smiled, pushing me over to Cooper's chair and setting me down. "I was thinking hip length or maybe a little shorter like where your belly button is. What do you think?"

I raised an eyebrow at her. There was no way Paige should go near my head and neck with a pair of scissors and ruin my soft hair. It may get annoying at times, but I liked my hair. Plus, what if Cooper wouldn't like my hair short? I stood up.

"No."

"Fine, but I will cut your hair eventually." Paige informed me before grabbing my hair and brushing. "But I'm still doing your hair."

Caving in, I gave her a little nod and allowed her to braid it. Different loops were made making it look like hoop earrings. It took a while for Paige to finish, but she finally managed to finish. A big beanie was placed on my head to keep me warm, and she held up a pair of cute black, knee-high boots. I slipped them on with ease and turned to her.

"You look so pretty! Your eyelashes are so long and black. You really don't need a makeup." My heart dropped, and I looked down.

My eyelashes was another one of Alpha Zaire's experiments. The experience was too painful since he had to pluck the lashes one by one. He had injected my eyelids a few times to achieve the color black. My eyebrows got the same treatment so they could match my hair.

Paige snapped me out of my trance and guided me towards a mirror. I looked myself up and down and smiled at how pretty my hair looked and how the coatdress looked on me. I had to admit, Cooper's sister knew exactly how to make someone look pretty.

"C'mon." She ordered, taking my hand, removing me from gawking at myself in the mirror. "Cooper is waiting for you."

I nodded and followed after her. For a pregnant girl, she sure had a lot of energy. I followed her down the stairs, clutching a pair of fingerless gloves. Why she would give me fingerless gloves was a mystery to me. While we were walking, she tossed me a scarf, which I quickly wrapped around myself.

If Cooper was taking me outside, then that would be my chance to escape. As I continued to walk, I started to sweat underneath the thick layers of clothing.

Finally, Paige and I arrived at the bottom of the stairs, and she moved away so I could see Cooper standing. He was holding a bouquet of beautiful white roses in his right hand. The navy blue dress shirt he was wearing was rolled down so it was at his wrists, and a coat was around his large frame. Grey pants hung low on his hips, but it wasn't exposing anything since his shirt was tucked in.

"Wow," I heard him whisper breathlessly.

Looking down at my feet shyly, I tried desperately to hide the smile that was creeping on my face. Cooper was looking at me dreamily as if I was like an angel to him. I bit my lip in order to make the smile go away. My eyes traveled the ground.

"You look amazing." Cooper gasped. My eyes snapped to his beautiful aquamarine eyes in a matter of seconds once his voice got my attention. I smiled at him.

"I know I did magic on her. Please take her away and enjoy." Paige grinned before walking away, leaving me alone with Cooper.

"Come on," my mate said, taking my hand and nudging me to follow him.

We walked the entire way out, but with the layers on me, I wasn't all that cold. We walked into the knee-deep snow with little trouble. When I seemed to fall behind a bit, Cooper picked me up bridal style so he wouldn't lose me. It felt as if I was in some kind of movie when the groom carried his new wife into their picket fence house.

About ten minutes later, we arrived at a clearing where there were no trees but a long sheet of thick ice. I looked up at Cooper, confused. He placed my feet back on the cold ground and stepped away. The clearing was beautiful to say the least, but why would Cooper take me here of all places? I didn't exactly enjoy the cold. I would love to look at the beautiful landscape inside a house, by the fireplace.

"Isn't it beautiful?" Cooper said, taking in a breath of air. "It's breathtaking."

I looked down at the ground, not wanting to talk. Every single thing just reminded me of what's wrong with me. All it did was hurt me on the inside, slowly killing me.

"Celia, you can't keep being like this." My mate shook his head and turned away from me once I looked up at him again. "You should be able to talk to me about things like this. If a baby is what you want, we can make something work."

"It's not that." I croaked. My voice sounded weird since I hadn't spoken in a while. My fingers twirled around each other when I looked down. I couldn't control how nervous I felt whenever I was around him. "I mean it is, but it's complicated. What *he* did to me ruined our lives."

Cooper ran his hand through his hair and tugged at it. "Please tell me you aren't thinking what I think you are thinking." He moved his hand out of his hair and looked at me. Slowly, he walked over to me menacingly. "Please tell me you don't want to get revenge and commit murder!"

I couldn't look him in the eye when I lied to him. "I wasn't thinking that."

There was a loud growl coming from my mate, and I flinched at the noise. It didn't take a genius to know that he guessed I lied. "You can't think that. Celia, you can't have his blood on your hands."

I looked down at the ground, ashamed, and bit my lip gently. Suddenly, a warm hand cupped my cheek, forcing me to look up into my mate's eyes. He'd been doing this a lot lately, forcing me to look up at him. His eyes were filled with disappointment. Why couldn't I for once make my mate happy?

"Here's what we're going to do." He breathed, taking both my hands in his. "We are going to enjoy this date together, and then we're going to head home, go to sleep, then talk to Trixie.

After that is over, I will have Adam back to form a plan to punish that disgusting man who shouldn't be considered an alpha."

Nodding in agreement, I turned back to the clearing that was covered in thick ice. Suddenly, I realized that the clearing was actually a frozen lake.

A smile formed on my lips, and I took a step forward. Cooper took my arm. Before I could question it, he held up two pairs of ice skates. No way.

See, there's a reason Ice Moon Pack was called what it was. After going through many books on the pack's history when I first got here, I learned a few things: the place was founded on a full moon, and this was the lake that the first members of the pack had come across. It was frozen solid and thought it was some magical ice land, hence the name. Blood Moon however was named for a different reason. Let's say it involved massive amounts of blood spilled on a lunar eclipse, also known as blood moon.

"I can't skate," I told him.

"Then I'll teach you."

And so he did.

I, of course, fell a hundred times. Whenever I did fall, Cooper would either laugh or catch me just in time. About an hour into skating, I finally managed to skate on my own without needing his help. It was exhilarating to be able to do something that my mate enjoyed, so I sucked it up whenever I fell. I really enjoyed spending time with him for once, and we had a lot of laughs together.

I grabbed him by the collar and held onto him while he skated. He was going really fast and it was hard to keep up with him, so hitching a ride was easier. It didn't take long for my mate to realize I was clinging onto him, and when he did he stop, I came crashing into his back. Almost losing my balance, I was about to fall, but I wasn't going down alone. Cooper fell down with me, and we laughed like maniacs.

I fell down with a grunt, with him hovering just above me. Snow was all in my long hair and stuck to my fluffy hat while Cooper's hair was sticking out. Looking around, I soon realized I was being straddled by him and he was looking intensely into my violet eyes. A blush rose to my cold cheeks, and I tried to cover it up but he just pinned my arms down.

Suddenly, a rustling noise from the trees caught both of our attention. Cooper's head snapped in the direction of the noise. He growled warningly. Since we were in the middle of the lake, there was no way to determine where the noise was coming from. My hand clutched onto the sleeve of his jacket for some sense of security.

"Don't move," Cooper whispered, scanning the area. "These aren't rogues, so don't even speak, or they'll know who you are."

I nodded.

We heard growls, and the next thing I knew, four Ethiopian looking wolves appeared angrily. Their fur was coated with black and red designs, some with two separate stripes, and others with tips of the two colors. I stared at them in fear.

"You are trespassing. Shift now." Coopers ordered. I jumped a little, but he held me down with his hands. "State your business."

The wolves growled but soon left as fast as they came. Cooper seemed to space out, and I knew he was mind-chatting with the scouts to get the trespassers. Quickly, he carried me bridal style as he scanned the perimeter. He didn't want me to leave his side. The thought made my heart leap out of my chest and a blush rose to my cheeks. Much to my disappointment, he placed me back on my feet right after.

"Come on, it's getting dark." The sun was pretty far away from the horizon. He was making up excuses. We still have an hour or so before it was sunset. He walked ahead of me, but I didn't move. When he realized I wasn't following him, he turned around and gave me a look. "Celia."

"Cooper, we both know why they were here and where they came from." I explained, crossing my arms over my chest to shield myself from the cold. "It's Blood Moon."

"We'll talk about this behind closed doors. Right now, it's not safe."

Chapter 15

Cooper had nervously been pacing the room as Adam sat in a desk beside Philip, third in command. The meeting office was down in the basement, I guess to prevent any distractions from other pack mates or keep everything between them before they announce their plan to the pack. Anyway, I was getting very anxious while I sat there, barely listening to them.

Philip slammed his fist on the desk before standing up and glaring at Cooper. My wolf got angry at that and let out a faint growl. However, Cooper obviously heard my warning. I'd sent him at least a dozen, and I'd already grown to hate his third in command.

"Why am I even here when you guys won't even tell me what you are discussing?" I yawned, looking at the time and seeing that it was already around ten in the evening.

"Fine." Phil sneered at me, and Cooper's eyes darkened at his tone toward me. I rolled my eyes when Phil looked back at my mate. "Tell her."

He sighed and sat down at the large desk. I was situated in a leather chair that was really taking a toll on my bottom since I hadn't stood up for three hours. Cooper looked me directly in the eye before speaking, "Enemy trespassers is an act of war. I have no choice but to accept this indirect declaration. Not to mention that your safety is at risk here."

"W-what?" I asked. Was he saying what I think he was saying?

"As long as Zaire is still the alpha, Ice Moon Pack is at war with the Blood Moon Pack." My jaw dropped at Cooper's words.

"W-war? Our pack, the definition of a hundred dollar bill, is going to war against a pack the size of a dime?"

Cooper seemed pleased that I had spoken well about his pack and couldn't seem to shrug the smug on his face.

"No one is risking their lives because of something *I* did!" I argued, placing my hands on my hips as I stood up. "This is my war against Alpha Zaire. He did terrible things to me and not this pack. I caused this. I will deal with him myself!"

"You didn't cause anything, Celia." Cooper's voice was low yet dangerous, and I held back a scoff at his behavior. If I had not wandered into his territory, Blood Moon Pack would've stayed away. "That pack won't stand a chance against our numbers."

"But killing innocent lives?" I argued, sending implausible looks towards the three men that watched my fit. "Children? Unmated males and females? Ones that have a family to go back to? How could you be so cold and cruel to take those lives away?"

"We aren't being cruel, Celia." Adam interrupted, looking at the scene that was unfolding. "We are trying to protect you and everyone else in this pack."

"That pack needs a better alpha anyway. Blood Moon won't survive long with Zaire in control. Cooper is a strong man and can rule people wonderfully. Anyone would follow him as a leader," Philip said. My eyes narrowed a bit when he complimented my mate.

"Stop your flirting, Phil." Adam warned, and then it hit me. How did I not see that Philip was into men? I was a bit annoyed that he kept looking at my mate. Now I'm just surprised. There were a lot of men in the packs who liked other men, but I had never seen one in the higher ranks. "Cooper's mate is two feet away from you."

Philip gulped and turned to look at me. "My apologies, Luna."

My eyes widened at the sudden realization that I was being called that now. I'd have to get used to that kind of power. I had wanted it so desperately before with Warner for my own protection, but now this was different. I felt like I had no future with Cooper, but now I felt like I did. There would always be a part of me that would regret my decision with Warner. Looking at Cooper for help, he cleared his throat and shook his head at his delta.

"Um…yeah." I stuttered, trying to figure out how to tell someone to stop flirting with what's mine.

"Send in that female Trixie. We need information now," Cooper said suddenly, and all heads turned to his voice.

"Fine. I'll get her." Phil growled and stomped out.

Everyone in the room remained silent as I stared at Cooper angrily. I may have suffered a great at Blood Moon, but I had bonded well with the children there. They had always been so cheerful when they saw me.

***

I sighed heavily and sat on the couch for a minute or two, exhausted from work—not to mention how I had dealt with the fourteen different needles injected into my arms. They were sore and numb from the different chemicals I had still flowing in my system. Looking down at my hands, I could see dried blood under my fingernails. I had dug my nails so hard into my skin that I must've pierced my own skin. Four small lines were on my palm, blood oozing out of them.

"Celia?" I looked up from my palm to see a little girl around eight years old, looking worriedly at me. "What happened?"

"Nothing, sweetie." I smiled, placing my uninjured hand on her cheek. "How about I make some plum pudding for you?"

She seemed happy and completely forgot about my injury.

Nodding, her beautiful raven hair swayed. She skipped off to the direction of the kitchen. I stood up with a little trouble and followed after her. If I could recall, her name was Savannah but liked to be called Savvy. When she was really little, I would tuck her in and assured her that the monster in the closet wouldn't get her.

"Hey, Celia?" Savvy called when I walked in, her green eyes shining bright. "I changed my mind. Can you play me a song instead?"

I internally groaned, but I couldn't say no to her adorable pleading face. Taking her hand in mine, I led her to the one place I could play the music she wanted. I entered the room and hushed her. The problem was low ranks were not allowed in this place. Peeking around a corner, I noticed the coast was clear and tugged Savvy along.

Sitting, I grabbed the instrument and turned to her. "What would you like me to play?"

"Greensleeves," Savvy whispered and sat a few chairs away from me. "You always play that so beautifully."

Giving her a sad smile, I rested the instrument on my shoulders and began to play her requested song. She swung her feet back and forth while I played and a grin was plastered on her face. I never played this for people, but one day, when she found me playing the song, I promised to play it to her so she wouldn't tell Alpha Zaire. I'd kept that promise for at least a year now.

By the time I had finished, Savvy was already beaming. I quickly stood up and grabbed her hand. We ran as fast as we could away from the music room and ended up in the kitchen. Our excitement and the time we *could spend together drove our quick movements. Savvy was full of so much energy, I struggled to keep up with her. The place was full of people, obviously waiting for me to cook for them.*

I sighed and released Savvy, but not before she whispered, "You play with so much emotion that sometimes I wonder what is really going on with you."

But I knew she was too young to understand, and with that, she disappeared in the large crowd.

***

I had always been one to love and appreciate music. Savannah was always trying to find a way to get the music room cleared. One time, she had said the house was on fire, and everyone ran like headless chickens. It was a hilarious sight to see, and I played for her for a long time that day. She had a brilliant mind and a good soul. For the longest time, I thought she was crushing on my brother.

The instrument I used to play her favorite song was a harp, and that's probably the only thing I missed from Blood Moon. I did miss Savannah; she was one of the children who were good. She was a loving girl and got along well with others. Compared to the rest of the children, she was an angel.

"Sometimes, I wonder why I even bother to help you pieces of snobby shits."

My eyes snapped up to meet bright sparkling green eyes that belonged to Trixie. She was smirking at us. In my eyes, I had to admit that she may even be stronger than Cooper.

Chapter 16

Trixie looked even more intimidating with her new outfit. She enjoyed evoking fear by wearing black and red clothing. She wanted to show that death was around her all the time. Eyeliner coated every inch of her eye. The black lipstick she had on before was now replaced by a deep red color that showed her white teeth whenever she opened her mouth. Mascara coated her lashes, making the greenness in her eyes stand out even more. This girl was confident, and her outfit proved it.

Trixie was pulling off a tight black skirt that hugged her butt and legs to make everything about her look good. A leather jacket covered a white tank top, which showed the perfect abs beneath her shirt. Different kinds of rings covered her fingers along with bracelets on her wrists. Zebra print heels rested around her feet, and I was pretty sure they were pumps. If I looked long enough, I could see a belly ring under her shirt that was peeping through. Everything about her just screamed dangerous.

"Close your mouth, honey, and thank you for bringing my bags to a very suitable room," Trixie stated, raising a teasing eyebrow at me. She looked up at Cooper. "You too."

I turned to see Cooper staring at her. I didn't enjoy my mate looking at her like that, so I purposely let a growl escape my lips. His eyes snapped to me, but his eyes softened and I knew immediately he wasn't looking at her like how I feared.

"Long time no see, huh?" A smirk was on Cooper's face, and my eyes widened. They knew each other like old friends.

"Haven't seen you since we broke into your school before the attack and put buckets of red paint above every door." She chuckled before sitting on the leather seat casually. "Happy to see your long lost best friend again?"

"Wait, I'm confused." I butted in, and everyone in the room looked over at me. "You knew her?" The question was directed to Cooper, but it was answered by Adam.

"Yeah, they used to get into so much trouble when the allied packs met up. I even joined some of the pranks they played on others. Those were the days, huh?"

"You mean when you weren't getting beat by my sister?" Cooper chuckled and looked over at Trixie and soon became serious. "How the hell did you survive?"

"My flirtatious skill. You get the idea." She winked at one of her guards behind her and turned back over to my mate. "But with my ability to run like my father, I was able to escape."

It all made sense. Trixie's father was an alpha, which meant she was part of a strong bloodline. However, she lost both her parents. Her mother must've been caught up in the battle, and Trixie's father was distracted. He couldn't save his pack members because his mate was in danger, and like every alpha, he only cared about her at that moment. Based on this past, it had been decided that no female could fight. If it occurred again, it could lead to the loss of another pack.

"But that isn't why I'm here." She smirked before standing up and looking at us all. The air thickened, and a deafening silence began. My ears were ringing. I was desperate to know why she came here.

"Zaire is beyond angry that Celia is your mate, and he's trying everything in his power to take her away from you. I've been closely monitoring his territory for months, and I've noticed that more and more rogues have been going in and out of his place. I was approached by a young female explaining she was going to Blood Moon for some meeting to destroy a criminal. It turns out, Zaire has been gaining help from your enemy packs, and even rogues, to take out Celia for the crime she committed—"

"Celia did not commit any crime." Cooper interrupted her.

Trixie rolled her eyes and crossed her arms in front of her chest.

"As I was saying, the crime she is *thought* to have committed has spread throughout Canada and in some parts of the US. People will start to think you're mated to a first degree murderer, Cooper. More rogues will join him, and it's only a matter of time before enemies of yours start to pop out of nowhere. Rogues don't enjoy following orders from others, but Celia's head has a pricy reward. Zaire wants war."

"Tell me something I don't know." I knew Cooper was getting agitated since Trixie seemed to be holding something else. Trixie looked at the ground and bit her lip. "Trixie, what aren't you telling me?"

"He doesn't want to just get Celia and make her pay for her actions."

Coopers eyes darkened immediately, but she continued.

"They're coming to take someone in your pack. They know that someone's pregnant."

"Who?" Adam asked. He looked confused.

"Paige." She began to twiddle with her fingers. "Alpha Zaire mentioned something that confused me, and it doesn't make sense to me but perhaps to you. He said that he wants to do what he did to Celia the same to Paige's child."

There was a long silent pause, and Adam's jaw dropped while my mate's clenched. My stomach grew queasy at the thought of what Zaire would do to the unborn child.

Cooper's eyes darkened, and he turned to look at his beta. Adam gave him a confused look.

"What do you mean? Paige isn't pregnant." Cooper looked between Trixie and his beta.

I couldn't hold it any longer and let out a small unpleasant snort, and they all turned to me. Cooper looked over at me with a hint of betrayal in his eyes, but I tried not to pay attention to how much that look hurt me. I didn't want my mate to be angry with me.

"Celia." Adam demanded.

"Do you know something?" Cooper gave me one of his heartbreaking frowns.

"I'm not supposed to say." I was always right when I said I was never going to be a good luna, and this proved it. I couldn't keep secrets from Paige and her mate Adam. "Paige said—"

"I told her not to tell you until you came back." Everyone's attention turned to Paige who was touching her flat stomach. She looked better since the last time I saw her. Her eyes flickered to Adam, but she made no move to go to him. Neither did he. "All four tests, and I got said the same thing."

"If only I had known." Adam looked at the ground in shame and put his head in his hands. "I'm such an idiot."

I looked over at Trixie and saw her roll her eyes before leaving the room, obviously not wanting to deal with family drama. The guards soon followed her, and now it was just the four of us staring at Paige, besides Adam who was too busy being guilty. I knew Paige didn't want this reaction from her mate since her eyebrows were creased with worry and she was gnawing on her lip. Tears were filling her eyes, and I knew she was upset because she accepted the baby but he wasn't.

"Adam…" Paige whispered.

"For the Moon Goddess's sake, how could have you knocked up my sister?" Cooper boomed, standing up from his chair, knocking it over in the process. "I told you not to mate her until she's of age. I mean, she isn't even an adult yet. She's a teenager!"

"She went into heat." Adam growled, removing his head from his hands. "What was I supposed to do? Let her suffer? I wasn't worrying about the probability of getting her pregnant."

"Guys, please stop fighting." Paige whimpered, holding her stomach as if she was going to be sick again. I scanned the area for a trash can but was unsuccessful to find one.

Both boys ignored her and were soon standing chest to chest. I knew Cooper was trying to get his beta to stand down, but Adam wasn't having that. They both growled menacingly at each other, and I went over to stop Paige from charging over. I took her hand and pulled her behind me. If a fight broke out, there was no way I would let her get hurt.

"How could you be so irresponsible?"

"Cooper, it wasn't just my fault!"

"Are you seriously going to blame my sister in this?"

"Last time I checked, her body and wolf needed me to relieve her pain! Although you wouldn't understand since you haven't taken any step with your *mate*." Adam spat and my jaw dropped when he said *mate* with such disgust.

"How would you feel if I sent you on a nice long trip for a year? You wouldn't see your son or daughter born!"

"I just got back! How cold and heartless can you be?"

"Stop. This isn't good for Paige or the baby!" I shouted, and shockingly they both stopped arguing and turned to look at me. I huffed, crossing my arms angrily.

"Thank you," Paige muttered, and I could practically hear the smile on her face since she was still behind me.

"Paige, can we talk?"

She nodded and turned to leave the room. Adam followed after her with mixed emotions on his face. I gave Paige a reassuring smile, which she returned back before her mate shut the door behind him.

I inhaled deeply before letting out a breath quickly. Taking in some courage, I turned to look at Cooper who was staring at me.

"You lied to me."

"Technically, I didn't lie." I explained, but he only let out a low growl in aggravation. "And you promised you wouldn't get angry at Paige."

"You kept a secret. That's the same thing." Rolling my eyes at him, I turned to walk away from him, but I was suddenly pushed against the wall, my stomach just kissing the wall. "Don't you *dare* roll your eyes at me. You made me promise not to get made at Paige, yes, but just didn't know what I was promising for."

"What happens if I do roll my eyes? You can't control me." My voice sounded stronger and fearless.

"I'll punish you." Liking how his words made my wolf stir in blissfulness, I spun around to face him. This was so unlike me. I felt stronger, and my power felt like it had multiplied more than a dozen times.

"Then punish me," I whispered seductively, and a purr escaped my lips the same time a low growl fled my mate's.

"I enjoy this side of you." Cooper grinned, placing his hands on my hips gently. I leaped in surprise, but it gave me a small hint of pleasure. "My luna."

Luna? Last time I checked, I was still an omega.

"I need to make an example of you because you don't lie to an alpha." The way Cooper towered over me caused a shiver to run down my back. I couldn't hold back the soft purr that escaped my deep red lips. "Now what should I do?"

"You can…" I got a little frightened from his serious expression. Was he really going to punish me for keeping his sister's secret from him? I mean, Paige was from his alpha's bloodline, so it's not like I could go against her plead anyway. "You can let this slide."

"Now why would I do that?"

His face held a mischievous glint, but before I could argue, his lips were attacking mine. It may be his kind of punishment, but it definitely wasn't anywhere near that. I wouldn't mind this being my punishment every day.

Cooper's lips moved hungrily on mine, and I couldn't help but let them move in perfect sync. It felt amazing to kiss my mate so passionately. Whether he was mad at me, I didn't care as long as we kissed like this all the time. Butterflies erupted in my belly, and I couldn't help but smile. His tongue trailed over my bottom lip, asking for entrance, which I teasingly denied.

My mate let out a growl in annoyance, but I still didn't let his tongue roam my mouth like he desperately wanted to. It was fun to torment him—until he shocked me completely. His hands roamed further down until they landed on my bottom. I gasped in surprise when he gave it a little pinch, causing my mouth to open without my consent. Taking the chance, Cooper's tongue roamed every single inch of my mouth, and I couldn't help but moan loudly. He chuckled and tweaked my bottom again.

Removing my lips from his, I slapped him playfully on the chest, which only made him chuckle. It was a wonderful sound coming from his perfect yet swollen lips. Rumbling up from deep in his chest, it was an amazing sound I couldn't get enough of. I loved his laugh; there was no denying how much I enjoyed hearing it.

I couldn't help but blush and giggle shyly. Cooper gently patted my butt and kissed my forehead lovingly. I always relished it when he was like this, showing rare emotions. He peppered kisses all over my face and took my hands while rubbing his thumbs along the top of them. It was obvious he was deep in a thought. I coveted to know what was going through his head, and there was only one way to do that.

"Mark me, Cooper."

Chapter 17

There were no perfect words to describe how surprised Cooper was. Marking was the second step in the mating bond. It was a way of saying 'I love you,' and just like people always say, 'Actions speak louder than words.' I wanted to be loved by him, and him only. There were no ifs or buts in this.

"Please, Cooper." I begged, clutching onto his shoulders gently, preparing for what I desired him to do. "Mark me."

"I can't, Celia."

His words felt like a bucket of ice cold water on my body. And every word dug deep into my heart. Tears prickled in my eyes, but I held them back. I pushed him away gently and turned away from him. Nothing was worse than a rejection like that. It hurt like hell. My heart throbbed painfully. I was tired of crying. I didn't expect my mate to do something this hurtful.

Not being able to say anything, I opened Cooper's office door and left. With my back facing him, I let the tears fall down. My body shook, and a soft sob left my lips. He didn't love me; I knew it. I tried so hard to push that thought away, but it really was true. Why else wouldn't he mark me to keep other males from touching me? I thought alphas were very possessive, yet here he was, putting me out in the open for any male to claim me.

"Celia, wait." My hand was taken, and I was jerked back into the room. Thumbs brushed my tears off my face. His voice hushed me, but I couldn't calm myself down.

"Just stop." I croaked, my voice aching from my crying.

"Celia, you have to understand." His voice also held a hint of hurt, but I expected it to be pity. Why would he even bother explaining? "Right now is just too confusing. My best friend got my baby sister pregnant. I just can't let that one go. Then there's you with so many problems. I—"

"Problems!" I snapped, pushing his hands off my face. "You know nothing about my problems. Am I just a person you tolerate because of my problems?"

"What?" Cooper must've noticed his mistake and shook his head. "No! No, you don't have problems. I mean, you do have PTSD, and I'm a little bothered that you can't have my children but you—"

"So you don't love me because of the things I am going through right now. And because I can't reproduce an heir for *you*!" I sneered, pushing on his chest for him to get away from me when he approached me. "I can't believe you! I can't even stand being in the same room as you!"

When I sprinted out of the room, Cooper didn't try to stop me again. He knew not to come near me now that I knew exactly what was wrong. It was all because of me. I would've been okay with that because I would get better in time, but now he couldn't even touch me because I could never have children!

I ran into the basement down the hall. There could be a chance I could be fixed. There must be a way I could make Cooper love me. I needed to find a way to produce a child for him so he could love me. Would he only love me if I produced an offspring for him? Or was he really after a child and was planning on taking the baby away from me after? Could he be that cruel? It hurt me to know that he would never put my needs before own needs and the pack.

My feet carried me to the pack doctor's office. I knocked frantically, hoping Cooper wasn't running after me. I didn't want him anywhere near me.

The door finally opened, and I walked inside, trying to catch my breath.

"Celia, what happened?" Sheila asked, taking my shoulders gently and guiding me to a chair. She gently placed me in the chair and sat down across me. "Please explain, hun."

I began to tell her about what happened only seconds ago. Tears filled Sheila's eyes, and then they were covered with rage. I knew she was upset with her alpha, and I couldn't help but be relieved that someone understood me. She stayed silent the entire time, occasionally handing me a tissue.

"Sheila, I'm begging you to find a way to have me produce children." I was looking at her desperately.

"There is always a way to produce a child through artificial insemination. All I need is both—" I interrupted her.

"No, Sheila, I want it done the usual way." I hinted, making sure she knew what I was talking about.

"You can try different medications, but they don't work for werewolves because we are usually extremely fertile." I knew she was stating a fact, but the thought of knowing all werewolves but me had the ability to produce children wounded me.

Tugging my hair angrily, I let more tears fill my eyes. It was surprising how my eyes were able to hold so much. I must have been crying for almost an hour.

There had to be something else. Anything really.

"But..." Sheila looked at her hands. I knew there must be something else, and I leaned in to hear it. "There's this witch that may be able to help you but with a price."

What, the Moon Goddess was a witch? I'd never heard or come across one, but if it could fix me, I wouldn't mind. I gave Sheila a pleading look for her to continue. She sighed and took out a phone from her pocket. I looked at it curiously since I had never had one. It really was a pretty device.

"I'll tell her to come here late tonight. Cooper doesn't like witches very much because of the deals they make, and he won't like this. I'm doing this for you, but if he finds out about this, he will have my head and then hers." She pushed a button and pressed the phone to her ear. All she said was. "Be here at midnight. Usual place."

Sheila hung up and gave me a reassuring smile. "Good luck. Meet her near the graveyard at midnight."

"But I don't know where that is."

"Then I'll show you."

***

It was late, and I knew no one was awake in the pack. Cooper had fallen asleep on the leather couch since I told him he wasn't sleeping next to me. That was all I said, and he nodded in understanding. Now, all I had to figure out was how to leave the room. I could use the bathroom and sneak through the window, but it's too far down to jump. I could tiredly get up and mumble to myself that I was hungry.

Picking the last one, I did what I thought was smart. I stood up and creeped out of the bed. Beginning my mumbling, I heard Cooper stir but soon relax again when he heard what I was saying. I left the room and slyly went down the stairs. There were a few creaks here and there, but I was able to make it to the bottom floor.

I left the house and followed the same path Sheila had showed me earlier. It didn't take long for the trees I had dodged to disappear and grey stones to show up. Each one had a name, and some had a rank if they were important. Most looked very old, but others looked brand new. A chill ran down my spine, and I tried to push away how terrified I was.

"You must be Celia." A voice croaked, and I turned around to see a woman dressed in something that reminded me of one of those beautiful Indian outfits. The skirt went down to her ankles, and I could barely see her chocolate skin and slightly grey hair.

"Yes, you must be the witch." Our conversation seemed very formal. "How did you know me?"

"Word travels about who you are. Even in the witch world." She stepped into the moonlight, and I noticed right away that her eyes were a foggy white color. I stepped back in fear, but she only chuckled. "I may be a blind witch, but I already know you took a stride away from me."

"I'm sorry, miss."

"It's Ayana." She walked forward, resting her hand on a gravestone. "Now what brings me here and you away from your mate?"

"I need help."

Ayana gave a toothless smile and popped her hip. I couldn't help but smile at her impression of trying to look young.

"Well, every wolf who contacts me needs help. Usually, it's to help find or track a mate, make their child's shift become less painful, and make them look younger." We both chuckled softly at the last one but soon grew sober instantly. "What is it that you need?"

I rolled my lips into my mouth and sucked in a breath. It's now or never. "My mate won't mark me because I can't produce an heir for him. I'm sterile, and I want that to change."

Ayana's eyebrows scrunched together in confusion. I knew what she was thinking, but I guess my silence was enough for her not to question it. My heart was hoping for any glimpse of hope, but she remained silent with her pale eyes looking aimlessly around. My eyes were growing watery from the wind blowing in my face, and I slowly began to get cold. If I got cold enough, Cooper would wake up and notice I was gone since our bond was still there.

"You want to produce children..." She seemed to be thinking very hard. My hands were growing clammy from my anxiousness, and I was starting to fear the worst. That was until she spoke music to my ears. "I can do that, but for a price."

"Anything." My mouth moved before I could even think about what would happen. She could ask me to hurt the pack, and I would never do that even if I was to lose something Cooper and I obviously wanted.

"If you are to ever have a daughter, you give her to me."

My heart stopped then and there, and my blood ran cold, colder than the winter air. Give my child away for my own selfish needs. Although it was possible that I could have a son, and I could tell Cooper I didn't want to have a child anymore. This would avoid any possibility of having a daughter after my first son is born. Now that I thought of it, I actually would want a daughter. She could look just like my mate. She could have his striking eyes. It could be possible my baby girl could look as beautiful as Paige. However, I needed to think about the future of the pack. Cooper needed someone to take control of the pack, and although Paige's baby could, Alpha Zaire was risking that child's life as well.

If I didn't do this, I may never know what it would be like to have a daughter or a son. Though I would be giving up my daughter, there was always the possibility of having more than one daughter. Could one sacrifice result in my happiness with Cooper? He could protect our first born daughter as well. It was all probability, but I had hope Cooper and our pack would protect our daughter. There was no chance that either of these would be dangerous. If I accepted the witch's offer, I could have as many children as I wanted to make Cooper happy. I hoped that giving up my daughter would bring a good life for her. Ayana seemed harmless. And if I declined, I would never know what it would be like to be a mother, and my mate would never love me.

Risk the life of my daughter or have no children at all?

I knew anything could go wrong, but I spoke anyway, "Yes."

Chapter 18

    I gazed at the small vial in my hand that Ayanna had given me. Being seated on the bed at three in the morning in Cooper's room in complete darkness didn't help with my decision. She had put a little spell in the contents of the vial, but I never asked what she had done. I was going to, but she just disappeared completely out of sight. There was no way I could contact her but through Sheila.

    The small glass bottle was filled with a glowing object that resembled a growing wolf fetus that was sleeping. The tail of the pup was forming, and a faint red luminosity was around it. There were several veins leading out of the blushing ball that were connected to it. All I needed to do was press the opening to my lips, and it would crawl inside me easily. I just lacked the courage to do just that.

    My heart kept racing, and I saw Cooper shift in his sleep a few times at the noise. Maybe I should talk to Sheila and see what she could do with it. There could be a way to study it and find out how it was made. Pulling the cork that kept anything from spilling, I slowly moved the vial to my lips. Before I could place it fully, I pushed it away and put the cap back on. I couldn't do it, not when Cooper was only a few feet away from me, sleeping soundlessly.

Do it. My wolf ordered, and I jumped at the aggressive tone she used. *This will make our mate love us.*

I knew she was right. We both knew this was the only way to make this bump in the road go away finally. If this worked, I would be left with my PTSD to deal with. The decision to make me fertile was screaming at me, but my body kept worrying. What if I had a daughter? I would never be able to just give her away without a fight. The deal was stupid. I never should've agreed to it. I never would've had to make such a complicated decision.

Hours went by and I was growing tired, but I couldn't stop looking at the wolf fetus. It was like it was waiting for me to make the decision that I knew I could never make. No, this would make Cooper love me. He would mark me and everything would be perfect. One child was all I'd have. I wouldn't risk having a daughter.

"Celia?" My eyes flickered over to Cooper who was rubbing his tired eyes.

I looked at the clock and noticed it was already five in the morning. Did he always wake up this early?

"Why are you up so early?"

He hasn't noticed the vial. Hide it. My wolf commanded, and I pushed the bottle under the covers quickly before Cooper could see it.

"What was that?"

My heart stopped, and I bet Cooper could see the panic written on my face. Hands growing clammy, I furiously began to wipe them on my pants.

"It's nothing. Just some medicine I was told to take by Sheila." I lied, looking around the room and away from his face. If I looked into his eyes, he would see right through me.

"You can't keep lying to me, baby. What is it?" Cooper moved over to me and sat closer to me. Carefully, he moved my hand ever so slowly and reached in the bed sheets. I looked away while he slowly took out the vial. Tears filled my eyes, and I looked at my hands. "What the hell is this?"

I couldn't look at my mate, so I just stared blankly at the door. Cooper would never forgive me if he found out I had made a deal with a witch. Hearing him sniff the vial in slow motion made my breathing hitch.

A growl came from Cooper, but I didn't move. "A witch! What did you do with a witch, Celia?" I couldn't say anything that would comfort him. There was no way I was able to lie to him, so I turned to look at him.

"You weren't going to love me unless I got it." My voice was filled with so much vulnerability. "It's a cure."

"A cure for what?"

I didn't answer. He grew frustrated and jumped off the bed before facing me. Placing the bottle in my face, he demanded. "What will this cure?"

"Infertility."

His eyes flashed in surprise and brought the vial down to his thighs. A tear leaked from my eye, and I furiously brushed it away. He stammered while forming the words to speak, "What?"

"You weren't going to love me if I didn't produce children for you. I found someone to help me with that. The witch, she gave me that."

Cooper shook his head furiously. "Witches don't just give werewolves things out of pity. Everything comes in a price."

Fear erupted in my chest, and I knew instantly that he had caught me. "What did you promise to give her? Money? Medicine? Silver? Herbs? What?"

Lie. My wolf barked, and I jumped once again at her antagonistic tone.

"A living being. Any living being," I stated.

Is that all?" He laughed humorlessly. "I don't believe your statement."

"It's possible that it won't be a living being either."

"You're not making sense, Celia." He angrily knocked over the chair where his desk was and ran a hand through his copper hair as he began to whisper to himself. "How could you be so reckless to seek a witch? But then again I have a chance of being a father, and how could I pass that up?"

Cooper took a step back and looked at the vial. I knew he was examining the wolf fetus. I held my hand out for him to give it back to me. I'd made my decision.

"Fine. If this vial allows you to get pregnant, I don't want you to take it until after we mate. I don't want to worry about getting you pregnant our first time together." Nodding my head in understanding, I watched as he put the vial on his desk and moved away from it. "I'm not happy with the deal you made with a witch. Don't ever to it again. You mentioned Sheila aided you, and she will be punished for her actions."

With that being said, he walked out of the room, letting multiple curses leave his lips. Cooper was angry, and I wasn't going to push him. Letting out a huff of air, I walked backwards and collapsed on the bed. I needed to sleep.

***

I felt older, more mature for some strange reason. Dressed in a summer dress, I ran around a little log cabin looking for someone. My search ended when I heard three giggles.

"Shush, Rylan. She'll hear you," a girl's voice whispered.

"Quiet, One Cent," a very powerful boy's voice barked, and I grew a little angry at the voice he had used to the girl. It was a tone of an alpha, but I knew he didn't realize it.

"I think I hear her coming." Another boy's voice quivered, and I sensed a bit of uncertainty which caught me off guard.

Suddenly, I was scooped in the air, and I was soon hovering above three small children. They were looking at the person holding me with awe, and the girl who must've been the youngest let out a giggle. The two boys chuckled, and the oldest held a smirk. I didn't know how I knew who was the oldest since they all looked the same age, but I didn't pay much attention. Instead, I was concerned about who was holding me.

"Run, kids! Momma can't get you!" The voice was entirely familiar, and I soon smiled when I recognized it.

The two boys grabbed the girls hand and ran off, laughing loudly. "Cooper! Put. Me. Down." I began to squirm under my mate's grip, and he soon placed me back on my feet. When I looked up at him, I noticed several different things about him.

A small stubble on his chin was there, showing a little maturity from him, but he still looked as handsome as ever. His hair was cut short, but it looked more like a buzz cut than anything. The muscles on his arms grew, if that was even possible, and a new tattoo was showing proudly on his neck. When I looked close enough, I soon realized what it was; it was a mating mark. Only alphas and lunas were allowed to mark each other.

The last thing I noticed was the gold ring on his ring finger that shone proudly in the light. This only meant one thing. Cooper and I had mated and were married like humans. Looking at my left hand, I noticed a bright engagement ring with a large diamond on it next to a matching wedding ring. I touched my neck and felt the groves of a mark.

"Come on, before they get away." He winked before sprinting in the direction where the kids had ran off to.

It must've taken us ten minutes to find the children huddled underneath a hollow log. Cooper had chuckled and pulled the two boys out. I *reached down and pulled the little girl out careful not to rip the bright pink and white checkered dress she had on. Propping her on my hip, I was able to notice her features.*

Her hair was like Cooper's, but she had my perfectly straight hair. She was very beautiful even, and I couldn't wait to see her get older. She had milky and fragile skin like me. Then I noticed her eyes. The girl's eyes were my purple ones that shone whenever the sun hit them.

I turned to look at the boys in Cooper's arms. The one on his right had tan skin and blond hair like I once had when I was younger. His hair was curly, much like Emilia's. He shared his father's aquamarine eyes, and I couldn't help but feel proud that he looked a lot like him. The boy on the left looked very shy yet extremely strong at the same time. His skin was tan just like his brother and had the same frame as him too. However, his eyes were a lot different. They were purple just like his sister's, and he had my white straight hair. It was amazing how much he stood out from his siblings.

"Say hello to Clayton, the oldest." Cooper shifted the blond haired boy on his hip. "And Rylan the second child. That cute little girl is Penelope." The cute boy with the white hair and purple eyes beamed at me before catching what his father said.

"Her name is Penny!" Rylan snapped.

"Yeah, her name is One Cent."

I smiled at Clayton's nickname for his sister and couldn't help but feel proud that they were arguing with their father, their alpha.

Cooper rolled his eyes and spoke again. "They're your pups, our children."

***

My eyes fluttered open, and I couldn't help but smile at the dream. It seemed so real. Each one held some feature of both Cooper and I. They were a perfect blend of us. Penelope, or Penny, reminded me so much of myself, and Clayton obviously got the strongest alpha gene out of the three. I could see him being an excellent leader of the pack. Rylan looked just as mischievous as his father.

Turning my head, I came face to face with an exhausted looking Paige. Her cheeks were all puffy, and she was cuddled close to me. I couldn't help but smile at her innocence, even if she was just a year younger than me. Her arms were wrapped protectively over her flat stomach. Brushing a curled lock out of her face, her eyes snapped open, and she turned to look at me.

"You were mumbling in your sleep, so I thought I should check up on you since you always have nightmares," she spoke, offering me a smile. "Are you okay?"

For the first time in a while, I actually gave her a real grin. "It wasn't a nightmare. It was a perfect dream."

"Tell me about it." Paige seemed overly interested, but I wasn't going to get a pregnant girl with crazy mood swings angry by denying her request.

That was when I decided to explain the dream. I never left out any detail of Cooper as a wonderful father who was always playful around them. Then I spoke about Clayton, Rylan, and Penelope. Paige couldn't get the smile off her face while I explained the dream in detail.

"You know what that's called?" Paige asked. and I shook my head. "It's called an *illumination dream*. Alphas get it so they know who their first child will be. Your mind chooses the names for you so you don't have to spend months thinking of the perfect name. The dream also tells you who the future alpha of the pack will be. The number of children in a single dream shows that you will either have twins or triplets, possibly more. The dream also tells you that you are ready to complete the bond with your mate and that you will be pregnant soon after."

"But I can't get pregnant until I take that." I nodded to the vial still glowing brightly on Cooper's desk.

"What is it?"

"I made a deal with a witch. Her magic is going to help me get pregnant." I let out a sigh and clutched my flat stomach. "Because I can't do it myself."

"You never know." Paige winked before sitting up in bed. "You could be fertile now for all you know."

I rolled my eyes at her and gently pushed her off the bed. She waved her hand for me to follow as she ran out of the room. Trying to keep up with a pregnant Paige was difficult, but now she was even more hyper than few weeks ago. I guess the revelation of her pregnancy was a good thing. It gave her back her strength and energy.

"Are you and Adam okay?" I had to ask since her cheeks were still bright red and her eyes were a little bloodshot as we walked down the hall together.

"He wasn't as happy as I wanted him to be, but he's accepted the responsibility of being a parent." Paige shrugged before giving me a slightly fake smile. I could tell a fake smile from a real because I'd used them before to Logan, my little brother.

We walked down the hallway and down the stairs. I had no idea where she was taking me until she jumped on the couch in the sitting room. Paige popped her legs up on the coffee table and kicked off her brown boots. Jeremy was in the room, snuggled to some fluffy object, sleeping and murmuring words.

What surprised me the most was when Paige poked Jeremy's cheek without waking him up. It was pretty funny when he snatched her hand and held it close to him. How could he be sleeping in midafternoon?

"Lazy omega, I tell you." Paige chuckled before using all her strength to throw Jeremy off the couch and onto the wood floor. "Payback really does bite back."

"Ow!" Jeremy stated simply, rubbing his arm that must've landed funny. "I only did that to you once. You've been doing this to me forty-seven times."

Paige just rolled her eyes and gave him a bored look. "You're the one saying I'm weird for having a snow globe collection when it's *you* who counts how many times I push you off the couch."

Jeremy muttered some curse words under his breath which she obviously caught. "Hey! Child on board here!"

He looked at me in confusion while I plopped myself in a very fancy arm chair.

"You're pregnant?"

I raised my eyebrow at his statement. I was surprised he didn't know. I assumed gossip traveled fast since packs usually had the knack for knowing all the personal details about their alpha. I wouldn't be surprised if the entire pack knew I couldn't have children without the vial Ayanna gave me. I mean, werewolves were usually extremely fertile, so this would cause a shock to everyone.

"Not here, Omega Boy."

Jeremy just rolled his bright blue eyes at Paige. If she wasn't mated, I could see them being the couple that fights playfully. "Me."

"Oh." Jeremy rolled his lips and shook his head, sighing in relief. "Good because I was seconds away from saying you looked like you were gaining weight."

He rubbed the back of his head, wincing in the process as Paige whacked the back of his head. Judging by the noise of it, I could only assume it was very painful for him. He scowled at her while she just relaxed back into her seat and patted her flat stomach. I really didn't see a difference in her weight. She was still very thin to me.

"Crazy, hormonal, mood-swinging bit—"

"I wouldn't finish that sentence if I were you, pup." The three sets of eyes snapped to the voice, and we all realized that Cooper and Adam were home. Adam was sending Jeremy a glare while he leaned against the doorframe, obviously angered by Jeremy's words. "Get lost, omega."

Jeremy made a move to get out of his chair, but I stopped him. "No, Jeremy, please stay." I begged, giving him a pleading look. This time, the low growl came from Cooper, and we once again turned to look at him.

"Scram." Cooper ordered, and just like that, Jeremy fled out of the room.

My mate walked over to my furious figure and stood over me. He examined my comfortable position, taking in every single detail. We had to interact sooner or later, and with the dream still in my mind, it wasn't helping.

"That's my chair, mate." Cooper's voice informed huskily, and I hid a shiver by pretending to cough dramatically. No wonder this chair looked so worn out and the scent in it was so comforting; it was my mate's favorite seat.

I made a move to get up, but Cooper beat me to it. He lifted me up by my hips, causing a squeal to escape from my lips. Instead of my bottom resting in a fluffy chair, I was plopped on a pair of muscular legs. Seated on Cooper's lap, I made another move to get up, but he just held me tighter to him.

"What are you doing back so early? I thought you had a perimeter run to do," Paige questioned, cocking her head to the side as Adam sat next to her and brought her close to his chest.

"What? I couldn't spend some quality time with my unborn child?" She sent him a glare when he didn't say anything about her. He gave a playful grin when he noticed. "But of course, I am forced to be around you since the pup is *ours*."

"You two make me want to throw up," Cooper grumbled, rubbing my back soothingly with his rough thumbs. I didn't know why I enjoyed the roughness of his fingers, but it did have a calming effect on both me and my wolf. There's only so much that could put my anxiety to rest.

"You make me want to throw up just by looking at your face." Paige shot back, and we girls giggled at her own words.

The rest of the day consisted of me resting on top of Cooper's lap. When I had to use the bathroom, he let me go, but I went back to him immediately since I missed his warm body. My chilled hands and fingers felt numb for some odd reason. Cooper had noticed and cradled them gently.

My eyes were getting droopy around dinner time, but I decided it was better to stay awake while I still had time to be around him. The tension we had early this morning was gone, and we both knew bringing up the topic would just cause another brawl. I actually wanted to live my little fairytale with my mate for at least twenty-four hours.

I must've fallen asleep while still in Cooper's arms because I jumped when the noise of footsteps was heard. My eyes didn't feel like opening, but I did hear what the person that had walked in was saying. I didn't recognize the man's voice, but he must be a pack member.

Cooper's arms tensed around me. "Slow down, Ronald."

The man spoke again, "The omega found his mate. And you won't believe who it is."

This time I opened my eyes.

Chapter 19

This little shocker was the reason we all stood in the hallway, staring at the newfound mates. Jeremy seemed a little shocked but couldn't move to her because of the alpha tone Cooper had used on him. I was very angry with him for that but would scold him later. Right now, we had some major things to discuss.

"A rogue, Jeremy? A rogue just happens to be your mate!" Cooper growled, taking him by the cuff of his collared shirt. Why he was wearing such a nice shirt was a mystery to me, and I knew I had to ask him about it next time.

"You know better than I do that she is more than just a rogue," Jeremy spat, causing everyone's eyes to go wide at his words. Did he seriously go against what his alpha had just stated?

"Don't play with me, pup, or you'll be locked away just as she is." My mate angrily pushed him away but told him not to go anywhere.

"I just so happens to be standing only a few feet away from you." A new voice snapped, and I looked over at Jeremy's mate. "Think, Cooper. You know what he's talking about."

This was getting a little out of hand, so I grabbed Cooper's forearm before he could charge over to Trixie. She didn't even flinch, but I knew why she wouldn't even bat an eyelash.

"Don't you dare touch her!" Jeremy exclaimed.

Cooper's eye snapped back over to him, and I had to hold my mate's arm to hold him back from punching him square in the jaw. All my weight was rested on his arm, and I knew if he tugged away from me, I wouldn't be able to hold him back. Luckily, he didn't take a step away from me, but I still feared for Jeremy's life. Disrespecting an alpha was a death wish that would never go unpunished.

"And once again." Trixie snorted, rolling her eyes. "'I'm right here."

"Trixie, don't speak. You are still a rogue in my eyes, and I won't hesitate to punish you for your disrespectful actions."

"Then why let me roam around your pack house like a guest?" Cooper didn't answer. "My pack was an ally with your pack before it crumbled, which is why you can't hurt me. That is why you will erase my rogue status and make me an honored guest of this pack."

"Fine." He turned away from her before he looked back and took a step towards Trixie. "But don't think for a second that if you mess up, you won't be kicked out of my pack in an instant."

The redhead rolled her eyes at him, and her arms remained crossed.

Like always, she was wearing a heavy makeup. The outfit she was wearing screamed sleazy, but I knew that was just her style. A pair of black ripped jeans that showed too much skin hugged her fit legs well. A hot pink crop top was on, showing perfect abs and a gold loop in her belly button. The top also showed her cleavage that I certainly didn't have, along with the black laced bra underneath. Purple lipstick was on her face, and powder covered any flaws she had on her face.

What I never noticed that wasn't on her before were the three claw marks on the back of her neck. It took a lot to scar a werewolf and was usually done with silver. However, these scratches must've been done by some kind of wolf that had silver claws, and I could only wonder how this happened to her.

"You cannot order me around, Cooper, when I'm one of the strongest alphas ever bred. It is in my nature to speak open with you, and it is my right. My father was an alpha, and you should treat me as one even if I don't have a pack anymore. Learn some respect for an old friend." I didn't enjoy the words she spoke and narrowed my eyes at her. "Oh, don't give me that look, future luna. You know he can be sour at times."

I knew the only reason she was talking like this was to speak to her mate, but I didn't appreciate any of the things she had said. Jeremy couldn't stand up for her because of his position, but Trixie could. She did what she had to do to prove she deserved to stay in the pack. She needed to stay with Jeremey, and the only way was to show that she was an alpha as well. I looked up to her for the courage and strength she had.

"Now, let me have my mate." Trixie snapped, looking over at her mate, Jeremy, with a flicker of gentleness.

This must be overwhelming for an omega because they didn't usually get mated to someone who had a higher rank than them. However, being mated to a female alpha must be as complicated as my relationship with Cooper. This may be better for Jeremy because his rank would increase and Trixie may form a new pack with him.

"Fine." Cooper nodded towards Jeremy and moved to walk away. I followed after him, but not before seeing Jeremy enveloping Trixie in a warm and gentle hug. Even with the two guards around her, he still managed to get closer to her. It shocked me how resilient the pair were, even after knowing each over just now.

I kept myself at Cooper's side as we went up the stairs. I could sense that he was annoyed, but I couldn't tell why. Did I do something? Was he thinking the same thing that I was?

We entered his bedroom, and I took a seat on his bed while he paced the room. Placing my clasped hands between my legs, I waited for him to do something. I pursed my lips, trying to be patient until he walked over to his desk where the vial was vibrantly glowing. I watched him stare at it intently.

Whatever he was thinking about must be important. I'd seen him stressed before but never this frustrated. Then suddenly, he pulled himself off the desk and turned to look at me.

"What?" I asked, cocking my head to the side.

"You told me that you were upset that I wouldn't mark you." I didn't speak because he knew that was exactly what I had felt. "Well, I've realized that a mating bond isn't just about producing an heir. I've learned to accept that."

I didn't know how to respond, so I kept my mouth shut. What was he saying? Was he going to change things between us for the better? I knew I was hopeful, but perhaps there was a chance we could be a wonderful mated couple if he progressed things.

"What are you going to do about it, Cooper?" I asked a little worried as he started to slowly walk over to me. It reminded me a lot of Alpha Zaire when he would walk over to me and hit me.

Soothingly, Cooper placed his large hands on each of my shoulders. He pressed our foreheads together, and I held my breath, waiting for something to happen. Slowly, his hands traveled down from my shoulders to my waist where he pushed me closer to him. His sweet breath fanned over my face, causing a chill to run up my spine.

"Cooper, I…" My mouth couldn't form any words once his lips crashed down to mine.

Like always, our lips moved in sync with each other, but it felt a little uncomfortable since he was still standing and I was seated on the bed. As if Cooper had read my mind, he pushed me so my back was pressed against the mattress, hovering completely over me. I didn't know why he was acting so strangely, but my wolf and I enjoyed it.

I wrapped my legs around Cooper's hips, bringing his body closer to mine. A low growl echoed from his throat, and I immediately knew it was his wolf. A purr escaped my lips that was caused by my own wolf, and I accidently let out a moan. The grip on my hips tightened, and I felt a sharp pain.

Once I removed my lips, I was able to breathe out. "Cooper, that hurts." This only made him dig his growing claws deeper into my skin. "Please stop, Cooper. You're hurting me."

He seemed to snap out of it because he moved his hands away. A small trail of blood trickled from my wound, and the look on Cooper broke my heart. I knew his wolf had taken over for a second, and the look in his eyes showed he regretted it.

"Celia, I'm so sorry." He tried to push himself off me, but I held him with my legs that were still wrapped around him. He gave me a confused look. "I didn't mean to hurt you. Okay? I should've kept him on a better leash, and I promise I will next time. My wolf just keeps bringing us apart with his dominance."

"It's okay." I really wasn't that livid at him, and I wanted to prove that to him. "I'm not mad."

"But I hurt you. Mates shouldn't hurt each other, and I just did."

Before he could say any more, I wound my arms around his neck and kissed him with so much force, I knocked the wind out of my own lungs. He groaned. I knew he was trying to keep his wolf at bay. The minute a giggle escaped my mouth, the back of Cooper's neck got hot.

He started to trail kisses across my cheek and down my neck. I froze the minute his teeth grazed over the soft spot on my neck. He noticed and moved his head away from me so he could look at me. His eyes were pitch-black, and I knew he was trying to fight his wolf again.

"Cooper?"

"Do you still want me to mark you?" My heart stopped at his words.

His decision to suddenly mark me now made me curious.

"What brought this on?" I asked suspiciously.

"I saw the way Trixie and Jeremy acted around each other, and I would give anything to have the same strong bond they have. I know we can have something stronger. A mark could make us stronger together." He explained, looking at me with hopeful eyes. "We can be the mated couple of the century."

"Cooper..." I tried to find a way to explain to him what I wanted.

"Just say it." He begged, looking down at my neck and then up into my eyes. His eyes gazing straight into my soul made me shift uncomfortably. "If you want it, tell me."

"Mark me." I begged, holding my lower abdomen closer to his warm body.

I'd heard many times that the process of marking was unbearably painful and usually made the one who was doing the marking break down. Even for a man, it would be slightly embarrassing to watch an alpha cry over his mate.

With that thought, he leaned and kissed the place where I knew he was planning on marking me. Butterflies erupted in my stomach, and I was beginning to grow nervous. I knew it would hurt, but he was supposed to distract me with pleasures.

Before I knew it, Cooper sunk his teeth deep into my fragile skin. A yelp escaped my lips, but I bit my tongue to hold out a scream. I still cried. The pain was excruciating. A mark was different for different mates, but I never thought it would hurt as much as it did.

Then he did the unthinkable, he grabbed my head with his free hand and brought my lips close to his neck. With the tears threatening to fall, I already knew what he wanted me to do. My mate wanted me to mark him. If I did exactly what he did, I would finally be a permanent part of his pack. I couldn't think of anything that would make me happier.

My lips attacked his neck, and I slowly let my wolf inch her way to the surface. First, my claws came out of my nails, and I felt my eyes growing a shade darker. Next, my teeth grew sharper and longer. Kissing his neck to give him some pleasure, then I finally pierced his skin.

Cooper's blood hit my tongue hard, and I couldn't help but let a moan out of how sweet it tasted. It's like a mixture cotton candy and caramel. A few drops of blood trickled down on my tongue, and I welcomed it with affection. A burning began in my neck. A sharp pain echoed in my body, but I tried to pay more attention to my own task.

I didn't let him have any of my omega DNA because it would only weaken him. Instead, I gave him a part of me that I liked. My golden eyes and blond hair were given to Cooper, along with the tan skin I possessed almost two decades ago. He shivered and winced a bit, but soon it was all over.

Pleasure erupted all over my body. I moaned my throat and pulled away from him so I could focus on everything he was doing to me. His teeth were still deep in my neck, but he also pulled away. My skin was searing with the heat he had given me, but he didn't stop. He trailed his tongue and lapped up any blood that had escaped my neck. I did the same to him and gazed up at him.

We both gave each other a smile, and he kissed my lips gently. He shifted so he was on his back and half my body was on his chest. My mark still throbbed uncomfortably, but I tried to let this moment last. I relaxed myself on him and let him cradle me.

"Are you okay? Does it hurt?" Cooper asked, lightly brushing his fingertips across my healing skin.

"It's fine. It's not that bad," I whispered while listening to his heartbeat. I felt mine beating with his and couldn't help but feel excited that the mating process was almost completed. He's perfect.

"You're amazing," he whispered while caressing the exposed skin on my arms. "And mine. All mine."

"For eternity." I finished, closing my eyes and letting out a huff of air.

We lay there in peace, listening to each other's heartbeats and breathing. My eyes felt droopy from the sight blood loss, but I tried desperately to keep them open. Since, I was an omega, my body took slightly longer to heal itself.

"You're tired," he said, planting a kiss on my elbow then up towards my shoulder. "You can rest. I don't mind it."

I shook my head on the pillow. "I'm fine."

For the rest of the day, we lay in each other's arms. Around midnight, Cooper was fast asleep and I was dozing off slowly. My eyes were growing heavy, and I welcomed the darkness begging to take over. However, before I slipped into a dream, I heard the door open with a low squeak, but I ignored it because of my drowsiness.

I dreamed about Cooper and I laughing in a field. They said that after the marking, the mated couple could slip in each other's dream and live it together. It's hard to decide whether I was in his dream, but the place we were in was unknown to me. However, I felt a stinging in my arm, and Cooper and I shared confused glances. I looked at it and saw a dot of blood on my skin. Hissing in pain, I touched it lightly in confusion. The pain appeared from nowhere.

Gasping for air, my body sprung up. I saw Cooper's eyes fluttering. He was as confused as I was. Quickly, he grabbed my left arm. Small trails of blood were slithering down my arm. I hurriedly grabbed a tissue off the nightstand to stop it.

"Oh my god." Cooper breathed, looking up and down at my bare arm.

Looking just as confused as him, I scanned it. I saw that something was glowing brightly under my skin, exposing the blood flowing through my veins. The blood turned gold and traveled from my forearm to my shoulder and downward. I lifted my shirt. I gasped in horror when I saw the light traveled further and further down. My eyes widened when it slipped into my baggy pants, and I cautiously looked down the fabric to see that it disappeared in my most private area.

"What just happened?"

Chapter 20

Once again, I was seated on the examining table in Sheila's office, waiting for some kind of reason why my body glowed and the little ball disappeared into my lower region. The entire thing made no sense to me, and I could only think of one thing. What if a spirit was transported into my body, or a demon? It's happened to wolves before, although it hadn't happened for centuries, but anything was a possibility.

"What happened to my mate, Sheila?" Cooper growled at the pack doctor who was examining the results of my blood test. She had been looking over them for a couple of minutes now.

"I don't see anything that has really changed." She shrugged, placing the clipboard on her desk. "I can always do another checkup on her."

"Alright, do what you have to do." He sighed, giving me a quick kiss on my forehead. "I'll be in our room."

With that being said, he left the office, leaving me alone with Sheila. I desperately wanted to go after him since our mating bond had gotten so strong, but the pack doctor's grip on my arm stopped me. She eased me onto my back. I didn't understand what she was doing until she came back with washed hands and was walking over to my most private area.

"Wait." I trembled, shifting so my legs were closed and away from her. "I don't want you to look at me."

"Darling, the glowing ball went inside you and stopped here." She pointed at my lower section, stepping up on a stool so she could reach my figure. "I've done many checkups on men and women. I've seen it all. Paige was here yesterday for her ultrasound."

I knew she was trying to get me to relax, which she somehow did. With her words, I allowed her to look at me, not before closing my eyes, of course. It felt very uncomfortable, but I tried to think of Cooper—his smiling face that only appeared when I was around, or his sleeping form next to me after he marked me.

Suddenly, the door was swung open. I was surprised it didn't fall off with the power used on it. I didn't open my eyes because Sheila was in the middle of my checkup. That was until I felt the presence of my mate. Opening my eyes, I was greeted with a furious looking Cooper.

"Alpha, you can't be in here." Sheila ordered. Never had she used his name formally around me, so it kind of surprised to me. I pulled my pants on and sat up while Sheila walked over to him so he would leave.

My eyes traveled down from his face to his tense yet muscular body. He was shaking uncontrollably, and his muscles were bulging. I couldn't help but stare at his sculpted chest and arms. That was until my eyes landed on the objects in his large hands.

"There is a traitor in this pack." He growled, almost cracking the syringe in his left hand.

However, the needle wasn't what my eyes were focused on. Instead, I was staring at the empty vial in his right hand. It was the exact vial that the witch gave me. The only way for me to conceive a child was in that vial, and now, it was empty.

Sheila stood there emotionless. Her eyes were wide. She checked my arm that had been cleaned of blood and looked back over to Cooper.

"Do you think someone injected the cure into her?" she asked. All eyes were on me now, and I really didn't enjoy the attention I was getting.

"Right now, we have no idea what the cure could've done to her," Cooper stated, walking over to me and picking me up. He carried me bridal style and walked towards the exit. "Pack meeting in ten minutes. Spread the word."

"But it's three in the morning!"

***

Right now, Cooper and I stood above thousands of exhausted and tired looking pack members. All ages were awake now, rubbing their eyes tiredly. Some were even glaring at their alpha without even realizing it. Paige was among one those people. Her hair was everywhere, and she was wearing what appeared to be Adam's sweatshirt. She was trying to hide her legs as best as she could from the unmated wolves, but she was barely successful.

Sage was cradled in my arms since Emilia was busy trying to organize everyone along with Patrick who was speaking with the elders. She was snoring soundly, and I noticed Cooper gazing down at me with pride as I soothed her back to sleep. Propped up on my hip, I tried to keep her from falling as best as I could. The petal pink feet pajamas hugged Sage and kept her warm so I didn't have to worry about her getting cold.

"For those of you who don't know my mate, Celia, is officially your new *luna*. Please treat her with upmost respect." Cooper's voice was filled with authority, and a chill ran down my spine. "Now, for the real reason I called this meeting."

Everyone seemed to give me a warm smile before looking back at their alpha. All eyes were on him, and they seemed to be more awake as they sensed the tension rolling off him. Cooper's anger was radiating off him, and I rubbed his bicep to calm him. It worked, and he leaned into my touch.

"Your luna's old pack has taken a dangerous step, and I have decided it's time to hit them back just as hard. They have penetrated our territory and caused multiple hassles in the pack. A peace treaty is almost impossible; there is no chance of us agreeing with them on anything." Coopers speech warmed my heart but caused me to worry. Where was he going with this?

"What shall we do, Alpha?" someone called out, standing strong and hefty. He had a dull brown hair with hazel eyes and was built like a bull.

"This is officially a declaration of war on the Blood Moon Pack." My jaw dropped, literally. I didn't expect Cooper to say that. A few members were shocked and were now fully awake.

"What?" I asked, completely mortified. "War?"

My mate only ignored me and turned back to his warriors. "I will call for a messenger to deliver the news to Alpha Zaire that we have declared war against his pack."

A man in his late forties emerged from the crowd and pledged to deliver the message. "It would be an honor to do it, Alpha. However, we must ask why."

"Alpha Zaire experimented on your luna, my beloved mate. He must pay for his crimes against her." Cooper looked down at me, obviously sensing my panic at this new revelation. "He beat her, starved her, and damaged her body in ways no werewolf should. He not only has mutilated a woman of our race but has brought dishonor to werewolves alike. He embarrasses our kind, and he must be put down."

"Cooper." I warned, feeling my heart race. This was such personal information, and it terrified me.

He ignored me. "They are hunting her down for a crime that was committed by his own mate. Both the alpha and his luna must face their punishment. This is personal now, and I hope that you defend her as I believe you would."

The man who spoke before took a step forward. "This pack will defend her until we draw our last breath."

I was upset with his proclamation. People were going to die, and their blood would be on my hands. They couldn't do this with so many people against them. I hated him for ignoring me like this and made my wolf howl in sadness. Only six hours ago, he had marked me.

"Good." Cooper nodded in thanks towards the man and scanned the large meeting area. "Now, all scouts are to report to our allied packs. I don't know who Blood Moon has allied with, and I'm unsure of the warriors they have in their army. Right now, all we can do is prepare for the worst."

The meeting was set to a close after each scout was told where to go and when. Our war wasn't going to start until after the holidays, which were just around the corner. My heart pounded with worry, and I could only think of the worst possible scenarios. Something could happen, and my mate could get hurt because of it.

Cooper turned on his heel and walked away from me. I scurried after him like a lost puppy until he arrived in our room after I handed Sage to a passing pack member. My head was spinning and was beginning to throb with extra worry. He was about to walk into the bathroom until I snatched his arm, holding onto it desperately. Stopping immediately, he slowly turned to look at me.

"What brought this on, Cooper?" I asked worriedly. Obviously, there was a reason for his sudden mood. "This isn't about the—"

"It is, Celia! Okay?" His voice was filled with worry and anger that only made me flinch away in fear. I didn't want to be scared of him, but right now, I was shaking. "Who knows what that cure did to your body. It could…" He paused, shaking his head and closing his eyes. "It could *kill* you for all I know."

"But we can have something." My voice was just above a whisper, but I knew Cooper could hear it. "We can have a baby together. We can start a family whenever we want. Just you and me."

Cooper walked over to me so we were chest to chest. He placed his large warm hands on my shoulders and rested his forehead against mine. His sweet breath tickled the fine hairs along my jaw, causing a shiver to run down my spine. It was pleasurable and warming to have him like this when only seconds ago, he wasn't far from shifting.

"And I would like—no—love that. All I ever wanted was to have a family with my mate, and I can't wait to see you carrying my pups one day." Our eyes locked, and I couldn't look away from the almost glowing orbs. "But your life and safety come first."

With that being said, he pulled away from me and walked into the bathroom, shutting it softly behind him. I groaned silently and collapsed on the bed. My neck still ached, and I was still tired. Sleep was calling my name, and I accepted it quickly. Without going under the sheets, I passed out then and there on the bed.

***

My eyes fluttered open, and I looked around at the light streaming through the drapes that covered the large window. I let in a breath of air before releasing it out quietly. I attempted to get up but was held down by a large heavy arm crushing my small waist. Sighing in pure blissfulness, I squirmed until I was facing a sleeping Cooper.

My mate's eyes were shut, showing how peaceful he could be. A tiny yawn escaped my lips, and I tried to hold a giggle in. I didn't want him to wake up from my voice. Thank the Moon Goddess Cooper didn't hear that.

That was until Cooper let out a husky chuckle. "Well, that was sexy."

I felt embarrassed at my yawn, and in that moment, I felt like kicking myself. It was not sexy at all, and my mate was a liar. In times like these, I wished we weren't sharing the same bed together. If we didn't, he wouldn't have heard my horrendous screech.

"I found it very adorable actually." His morning voice was filled sleepiness. "I marked you, which means I can hear your thoughts and you can hear mine. "Plus, you are part of my pack now, so we can mind-chat whenever."

"Oh..." I whispered before snuggling closer into his chest. His scent immediately filling my nose caused a sigh to escape my lips.

I can never get tired of his scent. My wolf howled happily before prancing around foolishly.

"Good because you're stuck with me forever." Cooper chuckled, skimming his fingers up and down my spine lovingly. I shivered noticeably, and he only smiled before speaking huskily. "I love it when you do it. It makes me feel..."

"Like the alpha that you are." I finished for him, kissing his soft right cheek.

"I was going to say that I'm fulfilling my duties as your mate, but that's ideal too." He smiled, continuing his little act of teasing.

Suddenly, the phone rang, and we both groaned. We both shared annoyed glances before he sighed and reached over for the phone and placed it over his ear. Several emotions crossed his face, including confusion and worry. I didn't like any of those. While he was on the phone, he stood up, running a hand through his hair in the process. Something was up and was obviously important.

"Alright, Philip, we'll be there soon." Cooper hung up and hastily got dressed. In less than a few seconds, he was dressed in a white wifebeater and grey jeans and quickly tied his shoes. "Get dressed, Celia. Something's happening. You and I both are not going to like it. I can tell you that."

"What is it?" I asked, tossing the sheets off me and getting dressed. Right now wasn't the time to worry about my mate staring, so I hastily threw on a sweater that went past my butt before tugging my other clothes off.

"Remember that rogue, some beta's son from Blood Moon?" he asked, paying no attention to my undressing since he was too busy getting ready as well.

"Yeah, Malcolm." I nodded, pulling on leggings before shoving my small feet into a pair of snow boots.

"Well, turns out he did something."

"What did he do?" My voice was laced with worry, and I knew he caught it immediately because he was in front of me in an instant. "What's going on? You're really starting to worry me. Is someone hurt? Did something happen?"

"I don't know." He sighed, gripping his copper hair in his large hands. "All I know is that Philip informed me that Malcolm escaped with the help of rogues. They left something in their stead, and I'm being called by my pack members to go outside."

"We have to go."

I took his hand and tugged him out of the room. I didn't care if he protested, but this was now my pack. There were duties I needed to fulfill, and that won't happen unless I proved myself to the members. I needed to be seen as worthy of my amazing and gorgeous mate.

"Well, I'm glad you find me gorgeous."

My cheeks caught fire. Cooper seriously needed to stay out of my head because if he could easily get into my thoughts while I was awake, he could easily do it while I was sleeping. That meant he could see and hear everything going on in the dreams that had kept reoccurring. And I knew it would only fuel his anger at Alpha Zaire, which could lead to a sooner war than I hoped.

"Please stop overthinking. You are starting to worry me," Cooper mumbled before taking my hand and walking in front of me. I stared at him in confusion. "I don't know what's going on, and I don't want you getting hurt."

Moving as quickly as we could out of the house, we scanned the perimeter. A crowd of shirtless men were all circled around something. People were shouting, and others were going out of their minds. Men pulled their mates behind them, hoping to protect them from what was in front of them. As soon as they caught the scent of their alpha, they all parted like the Red Sea.

"About time, Alpha," Philip stated, crossing his arms over his chest. "I was beginning to worry."

"What is it?" He barked, not feeling the need for any discussion.

"What you are about to see is something you won't see every day." Philip led us through the parting crowd until we arrived at the scene. "She just came here unnoticed by any of our patrols, same as the rogues."

It was a girl no older than sixteen. She was standing in front of us with big terrified eyes. She looked scared. The crowd around us let out a loud gasp before taking several steps back. She turned to look at everyone with worry before locking her grey eyes with mine. Shaking uncontrollably, she tried not to move a muscle as her beautiful orbs held fear and a flicker of hope.

"Please, help me." The girl begged, turning to look at me once more before staring straight into Cooper's eyes.

That was when I noticed what everyone was freaking out about. Not only did she have a small baby bump, but she was surrounded by shining metal around her. One was caught only inches from breaking the skin on her ankle.

"Is that…" I asked, staring at Cooper, hoping he wouldn't confirm my suspicion.

"Silver." He nodded, and my mate pushed me back among the crowd. "Get her out of here. She shouldn't be here to see this."

"But, Cooper—"

"I said leave!" he exclaimed, interrupting me.

"No!" I hissed, placing my hands on my hips and swatting Philip's awaiting hand. "You told me I was the luna of this pack, and you marked me proving just that! The pack comes first, and you know that! This girl is scared and pregnant if you haven't noticed. Let's help her!"

Cooper's jaw ticked angrily, and he turned to Philip. Before I could register what was happening, a muscular arm tackled my stomach, causing me to fall straight into it. Philip carried me as I squirmed closer to the pack house.

My mate told me I was the luna, and I was trying to prove I could be do it and be the luna they deserve. Now, Cooper just brushed me aside when I made a suggestion.

I was thrown uncomfortably on the couch and left alone. All I saw was Philip going outside to face the problem that Cooper and I should have done together. Letting out a huff, I crossed my arms and lied down on the couch. Looking up, I faced a very exhausted looking Jeremy. His hair was all over the place, and he smelled very strange.

"You okay there?" I asked, sitting up and facing him directly.

"I'm perfect." He yawned, running a hand through his hair and looking over at me.

"Why do you smell different?" I asked, looking at him strangely before staring back at him.

He chuckled and shook his head. "You are way too innocent for me to explain exactly why I smell different. But let's just say, it's the same reason why you smell a lot like the alpha."

I gave him a confused look. It took me a few seconds before I understood what he meant.

"Oh." A shiver ran up my spine in disgust, and I shifted away from him awkwardly. "I suggest you take a shower."

"Wait until you and Cooper—"

I cut him off before he could finish. "Don't even say his name! I am beyond furious with him!"

"Someone's having mate problems." I heard him mumble when I stood up. Growling angrily, I chucked the pillow at his head, hitting him perfectly the first try. Stomping out of the room and towards Cooper's, I shoved people who got in my way.

Why are you acting like this? my wolf asked, clearly knowing the answer to it.

I don't know, I replied, pausing in Cooper's room and wrinkling my eyebrows in confusion.

What was wrong with me? I hardly ever got angry easily. As an omega, I usually cowered and got scared, but right now, my blood was pumping with anger. It's not safe to be angry in a house. I could cause major damage. Trying to control my breathing, I soon relaxed and opened my once closed eyes. What was going on with me?

Chapter 21

My entire body ached for a weird reason, and I opened my eyes to be greeted with a bright light. I couldn't believe Cooper didn't come home last night. I must've stayed up until one in the morning waiting on him to come back. Something must've happened with the pregnant girl if he didn't bother mind-chatting any news.

A knock on the door snapped me out of my thoughts, and I sat up slowly in the bed to see who it was. It took a while to actually sit up because the muscles in my arms were tight. Hissing in pain silently, I opened my eyes to look at the figure.

Paige was beaming happily at me with a little image in her hand and a box in the other.

"Hey, Paige," I greeted casually, trying to pat down my unruly hair that already resembled a bird's nest. "Is everything okay?"

"I have two things to show you." She smiled, skipping over to me and collapsing in front of me. Shoving the picture in my hand, she squealed. "Guess who this is!"

The picture was black and white, and all that seemed visible was a little circle on the side. It didn't even look like anything. Scrunching my eyebrows together, I examined Paige. Why was she getting so excited over a little circle on a picture? Did it mean something to her? Should I say something?

"Um…" I paused, looking for the correct words. "What is it?"

"What is it?" she asked angrily, but she quickly composed herself. "What is it? It's my baby!"

"Really!" I beamed looking at the little circle again. "That's amazing! Is he or she healthy?"

"Yep," she said popping the 'p' loudly. "Sheila told me everything was fine, but I should try to limit the amount of stress for the next few weeks because now is a fragile part of my baby's development."

"Well, that's smart." I nodded. "Now, what's the other thing?"

"Oh, right." She chuckled before opening the little tin box. Inside it were different kinds of combs and scissors. "I know the signs about your heat coming in the next month. I've went through them myself. Any woman who has been through heat knows the signs. If you're feeling achy right now, then my suspicions are correct. I thought it would be a good idea to use this entire kit for when the time comes."

"A kit for what?" I asked hesitantly, dreading the answer.

"Well, I scheduled a waxing for you at three, and I've decided to cut your hair." She pulled out the pair of scissors. "This entire kit is filled with makeup as well to make you as gorgeous as you already are. I thought it would be a good idea to make you feel beautiful when the time comes around. You could use a girl's day after everything you've been through."

I cringed at the thought of waxing. I'd heard all the girls complaining about how painful it was to get one. They said it hurt and burned in the most uncomfortable places. It took me seconds to process the scissors in front of me.

"You're going to cut my hair?" I asked in shock, my mouth ajar.

"Believe me, you'll look beautiful. Now come." Paige grabbed me by my long hair and guided me to the bathroom. My eyes widened when I got a flash of what Alpha Zaire had done to me years ago.

***

"Wait!" I cried, clutching my long hair tightly. He was dragging me along the carpeted floor, causing rug burns to break on my milky skin. "Please don't! I'm sorry!"

"Stealing food?" Alpha Zaire growled, shoving me into the bathroom where a tub was filled to the top with murky water. "I let you stay in this house, and you let the thought of stealing food cross your mind! If your parents were here, they would be ashamed."

"I know, and I'm sorry! I'm just starving and thirsty! You never let me have a break, and I'm tired!" I knew my words were only going to anger him more, and that terrified me more.

My legs skidded against the marble floor, and a drop of blood escaped my head when it crashed into a wall. I lay limp, biting my tongue so I wouldn't cry out in pain.

All I took were leftovers: a bread and some sweet olives. I knew stealing was a terrible thing, but I hadn't eaten in more than a week.

He dragged me outdoors. My tiny body was soon lifted into the air and was tossed roughly into the lake. I hugged my body tightly, trying to conserve heat as much as I could in the freezing water.

"Please don't," I begged, but it was too late when I received a mouthful of water.

Water filled my mouth and lungs, and I struggled desperately to get out of Alpha Zaire's grasp. I tugged and pulled, but I was already begging for death. My head pounded from lack of air, and my eyes opened wide in the water. My mouth opened and closed, trying to get any hint of oxygen. The clouded water caused my eyes to burn and sting, but I couldn't find the energy to shut them.

I was then lifted out of the water, my body reacting to the new source of air. I coughed and sputtered, making my throat burn and itch. Before I could get my needed oxygen, I was back in the water, and the process repeated until I was overwhelmed with darkness.

***

"I called you as soon as it happened."

"She just collapsed. I didn't know what to do." I could hear Paige's voice shaking as she spoke. To who? I couldn't figure out.

"Why did she collapse?" The voice sounded distant, and I tried to reach it.

"I was going to cut her hair and make her pretty for you later."

"Celia! Baby, open your eyes," the voice said. I opened my eyes and looked around to see Cooper crouched beside me, shaking my shoulders. "Celia."

"Cooper." I breathed, allowing him to hug me as I cried on his shoulder. "I don't want to live like this. It isn't fair."

"Shush…" He whispered, stroking my back lovingly. "It's okay. I saw the whole thing through our mate connection."

Cooper shouldn't have seen my memories. He didn't deserve to know what I went through. This entire thing should be left in the dark. I had stolen that food because I was being starved to death. I had almost died that day. I had no other choice.

"Stop, Celia." Cooper ordered, and that instantly made my sobs turn into quivers. "This isn't your fault. None of this is your fault."

I dug my nails into his back, hoping for some support. He allowed me to soak his shirt with my tears. The memory was nerve-racking, and I could only imagine how angry he must be. Getting plunged into the water until you're almost dead was one of the worst ones. I could still remember how I struggled and kicked, trying so hard to break free from his firm grasp.

"What did you do?" I peeked over Cooper's shoulder to see him glaring at his sister. She looked completely confused. "You triggered one of her memories, Paige! Don't you see that? What did you do?"

We were still in the bathroom, and I was against the wall, closest to the door. Paige was still standing up, and Cooper and I were crowded together. The cool flooring was causing an uneasy feeling in my stomach, but I only seemed to hold onto Cooper tighter.

"Why don't you lie down?" Cooper whispered in my ear. "Come on." He swept me off the floor and carried me out of the room but not before sending Paige his famous glare.

"I'm sorry," I whispered, closing my eyes, feeling fatigue after my crying. "You deserve so much better, and I know you're still mad at me from yesterday."

"I'm not mad. I just don't like it when you talk back at me in front of our pack. To be completely honest, I can't think of someone better than you. Sure, you have some difficult stages, but you're perfect in every way for me, Celia."

"That's only because I was genetically changed to be perfect. I was made to suit Alpha Zaire's interests."

"No," Cooper said sternly, placing me gently on the bed. "The Moon Goddess put you on Earth so we could be together. You weren't created by her for *him*, only me. I know this may sound selfish and possessive, but you will only be mine. I won't share you with him, and he'll never get you. I don't know what you looked like back then, but I can promise you that you would've been just as beautiful as you are now."

I reached up from the bed and gave my mate a quick kiss on the lips. I covered my mouth with my sleeves in order to prevent myself from squealing. He grinned down at me before leaning down and planting his lips on mine. They were sweet and full of passion, and I couldn't believe this amazing man was my mate.

Promptly, he moved away and placed his warm lips against my forehead. Before he could walk away, I grabbed his hand and pulled him. He sat back on the divan. He looked at me in confusion.

"Do you think it'll happen soon?" I asked, showing him my worry.

"What will happen?"

My face felt like it was going to catch on fire with how embarrassing it was to have a discussion with him about this.

"Baby, what is it?"

"Do you think I'll go into heat soon?" I looked down at my hands, trying to avoid eye contact as best as possible. We'd never really talked about completing the mating bond, so speaking about it to him was a new thing for me.

"Hey," he whispered.

I met his aquamarine orbs with my eyes.

"It can happen any day or week now. I won't pressure you, but if you do go into heat, I can't trust my wolf. When it happens, I want you to stay in this room, and I'll have my father put me in one of the cells—unless you are ready."

I smiled happily at Cooper and gave him a small hug before lying back down. There were so many thoughts running through my head while he left the room. The main question being—was I ready?

***

Cooper

  I sat in my study in a room away from Celia. I sipped the bourbon in my hand, feeling the amber liquid burn down my throat. I was on my laptop looking up the scouts that had been on patrol the day Malcolm had escaped. Something didn't seem right because ever since the situation, those men had not been seen. I began questioning my pack's loyalty. These fears however could be sent to Adam, my beta, who would easily resolve this issue. He was quick to bring to light about issues I had in the past, and currently, I had personal matters to pay attention to. I couldn't keep putting my pack ahead of Celia.

  My free hand rubbed my pounding head, my thoughts racing from the previous encounter with my mate.

  Every single memory was so real. I could almost feel the pain that my beautiful mate had felt all those years. I could not believe her past was worse than what I had thought when I listened and watched her dreams, hoping she could be dreaming about future pups. Right now, the vial that had been injected into her should be fixing her inability to conceive. If it did work, she should've had her illumination dream already and should have told me.

  "How's Celia doing?" Paige asked from out of nowhere, his figure standing at the entrance of my study.

  I looked into her direction and replied, "I managed to calm her down. It would be best if she didn't get a lot of attention from people right now."

  Earlier when Paige notified me of Celia fainting, I ran as fast as I could to her. I thought she was upset with me because I had fallen asleep in my office. The second I entered her thoughts, I couldn't help but plan Zaire's death. She had been experiencing one of the most terrifying memories. He would pay for nearly drowning her. No wonder she seemed so jumpy at times. Perhaps it was something she never noticed she did, but a mate would. I worried for her as every day passed.

"You know her heat is coming soon, don't you?" Paige asked, crossing her arms at me and giving me a look. "As a girl who has been through it multiple times, she's starting to show the signs like mood swings, and cramps. Soon, she'll start burning up, and you'll have to—"

"I can't do that to her," I mumbled, walking past her. "And Paige"—I paused and looked back at her—"look what happened to you after your heat. My little sister is having a pup because she gave in to that *heat*. That can happen to Celia. We have a lot of things to figure out first before we can have a child on our own. Plus, I know she isn't ready for us to complete the bond."

My wolf growled in annoyance at my sentence and lashed out at me. I held him down. He knew I was right. Celia didn't want and wasn't ready to give herself entirely to me. I couldn't be quite sure yet if she was ready for the responsibilities to be a true luna. At the moment, she was a luna, but it was more of an honorary title since she was only marked. She couldn't take any of the responsibilities a luna generally would until we mated. In other words, we would have to be intimate with each other.

"And you know this how?" She snapped before turning around, but before she could walk away, she spoke over her shoulder, "How do you know she's not ready? I see the way she looks at you. She wants to make you happy, and in return, she wants your love. I will continue today with what we had planned because even if she won't say it out loud, she wants to spend time with people. And that person is me." After her words, she left me with my own thoughts.

I had been trying my best to stay out of Celia's head, but when I sensed her fear, I entered her mind immediately after. Celia worried me too much, and I couldn't help but fear something was always going on with her. She needed to be happy, and I wanted her to be, but everything I tried didn't seem work for her. It felt like everything I did was never enough.

***

Celia

"How about this one?" Paige asked. She was showing me a pixie cut picture on the internet.

"No," I said, shaking my head at her and falling back on the bed. We'd been trying to sort out a hairstyle for me, which had been very difficult. It was harder than it seemed.

"Well, then what do you want? Your hair would go with just about anything!" She beamed and scanned the internet for something with a little more spunk.

I groaned and rolled around a few times in Cooper's bed. It still smelled so much like him, and I just couldn't get enough of it. To be honest, I felt guilty when I left the house and went with Warner. It was wrong of me to even think I could survive without my mate. I thought it was time I did something for Cooper.

"Oh!" Paige squealed, snapping me out of my thoughts. "I like this one, and even if you disagree, I'm doing it anyway."

I didn't have time to look at the picture because she grabbed my arm and slowly guided me to the bathroom. She set me down on a chair set up in front of a huge mirror. Spinning me around, she left to get the laptop.

She walked back in happily and set the computer down on a table away from me so I couldn't see the hairstyle she chose for me.

She snipped my hair after scrubbing it good with different shampoos and conditioners. There were dozens of different combs and scissors aligned beside her. Products I didn't even know the name of were placed into my white hair.

When the scissors were drawn close to my eyes, I moved back a little, but Paige grabbed my head tightly. She cut diagonally across my face. The hair covered my right eye, making half my face disappear against the light shade. Paige placed the scissor just above my forehead, and then, I heard it snipped.

What on earth is she doing?

She grabbed a large brush and swished the hair on top of my head, but mainly to the right side. For the finishing touches, she grabbed my knee-length hair and cut it just below my breasts. I almost let out a cry of horror when all my hair went barreling down. I stared at Paige in revulsion. I didn't expect her to cut my hair that much.

Reaching over me, she grabbed the hair dryer and spent the next twenty minutes blow drying it to perfection. It probably looked terrible judging by how different it felt behind me. She fixed my part and put the shortened hair back over my right eye.

"You look so sexy." Paige squealed and grabbed a smaller mirror so I could see.

My long hair was cut to medium length, which was basically just right below my breast. The short hair that was covering my right eye actually looked good on me. I had also noticed that my head looked so much healthier, which was probably because off the products Paige used.

"Alright. Now that your hair is done, it's time to get you waxed." She giggled, clapping her hands together after putting all her tools away. "I'm sorry I couldn't do your makeup, but you know how time can be."

She dragged me out of the room and down the stairs. She was careful when Cooper walked by with a pair of earbuds in his ears listening to heavy metal. He was shimmering with sweat, and I could only guess he had been working out. He was looking down at his phone and appeared to be in a deep thought. I couldn't help but wonder what was going on, but he seemed frustrated. Due to this, he was too preoccupied to smell my scent. I was surprised he wasn't as alert as he usually was. Something must be wrong, but I knew he would be able to manage it. He was an alpha, and a strong one at that. Whatever was occurring would be resolved.

I was pulled down a different corner to avoid getting seen by Cooper. Paige explained to me that my makeover was supposed to be a surprise. But I thought it didn't make sense since I knew Cooper would be out doing perimeter runs.

He walked past us completely oblivious, and I couldn't believe he hadn't noticed me.

Rolling her eyes, we were able to make it out of the house undetected by any pack members. By the time we made it to the SUV, Paige was panting.

"You okay?" I asked, looking at her worriedly.

She just waved me off and started the car. "Being pregnant, I guess, takes a lot of energy. You'll know sooner or later." She gave a small smile at me before backing out of the driveway and onto the dirt road.

"I never got the chance to ask Cooper this, but I was wondering if you heard," I mumbled, letting her nod for me to continue. "There was a pregnant girl yesterday, and she had silver all around her. I was just wondering if she's okay now."

"She and her unborn baby boy are perfectly fine." She nodded looking at me with sparkling eyes. "Her name is Alyssa, and she was actually from a pack in the Caribbean. I don't remember the name though. Her mate was the alpha, but he was killed during an attack caused by witches. A group of rogues kidnapped her and brought her here. Sheila looked her over, and it's said she will have her baby boy around February. She said that the minute her baby's born, she wants to die to be with her mate. She's trying very hard to pull through for her baby, but we all know she won't last long."

Paige took a left turn before heading down a straight path.

"So the baby won't have anyone to take care of him," I whispered, instantly getting a feeling of dread.

"Cooper is looking for someone to adopt him. If there isn't anyone willing to adopt the baby by the time he is born, the baby will be sent to an adoption center in Bermuda." Paige explained, stopping in front of a small little building.

"Bermuda?" I asked, looking at her curiously.

"Yeah, I know, not the best place to run a pack, but that's probably why it's falling apart, especially now that their alpha's dead." She sighed. "I honestly feel bad for the poor unborn pup. Let's hope she gives it a name before she dies. We're hoping the baby survives the birth because it would be sad for the mother to go through that pain of losing her child. We want her comfortable when she passes. It is her wish to die, and anyone who loses a mate wants to be with their soulmate."

What confused me, however, was why the rogues dropped her off at the pack house? What were rogues doing with Alpha Zaire? It didn't make any sense. Suddenly, I wanted to know the reason, and I was determined to find out, even if I had to confront Alyssa myself. It felt like Paige was keeping something else from me.

"Do you know why she's here?" I asked.

"Cooper told me, but it's not anything big." She shrugged. As soon as she saw the expression on my face, she sighed. "It was just a scam. The rogues were trying to scare us. Bringing in a pregnant luna was the best thing they could think of. Since she's a luna and you're a luna, it was meant to scare you. It was almost as if they were saying, 'If we can do this to her, we can do this to you.'"

I remained silent after that and continued to look outside the snowy landscape. The car was moving fast, and there was no civilization within miles. Snow was everywhere from the tree to the ground, and even a little on the road. I turned back to look at Paige who was concentrating hard on her driving. She seemed more excited to go to the salon than I was, and her excitement grew once we arrived.

While Paige and I sat in the waiting room, I couldn't help but tap my foot repeatedly. To say that I was nervous would be an understatement because I'd never done anything this kind of thing before. This was different now that I had a mate to please. It wouldn't matter if I had to go through the pain of having my hair ripped off painfully from my skin. I knew it would be worth it.

"Calm down," Paige whispered, giving me a flat look. "The more you stress about it, the more it'll hurt. We can't have you getting indignant over your pain when it is this place's job to take good care of you."

"I don't even know what that word means." I hissed, tapping my foot repeatedly.

"You seriously should consider going to school." She chuckled, shaking her head. "Let's just say it'll hurt."

"Way to put my mind at ease."

My mate's sister only rolled her eyes and walked over to a woman at the desk. I sighed and decided to look through the magazines. While I was doing this, I felt something itching its way into my mind.

'Where are you?' Cooper's voice entered my head. I jumped in surprise and almost had an instant headache. *'I can't find you anywhere.'*

'I'm fine.' I promised, looking over at Paige for any help. Surely, she was already talking with Cooper in her head because an annoyed look was already plastered on her face.

'Where are you?' He repeated furiously.

'I told you. I'm fine. I'll be home soon.' I groaned and instantly received a questionable look from the old woman beside me. I smiled at her kindly.

"Celia Pierce." As soon as I heard my name called, I looked up at the woman and then at Paige.

Why would she put me down as Pierce when Cooper and I aren't even married yet?

The last time I checked, I didn't even have a last name. "Celia Pierce?"

Paige rolled her eyes and grabbed my shoulder. She pushed me towards the woman and gave her an apologetic smile and said, "She's a bit nervous. This is her first time to do something like this."

The woman just nodded and gave me an apologetic smile. "I'll give you a little heads-up, it isn't very pleasant, but I promise I'm a professional."

Following her into the back room, Paige bid me goodbye. She gave the nice woman a wad of cash. She whispered something to her and walked away. I was really starting to question my decision in accepting Paige's offer.

***

I walked out of the small building feeling in complete and utter pain. My legs stung, and so did my underarms. I got just about every single body hair removed from me except for the hair on my head, of course. Paige was walking confidently towards the car while I was trying hard not to make any sudden move. When it was time to get into the car, I gave Paige an incredulous look.

"Come on, Celia! The faster you get in the car, the faster the sting will be gone!" She sang before hopping into the car, honking the horn loudly.

I ducked my head down in embarrassment and slid into the car. It was uncomfortable at first, and I couldn't wait to get back to the pack house and take a few pain medications. The woman was perfectly calm and didn't seem at all affected with my body. She was, indeed, a professional, but I would never relive that experience again.

"You look like you saw a puppy tripped down the stairs!" She laughed, looking at me with a big grin. In return, I gave her my best glare. "Fine, I'll drive."

We spent the remainder of the car ride in silence. I was tempted to touch my legs to see how soft they were but decided it wouldn't be the best choice. My skin still felt numb and tingly, but I tried not to pay attention to it at all.

"Oh, yeah, here are some painkillers. I was going to give them to you before we left, but I forgot." Paige chuckled, handing me a white container while her other hand was on the steering wheel. I gave her the biggest glare I could manage.

By the time we got back to the house, the sun was setting, and all the lights were already on. We walked as quietly as we could into the house. My legs still felt stiff when walking up the stairs, and Paige tried to push me up as fast as possible.

"Alright, so here's what you're going to do," she whispered quietly outside of Cooper's door. "You're going to lie down on the bed in only one of his shirts and try to look as sexy as possible."

"I don't think I can do this." I looked like a brick was just thrown into my stomach. "I don't know how to be sexy."

"Just try it." She giggled happily. "And try not to make so much noise."

Before I could argue, she walked as quickly as she could down the hall and entered her own bedroom. I groaned and entered Cooper's, closing the door behind me. Much to my happiness, Cooper was nowhere to be seen. If I could recall, it was around the time the pack ate dessert together. That meant I had enough time to change into Cooper's shirt.

Throwing my sweater and leggings across, I walked over to Cooper's drawers with nothing but my panties. I scanned his drawers, looking for the right shirt. When I found one, I put it on and adjusted it so it covered my bottom.

The skin along my neck suddenly felt very hot and itchy. I scratched a few times, but that didn't make it feel any better. The itch traveled from my neck down to my mark where it throbbed and ached. I cupped it with my cold hands, but they were heated in a second. I could feel my face flushing. I put a warm hand on my blazing forehead. It made no sense to me why I was feeling this way when I felt perfectly fine just minutes ago. In the most private area of my body, I could feel it getting uncomfortably hot, and soon so was every inch of my entire body.

My thoughts were interrupted when the door opened, and I quickly jumped into the bed and lay there facing the ceiling. The shirt lifted up a little, giving *him* a perfect view of my bottom if he was looking. I was wearing panties obviously, but they didn't exactly hide much. I crossed my legs, feeling how soft and delicate they really were.

"You had me worried sick, Celia." Cooper sighed, his voice filled with so much relief. I felt guilty for making him worried but tried to push the thought away. "What have you been doing?"

The light was off, so he obviously couldn't see my new haircut. Groaning internally, I sat up in the bed and switched on the bedside light, creating a faint glow in the room. Pushing my hair so it was more in front of me, I heard him suck in a breath. The side fringe covered my eye, but I swished it away so he could see my face. I gave him a little smile and sat on my shins to kneel on the bed. Cooper's eyes roamed my face, taking in the new me.

"Wow." He breathed, having a dazed look in his eyes. "You look …I can't even put words to how beautiful you look."

"Then don't." With that, I sat up on my knees and grabbed his shirt, pulling him towards me. I was acting on instinct, which I should do more often. The mark on my neck was pulsing with my racing heart, and the burning was causing beads of sweat to form on my bare feet.

"Wait, Celia," Cooper whispered, taking in a big whiff. I uncontrollably began kissing his neck, biting his earlobe. The burning subsided for a second before it hit me hard in my lower region. I gasped when he lifted me by the hips and pushed me roughly on the bed.

My legs wrapped around his waist, bringing his area closer to mine. I moaned as he straddled me. Sweat formed along my chest, and I wiped it down with Cooper's warm shirt. The fabric felt way too hot on me, so I grabbed the hem of it and pulled it over me. However, before it could reach my head, Cooper sucked in a breath and pulled it down.

His eyes were completely black, and I knew mine were filled with the same kind of lust. My heart was racing, and I didn't know how to slow it down. Cooper sat up, but I didn't release my legs from his waist. He sighed in annoyance and unwrapped them hesitantly. The minute he touched my smooth skin, he growled loudly, shaking his head and trying to control his wolf. I could see him clawing at the surface because his canines were coming out, and so were his claws.

"You're in heat, Celia." Cooper explained, moving a few inches away from me. It felt like he was trying to distance himself from my frenzied body. "This isn't how your first time is supposed to be."

"I don't care." I whined, wrapping my arms around his neck and kissing him with passion. "My body hurts. It feels like hot coals are being crushed into the most uncomfortable places. Please just make it go away." I was begging now because the pain was starting to flood.

"Celia, I—" I cut him off angrily.

"Just make the pain go away!" I cried, burying my face into his neck and kissing the mark on it. "Please, Alpha, *my* Alpha. I want this."

With those last words, his eyes darkened, and he did exactly what I wanted him to do. He mated me, and I had never felt as complete.

Chapter 22

My eyes fluttered open, and the first thing I noticed was the warm breath sprinkling across my mark that Cooper had bitten again. I let out a little squeak when a warm thumb rubbed small circles around my belly button. I let out a groan when a shock of soreness hit my lower body. I pressed my face into the pillow. Although, I felt complete and blissful, I couldn't help but feel different.

A kiss on my shoulder brought me back to reality. "Good morning."

I couldn't hold the smile back anymore and turned my head to see Cooper leaning over me. A necklace dangled from around his neck and hovered just above my lips, shining brightly. His eyes sparkled with cheerfulness, and the grin on his was infectious. Never had I seen him show this much emotion before.

"Good morning." I returned. I tried my hardest to face him but had some trouble the minute I winced in pain.

"Are you sore?"

When I didn't answer him, his smile disappeared and was replaced with worry. "Shit, I'm sorry. I should've been a lot gentler."

"Shush." I cooed, placing my index finger on his lips to hush him. "I'm fine. I'm happy, and that's what matters right now."

I showed him I was okay by stretching up to plant a kiss on his lips. He pulled away briefly and leaned down again, giving me a longer, passionate kiss. His warm hands traveled across my exposed stomach, making me let out a tiny moan. His lips traveled down to my neck where he kissed the tender mark, causing me to shiver and arch towards him. He only chuckled and moved his head away so he could examine me.

"Well, you smell like me," he stated, nuzzling his head into my neck. "You're perfect."

I giggled and moved his hand off my waist so I could get up. Gripping the sheets tightly, I turned to look back at him. The comforter was just below my mate's waist, hiding his nudeness yet showing off his toned stomach. He moved his hand behind his head and examined my bare back as I sat up.

"Can you…" I mumbled, blushing a deep red. "You know, look away?"

"I've already seen you—" Cooper chuckled, shaking his head and examining my body some more "—multiple times. I don't think I'll see something I haven't already."

"I know," I murmured, tightening the sheets to cover my breasts.

"Then what's the problem?"

"Well, I just want …"

He leaned forward and yanked down the sheet so he could see me fully.

"Still as gorgeous as I remember." He beamed lazily, looking up at me. Reaching over, he grabbed me by my hips and dragged me, so I was on top of him. His warm hands resting on my hip caused some tingling feeling to ignite on my skin.

"Cooper." I gave him a flat look, which he only returned with a lopsided grin.

"Fine."

Letting me go, I grabbed the sheets and shoved them over his face. Moving as quickly as I could, I ran over to his drawers and put on one of his sweatshirts. Looking over at him, I saw him struggling to pull the sheets off his face. I went through his dresser and found a loose pair of boxers. Tugging them on, I leaped on the bed and crossed my arms onto my mate's chest.

"Hey." He croaked, sounding tired.

"Hi." I smiled, tracing patterns on his rough chest.

"I now know exactly why you were gone all day yesterday." My mate rubbed my forearm affectionately before looking down at me with his glowing orbs. "I have to say it quite pleased me."

I grinned happily before closing my eyes and letting out a breath of air. "I wish we could stay like this forever."

Cooper nodded in agreement and kissed the top of my head lightly.

By the time we got out of bed and took a shower, together may I add, it was around one in the afternoon. We were both starving and left the room to look for food. The house was strangely quiet, and I could only wonder why. We walked hand in hand down the stairs and were surprised to see all of Cooper's family members, sitting on the couches, reading together. They looked up at me, each with a smile on their faces.

"I knew it would happen." Paige smiled triumphantly before returning back to her book.

My face flushed, and I covered my cheeks as best as I could. Emilia turned her book around and sniffed the air. Adam looked at her strangely, and so did the rest of us. What could she possibly be smelling? Patrick was doing the same with his.

"Ah." Emilia breathed. "I can't wait for grandchildren…"

I covered my ears as quickly as possible so I couldn't hear the end of her sentence. She kept talking, and Cooper's eyes were bulging out of his sockets in embarrassment as well. When he looked down at me, he let out a noticeable sigh of relief and looked back at his mother. Her voice was drowned out, and I was internally laughing when I saw Patrick covering his daughter Sage's ears. She seemed just as clueless as me.

After a few minutes, Emilia's lips stopped moving and was now replaced with a curious frown directed towards me. At that exact moment, Cooper wrapped his arm around my waist and pushed me into him. Paige winked at me mischievously before walking over to me. Before she could even get the chance to take three steps towards me, Cooper let out a feral growl and pushed me closer to him.

"Don't touch her." His eyes were pitch-black now, and his canines were showing.

"Calm down," I whispered to him, rubbing my delicate hand up and down his muscular chest. He relaxed immediately and looked down at me with lustful eyes. I turned to my mate's sister. "Nice, Paige. You know how recently mated males can be with their females, especially since he is an alpha."

She shrugged her shoulders innocently and went to lay down next to her mate. No one stopped Cooper when he picked me up and led me to our room where we relived the night before. I assumed we weren't going to be eating any food for a while.

***

It had been a week since Cooper and I have mated, and it's been a week since I last left the room. He had prohibited me to leave the bedroom unless I had to take a shower where he usually joined me too. I was starting to go stir crazy from being in the same place for too long. My mate locked me in from the outside and kept the key with him. I'd looked everywhere in the room for a spare but hadn't had any luck.

Sage kept knocking on the door, but every time I try to answer it, only the knob would rattle. We could only talk through the door, which resulted in everyone thinking she's talking to herself since the walls were almost soundproof. Paige did the same thing, and she kept complaining how she had a little belly the size of a grape now. I couldn't understand why she was complaining since no one really noticed but her. However, the weight she was gaining from her cravings were making her insecure.

For a pregnant werewolf, the bump would typically show on the second or third month. Werewolf pregnancies were completely different from human pregnancies. While a human would show well into their second or third trimester, wolves showed a lot earlier. This was because for a werewolf to be born, the female must carry the wolf spirit and the human embryo inside her womb. It would appear as if she were carrying human twins, when in reality, she was only carrying one werewolf baby. The baby wolf spirit would take longer to develop inside the womb. Paige was basically trying to have two beings develop inside of her. The baby wouldn't stop being human until the third trimester where the two souls would combine together. It's a strange process, but it's just how it worked. Werewolf pregnancy was a strange thing.

"I mean, Adam didn't say anything before, but now I feel huge!" Paige complained from the other side of the door with both our backs rested on it. I could hear the wooden door creaking back and forth from our weight. "I think it's a boy now though."

"How many times do I have to say to you that you don't look *that* fat?" I chuckled, shaking my head before realizing she obviously couldn't see me. "Cooper's going to be the uncle, and I already declare it being a girl."

"Fine." She huffed, slamming her head on the wall, or so I heard. "I miss looking at you. Cooper has no right to keep you cooped up in there. I miss our little adventures," she added, and I could only imagine the smile on her face.

"I've been feeling very woozy lately." I added, closing my eyes and letting out a loud sigh. "It's not like I don't enjoy mating with Cooper all over again, but I need some fresh air. My body is really sore, and I don't think he realizes that."

"Well, tell him that!" Paige cried, making my sensitive ears ring. "Anyway, you're actually going through the process of being the luna of Ice Moon Pack. Being a fully developed luna doesn't just come to you overnight. That's why you're feeling woozy and such. My mom thought she was pregnant because she had most of the symptoms, but it was just her wolf getting used to her new strength. She even threw up once or twice, from what I heard."

"I never asked," I said. Changing the topic on a sudden thought, I asked, "What rank was your mom before she found the former alpha?"

There was a long pause, which unsettled me. I couldn't hear her breathing, and I knew she was holding it to help her think. I scrunched my eyebrows in confusion and stared at the door. I asked again, and once again she didn't answer. For a moment, I thought she had left, but I knew she hadn't.

Finally, she spoke, "A Rogue." My jaw dropped.

Is that why Emilia was always so kind to me? But I don't get it; rogues are always the aggressive type.

"Before her pack was wiped out, she was a delta's daughter. She was meant to be third in command."

I remained silent and looked down at my hands. That explained many unanswered questions. She walked with confidence because she had always been in a higher rank. Emilia was caring because she knew the difficulty of surviving as a rogue. It made sense why some were surprised and at the same time intrigued that I was Cooper's mate. His father found his mate who was a rogue, and Cooper did the same. It was as if history just repeated itself.

"She hardly ever talks about it though." Paige sighed, bringing me out of my thoughts. "A group of rogues destroyed her home, and she watched her younger siblings being unapologetically slaughtered. They were heartless, and my mother didn't open up to my dad when they first met. It's a lot like you and Cooper."

"What's a lot like us?" I heard Cooper's voice, and I could make out Paige scurrying off the floor towards her room. I leaped up just in time for Cooper to open the door and made it to the soft bed. "Hey, baby."

"Hi, Cooper." I beamed the moment I saw him. His hair was everywhere, and a thin layer of sweat covered his amazing body.

My mate had other plans. He pushed me down on the bed so he was hovering over me. There was a huge grin plastered on his face but was soon wiped away when I didn't react. His eyebrows scrunched, and he moved a few inches from me.

"What's wrong?" Cooper questioned, looking at me worriedly. "Are you hurt? Did something happen?"

I sighed, running my hands from his fit stomach up to his shoulders. Biting my lip, I sighed and closed my eyes. "I don't want to be in here anymore. I love spending time with you and us mating, but us mating all the time is taking its toll on me. I'm exhausted, so I would really appreciate it if I could let my wolf out."

Cooper's face dropped, and he plastered on a serious face. His lips were in a thin line, and frown marks were forming. His muscular arms were on either side of me, driving my wolf hormonally mad. She constantly wanted to mate with Cooper. Although, I knew she only wanted to mate to procreate; to her, mating was just something to be done for the propagation of our race. "Okay." He sighed, but soon a mischievous grin grew on his face. "I just feel the need to keep my beautiful mate out of the unmated werewolves' eyes. I want you all to myself."

"Cooper…" I breathed out, allowing him to kiss my shoulder affectionately.

"Let's go for a run."

***

The run was amazing, and I couldn't help but let my smile shine brightly. I really needed it. Cooper was playful with chasing me, and I was surprisingly able to keep up with him. I thought it was probably the new luna's power surfacing, significantly increasing my power. I'd never felt this alive in my entire life. I smelled the fluffy snow beneath my feet, relishing the feel of it. My feet had only been touching wooden flooring. It was nice for my claws to patter across the wet snow.

'I'm gonna catch you baby.' Cooper chuckled through our mind link, and I could hear his strong pounding heart grow closer. I knew how much he loved chasing me, so that's what we'd been doing for the past hour.

"*No, you won't!*" I giggled, sidestepping a tree to throw him off. Looking behind, I noticed he wasn't fazed by what I did and kept barreling towards me.

The new energy was overpowering me, making me have a triumphant smile. When I looked back, Cooper was no longer there, and I cocked my head to the side in confusion. Shrugging my shoulders, I turned back to look dead ahead but ended up ramming straight into a white blur. My wolf let out strange noises that hardly resembled a laugh while we kept toppling over each other.

Whenever my mate would shove me on the ground from my shoulders, I would always try to do the same and had been going at it for several minutes, trying to tackle the other and gain dominance. I let out a wolf-like laugh, never removing my violet eyes from those aquamarine ones. We were enjoying ourselves, acting like best friends who could be just as playful. It was amazing to have the kind of relationship where we didn't worry about making a fool out of the other.

Sighing in defeat from exhaustion, I relaxed and allowed Cooper to pin me down. We were huffing, both exhausted from our childish fun. He gave me a lopsided smile, letting his tongue hang out lazily. I gave him a wolfish grin. However, it probably looked like I was rolling my lips in. Taking me by surprise, my mate flicked his pink tongue out, sanctioning it to brush my snout. Shaking my head from his slobber, I shoved on his muscular yet furry chest with my black paw.

"You're so beautiful," he spoke to me through his mind, nuzzling his nose against mine lovingly.

Never removing eye contact, I flicked my own tongue out before slobbering up his white nose. His eyes flashed in amusement before rubbing his nose against mine all over again. We couldn't stop the laughter from escaping our muzzles, and soon we were howling with laughter. Cooper's pearl white teeth reflected off the snow, making them seem whiter than ever.

"And that's why I—" Before he could finish his sentence, a loud ringing noise echoed in my ears.

I shoved him off, shaking my head from the noise. Cooper seemed confused by my actions and jumped away from me in a flash. He didn't seem to find any potential threat after examining the area. He talked to his pack through his mind link and found out that nothing was wrong. He quickly shifted in front of me.

His lips began to move, but I didn't hear any kind of noise, just the ringing. It got louder and louder making, me howl in pain. Placing my paws over my ears didn't seem to help but only made it worse. I began snarling as if I were rabid, and this just got Cooper angry. Removing my paws away, he placed them in his hands and examined my ears.

As if it never happened, the noise stopped, and I dropped into my mate's arms, shifting into my human form. I let out a ragged breath as I relaxed against his warmth. His muscles tensed against my fingertips as I rested my hand on his shoulder. I was panting now, trying to regain my strength. Our chests were pressed together, but I knew Cooper wasn't paying much attention to that.

"What was that?" he asked, breathing in the deafening silence.

"Probably just another side effect from my PTSD." I sighed, relaxing in my mate's arms. "I think I had some sort of trigger." He nodded in understanding, but his concern didn't disappear.

"Couldn't be anywhere near romantic without some kind of disruption." He chuckled, trying to brush the situation off and hide the worry in his voice.

Hand in hand, we made it back to the pack house dressed in comfortable clothes. I let out a screech when Cooper pinched my bottom, making me cover my mouth immediately. He only gave me a wink before brushing past me as if he did it all the time. I rolled my eyes but followed after his muscular and fantastic body.

The attention he gives us is exciting. My wolf howled. Her happiness was evident in her voice.

And you make me feel different, I answered her, watching as our mate listened in, wishing for everyone in the house to be asleep.

Our mate did that all by himself. She beamed, leaping happily. *It's about time you got fun. I was getting bored in your small head.*

Don't forget—I chuckled, and Cooper gave me a confused glance before taking my hand and walking up the glass steps—*you are me as I am you.*

I smiled at my wolf and clutched my mate's hand tightly. He was changing me, and obviously for the better. There wasn't a single day that went by that I wasn't thankful I ran away from Blood Moon. If I hadn't, I never would've met Cooper, my amazing mate. There was no way I would've met his amazing parents, Sage, and Paige.

Cooper glanced down at me, pure admiration in his eyes. He stopped at the top of the steps and brushed the side fringe that covered my eye. We never removed our eyes from each other, and I couldn't hold back the purr that escaped my lips when electric shocks passed through my body. A low growl echoed deep within his chest, and I rested my hand on it to feel the soft vibrations. It was amazing how much his growls and rumbles were affecting me, making me want to do so many things that should be illegal to him.

It was then that I realized how much I needed him, but more importantly, how much I loved him.

Chapter 23

I sipped my tea in the sitting room, watching light snowflakes fall from the sky. It was getting late, but I felt this sudden need to stay awake. My wolf continued to nag, and the pit in my stomach felt worse. I knew something wasn't wrong. It was just that something felt new.

I felt a presence behind me, and when I turned around, I saw a shadow standing before me. I jumped in surprise, my mug getting knocked out of my hands when I stood up. I wrapped the cardigan that was over my shoulders around me as I studied the figure. It got closer to me, and I held a hand up.

"Who are you and what are you doing in the pack house?"

The figure tilted its head to the side before reaching over and flicking the light on. The lamp lit up the room instantly, and I finally got a look at the girl that was in front of me. She was wearing a sweater dress, the fabric clinging to her very pregnant belly. Her eyes were glistening with unshed tears, and my entire body relaxed.

"You're Alyssa, aren't you?"

Her doe eyes snapped up to meet mine at my words, and she nodded. "I couldn't sleep so I came downstairs."

"Well, for one, you can't sleep in something so uncomfortable as that." I gestured towards her attire, and a small blush formed on her cheeks.

"I'm sorry. I'm not used to this cold weather. My mate and I lived in such warm weather, so even seeing snow is a shock to me." Alyssa mentioned, placing her hand on her stomach. Her eyes averted down, and I could see the sadness looming in her.

"Why don't you sit with me?" I asked, gesturing to the tea-stained couch. Emilia was going to kill me the moment she saw this couch in the morning. "I can't seem to sleep either."

She nodded her head in thanks before taking a seat. I soon followed after her, but not before placing a blanket of the tea. I grabbed my now empty mug and placed it on the coffee table in front of me. I grabbed another throw blanket that rested behind the couch and placed it over both of our laps.

"How are you holding up?" I asked her, brushing my hair behind my ear.

"Once this baby is born, I want to die." I cast my eyes down at her words, but she continued. "It's not as sad as you believe. I loved my mate. We grew up together, and when we discovered we were mates, we were young and happy."

"But what about your son?"

"My baby doesn't deserve to watch his mother depressed as he grows up." She sighed, rubbing her stomach. "This is a sacrifice I'm making. Of course, I want to watch my son grow up, but he will only remind me of my dead mate."

"You're wise for your age." I complimented. Her words still brought sadness to my life. I wanted a family, and more importantly, I wanted to watch them grow up.

"I will always love my son and my mate, but the loss is unbearable." She placed her hand over my arm, giving me a reassuring smile. "I hope you never go through the pain of losing your mate, and I hope your children don't either."

The uneasy feeling in my stomach came back, and I tried my best to give Alyssa a soft smile. She returned it, twirling a ring on her left hand, seeming deep in thought. She looked terrible for a pregnant mother, and the glow Paige sported wasn't on Alyssa. She looked dull and miserable, seeming to only want her son to be born so she could die. It made me upset that she would die in this pack and let her son wander for a home the rest of his life.

"I've asked for seclusion until the baby is born and I die." She gave me a soft smile. "This is the last time I'll really communicate with anyone until I die and see my mate."

"I'm happy I got to speak with you." I commented, watching her throw the blanket off her laps and stand up. "I'll try my best to let your son find a good home, but there's only so much I can do."

"Don't worry yourself." She waved her hand in a dismissive manner. "You'll have so much to worry about you won't even notice I'm gone."

Somehow I knew, her words were right.

***

Another morning came. I stretched my arms, feeling the welcoming click that came from my shoulder. A groan broke from Cooper's mouth. I turned around to face him. My face was to his chest, and his own was resting on my head affectionately. His warm breath fanned around my ear and down my neck, making me shiver subconsciously. Usually, in the morning, my wolf was more awake and letting my wolf take in control, without transforming, of course. I rolled Cooper over so he was on his back and I was on top of him.

I glued my nose to his neck, feeling comfortable for being close to him. I didn't want him to know about the nightmare I had again last night. All I wanted was for Cooper to hold me close and never let go. My wolf convinced me to kiss his neck. I did, and because of that, Cooper's wolf woke up. I internally groaned but welcomed the sudden movement of him pushing me on my back and him hovering over me.

His once aquamarine eyes were now black, staring at me for a long moment. Finally, he broke the silence, but not the way I wanted him to. "You had a nightmare." It wasn't a question. It was a statement.

I sighed and turned my head to stare anywhere but at him. Of course, he would know. The mating bond had allowed us to see each other's dreams, and I knew he had been doing that every night. Every night he would see the same thing. My young abused self continuously getting tortured was not a good scene for him. If Cooper didn't see me being sprawled out on the surgical table with liquid silver running through my veins in my dream, he wouldn't be this upset.

"Yes," I mumbled, running a hand through my hair as tears welled up in my eyes. "I wish this would just stop. This entire thing is taking such a toll on my body. I wish so much that something would happen to us to make everything better."

"What do you want?" he asked, determination coating his handsome face. "I'll give you anything you desire. Just name it."

Our eyes locked again, and I sucked in a breath before holding it. Might as well get on with it. "I want a family. One that I can call my own. I lost mine many weeks ago, and I can't stand this different kind of loneliness I feel. You have a family that I could only wish I have, and it makes me envious that I can't have what my own mate has."

Cooper didn't say anything but just stared at me. I tried reaching into his mind, but I soon noticed that he had many blocks up, barring me. I wasn't emotionally stable to even try to get past the walls holding me back. That's when I decided to continue with what I had to say.

"My parents abandoned me to a horrible man that I could never call my father. Even if I find them one day, I will never forgive them for the years that I had suffered. You have a family that I can never truly have." I looked away from his eyes, but he only gently grabbed my chin to get me to look at him. "History shouldn't repeat itself. Children should have parents, and I want to be one."

Still, he didn't speak. I guessed he wanted me to continue, and I did. "I want to hold my baby in my arms and kiss his or her forehead before saying goodnight. I want to play with my baby and make its giggles bounce off the walls. I want to teach my baby how to walk, talk, and use the toilet right." By now I was almost in tears. "I want to do the things my parents were meant to do, not someone else."

A single tear escaped my eyes, and Cooper quickly brushed it away with his rough thumb. With utter humiliation, I couldn't look him in the eye after what I said, but a soothing touch to my hand brought me to connect with his aquamarine eyes.

"It would make me happy—no, scratch that—it would make me completely and utterly joyful to have you carrying my pups one day." Cooper seemed excited at the idea of becoming a father. However, before I let that dream come close to coming true, his smile faltered. "But it can't happen. Not when your life is still at risk with the war coming."

Sadness filled my heart, but I soon realized where he was coming from. Alpha Zaire was still coming after me, and I had the mark on my arm to prove it. The Blood Moon imprint in my pale skin showed that every day wasn't a safe one. We just had to wait until the war was finally over and done with.

"Okay." I nodded, closing my eyes and letting out a sigh.

***

I woke up to the sound of a bell ringing in my ear but brushed it off and cuddled closer to Cooper's relaxed and warm chest. His arm went around my waist in his sleep, and I breathed out before closing my eyes again. I wasn't at all welcomed with the light shining through the curtain in the room, so instead, I decided it was better to just sleep. However, someone had a better thing in mind.

My body was shaken up, and I felt two hands grasp my shoulder. "Wake up! Wake up! Celia, wake up!" With my eyes still closed, I felt the tiny body move over to my left and heard tiny screeches. "Wake up! Wake up! Wake up, Cooper! Wake up!"

All I heard was my mate let out a grunt before turning over, so his entire chest was on top of me. Nuzzling his head into my neck, I finally opened my eyes only to be greeted by the dim light from outside. Closing my eyes, I let out a yawn before snuggling closer to Cooper's warmth.

"No!" she cried, and I let out a huff. "You have to wake up right now!"

"Sage, go back to sleep," Cooper mumbled into my hair and faked a loud snore to try and convince her he was dead to the world.

"But it's Christmas!"

Cooper groaned loudly and moved over so he was on his back, dragging me along with him.

"No, it's not." He argued, shaking his head and finally opening his eyes. "I've only kept Celia in here for a week."

"No, it's been three."

Shock was written all over Cooper's face, and I rolled over so I was off his chest. I didn't even know I was in his room for that long.

"Fantastic," Cooper whispered before tossing the blankets off his body, covering Sage's face with it so she wouldn't see his nude body. I made sure she didn't look as he got dressed, but once he was fully clothed, he sprinted out the door. A sudden realization hit me, and I instantly felt guilty.

"I didn't get him a gift." I felt like the worst mate in the world. It was my first and official holiday with him, and I didn't even get him anything.

"That's okay! Cooper doesn't like receiving anything on holidays." Sage explained after she pulled the blankets off, showing her lovely bed head. "He doesn't give anyone anything. He just patrols around the territory all day."

My heart dropped, and I looked down at my hands. "Is that why he left so quickly?"

Sage shrugged. "Probably."

After our little alarm clock left, I sluggishly made my way to the bathroom and took a shower. I would be truthful and say I moped the entire half hour I was under the sprinkling water. The scent of Cooper was still in the air, and I let out a low purr. It smelled so manly yet sweet at the same time, bringing my wolf at ease.

Finished with washing off, I took some of my new comfortable clothes out of the dresser and changed. I was excited to at least watch as Sage opened her gifts from Santa and grin like a mad woman. It was a perfect time to get to see everyone so happy during this time of year. For me, it was different. This time of the year only made me miss my brother, and I could feel my heart throb at the thought of him.

I walked down the stairs, almost getting run over by a group of seven-year-olds dragging each other towards the large tree set up in our sitting area. All packs celebrate Christmas, which was very adorable since the tables seated for everyone in the pack was long and filled with food. It's usually just the feast, but it's more like a seven-course meal. Older women passed me carrying squirming toddlers, eager to get to see what Santa Claus had gotten them. Once they greeted me, they ran off humming Christmas songs and just about anything to do with the holidays.

When I entered the sitting room, small children were all lined up, holding a present in each of their arms. Sage was seated in the middle, clutching onto the gift for dear life. I grinned at her and sat down, placing her between my legs, and urged her to open it. She did with excitement and squealed at what was inside. It was a little doll that was the spitting image of her and hugged it tightly.

"Thank you, Santa!" she cried, and I couldn't help but hug her close to me.

That went on for several minutes, or what must've been hours since every child did open their presents one by one. I didn't get any, but that was expected, so I didn't make any comment. It was amazing to see how carefree and happy others were on this day. It was something I knew I would love and get used to.

"This one's for you, dear." Emilia appeared with a smile, holding out a little green box with a red bow on it. I took it with caution and smiled up at her.

"Thank you."

"Well?" She urged with a grin. "Aren't you going to open it?"

Pursing my lips together, I pulled the ribbon, allowing the fabric to fall to the ground. Snipping the tape with my fingernail, I peeled the wrapper. I lifted the lid and took a peek at what was inside. Gasping in shock, I put the lid down. A key was something I didn't expect. I was perplexed. What was the key for?

I must've spoken my question out loud because Emilia answered it immediately. "It's a key to a little cabin down South. It'll be perfect for raising a new family before returning back to the pack house. However, it's just a suggestion. You can raise your children in the pack house if you would like. Cooper doesn't know I'm suggesting this, so I would keep this to yourself until you decide."

"Oh, Emilia." I gasped, looking at her in complete shock. "I don't know what to say. This is so…" I couldn't even begin to say how amazing this was. I had never expected a present from anyone.

"Welcome to the family, dear." She beamed before kissing my forehead and Sage's and strutting over to her own mate. She sat on his lap and kissed his cheek, causing him to kiss her lovingly. I smiled at the old couple who were still in so much love and looked down at the golden key.

Would Cooper and I still be like his parents when we get older? Even without children? I couldn't help but smile at the thought of Cooper's large body snuggling a small baby in his muscular arms. It would surely be a sight to see. It honestly wouldn't matter if we had children as long as we're happy.

"Merry Christmas, love," a voice whispered in my ear, and I turned around to see Jeremy grinning down at me with Trixie wrapped in his arms. I was happy to know that Cooper had granted her a position into the pack. The holiday cheer must've made my mate more kind to her.

"Merry Christmas." I smiled and looked over at Trixie and repeated the same phrase. She returned it back and kissed Jeremy on the cheek before holding his hands and pulling him over to a group of children.

Over the course of the day, I received a lot of 'Merry Christmas' and 'Happy Holidays.' It was perfect to see everyone in the pack gathered together for this special day. However, I couldn't help but miss Cooper. I thought I would be able to spend some time with him and interact with his friends. I guess things never go as planned.

"Celia!" A voice screeched, and I turned around. When I was done greeting almost everyone in the house, I went to the kitchen and decided to help Felicity. As I looked up from the citrus fruit I was peeling, Felicity told it was actually called Satsuma. My eyes widened at the sight that I had to cover my mouth from laughing hysterically.

Paige walked over to me, or better yet, wobbled, with her arms wide open and a grin plastered on her face. My eyes darted directly to the large bump on her stomach she had gained since the last time I saw her.

"Paige?" I wasn't even certain if it was actually her because the baby bump in front of her covered entirely her once petite frame.

Placing her hands on her hips, she scoffed. "Yes, it's me, you idiot." She rolled her eyes and gave me a big hug, which was difficult since the baby practically punched me in the gut. "I told you I got fat."

The moment I released her, Adam came in and wrapped his arm around her waist, giving her a kiss on her temple and turned to me. He greeted me and walked off to help the men carry firewood, excusing himself kindly. Once he was gone, I turned to inspect Paige with a raised eyebrow.

"You sure you're not carrying twins in there?" I questioned, and she only laughed.

"Of course not." She waved, wiping a trail of sweat from her forehead, which was expected since it must have took her a lot of energy to move around. "It's just one."

"Have you been told the gender?"

A smile lit up of her face, and she clapped her hands, gathering the attention of some of the pack members who were trying to help with the preparation for the feast. "Yes, and it's a boy! They say the male grows quicker than females, so he will probably be born earlier than expected if he connects with his wolf soon enough."

"When is your due exactly?"

Paige smiled even more. "July 29th, but since he is developing quickly, the doctor says he might be born around the end of June!"

I was shocked. She had about six to seven months left looking as fat as she did. No offense to her, but I don't think I could do it. It was pretty surprising to know that she was only a few months in.

"I'm so proud of you!" I grinned, giving her another awkward hug, which she didn't seem to mind.

"And look at you!" she shouted, making the women in the room glance at her and sigh loudly. Obviously, they were used to her doing this. "You have gained too! You look so healthy now, and you even went up a breast size!"

I looked at her strangely and then down at my chest. Did she really look there? Was my increasing weight really that noticeable? I didn't want to become a whale just from eating so much. Cooper would not be happy about that, and neither would I. I wanted to be healthy for him so one day I would be able to carry his children.

"Paige, dear." A woman coaxed, rubbing her arm softly. She resembled a nurse, and I couldn't help but look at her curiously. Wasn't it Sheila's job to take care of all the pack members? "I think it's time to rest. I'll wake you up when the party starts."

Paige groaned but nodded anyway, wobbling out of the room and slamming the door behind her. I sighed and continued helping Felicity. Hormonal and moody, Paige was going to be tough to deal with for another six months.

Is there any way to get that baby out faster before she trashes the entire house?

***

After helping the pack chef and other pack members finish off the feast, I went upstairs to get ready. I couldn't decide what to wear, so I called Sage in to help me go through my newly supplied closet. She agreed and starting skimming through the closet, her cute velvet holiday dress flowing behind her. It was knee length and loose enough for her to walk in it. By the look of it, it was made of a very soft fabric. A strip of shining fabric went around her waist, along with a flower clipped near her waist.

"I found it, Celia!" she cried, and I walked into the closet where she was standing, holding a dress in the air, high above her head so it wouldn't touch the floor and get dirty.

"Oh, it's beautiful!" I grinned, touching it with my hand to feel the softness of the fabric. It had a little fuzzy texture to it. I took it quickly from her and ran off into the bathroom.

It only took a second to throw on the dress, and when I did, I gasped loudly. It had a strap that was about three fingers thick, which made me feel fairly comfortable wearing it. It was loose, and I was able to swoosh with it if I spun around. The color was a deep violet with a black leather belt in the front. A bow was tied securely where my belly button would be. It was one of the most beautiful yet festive dress I had ever seen.

I walked out and gave Sage a hug. She was holding out a pair of matching black flats that would perfectly complete the outfit. While slipping them on, we heard a knock on the door. The door opened, and I looked up and saw Paige strutting in, wearing a very loose red sweater and a flowing skirt that went down to the floor. She smiled at me and held up a curling iron and a makeup case.

"Oh no." I groaned, and Paige launched on my face.

Before I knew it, my hair was perfectly curled and my makeup was done to bring out my bright violet eyes. Paige did a little touchup on Sage, but since she was still young, she didn't put much on her younger sister. She didn't bother wearing any because she said she would only sweat it off after walking around for even a second. To say I understood was an understatement. There was no way I would've helped Paige fix her makeup if it ran even a little.

We left the room and descended down the decorated staircase which had been covered in red and green plastic wrap. The railing held multicolored Christmas lights, and by the time we had reached the bottom floor, I gasped in complete and utter shock. What once was a simple holiday-themed living room and hallway was now filled with different lights and funky decorations.

The moment I took another step, everyone stopped and turned to look at me. The first pair of eyes I saw was Emilia's. She was wearing a red cocktail dress with a black belt just above her slim waist. Her blond curls descended down her back and were clipped back with a jeweled bobby pin. She wore a pair of clear heels with small snowflakes on them. Once she saw me, she set her drink on a nearby table and strutted over.

"Girls, finally." She kissed each of our cheeks and took Sage's face in her hands. "Why don't you go play with your friends in the other room, sweetie, while the adults discuss adult stuff, okay?"

"Yes, Mommy." She grinned before skipping past us.

Emilia still had a smile on her face and began guiding me towards the kitchen where it was a lot quieter to talk. I didn't know why she brought me and not Paige, but I didn't want to question it. There was no use questioning a former luna.

"I'm sorry Cooper isn't here, Celia." She apologized, giving me a sad smile and released my hands to make me drink. "My son doesn't enjoy holidays because it's an easy access for the rogues. A lot of the men who patrol our borders tend to drink too much, and, well, they're an easy target. With you being here, I would've thought he'd celebrate with us, but I guess I was wrong."

"It's fine, Emilia." I waved her off, trying to keep on a good, fake smile. "I'm here with you and Paige, so I know I'll be able to enjoy myself."

She nodded, carefully looking at me and trying to determine something that I couldn't pick up on. Sighing, she picked up a fancy glass and poured a few drops of red liquid in it before adding a clear green liquor. After frosting it with green ice, she held it out to me and smiled.

"When Patrick left me on our honeymoon to help the pack with something, I helped myself with a lovely holiday apple martini." She winked before shoving it into my hands. "Might as well try following in my footsteps."

When she waved her hand dramatically, I noticed she only had one ring on her finger. Where was the beautiful one she usually wore? "Emilia, where's your other ring?"

Her eyes widened in shock and looked at her left hand. When she noticed what I was referring to, she let out a sigh of relief and turned to me. "I never wear it on festive days. Not only does it never match my outfits, but I almost always find a way to lose it."

I rolled my eyes at her as she walked away. I took a sip of the drink just to be polite. It was sweet and ice cold, and I did enjoy it. I had never tasted something so delicious before, so I took another sip just to relish it. I guess not having a mate around right now gave me some freedom.

After sitting at the dining table, I looked to my left and saw an empty chair with Cooper's name on it. I sighed and took a sip of the drink in my hand. The large room was filled with chatter, and I once again felt out of place. Even Jeremy was enjoying himself and speaking to others, and for an omega, he sure was social. Sadly, Cooper was supposed to be at the head of the table, and me beside him, but that didn't work out as everyone had planned.

The food platters were passed around, and I took it gratefully from Adam, whose plate was quite full with stuffing, turkey, and cranberry sauce. Taking the plate of the roasted turkey, I began piling food on my plate. Once I had finished, I took the vegetables from him and did the same. This went on for every dish I received, and soon, my plate was almost overflowing with food. When Adam handed me the stuffing, he raised an eyebrow.

"Are you bringing that to share with Cooper or something? That looks like a lot for someone your size. I don't even think I could eat that much," he inquired, looking at me suspiciously before turning back to Paige who had poked his cheek with her fork to get his attention.

I looked down at my plate before turning to Adam's. His portions of food were organized and well laid-out while mine were just piled on top of each other. I shrugged it off and dug in, feeling overly hungry since I hadn't eaten breakfast nor lunch. There was nothing wrong with me eating this much. Cooper said that if I ate more, my wolf would get stronger and somewhat larger. I just hoped I wouldn't gain a lot of weight after this.

When I took a bite of the turkey, I felt my stomach churn and felt the gooiness of it being undercooked. I looked over at Adam who seemed fine with his own even though his portion looked a lot like mine. However, I ate it anyway because I didn't want to be impolite to Felicity. She probably didn't mean to undercook the turkey.

I was the first to finish my plate, and when I looked up, everyone was still digging in while chatting. Feeling awkward that I was the first one to finish, I took a few scoops of the stuffing and cranberry sauce and ate it as slow as possible. When I looked up, Emilia was looking at me strangely. I turned back around when Paige called for her attention.

"I think I'm going to be sick!" Paige cried, covering her mouth before running as fast as she could out of the room. Adam groaned and stood up to go after his mate who was trying her best to run with her big belly.

Strangely, a few more women who looked pregnant stood up and ran out of the room. Their mates followed after them, growing worried since they all left at the same time. I glanced at Emilia who looked as pale as a ghost from what was happening.

I thought they probably ate too much for themselves and the baby they were carrying. Another moment passed before a few girls who didn't look pregnant at all stood up and ran out of the room, covering their mouths to hold back a vomit. I cringed at the sight and looked awkwardly as more mates ran after their wives or girlfriends.

"Get Cooper," Emilia said to her mate Patrick. "Something's wrong with his mate."

A moment later, Paige came back, looking strangely pale with Adam holding her up. He sat her down in her chair and sat beside her. When he turned to me, he looked a bit anxious. Worry lines formed on his forehead, which made him look a lot older than he actually was.

"Celia, are you okay?" he asked, placing his hand on his forearm. "You look a little pale."

A wave of nausea hit me, but I shook my head to get rid of it. "I'm fine. I just probably ate too much. Or it was the drink I had earlier."

"If it were from my mother-in-law, I wouldn't doubt she put something in it." He chuckled before looking back at Paige then back at me. "She's been getting sick a lot lately, but that's expected from a normal high-rank pregnancy. The excitement of the party riles most pregnant women up, and this happens every year. Everyone's fine, I promise."

"This happens every year?" I asked, looking around as the women who ran out came back holding their big bellies.

"Yeah." Adam nodded, giving me a small smile. "It's pretty terrifying, but werewolf pregnancies are pretty fragile when it comes to the holidays. We've surprisingly had a lot of pregnant women this year, but that's only because a new beta will be born, and a lot of families want their child to be their mate."

I raised an eyebrow. "So women in the pack are only getting pregnant in hopes that their child is the future mate of your and Paige's baby? Because they then they'd move a rank higher?"

"Messed up?" He joked, looking over at Paige who seemed perfectly fine and was eating more food. "Yeah."

"Never mind. Celia is looking better already. She probably just got startled." I heard Emilia cooed to her husband, resting her hand on his arm. "Everything's fine. Don't bother our son."

My heart sunk a little bit, disappointed that Cooper wouldn't come.

The night went on with only a few more women running to the nearest bathroom. Presents were opened again, this time from parents and family members. I smiled seeing Sage happy all over again. Paige received a lot of clothing and baby stuff for her unborn son. I couldn't help but laugh when she started talking to him. Adam did the same, asking him if he liked blue or green. I wasn't given any gift from anyone, besides the one Emilia had given me. I didn't mind. I was still happy without receiving any additional presents.

I was playing dolls with Sage on the floor when I was hit with another wave of nausea. Paige seemed to notice and slid off Adam's lap. She knelt as best as she could beside me and placed a gentle hand on my shoulder.

"Celia, are you feeling okay?" Her voice was filled with worry, and when I didn't respond right away, she looked at Adam. "Get my brother. Tell him something isn't right."

He nodded quickly and stood up from the couch. "No, I'm fine. I'm just a little tired."

Adam stopped, looking like he was debating whether to follow my request or his mate's.

"Sweetie, you look like you're about to throw up all over Sage," she whispered before pulling me up, which she shockingly was able to do even with her condition. "Come with me."

"Dessert is in a few minutes, girls, so hurry up," Emilia called while I weakly climbed the stairs, clinging onto the railing for support.

Before I knew it, the bathroom door was kicked in by Paige, and she helped me walk in. I was clinging onto her, which wasn't good for her since she already had to carry one human being in her belly. Dropping down to my knees, I clutched onto my stomach and cried out in pain. Tears prickled in my eyes, and a few droplets fell on the floor.

"Celia, you need to breathe." Her voice echoed in my head, but I didn't listen to her. Everything was a blur to me. "Just calm down. Cooper is almost here."

I started coughing disturbingly, and I felt myself being dragged towards the toilet and my head placed near it. I heaved the contents in my stomach before I could stop myself. Tears began pouring out. A small hand was rubbing my back, and I knew Paige was trying to comfort me for as long as possible.

"It's okay," she whispered, but I couldn't stop.

I had finally calmed down but didn't remove my head from the toilet. My body ached, and I felt like I had been ran over by a train. The dress I was wearing was drenched in sweat, and it uncomfortably stuck to my back.

Suddenly, I heard a loud banging behind me. I didn't look to find out what it was or who it was. I was breathing slowly now, with a small wheeze at the end.

"Cooper, you need to relax just a little bit." Paige's voice echoed, and I ran my hands through my damp hair. "She doesn't look good, and I don't want to risk you—"

"Risk me what?" He growled at her, and I heard her let out a whimper. "I would never hurt her. Now get out."

I heard the sound of scampering feet and a door being clicked softly. The presence of my mate calmed me down the moment I felt him sit beside me, but that didn't stop me from releasing more of the food I had eaten tonight into the toilet. Letting out another cry of pain, I began to find it hard to breathe.

"I'm so sorry you're going through this," he whispered, rubbing my back and thighs lovingly. I knew he was trying to help me, but strangely, it didn't work.

I barely managed to choke out. "I'm sorry, Cooper. You obviously wanted to be alone, and here I am keeping you here now."

"I didn't want to be alone." He chuckled, shaking his head. "I was planning a date tonight. It's something I've been putting off for a while now but…"

"Just please make this go away." I begged, hugging my stomach tightly.

"I can't. I'm sorry," he apologized, kissing my bare shoulder. "I thought you would've told me by now. Instead, you continued keeping it a secret."

"Keeping what a secret?" I asked, looking up at him for this first time. He was dressed in a fancy suit with a red rose tucked in the front pocket. His thick curls were pulled back neatly. However, a few strands were flopping down on his forehead.

I felt my stomach lurching, but I held back the bile that threatened to come out.

"You haven't noticed?"

"Noticed what?"

A smile made its way on his face. "You're carrying our child."

"Excuse me?"

"You're pregnant, Celia."

Chapter 24

Pregnant. That was the only word that went through my mind at that moment. I was pregnant. I couldn't decide if I was supposed to leap into loud squeals or bawl my eyes out. I wasn't emotional like Paige, so what did this mean? Was there something wrong with the baby? Or was it just me?

Oh my, I'll make the worst mother.

Sure I'd changed a lot of diapers, but I hardly paid attention to what I was doing! Now, I had to take care of a being that Cooper and I created! How was I going to cope with that? With the war that was fast approaching, Cooper would only be worrying about my safety. He could get killed if he was solely focused on me. He could lose focus trying to protect us if any possible battle started.

"Celia, baby, calm down." Cooper urged, looking at me with concerned eyes. "Everything will be fine. I promise."

Then it hit me like a bucket of cold water. What if it's a girl? Ayana would take the baby away from us. Cooper would never forgive me for allowing it to happen. I would be the reason he would never see our daughter again. I couldn't risk that. I couldn't have Cooper hating on me for doing something like that.

If it's a girl, I could get rid of it and blame it on a miscarriage. I couldn't risk anything happening to my daughter if Ayana came after her. What could Ayana do to her? I could also possibly give her up for adoption far away from where Ayana was. It would hurt me greatly, but it would protect her.

"Cooper, I can't have a baby," I whispered, completely frightened and terrified. I couldn't tell him I was afraid of it being a girl.

"It's okay," he mumbled, kissing my forehead softly. "That witch gave us something we can call ours—our baby. We owe her a debt that I don't think we can repay. Our life with our children will be priceless."

Our daughter. I wanted to say, but I kept my mouth shut. "What about the war?"

"I'll make sure you and the baby are safe. No one will know about the baby until after it." His aquamarine eyes sparkled with joy, and I couldn't crush it by telling him about the deal I had with the witch. It'd just have to stay in the dark for a little longer.

***

Christmas passed quickly, and soon, so did New Year's. It was all a blur to me, but that's probably because I stayed cooped up in our room, hiding the little bump that had already started to form on my stomach. I was growing worried. Even Paige's didn't grow that fast. Something must be wrong with him.

I decided to refer my baby as *him* to keep my mind from thinking about the deal. I'd been thinking about it for a couple weeks now. But with the impending war, I was starting to debate within me whether I should tell my mate or not. He'd be angry, but I wouldn't want him to get heartbroken because of me after I get rid of it if it's a girl.

Suddenly, the door kicked open. I turned around to face a blond curled monster—Paige. My arms were crossed over my chest as I stood, trying to hide my fatness. If Paige found out, word would spread like wildfire. Even Sheila didn't know, and I knew I was due for an ultrasound just to see how things were going.

"Celia, my darling," she greeted, using a British accent as she entered, swaying a little when the baby kicked. I mean, it literally kicked. I'm pretty sure I saw a foot stick out of her stomach. "Wow, he is getting pushy."

I only smiled and hugged her. I was wearing a comfortable sweatpants that hugged my body, hiding the little bump on my belly. Should I go shopping for something that would fit me better?

"Wait a second." Paige's mouth dropped open, and she stared at me in bewilderment. She seemed to be trying to figure something out "You're.. you look—"

My eyes widened, and I dashed over her, slamming the door shut and clasping a hand to her mouth. "Don't say anything. Don't tell anybody. No one can know that I'm pregnant," I whispered before removing my hand away from her.

"I was going to say you're looking nice today but…" Then the words sunk into her thick skull, and she couldn't have looked anymore surprised. "You're what?"

"Pregnant?" I cringed, looking around, worried that someone could hear us even though the walls were thankfully soundproof.

Before I could move out of the way, she lifted my shirt up and gasped at the size. I groaned and gripped my shirt to pull it down, but she wasn't having any of that. "How long?"

I looked down at the ground and mumbled. "A few weeks now."

She took a step back and stared at me. "You shouldn't be gaining this much already. It's not natural for you."

I growled, which was a first for me and turned away from her, running a hand through my pin-straight hair. Didn't she know I was getting stressed over this already? I couldn't handle all this worry, and it obviously couldn't be good for the baby. There were so many what ifs that I couldn't get my mind to calm down. I hadn't stopped worrying since I found out.

"Do you think I don't know that already?" I shouted, looking in the mirror and glaring at her through it.

"I'll call Sheila. She can sort this out."

"It's too late, Paige!" I snapped. "She's already preparing the medical supplies for the war. I can't just interrupt her now."

"Too late." She mocked me and headed for the door. "I already mind linked her. She'll be up in a few minutes."

I completely forgot I could mind link the people in the pack now that I was officially their luna. I must be playing the role terribly after keeping myself distant from the pack for so long. Everyone must be curious and a bit worried about how I was feeling. There's only so much a pack could handle before they would demand to see their luna. It's a proven fact that I wish wasn't true.

Only moments later, Sheila came in, out of breath and carrying a large bag. I raised an eyebrow while she unpacked her things. She placed a large machine on the table and clicked on a button showing a small computer screen. Not once did she glance at me or speak to me while preparing her medical tools. Different medical supplies were placed on the bed, a small smile plastered on her face as she did so.

"Sheila, what is all this?" I questioned, looking curiously at the metal bars scattered everywhere.

"This is my personal carry-on ultrasound." She grinned, taking my hand and shoving me on the free side of the bed. "I suggest mind-chatting the father before I begin."

Sheila left to wash her hands so that she wouldn't get me sick if there were any kind of germs that she had encountered on her way to my room. It was strange to think that we were in a room where a teenage boy used to live, now man. Now, man has turned into a father. Our family was growing, and I couldn't help but feel excited.

Cooper? I asked my mate using mind link through our personal bond. There was no way I would risk a moment using the pack bond because it was possible for one of the members to sneak their way into our conversation.

Yes, babe? Is everything okay? Is our baby fine? Are you feeling sick? I could pick up something. I'm pretty sure Paige has something she could give you. Are you craving something? I'm not far from the store. I was bombarded with Cooper's worried voice, and I could only smile at his protectiveness over us right now.

Everything is fine, Cooper. I cooed, watching as Sheila came back into the room with a small smile on her face. *But I think you may want to be here for this. Shelia is giving me an ultrasound any minute now.*

I'll be right there. He sounded excited, and my smile only seemed to grow just a bit.

"Celia, sweetheart." Sheila knelt down beside me and gave me a serious look. "What did you promise, Ayana? I know she didn't give you that vial from the bottom of her heart. I won't tell Alpha Cooper, I promise."

Tears filled my eyes, and I couldn't even look into her own as I mumbled, "Her."

"Her?" she asked, looking at me strangely. "Who? Who's her?"

"If I have a girl, Sheila—" I took a deep breath in and let it out. It was so difficult to tell her. She'd never look at me the same. "Ayana will take *her* from me, from us, from the pack."

Sheila's mouth dropped, and her hand went to her mouth immediately. I knew what she was thinking, and I stopped her before she could say anything.

"It's not like I want to give her away, but I really wanted to make Cooper happy, and our relationship was stressful, and I just wanted to fix it. But I didn't even take the vial. I mean, someone injected it into my body so—" I stopped dead in my tracks.

Not many people had known about the vial, so someone close to me had injected the cure forcefully. This only meant that someone wanted this to happen; a pack member wanted to hurt us. The only question was—*Who?* What kind of person would want something like that to happen? I had been kind to everyone I had met. Or at least tried to.

"I'm here."

Shelia and I both looked up when Cooper came in breathing heavily. His shirt hugged his muscular body perfectly, and I couldn't help but feel my mouth water at the sight of my mate.

"Good! Then let's get started." Sheila clapped her hands excitedly and began doing several things with the machine.

Before I knew it, there was a cool gel placed onto my stomach. Cooper looked at me with such love and affection. How could someone like me have him as a mate? The way he looked at me made me feel like I was the only person in his eyes.

Maybe he'd still be able to look at me like that when I told him the truth about my deal with the witch.

"Alright, so I see one." Sheila points to a fair sized dot on the computer screen, giving me a joyful look. "The readings say it's a boy."

I sighed in relief until she let out a loud squeak.

"What? What is it?"

"You have another little guy in here too!" She beamed before looking at it closely. "It looks like a boy too."

"No girl?" Cooper sounded a bit disappointed but didn't say anything else. It broke my heart a little to see his face. Did he really want a girl? I always saw him as the dad who threw baseball around with his sons instead of allowing his daughter to paint his nails because she's daddy's girl.

"Not that I see." Sheila nodded in my direction and gave me a smile before standing up and wiping my stomach. "With twins comes a large stomach, so don't be frightened when you gain twice as fast and twice as large as a normal pregnant woman. It's quite common for high ranks to conceive multiple babies to ensure another heir if one died. Unlike normal human pregnancies, your baby will grow fast, and you'll gain so much that in about three months, you must stay on bed rest for the remainder of your pregnancy."

I nodded in understanding and watched as she packed her things. It was quick, and she left without another word. Cooper was seated on the bed, looking at me expectantly. Something was wrong with him. I just couldn't put it together.

"When were you planning on telling me?" he asked, looking at me dead serious with his hand resting on the little hairs that seemed to be growing from his chin.

"Tell you what?" I asked, giving him a confused look. He couldn't have heard the conversation right?

"That you would've given our daughter away for something like this." He growled, and I jumped at his tone. "You should be thankful we're having boys, or I don't know what I would've done."

"Cooper—"

"Don't 'Cooper' me!" His voice raised. I looked down at the ground. "How could you not tell me when I asked you? I would've gotten rid of that vial long before this happened! You lied to me, Celia. You lied. You're my mate, and you couldn't even tell me the truth. I heard you speaking to Sheila. You can't lie to me about it now."

"I wanted us to be happy." I cried, feeling tears coming out of my eyes like a waterfall. "I told you how much I wanted a family. A baby was all I ever wanted, and there's no need to get all worked up because we're not even having a daughter."

"How about in the future?" Cooper questioned, flopping his arms dramatically. "What if you get pregnant again and it's a girl this time?"

"She'll be a secret. Only our closest friends and family would know about her." It was hard to try to fix things when they were already falling apart.

"So she'll be a prisoner in her own home?" His eyes rolled, and anger boiled inside of me when he did that. I hated it when he rolled his eyes. "You, of all people, should understand what that's like. History will *not* repeat itself."

"I know," I whispered, looking down at the floor ashamed.

He let out a sigh before leaning down to where I was and kissing my stomach softly. A small smile formed at his love already for the pups. Cooper may be angry at me, but any little fraction of stress could risk their safety. Usually, the male had the ability to help, kissing the bump to give them more strength.

"I want this with you," he whispered. "You made this decision on your own, and I'm frustrated with you, but our sons are our life now."

We stayed in silence, Cooper listening to the rapid heartbeats of our children. None of us spoke, not wanting to ruin the flicker of calmness we all had. I rested on the bed while he was lying down with me with his head rested gently on my bare stomach. My swelling tummy seemed to grow just a bit since this morning, possibly a half centimeter, but I noticed more than my mate had.

"Alpha!" We both jumped at the loud voice and looked towards the door. Cooper grabbed my shirt and tugged it down to cover my stomach. He grabbed the blankets and threw them over my stomach to hide the bump from the person running down the hall.

"Come in." My mate's voice was filled with so much authority that it made me shiver.

The door burst open, and our heads snapped in the direction. "Alpha Cooper." The teen sighed in relief before trying to catch his breath. It was the same boy from when Trixie came. I guess he was the messenger of the pack.

"What is it?" Cooper looked worried. I hated to see him worried, so I reached up and placed a small peck on his cheek.

"We have wolves plowing their way through the territory. Dozens of them. They're coming in hot, attacking anyone they see. We already have a few wolves injured around the border. They came out of nowhere, but we all recognized the scent."

"Zaire," Cooper and I both whispered at the same time. My heart dropped and was replaced with fear for Cooper and our pups. My mate could be hurt if he went out to fight. I wasn't prepared to lose him. What if something would happen to him?

"Gather the females and rush them to the safe house. This is an unexpected battle. They went for a surprise attack, which is against our race's war laws. Go now!" Cooper ordered. He stood up and helped me get up.

"Yes, Alpha." He nodded before sprinting out of the room. With the door open, I could hear the pattering of feet and the panicked voices of mothers searching for their children.

"Celia," Cooper whispered, softly rubbing my arms lovingly. "I have to go. The pack needs me, and you need to be kept safe."

"But, Cooper—" He only interrupted me with a small kiss on my lips.

"You have to keep them safe." He cooed, trailing one of his large warm hands to my stomach. "Stay safe as well."

I only nodded, fearing he would be gone and never return. This was the most difficult part, saying goodbye with such little time. We needed much more time.

"I've wanted to say this to you for so long, but the timing never seemed right." He chuckled humorlessly. "But hey, our timing has never been the best."

I let out a small breath of laughter and shook my head. He was completely correct. We both met when I was hurt, practically dying from being destroyed and beaten down with no hope left. He had been with a human even when we had met. Our first date was ruined with Blood Moon Pack members sneaking into the territory and confirming to Zaire I was here. I couldn't get pregnant. Then there was the moment we found out Trixie had shown up with information that terrified everyone. I had a cure that was mysteriously injected into me. Then finally, I get pregnant with two boys.

"I love you."

My heart jumped. I looked up at Cooper. His eyes were watching me carefully with hope and exactly with the way he felt. He loved me. My handsome and perfect mate loved me with all his heart. I didn't know how I had missed all the times he had tried to tell me, but the timing, like always, wasn't the best. It didn't matter though because I knew the second he said those three words, I felt the same.

"I love you too."

The moment, like all of our own, was ruined when children scampered past us, accidentally running into us. They apologized but still ran with fear to look for their families.

"I'll see you soon." It wasn't a question, more of a reassurance, and I nodded. "Felicity!"

Felicity appeared from around the corner, heaving breathlessly. Her eyes were filled with worry and of something else that I couldn't quite understand. "Yes, Alpha?"

"Escort your luna to the safe house. Make sure she isn't hurt in anyway, or I'll have your head." Cooper's voice was filled with anger and worry, obviously not directed at either of us. He reached over to me and took my hands in his before kissing me passionately. "Go now."

With one last look, Cooper ran off, clutching the collar of Jeremy's shirt and taking him with him. He had been talking to Trixie who had a few tears falling down her face. I looked at her with sadness before turning to Felicity. She took my elbow and swiftly ran down the hall with me being practically dragged.

All the female pack members were running out the back door when we finally managed to make our way down the staircase. Men were tugging their shirts off as they walked out the front door before shifting, preparing for battle. Boys, as young as sixteen, were fighting and running out, bidding their mothers goodbye and following their fathers. I couldn't imagine myself being that mother who had to worry about their child.

Then it hit me. When both my sons got older, they'd be involved in wars while I, as a luna, would be locked in a small underground safe house, praying for the best. I didn't think I would be able to cope with them being in such a dangerous environment.

Felicity tugged on my hand, looking at me with annoyance seeing as I had stopped to watch the mothers bellowing. When I had come to my senses, I allowed her to drag me out the back door, following the panicking women. I looked over a few shoulders to see Emilia guiding the long line of women in the front. She obviously knew where she was going.

When I took another step following the line, I felt Felicity make a ninety-degree angle right. I looked at her strangely. Wasn't that direction the correct way? I couldn't remember there was a separate place for the luna to hide, but this was a different pack than Blood Moon by a lot.

We ventured further into the snow, my feet leaving gaping holes in the untouched snow. I remembered Cooper explaining to me how difficult it was to fight in snowstorms, which was what the packs were doing right now. The wind began to pick up as we ran deeper into the forest, the lights of the pack house growing dimmer. I looked up, seeing the stars just starting to announce their presence.

"Felicity, where are we?" I asked, feeling a small shiver run down my spine. Something didn't seem right. Even my wolf agreed.

"We're almost there." She snapped, raising her head up in the air and sniffing.

I did the same and stopped dead in my tracks. How could I not know what was going on?

I tugged out of Felicity's hold, which had gotten tighter the further we had gone on. My face wrinkled in disgust as I watched her turn to face me. Taking a step away from her, I tried to find my voice, but all that came out was a weak croak.

"Who are you?" I asked, seeing as her eyes were looking crazy and her usual neat hair was everywhere.

"We have to go," she shouted, throwing her arms up before placing them back down. That was when I noticed it, right near her elbow. It was the same thing I had.

"Oh my god," I whispered before backing further away from her. "You know Alpha Zaire."

She snorted unattractively before lifting her arm up to show me the blood moon carved into her arm. "Of course I know him."

"What did he do to you?" I asked, looking around the desolate snowy landscape.

"I did nothing. This was done a long time ago when we were kids," she stated simply, but it made no sense to me. What was she going on about? Had she known Zaire since they were younger?

"Who are you?" I repeated, feeling a new gust of wind slap me across the face.

Felicity grinned evilly, and it almost looked familiar as if I had seen it before. "I'm Zaire's older sister. I've been spying Ice Moon for years, collecting one unfaithful pack member at a time for this exact moment."

Next thing I knew, wolves popped out from behind trees, snarling and growling angrily. However, only one wasn't in their wolf form, and I recognized the individual immediately.

"Zaire."

Chapter 25

I took a step back, not knowing what the vile man would try. I was surrounded, and there was no way for me to run like I had done when I first tried to escape him and his cruelty. It's hard to believe I'd been rid of this man for so long, only to have to see him again, faced with so much betrayal. I had hoped we would never cross paths until I saw his head removed from his body.

Zaire was just like I had left him, dark brown eyes with bright yellow specs in them, showing a flicker of his evil inside. His black hair was gelled back, away from his forehead, like how criminals from the human world generally looked like. Standing in front, he had nothing on but a pair of jeans which hung dangerously low on his hips. A small beard had started to form on his jaw and all the way up to his hairline near his ears, showing how much he had begun to age.

A few feet away was the she-devil herself—Carly. She was wearing nothing but her mate's shirt; and she wore it proudly. Her platinum blonde dyed hair was loosely swishing in the wind, catching flakes of snow falling from the sky. Her tanned skin flaunted and mocked me, proving how much I had once looked slightly like that. However, I nowhere near envied her. She killed my brother.

"Glad to see you in the flesh and breathing, *baby girl*," Zaire finally spoke, looking me up and down. "You look fairly different."

"Brother." Felicity greeted, holding her hand out for him to take. He looked over at her and scowled.

"You haven't contacted me in two months. I was beginning to worry," Zaire simply stated, giving her a disapproving look.

"I've been trying to keep a low profile." She explained before looking over at me and roughly taking my wrist. "As a peace offering, I got your murderer, and let me tell you, she has become a little slut here. She mated with the alpha here and is currently very pregnant."

Zaire grinned evilly at me before taking a step closer, so did the rest of his pack members. "Pregnant?" He looked back at his sister. "I was quite sure I made her barren."

"She asked help from a witch and was given a potion to help her produce." The evil glint in Felicity's eye didn't seem to leave. "I injected the cure into her while she was sleeping and let nature do its role. I assumed if you couldn't get the beta's child, the alpha's would be better. This is killing two birds with one stone."

"We can kill the baby first," Carly spoke for the first time since we came face to face. "Let her and that *alpha* suffer by losing their child. Then we come back and kill both of them. Celia deserves to feel pain for killing the child in our pack."

"No." He commanded his eyes glaring at his mate. "My sister was smart to do this. I want to try my experiments more, and I wonder what an unborn werewolf would become."

I took a step back, wrapping my arms around my stomach as if to protect them. There was no way I could let them harm my babies. Losing them would be like losing myself.

'Cooper?' I knew talking to him through our mind link would be distracting to him while the fighting was transpiring, but I needed him. I couldn't let Alpha Zaire kill our future sons.

'Celia, where are you? My mother just informed me that she couldn't find you, and I thought the worst! Please, for the love of the Moon Goddess, tell me you're safe!' His voice was panicking. I could hear it.

'Felicity was the one who injected me with the cure. She's been the traitor the entire time. Not only that but…but she's Alpha Zaire's sister.' I couldn't help but stop the small quiver that escaped from the link. I didn't mean for it to hit him hard.

'Celia.' He paused, and I could hear the uncertainty of his voice. *'Please tell me you're not there with her, that he isn't near you.'*

'He's here,' I informed him, but before he could start yelling, I spoke again, *'He's threatening the pups, you, and everyone we know. I can't lose you…lose them. I've already lost my brother to that man and his mate.'*

'I'll be there soon.' Cooper ended the conversation but kept his wall down obviously so I could inform him if anything were to happen.

The snow and wind began to pick up, blowing everyone's hair around. This drowned out the conversation the three were having, and I yanked my hand out of Felicity's hold again. This caught her attention, which soon gathered the others. They seemed to have remembered I was there and the growls of the rival pack erupted once again.

Before I could register what happened, Zaire leaped at me, his hand wrapped firmly on my throat, blocking my windpipe. My head felt like it was going to explode as I clawed for oxygen. Scratches began to form on his hand from my nails, but he didn't loosen his hold on me, only tightened it. The growls died down, and all there was to be heard was the faint noise of my gargling. A ringing in my ears grew louder and louder as the need for oxygen grew.

"Put her down!" The grip loosened a bit at the voice, and I let in as much air as I could.

My heart picked its pace up again at the sound of *his* voice.

"What makes you think I would?" Zaire chuckled, sizing him up before going at my throat again.

"Because her mate would obviously kill you."

If I could breathe a sigh of relief, I would, but that apparently wasn't happening as I turned to look at my savior. There Warner, alpha of the rogues, stood, looking down at me with concern with hands on his hips. He was fully dressed. His scar from when we had first met was still noticeable but was fading. If I were someone who had never met him before I would've thought he was a businessman.

"Run along, *rogue*. This is none of your business." Zaire's nails began to dig into my skin, making me let out a choked yelp.

"Actually, I think it is, seeing as she had been a temporary beta for me and we are fairly good friends." I had a feeling he knew exactly what he was doing. Warner was distracting everyone while Cooper was looking for me.

"Any friend of Celia is a dead man." Zaire growled before nodding his head to a few of his wolves. They sprang into action, leaping on Warner and biting into him. He shifted immediately and began to fight them. "Now, where were we?"

I gathered up enough energy to spit in his face. He only jumped, allowing me a little air before it was later taken from me. Groaning softly in irritation, I lifted my knee up to his gut and was finally released. Before he could take me again, I felt the presence of my mate and quickly ran over to where he had finally stopped to catch his breath.

Cooper was still in wolf form. He let out a warning growl towards Zaire but tried to refrain from viciously attacking him. I told Cooper through our mind link that I needed to give him a clarification before my mate could kill him. The man who ruined my life deserved an explanation.

"Now you better listen to me." I snapped, causing just about every wolf to stop what they were doing, even the ones who were fighting Warner. I turned to Alpha Zaire. "You don't know what happened that day. What your *mate* told you is all false."

"You watch your tongue you, little omega! Carly would never consider lying to me because she knows the consequences!"

"Oh, really?" I shouted, feeling myself getting angrier with each passing second. Cooper rubbed his wet nose on my hand to soothe me, which worked for the time being. "Did your mate tell you what exactly happened? That the only reason Logan died was because *she* wanted me to feel the same thing she felt when you paid more attention to me and less to her? You were so caught up experimenting on me that you had neglected your own mate, and because of this, she wanted to hurt me. She wanted me to suffer, and she did it by killing my brother. You are mated to a murderer."

Zaire turned around to look at Carly whose arms were crossed over her chest. I could tell by the way their expressions were changing that they were talking to each other through their mind link.

"She had no right to kill him, and I am truly sorry for that." He sighed, looking disapprovingly at her. "But you have no right to leave my pack, and once I pass the death sentence on her, I would need another mate."

Everyone knew where this was going, but before I could utter a word, Cooper pounced on Zaire, knocking him to the ground.

Clearly, Zaire wanted me as his mate to replace Carly, even after knowing Cooper was my own. It was disgusting to hear him say that he was going to kill his mate, and everyone knew how painful that would be for him. How could he say something like that?

"No!" Carly and Felicity shouted, but it didn't stop Cooper from finishing what we all knew would have started.

Zaire let out a scream before his head was ripped off from his body. I shrieked from the amount of blood that poured out of the gaping hole and allowed the bile that rose from my throat to escape. Everything that had been in my stomach left the moment I saw Zaire's head roll into the snow.

Carly cried out, clutching her chest. The bond was breaking between the two, and she was now left with half a soul. She dropped to her knees, letting out a loud wail as tears ran down her cheeks. I looked away from the sight, closing my eyes tightly, only to listening to the sobs wracking through the girl who just lost her mate. I almost felt sorry for her, but she didn't deserve any sympathy.

I felt Coopers' nose touch my hand, and I opened my mouth to see him watching me intently. That was until all the wolves surrounding us took one step forward. He crouched down in a protective stance, waiting for either of the wolves to make their first move. To our surprise, they all bent down, their ears pinned back and necks showing. It was only then that I realized they were submitting to Cooper, surrendering and officially ending the war.

"You killed him." Felicity's voice was filled with so much anger directed at my mate. Her cheeks were red and tearstained, along with swollen eyes and flaring nose. "You killed my brother."

"An eye for an eye." Cooper snapped, and it was only then that I realized he had shifted and was now standing stark naked in front of all of us.

"I didn't kill Logan," she whispered, taking a step back until her back had hit he nearest tree. "She did."

We all looked over at Carly, who was crouched on the floor and running her hands through Zaire's hair. It was sickening to see as she affectionately pet her mate's decapitated head. Her eyes were wide and crazy for the loss of her mate. She turned the bleeding head and softly kissed his cheek before whispering something even I couldn't catch in his ear.

She then began to dig in the snow, not noticing my mate was approaching her. We all knew she needed to be killed. After the sorrow faded, anger would form, and she would go on a killing spree. Zaire wasn't worth the deaths she would cause. He had already murdered enough people as it was. I didn't want to see anyone dying because of their unfortunate bond.

Carly had a gleeful smile on her face, which startled most of us. She held up a stick and snapped it in half. A sharp point formed on one of the two pieces, and she tossed away the dull one. After that, she looked up at the night sky and let out a sigh before bringing the sharp stick up to her throat. No one stopped her because we knew it would be done either way.

A choking sound came from her as blood ran down her throat the more she ran the stick across it. I closed my eyes, not being able to stand the sight of someone's life slowly fading. All I heard was the soft thump of her body and the metallic scent of her blood when I finally opened my eyes again.

The woman who killed my brother was dead.

Chapter 26

Cooper had called for Adam to cuff Felicity, and soon, we were making our way to the clearing where the fighting took place. The snowstorm had passed, and now it was a lot clearer to see what had actually happened. Zaire's and Carly's bodies were taken to be dealt with later. Right now we had to mourn the members we had lost in our pack.

When we finally arrived in front of the pack house, I couldn't help but feel relieved. As I looked around, some pack members had already started clearing the bodies while the rest were tending to the wounded. Remarkably, I could see that the battle had not claimed many lives. Fighters were cleaning up, and the scouts were making their way back to keep the perimeter safe. Others were hugging family members and friends. Some were grieving for their losses, and some were just felt blessed to have survived. A mother who had bid her son goodbye was holding her mate and child tightly, joyful tears running down her cheeks.

Maybe life with two sons wouldn't be as difficult and complicated as I thought. If all pack members, regardless of their rank, could take care of their young just as perfect as the higher-ranked members, maybe there was hope I would be great at being a mom. I would finally have someone to call my own, someone I created out of love with my mate. I knew that the love I had for Cooper would never fade, and our sons would only strengthen us.

"What are you thinking about?" Cooper asked, softly kissing my hand that he was holding before locking eyes with me. "I don't want to invade."

"I'm thinking of being a mom." I nodded my head in the direction of the mother who was reunited with her son. "I can't help but think that maybe I'll be like her. Maybe I'll be someone who can hold their baby close no matter how old they get."

Cooper only smiled, and I arched an eyebrow in confusion. "You're such an amazing luna. You treat my baby sisters exactly like a mother would her pups. I'm proud to call you my mate."

My mate finally stopped at the small staircase to the front door and turned around to look at everyone. The Blood Moon Pack fighters were all rounded up in a small huddle, surrounded by a few of our guards. None moved, and it looked like they weren't even breathing, just waiting for Cooper to state their punishment.

I looked over at the familiar faces, remembering how each one had watched me suffer yet none had tried to help. Seeing them now filled with regret made me nod in understanding. They knew what they had done was wrong, but I couldn't blame them. Zaire was not fit to be the pack's alpha, even if it ran in his blood. The pack was never a pack and was more like a herd of sheep, unsure whether to trust their shepherd or not. Fear was what the Blood Moon Pack thrived on, and it was something I knew should never happen again.

"Blood Moon," Cooper called, immediately gaining the attention of all the members, even our own. "I know you understand that this was a war of greed and useless anger directed in the wrong places. Fingers had been pointed to ease the pained but destroyed the weak. You have lived and followed a man of destruction and poison."

Not once did Cooper release my hand, and throughout his speech, I scanned the area. Paige was holding Adam's hand, her body leaned in close to him, and his large hand placed firmly on her large stomach. Sage was holding a few of her friends' hands, trying to reassure them that everything was perfectly fine. Emilia and Patrick, the former alpha and luna, were holding each other close, watching with pride for their son. Finally, Jeremy and Trixie were cuddled close but still watching the scene unfold.

"But I cannot take such a large number to my growing pack. I understand I was the one to kill your alpha and should be the one responsible for the pack, but I can't do it. From this moment on, a man who kills an alpha will not take the pack but will return the pack to someone more deserving. And someone here today is far more worthy of the title of being an alpha."

Where was Cooper going with this?

His eyes raked through the crowd, and I tried to see where he was looking.

"Jeremy." Gasps were heard as they looked over at the omega of the pack.

"You are mated to a woman of high rank, with the blood of an alpha, who was supposed to take up the role of her deceased father. She deserves to be a part of a pack again, and with this—" he cleared his throat "—I, Alpha Cooper Pierce of the Ice Moon Pack, give you, Beatrix Howling, the alpha title of Blood Moon Pack. You may choose your beta and delta in better circumstances and a new name for the pack."

"I, entitled Alpha Beatrix Howling, accept your proposal and have hereby proclaimed the Blood Moon Pack to be rechristened as Blue Crescent Pack."

Everyone smiled at her decision to use her old pack name she was meant to run.

Claps rang out, and everyone cheered before allowing Blue Crescent to meet their new alpha. Before I knew what was happening, Paige ran over to me, enveloping me in a big hug. She nearly knocked me over with her large stomach that was making her sway from side to side at times. She began crying hysterically, letting sob after sob rake through her body.

"I thought something happened to you! I was so worried." She bawled, clutching onto me tightly.

"As if we need another pregnant woman in one area." Adam chuckled, snaking his arm around her waist in an attempt to calm her down. "Hush now, babe. You can't put stress on yourself right now."

I groaned. "Does everyone know?"

"Yeah." He nodded before eyeing my stomach. "You're a little larger than Paige had described, but everyone has seemed to notice the little guy in there."

"There are two boys in there," Cooper corrected, sending me a broad smile.

"Two little Coopers running around?" Adam groaned. "I can hardly wait."

I rolled my eyes and squeezed Cooper's hand before dragging him over to his parents. They both gave him a hug before giving me a gentle and careful squeeze as well. Emilia began to gush about baby stuff, and I couldn't help but laugh at her excitement to be a grandmother to our sons. Only a few moments later did Sage come over, holding her arms up for me to pick her up. I sighed and bent down, so I was at her level.

"I'm sorry, Sage, but I can't carry you. I won't be able to for a while." I cooed, pinching her cute little tummy.

Her eyebrows scrunched together in the cutest way. "Why not?" She even added a little stomp to the foot to add emphasis.

"Because I can't carry three little babies, not when I already have two boys." It seemed that my words made absolutely no sense to her.

"What do you mean?"

"Why, I have two boys growing inside my belly." Sage's face brightened up, and she leaned in to give me a hug.

"I'm going to be an auntie!" she cheered, and I couldn't help but laugh at how adorable she sounded.

"Yes, Sage, you are." We hugged for a little longer before dusk started to arrive and exhaustion hit everyone.

I kissed everyone goodbye and followed Cooper, but not before hearing the death toll during Cooper and Patrick's conversation. Seven dead and fourteen wounded. It was a fair amount seeing as we had hundreds of excellent fighters that battled against Blood Moon. That pack hadn't been so lucky, with a five hundred and nine death toll and another half thousand injured. Our pack got lucky with not as many losses.

My mate turned around and scooped me up before I could take the first step towards the stairs. I squealed, covering my mouth after the bizarre sound had escaped me. His aquamarine eyes twinkled as he gazed at me lovingly while carrying me up the long staircase. My violet ones stared at him with admiration of him acting like this, even after the eventful day. He had killed Zaire for me, and he knew I would never be able to end his life myself. He showed me that I didn't deserve to have blood on my hands. He was ready to do it for me since he had already killed multiple rogues and rival pack members to protect Ice Moon.

After a few seconds of climbing the stairs, with me still secured in his arms, we finally made our way into our room. For once, the bed wasn't made when we walked in, and our clothes were lazily sprawled across. Everything had been left where it was when the war started.

"So how are our boys holding up?" Cooper asked after closing the door and bending down, so he was eye level with my slightly larger than normal belly.

"I think they're fine." I grinned, running my hand softly across where my children were currently growing.

"We still need names. My mother has been bombarding me with questions through the pack link ever since she found out." He chuckled, and the smile on his face was justly genuine.

"I told Paige about the dream I had before I got pregnant, and she said it was an illumination dream." I sighed, running my hand through Cooper's thick, soft curls. "I've already decided the boys' names."

"Oh, really?"

"Yes." I nodded while he stood up straight in front of me and placed his large hands on my small hips. "Clayton, the oldest, and Rylan, the youngest."

His eyebrows rose in surprise. "Not going original like Henry or Samuel? All the previous alphas were named after other alphas from this pack. I was named after my great grandfather."

I shook my head. "I gave it much thought, and I'm keeping them. We need to break tradition."

"Well, what if I don't like them," he asked seriously, moving so his lips were only a few inches away from mine.

My violet eyes locked with his bright aquamarine ones, and we had a small staring contest as I replied, "Well, then too bad."

"Too bad?" Cooper raised an eyebrow at me. "What happened to both parents making the decision for the name?"

"Do you seriously not like them?" I asked, scrunching my eyebrows sadly. I really thought the names were nice and unique. Did he seriously want their names to be common?

"I was joking, Celia," he said with a soft laugh that caused chills to run through my body. "I love them."

I sighed. "You scared me."

My mate reached down and planted a long soft kiss on my forehead while he held me. "I'm sorry."

"I was joking." I copied, looking up at him with shining eyes. "I wouldn't have changed the names even if you hated them."

"And this is why I love you."

My heart jumped, and I gave him a large grin. That was the first time he had said those three words after the fight. No matter the circumstance, it still made my body shiver. I guess this was what it felt like to be loved, and I wouldn't let it go.

"And this is why I love you."

I reached up and planted a small kiss on his lips. Like always, they tasted sweet and still held the spark we always had. This was what I wanted the most—my mate, my family, and the happiness and love I was surrounded by. Alpha Zaire and Carly were a dead mated pair, wrongfully destined to be together. But Cooper and I were meant to be. Running the pack and finally starting a family together—nothing could go wrong now that we were together.

"You guys are so damn cute."

Both of our heads turned to see Trixie smiling kindly at us. It wasn't like her usual smirk that had been plastered on her face since we met; it was a real one. Jeremy stood a bit to the side but not touching her since he had a faint blush dusted on his cheeks. They were both leaning in the doorway on each side but hadn't entered the room.

"Can I help you, Alpha?" Cooper asked kindly, and I had to hide the smile that threatened to drop when he said those words. He sounded so normal and sweet saying those words.

"Well, as you know, both of our parents are long dead," Trixie explained, and her smile dropped a little when she thought of them. "And I guess it only seems fair to…to…"

"To ask for your blessing." Jeremy finished, running his tongue along the two piercings on his bottom lip. I raised my eyebrow at the new accessory on his face, though it did suit him.

"Blessing?" I questioned, looking strangely at both of them.

"We want to get married just like humans do," my good friend Jeremy said. "We're expecting a pup soon, and we wanted it to happen before he's born."

"You're having a baby also!" I asked, looking over at Trixie wide-eyed. She nodded shyly, and I struggled out of Cooper's hold to hug her. "Why didn't you tell me?"

She shrugged in my embrace. "The timing never seemed right."

"The timing is always right because you love him and he loves you so much. I give you my blessing to get married because true love never fails."

"When did you become so wise?" Trixie asked, removing me from her but resting her hands on my shoulders.

"Since I found the same love you have."

Chapter 27

"I see you're on bed rest." Paige grinned, her eyes sparkling.

I looked up from the current book I was reading and glared at her. She was leaning against the doorframe, trying to hold the weight she was carrying. Of course, she could stand. She was only carrying one little baby. It was unfortunate for me since I had to carry two and had to endure being kicked and punched round the clock.

"Don't even mention it. I am not happy with Cooper's arrangement." I snapped, licking my finger dramatically and flipping the page.

It had been well over two months since the war, and the pups were now full-sized in my belly. All I had to deal with were their two wolf spirits connecting with the human child I was carrying. It was stressful for me because if one of the wolf spirits died inside me, the human child required to have it would too. Another problem was if the human baby died as well, the spirits would die. If the two wolf spirits went into the same child, then both children would die. A multiple birth came with more challenges than a single birth. Right now, there wasn't much I could do but hope for the best.

After finding out I was pregnant on Christmas, Sheila officially told me how far along I was. Now, two months later after the war, I was now about four months pregnant. She had informed me of my due date, but it was a little strange. I mean, they were supposed to be born on Thanksgiving, which would be my tenth month. That's a month longer than the normal nine months. I had asked Cooper about this, and he had explained that a wolf baby, unlike a human baby, would need more time to develop its strength. Considering he's an alpha, our sons needed more time to develop to be sure they would inherit his alpha blood, thus securing the bloodline. It made no sense to me, but I guess that's that. With twins, the process would usually take longer for the bonds to form. The extra time would also provide the Moon Goddess to make the decision for our sons. She controlled what was happening inside me, so she decided when I would give birth.

"Calm your hormones." Trixie laughed at Paige's comments and wobbled in.

"Shouldn't you be resting?" I asked, my eyebrow raising at my mate's sister.

Paige's baby was due around the end of June, maybe July, but it all would depend on her boy. I thought she was six months along, but it's difficult to remember with almost all the women I talk to being pregnant. Every pregnant female preferred to have a girl because then they could match their daughters with my sons and move up a rank higher in the pack, which I couldn't really blame them for. Cooper got really mad over it, but I managed to calm him down.

"Yeah." Paige shrugged before taking Trixie's hand and lying down on the bed with me. "But I hate my room. It's crammed with so many baby gifts."

Paige was given a surprise baby shower a few weeks ago, much to her annoyance. Her hormones caused enough problems at the restaurant since she thought Adam was going to propose to her. He didn't, but she was still happy the pack was celebrating her little accident at such a young age.

"Mine too ever since we told the pack we're having a boy. Jeremy doesn't know what to do with them." Trixie added, patting my hand gently. She wasn't as large as me and Paige, but she was only carrying one baby.

After the war, Trixie and Jeremy went with the warriors to scope out their new land. She found some of her old pack members from when she was little and invited them to join. They accepted without a second thought. Only a few people from Blood Moon left after having the name changed and location being expanded. They turned rogue and joined a pack of rogues in the east.

Not only this, but the mated pair got married soon after. They went on a small honeymoon to a place called Bermuda and requested for their beta to watch over the pack. This beta was Malcolm, my old friend who had threatened my life. I was surprised by Trixie's action, so I went to confront him about it. After a long discussion with him, he told me that he never trusted Alpha Zaire. The rogues that had rescued him were part of Warner's pack. Malcolm used his position in Blood Moon to tell Alpha Zaire to hire rogues, sparking the idea. Malcolm explained that he was protecting me, explaining that the rogues Alpha Zaire had hired were only loyal to him and Warner. Some turned against him, but others remained loyal to him. The reason for his protection was that the girl Savannah I had played music for didn't believe the accusations against me. For some reason, he believed her. Cooper let him go so he could reclaim his position and be a well-appreciated ally with Trixie's pack.

In the end, Malcolm told me he killed his father and took position as the pack's beta. His father was a cruel man, from what I remembered, and had known about Zaire's experimentations on me. He was serious on straightening Blood Moon up by gaining Alpha Zaire's trust so he could later on kill him, but that didn't exactly work out as he planned. Still, he was glad to be serving a better alpha and felt blissful to be their beta.

Warner went back to his rogues and said he was abandoning them. Later that same day, we found him at our doorstep begging for a place in the pack. I couldn't refuse, not after he tried to save me during the war. Cooper allowed him to be a leader of one of our hunting parties, and he accepted it kindly. He was finally a happy man, but something seemed off about him. He kept mentioning his missing mate, and I promised to help him find her.

"You're lucky, Trixie." Paige sighed, knocking me out of my thoughts. "You got engaged and married in less than two months.

"What can I say?" she said. "It's now or never."

"Is Bermuda pretty?" Paige had never left the pack. Being an alpha's daughter and the beta's mate forced her to stay cooped up in one single pack. She had never seen anything more than snow.

"Gorgeous!" Trixie emphasized, tossing her hands up in the air. "There's sand and sun—oh, and we even bought a little summer home so we can go there whenever our kids are born."

"That must be amazing." I smiled, taking her hand and gently patting it. "A summer home would be a great vacation spot after school ends for your kids."

"It's amazing to finally settle down."

We lay in silence for a little longer before both girls had to take their medicine for their baby. I closed my eyes and decided it would be a great time to finally get some rest. The boys seemed more active at night than the day. Cooper was usually gone when I was asleep, and I was awake he's asleep. This had given me a limited chance to see him.

"Oomph!" I said, feeling a powerful kick from one of the boys. They loved to bother me whenever I wanted to snooze.

"Alright there?" I heard someone say. Could I honestly not get one second of peace as a pregnant woman?

"Hey, Cooper." I sighed, holding back a yawn that threatened to leak from my mouth. "I thought you still had some things to take care of?"

It had gotten a little warmer, so now he was always wearing tight-fitting shirts that showed off his muscles. I was happy and proud to call him my mate. He really was an amazing guy.

"Did you seriously forget?" He snorted, and I raised an eyebrow at him. I couldn't recall having any right to move from this bed. "The appointment with Sheila?"

"That was today?" I asked, looking at him strangely. "Really?"

"Yes!" He beamed, leaning down to give me a quick peck on the lips. "She's coming up now."

It only took Sheila a few minutes before she walked in, carrying a heavy load on her back. She looked like she was struggling a little, and I wished I could help her. With such a short body and small frame, she must really be having some difficulty. I looked over at Cooper, who still had a smile on his face.

"Sorry it took so long." Sheila gasped, slowly dropping all the bags on the floor. "All set, Luna?"

In the past months, more and more people had been casual with calling me *Luna*. The only person who never did was Sage, because she was too young to understand much, and Cooper.

Occasionally, he would address me as the luna to the pack, but never actually said it directly to me. That made me feel extremely special.

"There is so much buzzing about your two boys." Sheila clapped excitedly, sitting on the chair that was next to my bed. "The word has officially spread around the entire world."

"How have you been feeling?" Sheila asked, stepping into her doctor phase.

"They keep kicking whenever I try to get some rest. I don't know why they're being so restless." After my brief explanation, Cooper gave me a worried glance.

'You haven't been sleeping?' He linked, a private talk for just the two of us.

'We'll speak about this later.' I didn't want to be having two conversations; it was a little hard to keep up with.

"That is normal…" Sheila trailed off, and I could almost taste the *but* coming. "But they shouldn't be kicking all the time. Mind if I take a quick glance?"

"Go ahead." I smiled kindly, taking Cooper's hand moments after he went to shut the door that was left ajar.

Sheila began checking me with her equipment, and as she did this, I gave Cooper a squeeze. I hoped nothing was wrong. Risking losing either of them would be heartbreaking. I didn't want to go through something like that again. Losing a family member such as Logan was enough to make me never want to let anyone go. I'd already lost so many.

The cool gel was placed on my bare stomach. I hadn't even realized my shirt had been lifted up, but I noticed Cooper's hand trailing along the sides of where the pups were. His had been the one to lift my shirt. I shivered a bit at how cold it was, then closed my eyes and tried to relax. Usually, when I did, there would be a kick.

"They seem to be sleeping at the moment." Sheila chuckled, and I opened my eyes to have a look at the monitor.

There they were, our little bundles of joy, sleeping closely together. Their hands were touching in an affectionate way as they napped. Of course, they decided now was a good time to rest. In front of them were small quarter sized circles where the development of two wolf spirits were showing.

"Their wolves are looking fine too." Sheila nodded happily, giving me a brief glance. "Their tails have just started to form. The snout is a little cute button, and—"

Sheila paused and crinkled her eyes together in wonder. Leaning forward in her seat, she held her breath as she moved the little remote on my stomach. Cooper and I locked eyes, both showing each other worry. We squeezed each other's hands in order to reassure the other that everything was going to be okay. After that, we turned our heads to see a smirking Sheila.

"What's wrong?" I was beginning to worry. One problem and I knew I would officially lose it, or worse.

"They have Cooper's craftiness and Celia's secrecy." This woman was beginning to scare me. "They hid it pretty well. I must say. Perhaps my equipment for your ultrasound had been faulty. This is the first time I'm using my new equipment I got a few days ago."

"W-what are you talking about?"

"You are carrying triplets."

My mouth dropped. It was more shocking than finding out I was pregnant. However, triplets? That's a really big step. I hadn't even had enough energy to squeal or jump. It must be a weird thing judging by the way Cooper was looking at me.

"Three boys? That's a bit unexpected. Did the Moon Goddess seriously believe we would lose at least two of them?" Cooper spoke this time, already getting over his own shock.

"Well, it looks like a..." She looked over at the screen closely. "Oh no."

"What? What is it?" Cooper growled, letting his eyes darken a bit and his claws dig slightly in the hand he was holding.

A look of horror crossed Sheila's face, and she vigorously shook her head. "It's a girl."

"What?" I shouted, feeling my heart drop into my stomach and my eyes fill with tears. "No. No. This can't be happening."

"Oh my god," Sheila whispered, putting her hand over her mouth and closing her eyes as a single tear escaped. "You are having a daughter, which means her fate is sealed. I'm so sorry."

The room was silent as she left quietly. I wiped the gel off my stomach and gently pulled my shirt down. The pack doctor left with one last glance before wiping another tear and looking down at the ground. All I could hear were the small pattering of feet from downstairs from Sage and her friends playing.

"Celia," Cooper murmured, releasing my hand so he could kneel in front of me.

"What are we going to do, Cooper?" I looked into his darkening eyes while mine pooled tears. "I-I can't lose her. She doesn't deserve to be paying for my price, and if anything happens to her—"

"We'll find a way. We always do."

"When!" I shouted, pushing on his chest to get him at least an arm's length away from me.

"One step at a time, babe." He sighed, rubbing his thumbs along my thighs and caressing them gently. "She'll be a secret. You, me, and Sheila are the only ones who should know about her. Our pup will be fine, but we will have to hide her in order for her to be safe."

I shook my head. "It isn't fair for her. She deserves to be happy and live a full life without misery."

"All we can do is pray for the Moon Goddess to do something."

With my stress levels rising, it didn't take long for the boys to wake up and immediately start moving around. My best guess was they were protecting their sister, which made me have a sense of pride that even at a young age, they already cared about her. In the future, I knew they would go out of their way to help her in any way possible, even if it meant keeping it from their parents.

"What about a name?"

"Can I pick this time?" Cooper teased, giving me a devilish smirk before clearing his throat loudly.

"Only if I like it." I sighed, trying not to let this affect me so much. I tried telling myself that our baby would be fine, but I knew deep inside, our life was going to crumble.

"How about Penelope?"

I didn't have to think twice at the name, I knew it was the name she was going to be given anyway. "I love it."

"As much as I love you?"

"Not even close." I breathed, leaning up and kissing his mesmerizing lips. "Our love is like a spark that started off dull but grew to become a fire."

"Have you been reading a lot lately?" My mate snorted, trying to lighten up the mood a little more.

"I think it was a form of figurative speech, yes." A breath of air left my lips, and I tried to fight the tears that wanted to spill.

Penelope would not be taken from us.

The debt would have to be paid off by something else.

I could only hope.

"You okay?" Cooper asked, moving his arms out after giving me a long sensual hug. "I don't want you to be stressing over this. I will handle it, I promise."

I nodded and allowed him to kiss me softly. "Get some rest okay?"

Smiling, I once again kissed him and lay down to get comfortable.

***

Today was Felicity's trial, and everyone was gathered to hear what Cooper was going to do. I had been placed off bed rest just for this occasion. It was hard for some people she was close with to watch her under scrutiny. They all had tears in their eyes, while some had disgusted looks.

I turned my head and looked away from Felicity's judgmental and challenging eyes and looked at my family instead. My heart went out to her mate, whom Felicity had never met. It's sad to think he would've had a traitor as a mate whom he should love, and that was the only thing I regretted while she approached us, hands cuffed and guards surrounding her.

"Felicity," Cooper said, clutching onto my hand tightly as he spoke.

"Cooper." She snarled, earning herself a wave of growls for not addressing him properly, and for her harsh tone towards him.

My mate didn't seem fazed by her rudeness and continued. "Do you know what you have done?"

"Yes," she simply stated, not showing any sign of emotions and didn't even break eye contact with Cooper. "I betrayed the pack."

"Yes, you did, and you will be paying for that shortly." He sucked in a breath before closing his eyes.

'Take your time.' I linked to Cooper, squeezing his hand firmly.

'You shouldn't even be here.' He sighed but not taking his eyes off Felicity.

'I know. I'm sitting. Don't worry. I won't hurt myself or anything like that.' I reassured him before paying attention to what was going outside of our heads.

"You are tried with endangering the welfare of the pack, risking your luna's life, assisting an enemy pack, and overall treason." Cooper's voice was filled with authority as he spoke, and I knew it affected Felicity just by the way she jumped and squirmed. "You will be sentenced to death immediately and privately."

I internally let out a sigh of relief. There was no way I would've been able to watch as they killed her in front of the pack. Instead of watching, I would probably wobble away as fast as I could go.

"Take her away." The guards nodded and dragged Felicity away and closer to her death.

Felicity died two hours later from a silver injection. There was no funeral. There were no tears.

Chapter 28

"Get him out right now!" Trixie shouted at the top of her lungs as she pushed. I cringed, worried I would be the next person to give birth and would have to go through the same pain. Much to my fear, I was due any day now.

Jeremy and Trixie wanted us to witness the birth of their son, but it only made me worried about the upcoming days. We traveled from Ice Moon, while I was pregnant, to Blue Crescent in a matter of hours. Cooper hadn't left my side once and was clutching onto my hand tightly.

"Just a few more pushes and he'll be welcomed into the world." The pack doctor encouraged as she told Trixie what to do.

Cooper and I were in the delivery room, keeping our eyes on Trixie and not what was happening. Sweat was dripping from her brow, and her hand had gotten insanely clammy as she held onto me. Cooper's hands were on my waist, holding me up since my legs could hardly carry the weight I was carrying now.

I cringed when Trixie let out a piercing scream, and Jeremy looked utterly worried. She had been crying and screaming for hours now, in labor and unable to give birth. It was terrifying to watch her struggle, but the doctor just said she needed to keep pushing and try to relax as much as possible. Obviously, her coaxing wasn't going anywhere.

I knew Cooper was silently hurting inside because this was his childhood friend in pain. He knew her since she was little, and here they were years later. It was amazing to believe how fast time went.

She was panting now, trying hard to get in as much air as she could. It went like that for a few more hours before *he* was finally born. We had to leave immediately because it was known for a newly mother wolf to attack anyone within a few feet from her baby, so we left to let her rest. Jeremy was finally a father and we would know his son's name soon enough.

"Can you call Paige?" Cooper asked as we sat in the living room. A few pack members glanced our way but shrugged it off, obviously knowing we were only visiting.

"Why can't you?" I snapped but instantly regretted it. We were getting closer and closer to my due date, and I was more and more on the edge with Ayana coming to take Penelope away.

"I'm sorry. I will."

He gave me a brief smile before walking away with his phone in hand. I looked at him curiously since it was strange that he wasn't using the pack link if it was business. What could he be doing? I shook my head. There was no reason to question him. Pulling out my own phone, I called Paige.

"What?" She breathed, sounding as if she had run a marathon.

"Hello, Paige. It's Celia." I laughed. There was no use mind linking with her, since she hated getting distracted by it.

"Oh, darling! How's Trixie?" Shifting uncomfortably in the sofa I was sitting on, I thought it would just be better to lie down on it. Jeremy and Trixie wouldn't mind, considering my children were making it difficult for me to breathe.

"She's doing fine. The baby was just born so we walked out. How are you?"

"Ugh." She groaned, and I could hear the movement of pots and pans moving. "Shaw won't stop crying. I've done everything—breastfeeding, diaper changing, and bathing him. He hates me, I swear!"

"He's your son. He can't possibly hate you." I snorted, looking at the clock to see it read six in the afternoon. "He probably just misses his daddy."

"I'm here too." Adam's voice rang in the background, and I couldn't help but let out another giggle.

"Tickle him or read him a book." I added, trying to give some ideas into them. Cooper walked in a few minutes later with his phone being shoved in his pocket. "I need to go. I'll see you when we get back."

"You are no help!" Paige shouted just as I ended the call.

"Hey, Celia," Cooper said, walking over to me and crouching down in front of me. I sighed, taking his hand and pressing it on my large stomach as I rested on the couch. "How's my wonderful nephew?"

Shaw Halo Harland was born a couple months ago and was driving Paige crazy. Mainly because he was so much like her and craved so much attention that he never stopped crying. His eyes were aquamarine like Paige's, and he had Adam's dark hair. His skin tone was fairly tan yet had a little freckles dusting his cheeks. He may have looked completely adorable on the outside, but he sure was a little spitfire.

"Causing trouble just like his mother. Who was that on the phone?"

"Wouldn't you like to know?" He cooed, kissing me gently on the nose. "Don't worry about it."

"Would you guys like to see how he's doing?" The pack doctor entered, carrying her clipboard and looking curiously at us. "You'll have to be quiet. Trixie is calm enough to allow visitors."

"Alright then, thank you." Cooper helped me up slowly, making sure not to hurt the pups who had finally stopped kicking with what little room they had. "We'll see them now."

Walking hand in hand, Cooper and I approached the door and stepped in silently. He helped me sit down in the chair not far from Trixie and went to go stand by Jeremy. The scent of cleaners was still evident in the room, but I tried to ignore it by looking at the baby in Trixie's arms.

Trixie was stroking the small head, smiling down at him affectionately. His eyes were closed he slept. A smile twitched on everyone's lips while watching what was taking place. He let out a small squeal as he squirmed in his sleep. It was a beautiful sight to see.

"What's his name?" I hushed, and Trixie's eyes snapped to mine in a guarded way. Her wolf was mainly in control, and right now, she couldn't be trusted, but she was still healing and would need a few more hours before moving.

"Lucian Theodore Eclipse," they both answered, and I couldn't help but let the smile grow. It was a perfect name for him.

"He's beautiful." It was true. He looked just like Jeremy.

"His mate would be contented with his looks alright." Cooper added, letting out a little joking laugh.

"Let's not worry about that until he's old enough to even find her." Jeremy spoke, looking lovingly at his mate for approval.

"Agreed," Trixie said, running her thin fingers along the shape of Lucian's head.

The rest of the day, we spoke in soft whispers, talking about the baby's room and where he'd be going to school to. When I got the chance, I finally gave them the stuffed bear I had gotten him. It was a dark brown bear with bright green eyes and a tuxedo on. Trixie squealed when she saw it, obviously gaining back her strength and control of her body from her wolf.

After a while, I went to get some food and had Cooper walk me towards the kitchen. When the mated pair had taken the pack, they rebuilt and remodeled all the houses the way they wanted it to be. The torture rooms were removed, and Zaire's studies were destroyed completely. The alpha house was built cutely, and the pack house was larger than before. Most members lived in the town nearby, but some wanted to help out and live closer to their alpha's.

Cooper went through the refrigerator while I watched. Now, since I hadn't been allowed to cook, getting home-cooked meals were rare in the pack. Most of the women frequently brought food over, but it was usually the common food like spaghetti and lasagna. I was craving something better. My mate couldn't cook, so he only made peanut butter sandwiches whenever he could.

"There you go, babe." He smiled, placing the food in front of me. I raised an eyebrow.

"You do remember that a peanut butter and jelly sandwich also requires the jelly and the peanut butter, not just bread." I chuckled and watched as he groaned and took the food back. He was distracted for some reason, and I couldn't figure out what it was.

I watched him as he prepared the sandwich, explaining every detail he had to do. It was like teaching a four-year-old when it came to food and preparation. The smile on my face didn't disappear when he came back with the real food.

"Celia?" I turned my head to the left at the noise and noticed a raven haired girl staring back at me. Her brown eyes twinkled when she spoke and stared up at me with admiration.

"I'm sorry?" I quizzed, looking strangely at her. She couldn't be anywhere older than eight, but she did look oddly familiar.

"You don't remember me?" The hurt in her voice was clear as day, which made me feel guilty that I had no clue who she was.

"I've been through a lot, sweetie. If I met you in my past life, I probably have forgotten."

As the pregnancy progressed, my PTSD smoothed out, and I hardly ever had flashbacks. I was now a hundred percent healthy, and I wouldn't let anything ruin that. There wasn't any time to ruin that now that I was carrying triplets. It was difficult enough to deal with everything that had happened a few months ago.

"It's me, Savannah!" She squealed, and my mouth dropped while Cooper looked at me oddly. "Savvy. Remember now?"

"Oh my goodness, sweetheart!" I practically shouted and tried to stand up as best as I could in front of her. Cooper rushed over to me to take some of the weight I was carrying by lifting me slightly off the ground. "I didn't even recognize you. You got so big."

"I'm only seven." She raised an eyebrow at me, which earned her a growl from my mate and made her jump.

"I'm sorry. He can be difficult sometimes." I cooed, kissing Cooper lightly on the nose. "How've you been?"

"Good!" she screamed which made me step back at the sudden noise and dig my heel into Cooper's foot. He winced but didn't say anything. "I just wanted to say congrats on the two boys you're having. What are their names?"

"That's a surprise for everyone." I smiled, flicking my finger on her nose and grinning evilly. "No one will know until they're born."

Savannah soon left, saying she would be seeing me around more now that baby Lucian was born. I didn't want to say I had my own children to take care of, so I just nodded and let her run off when a group of her friends called her over. It took me a second to notice that there was some power radiating off her. It was familiar, but I couldn't put my finger on it.

"That was cute," Cooper mumbled into my hair, kissing just below my ear from behind me.

"You'll be seeing someone like her around." I hushed, looking around to make sure no one had heard.

"I don't think I'll be a good dad." He sighed, and I almost felt bad for this little insecurity.

"No you won't." I whispered, trying my best to spin around and wrap my arms around him. It was a little awkward because our chests were firmly separated with my big belly. "Because you'll be the greatest dad in the world."

"Way to make me feel better," he said, and I could hear the sarcasm in his voice.

"Just you wait. They'll be here before you can say Thanksgiving."

Chapter 29

I cried out in pain, squeezing Cooper's hand tightly as another contraction went through my body. The babies decided now was a wonderful time to be brought into the world. It was Thanksgiving, and I had finished preparing a meal for everyone when my water broke. Emilia nearly passed out from excitement and Paige was laughing as I withered in pain; I had laughed at her a bit when she gave birth to Shaw because of her unique facial expressions.

Now I knew slightly how she felt while I was carried down the flight of stairs, moments away from giving birth. Cooper had been on patrol with Adam and a few higher ranks like Philip. Cooper's father, Patrick, was in charge of the pack for a small amount of time while they were gone.

I knew he was trying to be careful not to bump me into anything while we descended the stairs, but my cries of pain were enough to distract him. I did my best to muffle the screams in Cooper's bare chest, but it really wasn't working. We were given worried glances by fellow pack members, not really understanding what was going on. Yes, I was about to deliver, and yes, I was, in fact, in pain.

"And you laughed at me when I had my contractions." Paige scoffed, meeting us at the bottom of the stairs, holding a sleeping Shaw in one arm and a bottle in the other. "I must say, you look hilarious."

"You're not helping, Paige!" I shouted before crying again when another contraction hit. "Oh, Moon Goddess, you better be prepared for this." I breathed under my breath, earning a small glance from Cooper.

"Just keep breathing. Sheila is waiting for us in the delivery room." Cooper encouraged, giving me a brief and kind glance. "They'll be alright. I promise."

"I mean, I heard it's possible you could die during this hard time. You babies will be alright but—" Paige said.

"Shut up!" Both Cooper and I snapped at her, which made her jump a little in shock. She smiled and shook her head. She left quickly so she wouldn't upset me further.

Except for my frequent whimpers and soft screams, the rest of the way to the delivery room was overall silent. I should've taken that birthing class that both Trixie and Paige took. But compared to them, the pain I was going through was on a whole different level since I was giving birth to triplets. They both only had one.

Before I knew it, Cooper gently laid me down on a soft bed. Sheila was still preparing things and getting monitors out in case complications from the birth arose. My hands were getting sweaty around Cooper's hand and so was the one gripping the sheets around me. Unlike the usual births of a future alpha, I didn't want anyone to be recording mine or being near me. This was mostly for Penelope's safety. If one knew, so would the entire pack and later, Ayana.

Sheila gently and swiftly removed my underwear, and it was at that moment I thanked Paige for giving me the idea to be wearing a loose dress all the time. My legs were spread, and I looked over at Cooper for any sign of reassurance. He gave me a nod, and I let in a slow breath before turning to Sheila. She was finally done and ready to begin.

"Alright, Celia, now all you have to do is breathe and push." Sheila encouraged, looking up at me and giving me a small smile. "Everything will be fine."

"It's okay, baby. Just keep doing what she asks." Cooper soothed me, running his hand up and down my arm.

"Push."

I cried and screamed in pain while I did as she said, digging my nails sharply in Cooper's hand. He winced but didn't say anything and gave me an encouraging smile. How was I going to give birth to three? I was already having difficulty with the first baby.

"One more time, Celia. I see the head," Sheila said briskly.

I pushed again. My forehead was damp. I was sweating just about everywhere. The scent of both Cooper and I combined hit me, and I heard the little wail of our baby being born. I sighed but still felt the occurring contractions telling me I still had to keep pushing.

"It's a boy." Sheila held him to me and turned to Cooper.

He nodded, and my mate held his hand out and took our firstborn son. His aquamarine eyes sparkled while he looked down with pride, and he couldn't wipe the grin off his face.

"Clayton."

"Nice to meet you, Clayton." Sheila cooed softly while I breathed heavily on the bed. "But Mommy needs to get the others out before she could say hello to you."

Cooper hesitantly handed our son to Sheila, and I had to hold back a growl when my wolf tried surfacing. Now was not the time.

Sheila left the room briefly, saying our first baby needed to get cleaned up and checked over to see if he was okay by the other pack member who was helping her. She promised she would clean and check our daughter herself to keep the pack members from finding out. She came back in, and we resumed.

Next was Rylan. He came out a lot quicker than his brother. Cooper swiftly told Sheila his name. I was gasping for breath now, huffing and puffing as I struggled. It broke my heart to have him taken away, but I had to focus on his sister. I wasn't given a chance to hold either Clayton or Rylan because I had to quickly gather my strength back to push again.

"You have to try to be as quiet as possible. Okay, Celia?" Sheila whispered. "No one should know she's being born now."

"Just keep pushing," Cooper whispered as I was forced to bite his thumb to stay quiet. Tears were in my eyes and falling freely now that I was really struggling.

"You are never doing this to me again, Cooper." I breathed, biting him again and feeling my canines start to show. "You hear? I don't want to get pregnant again."

"Yeah, I really don't want to see you in pain like this again." He chuckled humorlessly before letting out a small yelp when my sharp teeth broke his skin.

"Push again, Celia!" Sheila growled, lowly looking down at me with crazy eyes. "She's right there. I can already see her."

"I can't." My energy was depleting, and I knew these last few pushes were going to completely drain me.

"Just a few more and I promise it will be over." She smiled kindly, and I closed my eyes and did what she said.

I heard a little wail before it was muffled by Cooper coming in and trying to keep her cries low. My body felt numb, and I closed my eyes and tried to catch my breath. It was done. It was finally over. As I felt my body beginning to recuperate, I only hoped my children were healthy.

"Luna." I looked up, and Cooper's eyes widened as he hid Penelope with his body.

A pack member was standing there, holding both boys with two small ankle bracelets on them. From what I could see, it had a name, color, and a time of birth. "They're all healthy and perfectly fine. They're just missing their mommy."

I weakly held out my hands, and she happily handed me my children. While this was happening, Cooper slipped Penelope over to Sheila, and she ran off to give her a checkup.

Clayton absolutely looked beautiful. He had the same eyes as Cooper, and I could see little blond curls forming on his eyebrows. They were small and thin, but as his mother, I could easily catch the most minor details on his face—even the little birthmark the size of a dime just below his ear was easy to see.

"Hi, Clayton." I cooed, giving him a little peck on his nose as he closed his eyes and went to sleep. "Mommy's here. Go to sleep."

"Hey, buddy." Cooper was grinning, kissing him on the forehead before turning to Rylan. "Rise and shine, Rylan."

Rylan let out a little squirm from his nose and struggled to open his eyes. He was a sight to see. I slowly put my finger into his open hand. Slowly, he closed his hand around it and squeezed it rather firmly. I allowed him to get a good look at me as best as he could and hummed a little melody for him just to get used to my voice. He seemed content and closed his eyes immediately.

"You're so beautiful," I whispered, and he really was.

Rylan was nowhere near close to his a minute older brother. His hair was white like mine, and his skin was a lot paler than Clayton's. Before he went to sleep, I could see his eyes were a sparkling violet just like mine but had little less shine, which made it seem darker. Other than that, he was a little less plump and didn't move much.

I handed Cooper our son Clayton, who was fast asleep but was rested wrongly on me. My body was still tired, but I was trying to stay up for Penelope's sake. She deserved to feel her mother before she had to be kept safely in our room while the rest of the family members shared in this very exciting time with the Clayton and Rylan.

"I have her," Sheila whispered, looking around to make sure that the coast was clear before bringing our daughter in. Penelope was all bundled in a little pink blanket, and from what I could tell, she had a lot of energy in her.

"Oh wow." I breathed, taking her in my arms and holding her close. Cooper took Rylan's sleeping body from me and sat down comfortably in the chair beside the bed. "She's gorgeous."

"That she is." Sheila smiled before going to the door. "I'll wait outside so no one comes in."

"Thank you," Cooper said before stroking the back of both boys' heads with his large hand.

Sheila left quietly. I could hear the noise from the people outside, wondering what the children's names were. She closed the door quickly and softly, trying not to wake the boys up but also not to let anyone see Penelope. I let out a breath, relieved that no one had seen her and unwrapped a few wrinkles of the blanket that covered her face.

"Welcome to the world, Penelope."

She let out a happy 'goo' sound and kicked her feet around. I smiled and felt the tears well up in my eyes. My baby girl was a lot smaller than her brothers, and I was afraid something like a little kiss on the cheek would hurt her. She was so beautiful, and it was a shame she couldn't be seen by anyone. Maybe when she turned sixteen, she would see the outside world of the pack and not have to worry about Ayana. Though she never said she would leave us alone, I was confident our daughter would be strong enough to protect herself. Not only this, but I was hopeful by then she would have a mate who would protect her from Ayana.

I sniffed. "It's Mommy." Reaching down, I kissed the top of her head, feeling a single tear drop down onto her nose. I wiped it away when I looked down at her.

Our skin touched, and I realized just how cold she felt. It only encouraged me to hold her closer, but even I felt myself growing weak. Our family would be fine. My family would be happy together, no matter what. I shouldn't worry about her being taken away from me. I wouldn't let it happen.

"She can't be by herself while we're gone, Cooper," I said. "Our baby doesn't deserve to be all alone all her life."

"Give it a few days. We can figure something out," he whispered, trying to blink back a few tears that threatened to fall. "We will keep her from everyone for now. If Ayana doesn't show up in the first year she's born, we'll show everyone Penelope and explain everything. I know we didn't agree on this, but we need our daughter to live a good life."

"That isn't fair." Penelope's eyes opened wider at my voice, and she gave a big grin before waving her arms around. "This is all my fault. I should've never made that deal."

"But we never would've had our family." Cooper soothed me, running his hand up and down my arm with a struggle because he was still carrying the boys.

"You don't know that," I said briskly.

Cooper didn't answer. Sheila could've been wrong the entire time. I mean, doctors weren't always right. There could've been a slip up or something. This deal never would've had to be made. I could've been less stressed and worried about what could've happened.

"A week." I urged, kissing Penelope gently on the forehead. I looked up at Cooper. "A week until we tell the pack about her. I don't want to live in fear of Penelope being taken from me. That's something I don't think I would be able to survive."

"I know she deserves better," Cooper finally said, cuddling the boys closer to his chest. "And I don't want you to blame this on yourself. This was a deal you made, but it was Ayana who bargained with you for a family."

Tears fell down from my eyes, and I sucked in a long breath to prevent myself from sobbing. "I just don't want to be like my parents."

"Hey, look at me," he said, bringing his thumb under my chin and lifting my head up a little. I brought my eyes to his. "You will never be like your parents because unlike you, they didn't fight to keep their family."

I didn't say anything, just closed my eyes and let out a breath of air. We would never lose Penelope. I'd rather die than have Ayana take her away from us. Maybe we could arrange a new deal, one that would be more beneficial to her than our daughter. If the time came, I'd kill myself just to give our daughter a chance to grow and have her own family.

***

I woke up to the sound of my babies crying. I rolled over in the bed growling. This was the third time that I had woken up tonight, and Cooper wouldn't even wake up. He's lucky he's a heavy sleeper and didn't have to change the diapers or feed either our sons or daughter. I should be pestering him, but he was supposed to wake up in the morning for his duties.

He took a week off to spend time with our new family. I knew he didn't mind looking after Penelope while I had to show off our boys to people. Most wondered why he wasn't with me. I was forced to lie to them by saying that Cooper was sleeping, but the truth was that he was with Penelope the entire time keeping her from crying and screaming.

Paige was overjoyed to be Rylan's godmother, and Adam, his godfather. I knew it was a good choice since Paige was also the middle child. It just seemed to fit our decision. Sage found out soon enough that I gave her the role of being Clayton's godmother, and when the time came when she found her mate, he would be Clayton's godfather. She was hardly involved with pack politics, but since her sister was the mate of a beta and her older brother was the alpha, I just thought that she needed another title than the former alpha's daughter.

Emilia and Patrick were officially grandparents. As planned, no one knew about Penelope, and they hardly suspected anything. We got really close when both boys were crying and Penelope giggled. I had to explain to them that it was probably just a hiccup. I didn't like lying to family and friends, but my daughter should always come first.

"Hey, Penelope." I soothed her, picking up the crying girl and holding her in my arms.

Ever since giving birth, I had been wearing nightgowns to bed because it was comfortable to sleep in. When it was really later and everyone was asleep, I sometimes carried Penelope with me in the chair.

"This is the third time you've woken Mommy up now." My lips touched her forehead, but she still continued to cry. "What's the matter this time?"

At midnight, she needed a diaper change, and at two, she was hungry. It was already three in the morning, and upon checking her, she seemed perfectly fine to me. I checked her diaper and found nothing that indicated she needed a changing. I fed her an hour ago, and she went to sleep immediately, so that wasn't it. She wasn't coughing, so she couldn't be sick.

"She okay?" I turned around to see Cooper rubbing his eyes. "I heard you get up, and your wolf woke up my own."

"I'm sorry. You can go back to sleep," I whispered and turned to look at our baby in my arms. "I don't really know. I fed her an hour ago, and her diaper's clean and fresh."

"Let me hold her." Before I could protest that he needed sleep, he took Penelope in his arms and got a good look at her. She stopped crying immediately.

"And you worried you would be an awful father." I scoffed, turning around to check and make sure the boys were still sleeping.

After sneaking Penelope into our room, we locked the door. Each of us had a set of keys—one for our room and one for the nursery that was still being prepared next door. Occasionally, Cooper would slip pink into the room for Penelope, so she wouldn't be surrounded by just blue. The children would be raised in a singular room before they were given their own rooms when they were older. The only problem was that no one knew we had a daughter, so gifts were only for baby boys. I wanted our daughter to grow up believing something was hers. That was when we decided we would sneak pink toys and clothing for our daughter.

Paige seemed suspicious about the entire thing, but I only told her they were newborns and needed to be treated as such and that the colors generally didn't hold that much meaning.

"Either that or you're a worse parent than me." Cooper teased, which only earned him a gently whack on his bicep since he was holding Penelope.

"Just keep doing what you're doing." I kissed him gently on the cheek before going around him and heading back to bed. It was time I got some deserved sleep.

A few minutes later, Cooper joined me in bed saying that Penelope had fallen asleep the moment I left. He laughed and kissed me softly on the lips before tossing the bed sheets over him. I rolled my eyes and shook my head moments before closing my eyes and finally falling asleep.

I'd tell the pack about Penelope this morning.

Chapter 30

I closed my eyes, letting the few puffs of snow hit my face. My thoughts were clouded with worry, but I knew it was the right thing to do. Cooper was preparing, getting the pack organized so no one would be able to leave so we could explain the circumstance and the necessity to protect our daughter. Everyone, besides the scouts, was asked to meet in the auditorium. It was stressful, especially for me, but it had to be done.

"I knew I'd find you out here." A voice chuckled lowly, and I opened my eyes only to be blinded by the sun. After adjusting, I saw a face in front of me.

"I thought you have duties to fulfill." I snorted, sitting up and dusting the snow off my fluffy soft coat.

"What?" Jeremy squeaked. "I can't visit an old friend?"

"You have a son to take care of." I pointed out, giving him a smooth glare. He shouldn't let his mate take care of the pup alone.

"Well, you have two." His laugh was almost enchanting, and I couldn't help but let out a giggle. There was a long pause before he spoke again. "I heard about the meeting you're having. Are you pregnant again or something?"

I glared at him. "I am never going through the pain of childbirth again unless Cooper happily agrees to do it himself."

"Males can't give birth."

"Exactly."

He laughed before collapsing beside me, causing the snow to fly up in the air with his large frame.

When Trixie became the alpha, it didn't take long for her to pass the title and responsibilities to Jeremy. Seeing him now after quite some time, I noticed that his shoulders became wider, and his arm muscles doubled in size. He still had his snakebites, two piercings under his bottom lip, although I had pestered him to get rid of them because it could be a bad influence for his growing boy.

Trixie lost all the baby weight quickly and once again showed off her exquisite body. Jeremy didn't seem to mind, as long as no one looked at his mate wrongly. She had a mind of her own and was eligible to do what she wanted. He wasn't exactly joyful to have her flaunting everything, but he loved to see that side of her.

"Are you going to be staying for the meeting?" I asked, worried how he would react if he found out this entire time I had a hidden daughter.

"Trixie brought Lucian. They're inside, so yes."

"Both of them are here?" I asked excitedly, hopping up from my sitting position.

"Yes…" He looked unsure as he stood up.

I sprinted out of the backyard and towards the pack house. I wanted to see Lucian now that he was older. Who knew how big Lucian got. My legs carried me up the few steps and closer to the door where a crowd had gathered. Excitement bubbled inside of me, making me push past just about everyone.

"Hi, Lucian!" I squealed, running over to where Trixie was holding him close. My hand pinched his rosy cheeks as he smiled up at me, flailing his sock-covered feet around.

"What about me, Celia?" Trixie asked, faking hurt. A few members left, not wanting to hear our exaggerated girl talks.

"And Trixie." My tone held boredom, and my friend hit me playfully on the arm before holding her son to me.

"Hi, sweetie." I cried, kissing Lucian all over his face. He let out a baby shriek and let his hands roam my face. "You got big, didn't you?"

"He's only a few weeks old, Celia. I don't think my son can answer you." My eyes rolled at her comment. "How are Clayton and Rylan?"

"They've been waking us up a lot. I keep telling Cooper I'll take care of them, but only he can put them to sleep. It's difficult when he has duties the next morning and is up all night taking care of them." I explained, tickling her baby's feet.

"You need a week out." She smiled, taking Lucian back into her arms. "When we were younger and our packs would meet, Cooper and I would go to this really nice cabin and hunt in wolf forms. It's secluded, and you could definitely relax there."

"Where is it?" I asked, crossing my arms. In my head, I could feel Cooper trying to get through the wall, but he needed to be ignored for now.

"It's in the US in Maine."

"What about my kids?" My only fear was them getting hurt while I was gone. I would never forgive myself if anything would happen to them just because I wanted a week with my mate.

"Emilia and Patrick can take care of them, or they can spend some quality time with their daddy's best friend." She raised her free hand. "I will gladly do it."

"I'll speak to Cooper about it." I thanked her and left to see what Cooper wanted.

The meeting was in an hour, and I still needed to get ready. I didn't even realize how much time I spent talking with Trixie, but that's understandable since we had some strange bond with each other. Call it friendship, but I'd never had something so much like family than with her. She's the sister I never had.

I passed some pack members who gave me a small smile or a greeting. Everyone was here now for the pack meeting. They probably expected some big news, like us getting married or having another baby, but it was bigger. The secret about Penelope was bigger any other secrets I had kept before.

When I finally reached our bedroom, I was completely out of breath. After multiple attempts to steady myself, I opened the door and snuck through the small crack I made and shut it quickly.

"Oh my god." I breathed, closing my eyes and placing both hands on the door for support.

The second I turned around, I was crushed against the door which made me squeak in surprise. Hands traveled down my shoulders and on my hands before firmly gripping my waist. I gasped when I felt lips sucking on my mark. I bit my own lip to prevent myself from moaning. I didn't open my eyes. I didn't have to. I knew who it was.

"Cooper." I panted, running my hands down, my fingertips brushing his solid muscles on his stomach. He growled in response before removing his face from my neck.

"Got you." He chuckled and kissed my forehead lovingly.

"You got me." I rolled my eyes and looked up at his extremely tall frame.

"Can't I have a little fun?" He shrugged, turning away from me and heading over to the cribs.

Crossing my arms, I shook my head and soon followed him.

"Hey, Penelope." I soothed, scooting past my mate and reaching my arms out to hold our girl. "Mommy's back."

After drowning her in kisses, I looked at her in my arms while cradling her around. She was glowing with happiness once she showed her toothless smile to me. Putting her close to my face again, I nuzzled her nose and pecked it softly. She was gorgeous in her little velvet dress, the one almost identical to the one I wore on Christmas.

"She's beautiful," I whispered, looking at the perfect combination of Cooper and me before us.

"She gets it from her mother," Cooper whispered in my ear before kissing my temple and scooping the two boys up in his arms.

Clayton protested, wiggling in his father's arms while Rylan cheered in happiness. I smiled, realizing how different they were. It was simple to tell who got the alpha gene and who got my omega gene, but they looked the same. Penelope was difficult because she had her mood swings but would also be happy seconds afterward.

"What if this is a bad idea?" I asked, looking up at him with glazed eyes. "I want to keep her with me forever."

"She'll always be with us." Cooper leaned over to kiss Penelope's head before kissing my own. "I promise everything will be fine."

Realization hit me that I had to get ready, and I placed Penelope back in her crib. "I need to get ready."

I ran out of the room and into the bathroom, grabbing a few hairpins along the way. Stopping in front of the mirror, my hands guided their way through it and took most of the knots out. All my twirling and clipping was complete, and I finally had a formal looking bun at the top of my head. After making sure no hairs would fall out, I went back into our room.

Cooper was leaning back in a rocking chair, a gift from my baby shower, and was holding Rylan as he cried. He watched me closely while I sprinted to the closet, grabbing the first dress I saw. It was navy blue dress with a low neckline, but it would have to do. In seconds, I was stripped down and nudging my way into the tight cocktail dress.

Tossing the clothes I had worn aside, I skipped barefoot in the direction where my shoes were aligned neatly in the corner. I could still feel Cooper's eyes boring into my body and had a difficult time not being affected by his gaze. The heels I slipped on were silver and matched the built-in belt around the curve on my waist.

"Alright, I'm ready." I breathed, closing my eyes and stopping directly in front of my mate.

He looked over at the clock. "Seven minutes."

"You timed me?" I shouted, debating whether to throw a shoe at him and risk waking Rylan up or not. "Also, you seem very affectionate to me today. It's not that I'm complaining, but we need to do this."

"Just wanted to distract you a second longer." Cooper sighed before standing up and kissing my cheek. "Everything will be fine."

He picked Clayton up before looking over at me and leaving with the two boys. I breathed and turned to look at a giggling Penelope. She had no idea what may happen after this. Let's just hope everything would be fine like Cooper had said. It's only a matter of time before Cooper told me in our mind link to bring her down to meet everyone.

Our plan was for Cooper to bring the boys down to the pack first and speak to everyone about our situation before I came down. He had explained the bits and pieces about my past for everyone to fully understand what was going on. After that, he would tell the pack of my infertility and why I couldn't have children. It was painful to relive it and I didn't want to bring it up to the pack, but it had to be done. When everything was explained, Cooper would say he had one more secret to reveal, and I would come down.

That's when I waited. Cooper let out mind link open the whole time so I would know every single thing he was saying. Throughout the speech, Paige had kept sending me little messages, telling me that she's there for me and that everything was fine. I thanked her with each one assurance, but when she suddenly stopped, I grew worried. That was when I was bombarded with different pack members asking if I was okay and where I was until Cooper told me through our mind link to come down.

My arms reached out to hold Penelope, and she didn't make a sound, probably because she could sense what was going on. I kissed her one last time on her head before opening the bedroom door. It was freakishly quiet as my feet carried me down the hall and closer to the stairs. Faintly, I could hear Cooper talking from the bottom floor and the gasps and murmurs that spread throughout the walls. This was it.

"Celia and I...your luna and I, your Alpha, have one more secret to share." Cooper's voice boomed, and my heart grew louder, obviously overpowering Penelope's slow smaller one.

I gulped, my hands growing shaky while holding our daughter. She let out a small groan and a yawn before staring up at me. I didn't know if it was her twinkling purple eyes or the little smile that reassured me that everything was going to be okay, but I grew calm. My own daughter was trying to comfort me, even at such a tender age.

Looking down at the small steps leading to where Cooper stood, I could make out the large group of people looking curiously around the room. They probably heard my beating heart. They looked confused. I couldn't blame them.

The pack looked up and stopped all movements when my heel landed on the step. Cooper turned around to look at me and held out his hand. I took it with Penelope in one arm.

Everything was silent as I glanced at our beautiful daughter once more before handing her over to my mate. All jaws dropped, and some had a betrayed look on their faces. I gulped and laced my hands together in front of me. I looked down on the floor, and faintly heard Cooper kiss our daughter's cheek.

"This is our daughter, Clayton and Rylan's sister and granddaughter to Emilia and Patrick. She was born on the same day as her brothers." That was usually how a new member from the higher rank was introduced.

"Godchild to my brother Logan and his unknown mate," I whispered, bringing my hand to Cooper's and blinking back the tears.

"When Celia, your luna, couldn't have my pups, she made a deal with a witch." Everyone gasped, and I couldn't even look up at my pack because of how disappointed I was with myself. "The witch gave her a potion so she could bear a child, but with this offer came a price. She has to give up her firstborn daughter and give it to the witch. If she hadn't agreed to the term, then my sons and daughter wouldn't be here. I wouldn't have an heir to take my place as your alpha in the future."

Everything clicked in the pack's minds, and everyone stayed quiet. Cooper nudged me, and I sucked in a breath before looking up. All of our members were on one knee and bowing their heads in respect towards…who? I looked over at my mate in utter confusion. He smiled and lifted Penelope back into my arms.

They accepted her. It was now obvious. She was smiling and giggling in my arms. I laughed, feeling the tears pool down my cheeks while I gazed at her. The pack would protect her. There's no doubt about that.

"I knew it." A voice boomed, and everyone turned around at the sudden sound.

Chapter 31

I pulled Penelope closer as the figure came barreling towards us. Cooper brought me closer to him, but that didn't stop a pair of arms from encasing me. Ripped out of my mate's arms, I let out a squeak when I was lifted up in the air. The arms squeezed tightly, and I could practically feel my eyeballs about to burst out of their sockets.

"I knew you were having a third child." The woman cried, and I couldn't help but roll my eyes.

"How did you know, Emilia?" I asked, and Cooper angrily took our daughter from my arms. That got me wondering where Clayton and Rylan were. My eyes scanned the room before I found Trixie and Paige cooing the life out of their children and mine.

The room had grown less tense, and each pack member would interrupt our conversation saying they wouldn't speak a word about Penelope. Cooper kissed my cheek before walking off to join his sister and best friend. That left me with just his parents. Wonderful.

"You were as big as a whale, darling!" Emilia emphasized, raising her arms high above her head to show my size. "But a *girl!*"

"Yeah." I breathed, turning around to see Cooper chatting with his closest friends. I never really got to know them, but the men seemed to be congratulating him.

"I am truly sorry about what's been placed on you. With everything you've been through, you sure are strong." Emilia placed a hand on my shoulder and gave it a reassuring squeeze. "We'll have guards around every entrance and one stationed at your bedroom or hers."

"I'll have to talk to Cooper about it." I smiled before kissing her softly on the cheek and giving Patrick a friendly goodbye wave.

Murmurs were sparking up as I fished my way through the large crowd of chatting people. If I were still the little omega I once were, I would've run out as fast as possible, but being mated to Cooper had given me a new way of living. I was hardly scared anymore, unless it's for my three pups.

"Hi, my beautiful daughter." I snatched Penelope out of Cooper's hands before he could even realize, and I kissed her gently on the cheek before looking up at my mate. "Hi."

"Hey, babe." He grinned, placing a kiss on my forehead before turning back to the man he was speaking to. "Everything's set right?"

"Indeed, Alpha." He nodded before bowing his head in respect and scampered away.

I turned to face my glorious mate. "What was that all about?"

"Nothing," he said before turning around and walking over to a group of men calling for him. I sighed, realizing he was busy and turned to talk to Paige and Trixie.

They greeted me kindly before both their mate came over to them and scooped them up and ran off. Hurt pierced my heart when both Adam and Jeremy walked off with both women screeching at them. I looked down at both of their boys lying on the mat chewing on their toys. Shaw and Lucian were cooing, their hands flying all over the place. My sons were there as well, laying in their little pens as they squealed.

I took Rylan first, since he was slowly rolling around, which was dangerous, and scooped him into my free arm. Penelope was rested in my hands as well. When I reached for Clayton, I had a hard time bending down to get to him. A huff left my lips, and I twisted in an awkward way which earned me a slight pain running down my back. I winced but tried again.

"Need help?" I didn't get to answer the voice before Clayton was lifted up. Slowly, I stood up, dusting off my dress in the process with the back of my hand.

"Thank you." I smiled before coming face to face with an old friend. "Warner." It was astonishing to see him here, but I didn't mind much.

"How's my former beta doing?" He chuckled since that part of my past had turned into an inside joke. Looking down at Clayton, he spoke again, "I must say he's got his father's kind eyes and his mother's smile."

"You're too kind." I rolled my eyes before struggling to get my son back in my arms. "Yeah, I trust you're strong enough to hold him."

"Such trust you have in me." Warner smirked, tickling Clayton under the chin, earning him a loud cry of happiness from my son.

"You saved me. Remember?" I asked, reminding him how he prevented Zaire from choking me to death and stalled him, giving Cooper enough time to save me. "I never really got the chance to thank you."

"I think given that Rylan's middle name is *Warner*, it's a dead giveaway that you were grateful for my help." Of course, a sly former rogue like him would find a way to sneak a peek at the birth certificates. They were in a safe in Cooper's office for safe keeping. Every child born by an alpha bloodline had a certificate that was stashed for safe keeping. It prevented any person from trying to take the pack if they believed the alpha wasn't part of an alpha bloodline. "Don't look at me like that. I found it flattering."

I rolled my eyes. "Don't you have a mate to look for?"

Warner's face grew serious. "You mean the one that was pregnant with my son and fled the day she told me? It's been a year now, and I can feel that she has passed away."

Her name was Josephine. She was more of a tomboy and went by Jo. She was beautiful from what he told me and from what I heard. She was very submissive and was a maid in a few of the elders' homes. It would've been great to meet her. Finding his son was his biggest concern now that she was gone. Luckily, he was handling her death well. I had the suspicion that he was staying alive for his child, hoping one day they would meet.

I didn't know Jo personally, but looking back, I missed the signs. When I had attempted to become Warner's beta, he had given in so easily to having me go back to my mate. At that time, Jo must've been gone and he must've felt her pain. At that time, he must've also felt her death. This was the first time he had really mentioned what happened. All I knew about him was the fact he had a mate. I just didn't know how terrible it had been for him.

"I'm sorry. I never should've brought her up." I sighed. "I'll see you soon, okay?"

"Yeah." He nodded before fleeing. It was wrong of me to even bring up the idea of his mate.

A pack member greeted me before giving Clayton to Emilia, who happened to pass by me again and took him without a second thought. I asked her to take the boys for a little longer while I showed everyone Penelope. She deserved a bit more time with the pack before having to take her nap. She would be sleeping soon.

I walked off, saying goodbye to Clayton and Rylan. It was hard leaving them, but Emilia was a mother of three, just like me, so I didn't have to worry much. Pack members greeted us as I searched for Cooper. He just disappeared, and this got me worried that something had happened. The pack had accepted Penelope, and now my mate had gone missing.

Paige and Adam were nowhere to be found, and Shaw was in Sheila's arms, being fed. It was the same thing for Jeremy and Trixie; their son was being held by his great aunt. Lucian had gotten a lot larger since he was born, and he turned out to look more and more a lot like Jeremy whenever they came to visit.

I found the kitchen and let out a sigh of relief when it was a little less crowded than the auditorium. However, Cooper wasn't still there. He couldn't have gone up to our room or his office because he had taken the day off from his duties to spend time with us.

"Celia!" I turned at the voice from outside and quickly went to the window to see the messenger boy running out of the forest.

Scanning the room, I asked someone to hold Penelope. I gave it to one of the higher ranks to be watched after before running out of the house. Whatever was going on had to be important, otherwise he would've gone to Cooper for more help.

"What is it?" I said once I made it outside into the chilly winter landscape.

He gasped for breath, before speaking. "Alpha Cooper needs to see you at the lake."

"The pond?" I questioned, confusion easily heard in my tone. "Why would my mate want to meet me there? Is he okay?"

"He only spoke to me through the link, Luna." He apologized before dusting off the snow that coated his clothing and brushed past me to go inside.

My feet carried me quickly to the direction of the lake. I remembered following Cooper out there many times before and during my early pregnancy. It wasn't difficult until I had really gotten larger. We skated together and even had the hockey game he promised. It was fun, to say the least.

It was difficult to even try to walk in the snow in heels, so I kicked them off and walked barefoot. Obviously, it was cold, but since I had officially became a luna, my body heat and resistance to cold had increased over time. I wasn't as warm-blooded as Cooper to the point where I'd wore t-shirts all the time, but I hardly felt my hands growing cold and blue.

I looked up, the sun was in the middle of the sky and shining bright with its yellow hue. There wasn't a cloud in the sky, which was pretty uncommon since it was always snowing. Snow sprinkled from above. It looked almost magical while I walked around looking for any sign of my mate.

After arriving at the pond, I heaved a sigh of relief when I saw Cooper standing right where the frozen water and the land met. He was facing away from me, fidgeting with the collar of his shirt. I could hear his heart beating rapidly, which worried me because it was usually at a very steady pace.

I stepped on a twig, which caught his attention. He turned around. A grin showed up on his face when he saw me. His heart rate seemed to slow down after seeing that I had arrived, but still, he looked overly nervous. I grew worried but didn't speak up when he held his hand out to me. Taking it greedily, we edged our way onto the ice together.

Whatever he was nervous about seemed to go away because he was finally calm and swinging our conjoined hands back and forth. The ice below us seemed to be holding our weight perfectly fine now, but I still had an itch that we could fall through and die. My grip on Cooper increased dramatically after that thought.

"Why did you bring me all the way here when we have three little bundles of joy back at the house?" I asked when we were about halfway in the middle of the lake.

"You'll see when we get there." He pointed to the small spot on the lake.

We were in complete silence the rest of the time we walked. No words were needed to be spoken because we had the rest of our lives to talk about just anything. We had shed enough tears and shared enough laughs to afford a moment in silence.

After Logan's death anniversary, I was a few weeks from giving birth, which was difficult for me. I wasn't supposed to visit his grave and grieve, but I had Malcolm sneak me into his territory and allowed me to see my brother's grave for the first time ever. I wanted to go alone, but Cooper found me ten minutes later, face beet red and fists clenching. That was, until he noticed my sadness and stayed with me the rest of the night, not that he could even stay away from me for such a long time while I was in pain.

I was pulled out of my thoughts from the day my brother died when we stopped walking. That finally gave me the chance to look over everything he had done. Now I understood exactly what he was talking about with some of the pack members earlier and why he was asking if things were *prepared*—why he got all the high ranks, besides Emilia, to leave and ignore me. It was all because of what was in front of me. They were too busy making *this* to even talk to me. Paige would've obviously slipped and told me that's why Adam snatched her away as fast as he could.

In front of me was a baby blue blanket neatly laid out on the ice. A few battery-operated candles were spread out, creating a romantic feel to it. Holding the blanket down was a little basket filled with a bottle of wine, a loaf of bread, and what looked like a pot of soup.

I gasped, completely surprised by how much effort Cooper had put into making this look so beautiful, but what was it for? I couldn't remember if it was a holiday. Christmas was in another couple of weeks, and it wasn't even my birthday.

"Happy anniversary," Cooper said from behind me. I looked up at him, confused.

"We met before December," I stated matter-of-factly, giving him a worried look, like he had gone crazy.

"No, today was the day we first *mated*."

I blushed, immediately remembering all the preparation Paige had done to get me ready. It was hard to believe he had remembered it when I had completely forgotten. I guess I was too worried about introducing Penelope to the rest of the pack.

"Oh…" I looked down again at the ground. I was an awful mate to forget something important like this.

"Let's just eat." Cooper smiled, guiding me to sit down on the hard blanketed ice.

I moved so my dress didn't lift up when I sat down, and I got comfortable while Cooper poured the wine. It was relaxing while we sat and looked out into the forest. It was times like these when I forgot about all the harsh things the world really had and focused on the one person that would always make me happy. Nothing could possibly ruin this moment.

"So, who planned this?" I asked, taking a sip of my wine while he cut the bread and handed me a piece.

"I did. Everyone else just offered to help their luna be happy." His words touched me. I never knew how much the pack really loved me.

We were silent for a while until he spoke again. "This was actually supposed to be our first date, but with everything that had happened and then you giving birth, I never could really get you out of the house."

I rolled my eyes and leaned over and gave him a little kiss on his lips. "It doesn't matter. I love this."

We talked, and as I was finishing my bowl of soup, Cooper seemed to watch my every move. He was just staring at me, but I didn't seem to mind since he was almost always doing that, admiring me. It's his usual thing, especially at night when I was seconds from falling into a deep and peaceful sleep. Although, this time seemed a little different.

While spooning up the remainder of my soup in the bowl, my eye caught something. Whatever it was in my soup had not looked edible. Cooper appeared to be holding his breath when I put the bowl down and fished my finger through the spinach and chicken that was left. After a few seconds of searching for the item I had seen, I brushed against something hard. I tried my best to scoop it up.

With little struggle, I held it in my hand and gasped at the sight.

Chapter 32

It was completely and utterly beautiful to say the least. Memories flooded back to the staircase filled with photos of Cooper's family tree. Tears threatened to leave my eyes while I stared at *it*. I sat up to get a good look at it. When I did, Cooper was on one knee, keeping his gaze on me.

Slowly, he took the ring from my hand before speaking those four words: "Will you marry me?"

At that exact moment, I let out a small breathless laugh before nodding my head and lunging at him. "Yes," I whispered.

It all came back to me now, and I finally understood why Emilia was missing the ring on Christmas. He must've wanted to ask me on that very day, but I was really sick and I was vomiting just about everywhere at that time. Every time he had disappeared for something unknown, it must've been for this exact reason. The timing never seemed right. It never was for us at all. However, now could not have been better. This day was the perfect day.

The ring felt cold around my finger I looked down at it with admiration. It was Emilia's ring, alright—the same ring that was outlined with navy and teal blue, with a white gold band that held the rare and expensive gem; the ring from Ice Moon that had been passed on for the pack's luna for centuries.

"Oh, Cooper, it's beautiful." I breathed, thinking that if I touched it, it would fall of my finger and cut through the ice, never to be seen again.

"It is a few hundred years old." Cooper grinned, not being able to wipe the smile off his face. "I was a little worried you wouldn't like something that old."

"I would've taken a soda cap as a ring if it meant being married to you." Our lips were only inches away, but we still continued to talk.

"Technically, we aren't married. We're engaged."

"Then, I guess I'll soon be Mrs. Pierce."

"I guess you will be."

We still stood there, wrapped in each other's embrace. Neither of us wanted to let go. I swooped in for a kiss. Never would I forget how he made me feel, how happy he really made me. I loved him. I truly and unconditionally loved him. There was no denying it now for how much he meant to me. I owed him more than I could give him, and I would spend the rest of my life proving to him I was worth being his mate. It's my turn to make him as happy as I was right now.

"I love you so much," I whispered, making sure my arms were still tightly linked around his neck.

"No, you don't." He chuckled, and I looked at him, confused for a second. "I love you more than air, more than water to keep me quenched, and food to keep me satiated. I love you more than my very own existence."

I could hardly hold back from kissing him after his sentence. Our lips met in a fanatical and loving way. Nothing else was needed to be spoken because he was all I needed right now.

Several more love phrases were spoken, but after kissing for the next few minutes, we finally broke apart and listened to each other's steady beating hearts. He was a lot more relaxed than before, but now it was over and we were finally happy, as fiancé and fiancée.

"What kind of ring is this?" I asked, spinning it with my other hand on its finger.

"It's actually an Australian black opal." He smiled, resting his chin on my head while I sat in between his legs and facing the snow-covered trees.

"It doesn't look like it was meant to be an engagement ring," I spoke truthfully, noticing how different it looked from Trixie's original diamond and white band. It couldn't be silver because it wouldn't exactly be eligible to be worn.

Cooper chuckled, moving a loose strand that had fallen out of my bun. "It was meant to be the first luna's gift from her mate after the alpha had found her. Her name was Annabelle, from the pack history books. Because of her selfless heart, she didn't want to have the ring for herself. She gave it to her only daughter's mate. She told him to propose to her daughter with *that* ring. The tradition has lived on for centuries."

"So there's a story behind it." I smiled admiring the ring. "How striking."

The rest of the evening was spent with Cooper and me eating the rest of the soup. I checked every spoonful to make sure he hadn't slipped a necklace or bracelet in when I wasn't looking. Today was already filled with so many gifts that I didn't think my heart could take all the affection and love from him.

When it got dark, the candles created the most beautiful and romantic feel. He handed me chocolate-covered strawberries and a cup of my favorite hot chocolate with a hint of cinnamon in it. When I got some cream on my nose, he kissed it away, making my laughter echo through the trees.

Today was turning out a lot better than I planned it to. My mate and I were happily together, and our pack had happily accepted our daughter. There was no threat of war battling its way towards us. I hoped everything would stay this way.

Logan had always been on my mind. Sometimes he would be, had Carly not killed him. Sometimes I would wonder about his unknown mate. Maybe one day I could go to a witch, one who wouldn't make deals, and ask her to help me find my brother's mate. I would love to speak to her. She deserved to know how her mate had sacrificed his life for mine by avenging what he thought was wrong.

I guess I owed Logan because without him, I never would've left the pack. If he had never died, I never would've found Cooper. Because of his sacrifice, I had the chance at being happy, and for that, I wanted to do this for him. I wanted to find his mate, so she could move on.

However, until the time came when everything was settled, all I had to do now was be here for my family, my pack, and my amazing mate.

***

"He did not!" She groaned, falling onto her bed while I skimmed through a child magazine.

"He did so," I stated for the hundredth time, flipping the page about what foods were not good for an infant to eat.

"How come I'm the only one who is suffering through this?" Paige groaned, looking at her bare ring finger. "I'm the only one who isn't engaged or married."

Paige and I were lounging in her room. She was on the brink of tears in her pillow while I sat comfortably next to her. I had gotten annoyed with her sulking and decided it was best to just ignore her while I read. The information on the magazine was more important than her moping since it was about what my children should or should not eat.

"Did you know that you shouldn't give a child a tablet until they are at least fifty pounds?" To be honest, I didn't even know that, and I had read plenty of pregnancy and child health books.

"Will you shut up and actually listen to what I have to say?" Paige snapped, giving me an infuriated glare. "You just got engaged not even twenty-four hours ago."

"Maybe Adam is waiting for the right time and way to ask you," I said kindly, placing the magazine down and sparing her a look. "Plus, you're a year younger than me."

"So?"

"You don't really have to rush into marriage when you just recently became an adult." I explained before sitting up to play with Shaw, who was kicking his blanket around with his feet.

"But we have a son, and I'm basically a mother now. I should be the one with a rock on my finger."

I turned to look at her while bouncing Shaw on my hip. "Are you forgetting that I'm a mother, and so is half the population of members in the pack right now?"

Paige was slowly starting to act more like a spoiled brat, a lot like her previous pregnant self actually. I couldn't tell if she was again, because she'd only worry over gaining weight, which she had after having Shaw. Every one of us gained a few pounds from our pregnancies. I had the most with having triplets. However, with my fast metabolism, I was able to burn it pretty quickly and look just like I had before. She wasn't so lucky and had more than an inch to pinch.

Life had finally shifted into the life I'd always wanted—three kids and hardly a care in the world. When summer came, we all took the opportunity to go to the cabin Emilia had given the key to me for Christmas. It wouldn't be as bad as what I had worried, since I wasn't pregnant and I would be able to enjoy it. Still, we were all officially a year older and needed time to mature by being full-time parents.

"Besides, not everyone has time to get married the human way," I stated, handing Shaw back over to her.

Ever since Penelope was introduced into the pack—well, since yesterday, Cooper had added more security around the pack house and perimeter. Everywhere I went with Penelope, either someone was pretending to put a book back on a shelf or eating some kind of food. I knew they were watching my every move only for the concern of my daughter, but it was unnerving. I tried not to let this bother me since it'd only been a day. It may be like this for the rest of our daughter's life, and I would have to get used to the additional protection on her. I was worried beyond belief of what could happen.

Adam had been far too busy to spend time with his son, which I'd noticed. Shaw was either being held by Paige or Emilia, who loved her firstborn nephew with passion. I wondered how it felt for her to suddenly be a grandmother so soon. Everyone knew all of our pregnancies were unplanned, but I felt she deserved to be prepared. Well, none of us were.

"I come baring gifts!" The door opened, and in came Trixie with a grocery bag filled with several different contents.

"Where's Lucian?" I asked, looking her up and down, wondering if he was somewhere on her body. That adorable boy was attached to her constantly, wanting his mother's attention. She also would carry him in a baby carrier over her back or chest. To me, it was a hilarious scene to witness.

"He's with his father." She beamed before collapsing on the bed. "Where are your kids?'

I shrugged. "Some pack member offered to bathe them and give them a nap. She was a sweet girl and explained she was about to be a mother and wanted some experience with children. I couldn't just say no to her."

Trixie and Paige began devouring chips, pretzels, popcorn, and ice cream while I spoke. It made me curious why Trixie was eating so much. I mean, she just got the baby weight off. When I decided it was time to participate in our weekly gatherings, I tipped the bag over and looked at the contents that spilled out. My eyes widened, and so did Paige's.

I was the first who was able to grab the box before anyone else. "What is this?"

"I feel like I'm going to faint!" Paige cried, turning away from the rectangle box in my palm.

"Stop looking at it like it will kill us all!" Trixie cried. "Jeremy and I agreed on having a big family, and we wanted to get started right after Lucian was born."

"Couldn't wait a year or two?" Paige shouted, seeming the most affected. It was slightly understandable since she could hardly handle her crying baby all the time. The thought of another one was obviously stressful for her, even if she wasn't the one who wanted to get pregnant.

"The test already told me. I took it right before I came."

"And," I drawled out, praying for the best that this was what she wanted.

Trixie's face broke into a grin. "I'm having another baby."

"Does Jeremy know?" I interrogated, giving her a stern look.

"He was the one who was suspecting, and he was with me when I took the test."

Much to my happiness, this was what made me happy. Everyone's lives were falling happily into place.

Chapter 33

I ran up the stairs, my heart hammering in my chest as the fire spread. Cooper was calling after me, begging for me to leave while he saved them. My stubbornness of being a luna set in, and I didn't listen. People were running down, making it difficult for me to get through. They each gave us concerned looks.

A wooden plank fell in front of me, blocking my path. I jumped over it while Cooper did the same, him hot on my tail. The tears falling down my face were blocking my vision, which caused me to trip over my heels. I looked at them and kicked them off and remained climbing the stairs.

When I finally arrived in the room, my heart stopped at the sight in front of me, and Cooper rammed accidently into my back making me almost fall to the ground.

"No," I whispered.

***

"Wake up, Celia! Wake up! Wake up!" My shoulders were gripped, and I let out a whisper of curses and curled into my only heat source. My heart was still racing from the nightmare I had, but for some reason, it felt like a sign.

The weight was off my body, but the shrilling child's voice went again. "Cooper, wake up! Wake up, big brother! Wake up!"

"Every year." Cooper groans with a huff before opening his eyes, glaring at his little sister.

She had gotten so grown up in the past year. Her hair had gotten longer and reached her waist, while her legs did the same. Sage was going to be very beautiful when she got older. I could see all the boys chasing after her. My soon to be sister-in-law better have an amazing mate who would treat her right.

"I'm up!" Cooper shouted, making Sage leap off the bed and over to our sleeping children. I smiled, kissing Cooper on his lips before getting up.

She was just tall enough to look through the bars to see Penelope sleeping soundly with a cute pout on her lips. They were puffed out, but my daughter still looked as beautiful from when she was born.

Sage turned to look at me and grinned. "Merry Christmas!"

Today was just about a month since the triplets were born. I brushed Sage to the side and unlocked the little latch that kept the crib from opening. All three infants were sleeping soundly, and I turned to look at Cooper who rolled on his stomach and stayed in his current sleeping state. Rolling my eyes, I picked Penelope up first, cradling her so she was in front of me.

At that moment, she opened her eyes and started wiggling happily at my face. I loved how she reacted to how I looked and knew immediately that I was her mother. A sense of pride filled me, and I couldn't wait for her to say her first words. My guess was it would be *momma* since I spent more time with her.

"Merry Christmas, sweetie." I grinned, rubbing our noses together and making her squeal in happiness. I looked down at Sage who had a frown on her face. Careful not to bump Penelope on the crib, I knelt down in front of Cooper's sister. "Merry Christmas to you too, darling."

Sage cried in happiness before kissing me on the cheek and running out to get ready. It was dawn, and I knew I was going to be in for a long day if she was this hyper. I'd asked Emilia if she gave her coffee in the morning, and she swore she had never given her youngest daughter a drop of caffeine.

I heard the tumbling of sheets and stood up the same time Cooper did. He stretched and flexed his arms, turning his neck to allow a satisfying crack. Sighing in relief, he stood up before tossing on a pair of checkered sweatpants and walking over to me.

His tall and large frame stood in front of me in no time, and the first thing he did was give me a sweet, long loving kiss on the lips. I smiled into it before kissing him back a few times and pushing him away. He growled, snatching my free arm that wasn't holding a baby, pulling me back to him.

"Don't I get something?" he asked, pretending to sound hurt. Penelope whimpered, obviously not understanding that her father was playing.

"You could get another kiss, but I think this is better." Yanking my arm free, I bent down to take hold of Clayton, who was still oblivious to his surroundings. Giving my mate a grin, I placed his son in his arms and did the same with Rylan.

"Seriously?" he asked, directing his head towards the bed. I knew exactly what he was thinking and shook my head. "Why not?"

"Because..." I turned my back to him and headed towards the exit. "I actually want to spend time with my entire family this Christmas."

"Technically, we did last year."

"Yes, you holding my hair while I leaned over a toilet sure was a family get-together." I rolled my eyes and opened the door.

The door was suddenly slammed shut, and Cooper let out a low growl at me. I only growled back and moved his hand away so I could leave. When he didn't budge, I slipped through and walked down the hall.

I was dressed in a very loose and comfortable night gown. A cardigan was thrown over my shoulders since all that held the dress up was a spaghetti string and it was winter. My newly cut hair was in two ponytails, with my side fringe still loosely flowing as I strode across the wood floor. My hair was like it had been before I was pregnant with just a few less layers. They had been difficult to manage, so I just let Paige change it up slightly.

Descending the stairs had gotten easier since I had a better grip on Penelope and a platform was placed so I wouldn't slip. Walking on glass was dangerous with a child in my arms, and I didn't want to risk hurting my baby girl. I would rather die than have something bad happen to her.

Like last year, the house was beautifully decorated, and I gasped at my surroundings. Lights were hung, so were candles and mistletoe. There wasn't a corner left dull or a light not working. It really was lovely.

"Look, Penny," I whispered to my daughter, and she instantly opened her eyes again at my voice. Her violet eyes sparkled with excitement when she saw all the colors and lights. A happy shriek filled my ears as she kicked her feet up and threw her arms around.

"Let's go see what Santa got you guys." Cooper nuzzled his nose with Penelope before kissing me on the forehead. He was carrying both boys in his arms.

We spent that morning opening presents mostly for the pups. They all got cute outfits and toys to chew on when they got a little older. Penelope mainly got fleece dresses to keep her warm at all times. Rylan and Clayton each got overalls and sweaters that I knew would make them look absolutely adorable.

The meals came and went, and in the evening, the adult party was in full swing while everyone was preparing for diner. While I was having a difficult time trying to figure out what to wear, Cooper was already ready, dressed in a dark green button up shirt with black pants. He had the few buttons at the top loosened, giving me an eyeful. Both our sons were dressed, matching in a pair of green and red overalls.

Penelope was in a diaper, lying down on our bed while Cooper tickled her stomach. My mate didn't hurry me, seeing as I was only dressed in my undergarments and was giving him a view. I really didn't care since I wasn't self-conscious of my body anymore.

"How about a cream white color?" I asked, turning around and holding a skirt and top.

"That looks nice." He nodded, not even looking at the outfit.

"You said the same about the other four outfits I've shown you." I groaned. "I don't think this would complement my white hair though." Sighing, I put them both back on the hanger.

"Because you would look good in all of those clothes you've shown me." Cooper grinned before gently picking up Penelope and standing up so he was in front of me. "You are beautiful."

I bit my lip before turning around at the other different dresses, blouses, and skirts. My eyes finally landed on one I knew would be perfect and snatched the two clothing choices. "So this?"

His eyes scanned over the black sequined top and navy blue skirt. There was a white fur coat that would keep me warm if I got cold in the house. "Perfect for this."

I hadn't realized Cooper had pulled out a black box which only made me glare at him. "I thought we agreed on no gifts."

"You agreed. I didn't." The box was placed in my free hand. He opened the box for me.

My hand that was holding the clothing dropped, and it instantly clasped to my mouth. Inside the box was a pair of ribbon diamond earrings and a necklace. It was all silver and looked like it would definitely match my outfit.

"Oh, it's so beautiful, Cooper," I whispered as he took them out with one hand holding Penelope. I took the jewelry from his free hand and clipped them on my ears and around my neck.

"They don't compare to you," he said and pulled out another box from his pocket. "Don't tell the boys, but I got another gift for Penny."

"Is Cooper Pierce already wrapped around his infant daughter's finger?" I teased, kissing him on the cheek and taking Penelope so she could see what he got her. "Look, baby, look what Daddy got you."

She let out a little yawn before opening her eyes. There Cooper unclipped a cute little velvet box, revealing a pendent with a running wolf encrusted in purple gems that I had assumed were fake. Our daughter let out a little squeal but did nothing to reach for it. Cooper and I both laughed, and he pulled out the long necklace.

"It looks a little big for her." I laughed, watching as it almost fell off her body.

"She'll grow into it eventually."

After our little moment, I got dressed and slipped on a pair of black heels. Thankfully, they allowed me to be a few inches taller. Cooper laughed before helping me slip Penelope into a matching outfit.

We made our way out of the room and down the hall. It was mainly for adults, but there was no way I was taking any of the three children out of my sight. I was carrying Penelope while Cooper had his arms full with Clayton and Rylan. I chuckled but didn't bother helping.

"Oh, Celia, you look beautiful!" Emilia cheered, holding two champagne glasses in her hand. She was dressed in a floor-length scarlet dress with a slit going down her left leg. Her outfit matched her neatly curled hair. She looked classy and sexy.

"You look amazing as well." I kissed her cheek, while she did the same. She eagerly handed me the two glasses she was holding and scooped Penelope from me.

"Oh you look gorgeous, One Cent Penny." I laughed at the nickname she chose for her only granddaughter. "You'll be as beautiful as your mother."

"Mother." Cooper groaned, seeing as she was gushing over our daughter about everything.

"I promise you, baby girl, when you get older, we will go shopping and get our nails done together." Emilia rambled on while Penelope let out a little drool slip from her mouth. I couldn't help but let out a laugh. "Oh, you'll be so spoiled."

"Mother!" Cooper growled lowly, which only earned him a scowl from her. "Mom, why don't you go find Dad. I think you've had a little too much to drink."

"Okay." She smiled before taking the glasses from my hand and handing my daughter back to me. "Have fun, you five."

Cooper rolled his eyes and walked with me to the dinner table. Everyone sat down when their alpha took the lead. I sat next to him while Paige sat across from me. On the other side of the table was Patrick who sat proudly across his son. This was the first time in a long time Cooper was joining the pack for Christmas.

Like last year, a few pregnant women got up throughout our dinner, excusing themselves politely and running off. They were then followed by their mates. Thankfully, neither Paige nor I got up, showing that neither of us were pregnant. Unfortunately, Trixie had to celebrate this holiday with her own pack, and I could only imagine what she was going through right now.

I carefully breastfed Clayton, making sure none of the unmated wolves got a glimpse. Cooper was trying to eat his meal while holding both Rylan and Penelope, but I just laughed as he suffered through it.

A young girl, holding her mate's hand, was seated next to me and kept asking me what it was like to do certain things with my children. The girl's name was Amazon, which was a unique name. I had never really heard a girl go by that name. She went by Amie, and I could completely understand why. Every time she asked me a question about pups, her eyes would sparkle, and I knew right away she desperately wanted to have a child.

"He always laughs at me." She cocked her head to the side. "Whenever I tell him we'll have a girl as our first born."

"And you think it's true?" I asked, giving her a smile. Amie nodded eagerly. "Have you thought of any names?"

"I met my mate in London and had our first date at a secluded harbor, so I was thinking London Haven." Her eyes once again shone, and I couldn't help but beam at her.

"That's a beautiful name—" I paused "—London Haven."

At that exact moment, Clayton seemed to move restlessly in my arms. I groaned and excused myself for a moment while I helped him calm down. His kicking finally stopped when I handed him over to Cooper and took Rylan.

I looked over at Cooper as he supported both of our pups' heads and still managed to eat. Rolling my eyes, I continued my own dinner while I fed Rylan, letting out a growl when a teenage boy let his eyes wander. My mate didn't seem to notice, thankfully, and I began eating in peace.

Dinner flew by, and once again gifts were being unwrapped from family members. I received a few from Emilia and Patrick. And most of the gifts I had received were either jewelry or shoes. I had enjoyed watching all the kids cry out in happiness when they got a new book or video game system.

I saw Paige handed Adam a small box. When he opened it, the box revealed an expensive looking watch. He grinned mischievously and handed her a velvet box.

She looked at him skeptically and snapped the lid open. Paige let out a loud gasp and almost dropped the entire thing. Everyone crowded around to see what it was and many clapped when it hit us.

Adam was proposing to Paige.

"Yes!" she cried and hugged her mate with all her might.

Emilia was holding Shaw so he wouldn't interrupt their little moment. Paige turned to me and showed me her ring. It had a light blue diamond heart resting on the gold band. It was beautiful.

When I gave her a thumbs-up, she turned back around and kissed Adam with all her might. I couldn't help but laugh as his eyes bulged out when both of them fell to the ground. They both laughed and continued to make out, much to the children's complaints.

"Alright, quit it." Cooper's voice boomed, using his alpha tone to get everyone to listen. Adam did what he said and glared at his best friend.

After the cute marriage proposal, we were given a few more gifts such as wine, and Paige even snuck a little lingerie to me. I glared at her, but she just shrugged and pounced on her mate when they went to leave. Both Cooper and I rolled our eyes.

"Ready to go to bed?" Cooper asked, standing up and dusting his dress pants off.

"I'll be up in a minute." I gestured to the cup of tea that was in my hand, and he leaned over to give me a kiss.

"Goodnight."

"Night. Love you." Our lips touched again, and he gave me a big smile before leaving.

I sat contentedly on the couch while the fire flickered in the fire place. Emilia came in a few minutes later and sat in the seat next to me. We both exchanged smiles but didn't speak. Cooper had taken the triplets upstairs when he went to bed, which gave me a little while to relax before either of them woke up.

When I felt myself growing tired, I wished Emilia goodnight and left the room to put my tea cup away in the sink. Before I could reach it, however, I accidently loosened my grip on the handle, and it went barreling down to the ground with a loud crash. My voice let out a loud squeak from the sudden noise. I let out a groan when I realized I had to clean it up.

Footsteps came from upstairs, pounding loudly on the wood. I held my breath when they stopped and turned around to see Cooper looking worried and terrified. When he saw me cleaning up the shards of glass, he bent down to pick them up with me.

"Oh, Moon Goddess, Celia, you scared me." He sighed before placing the small glass pieces in a napkin.

"I'm sorry." I breathed and kissed his cheek gently.

We were silent since it was pretty late at night until we smelt something burning. At that moment, both of us froze and I turned to look at Cooper with a mortified expression on my face.

Dropping the glass, we ran out of the kitchen and stopped dead in our tracks.

Flames were everywhere, and pack members were running out of the house like headless chickens. I turned around to see Sage holding Emilia's hand and running as fast as she could out of the house. Smoke filled the room, and men were walking in carrying water hoses. But the water seemed to do the opposite of what it was supposed to do. It only made the fire spread.

"It's the witch." Cooper growled, sniffing the air and looking around. "Ayana."

"Oh my god," I whispered, covering my hand over my mouth. "Penelope, the pups, oh my god." With that thought in my head, I ran past Cooper and towards the stairs.

I ran up the stairs, my heart hammering in my chest as the fire spread. Cooper was calling after me, begging for me to leave while he saved them. My stubbornness of being a luna set in, and I didn't listen. People were running down, making it difficult for me to get through.

People were more concerned for themselves as the pack house caught fire. This left our children unprotected, especially Penelope. I figured Cooper had been watching them, but after hearing the crash, he assumed something was wrong. He put me first, and now we were both paying for it. I was fearing not only my children's lives, but Penelope's safety.

A wood plank fell in front of me, blocking my path. I jumped over it while Cooper did the same. He was hot on my tail. The tears falling down my face were blocking my vision, causing me to trip over my heels. I looked at them and kicked them off and continued to climb the stairs.

When I finally arrived in the room, my heart stopped at the sight in front of me, and Cooper rammed accidently into my back, making me almost fall to the ground.

"No," I whispered, feeling the déjà vu from my dream.

The room wasn't on fire and looked exactly like how we had left it. However, there was a figure in the room, running her finger along the cribs. It stopped and turned around to face us. My heart shattered as I looked at Penelope in the arms of the one person I had feared.

"Ayana." I hissed as the door closed behind us, locking us in the room.

Chapter 34

Ayana was dressed in a black robe with a black hood that had almost hid her face. However, I could still see her fogged eyes, proving that she was in fact blind. I looked over at him to see his jaw tick, and his fists clenched and unclenched. A low, deadly growl escaped his lips which made her jump in surprise at the noise.

"Pleasure to meet you, Alpha Cooper, and it's nice to hear your voice again, Celia." She let out a toothless smile and turned to where she thought we were, which was a little more to the left. "Your daughter feels beautiful." To our disgust, she ran her hand along Penelope's face.

"Don't you *dare* touch her!" I seethed, taking a step forward, only for Ayana to push me back with her magic so I was pinned against the door.

Cooper growled and charged at her, only for him to receive the same fate I did, only rougher. He groaned. We were both standing, sizing her up to find any form of a weak spot.

"Let's make another deal." I cried. "Please, I beg of you."

"I don't listen to dogs who beg." Ayana snapped before clicking her fingers. Wind picked up in our room and began to circle around her and Penelope.

At that moment, Penelope woke up from her slumber and let out a cry when she realized I wasn't holding her. I went to run again but ended up having the curtains restrain me. Tugging and pulling only made it worse. I looked at Cooper for help. He made another move, and Ayana lifted her hands up, creating cuffs that held him to the door.

"No!" I cried, feeling more tears spill. "Please don't take my baby! I need my daughter, my Penelope. You can't do this."

"We made a deal." Ayana laughed, holding Penelope closer to her.

"You heartless, bitch!" Cooper snarled, and I turned to look at his glowing eyes. His wolf was coming out, surfacing to the point that his teeth were growing and his claws were fully grown.

The wind had now created a tornado around Ayana and Penelope, and I could hardly see them anymore. My tears were pushed off my face due to the wind, and my white hair was flying everywhere. This couldn't be it. This couldn't be the last moment I see my daughter. I wouldn't allow it. I would never forgive myself.

"Good luck finding her where the darkest place is, where the sun shines brightly." Ayana hinted, and at that moment, with one howl of the wind, everything stopped.

And they were gone.

Ayana was gone with my daughter, Penelope. The room felt empty and silent except for the cries coming from both the boys in their cribs. The biggest emotion running through my veins was regret. I wished I could go back in time and prevent the introduction of Penelope into the pack. If I did not introduce my daughter, this never would have happened. My daughter could've been saved.

The curtains had released me, and Cooper was free from his restraints. At that moment, I dropped to my knees as realization hit me.

"No." I sighed before going rabid with tears and shouts. "No! No! No! Please…"

My lip trembled, and I let out a loud cry, banging my head against the floor. Cooper bent down and took my body in his arms. He cradled me, trying to give me some support, but the shaky breath and soft gasps told me he was crying as well.

"Penelope. No!" I cried. "My baby. No!"

"Celia…" Cooper whispered, trying to help me get up. I pushed his arms away and lay down on the floor, banging my head against it. "Celia, please…"

"Why? Why am I so stupid?" I bellowed, shaking my head. "I'm so selfish. I never should've made that deal! This is my fault. All my goddamn fault."

"Baby, Celia, just—" I stopped Cooper from completing his sentence and sat up.

"What are you going to say?" I shouted, pushing him away. "That it isn't my fault that my daughter is gone? That I may never…That she could…" I couldn't finish any of my sentences.

Tears trailed down my own mate's face. "We'll find her."

"How?" I cried. "She's a witch! She can just jump from place to place without leaving a scent to follow."

"The necklace I put on Penelope has a tracking device in it." Cooper rushed out.

"Oh god." I breathed, closing my eyes, trying to calm myself down.

But when I opened my eyes, I almost screamed in frustration when I saw a little shining circle in the middle of the floor. I crawled over to it and suddenly burst into tears. My hands picked up the necklace, and I gazed at the running wolf pendant. It was our last hope, and here it was, not on Penelope.

"Celia?" Cooper ran over to me and looked at my hands. "No…"

My eyes could no longer shed any more tears. I ran my hand across the beautiful piece of jewelry. This was it; this was the only thing I had left of Penelope, my daughter. She was gone, and I would never be the same again.

"Celia! Answer me!" He shook my shoulders, but I just looked at him with empty eyes. "Celia…please, baby, talk to me. Please? I can't…I can't see you like this."

"I'm so sorry," I whispered. My voice was so soft that I feared he didn't hear me, but with his heightened senses, I assumed he did. "I'm so sorry for everything. I love you."

"I love you too, baby," he whispered before engulfing me in a bone-crushing hug as I wept on his shoulder.

All at once, I realized that the house had been on fire and weaved my way out of Cooper. I almost toppled over from how weak I was from crying but managed to catch myself. The door was swung open as I pulled on the handle and was immediately hit by fire and smoke. Blocking my face with my arms, I turned around at Cooper who was quickly gathering Clayton and Rylan.

I took Rylan from my mate and rushed as fast as I could down the stairs. Penelope's necklace was still in my hand while I ran, dodging fallen planks and broken glass. I didn't speak, not to Cooper, not to our wailing son. Cooper was trying to get in front of me so I wouldn't get hurt, but it took one glare at him and he stopped.

The Christmas decorations were burning, and the lights were starting to pop. I screeched but managed to make it out of the house fine. The moment we exited, the fire stopped. It wasn't snowing, but we were still knee-deep in snow as we stared at what was left. The house was reduced to a pile of smoldering wood, rubble, black and grey ashes, and items that had surprisingly been spared.

Looking around, I noticed that everyone had made it out okay. The pack members living nearby were running over to assess the damage. Emilia ran over to us with tears in her eyes and hugged both of us. Paige and Adam were watching the scene unfold, holding Shaw close to their chests. Patrick rubbed his mate's back, trying to comfort her as best as possible. That was, until Sage noticed something.

"Where's Penelope?"

At that, Emilia released Cooper and I. She stared down at Clayton and Rylan in our arms. Her eyes went black, and she looked into my tear-filled eyes. "Celia? Where's your daughter?"

My lip quivered. I couldn't manage to speak any words.

"Ayana took her." Cooper growled angrily. "Penelope is in the hands of that witch."

"Oh my god." Paige gasped, covering her mouth with her hand.

"No…" Emilia choked, looking over at the shocked pack members. "Did she say anything?"

"She said, '*Good luck finding her where the darkest place is, where the sun shines brightly.*' I don't understand what that witch meant," my mate said, looking down at Clayton and Rylan with sad eyes. "They'll never get to know their sister."

"Darkest place where the sun shines brightly?" Emilia repeated several times but never came to a conclusion. "I don't know."

"This can't be over!" Paige shouted, possessing a look of anger on her face. "We fight! We will find her! Our pack has never lost a war, and I plan on it staying that way."

"Paige, enough." Cooper seethed, holding me close with his free arm. "Celia, please don't cry."

I wiped my tears away and pushed past everyone. Rylan made it into the arms of Adam, who was staring at me with sorrow. My cheeks were raw with tears and felt numb. I couldn't do this. I couldn't. My life was over. I failed as a parent, as a luna, and as a mate.

But I didn't deserve to live like this.

I lost my parents before I even got to know them. I was left on a doorstep with only a name. They had never cared for me and didn't want me. It was like I was nothing to them, and I instantly knew when I was old enough that I would never forgive them. My parents were nothing to me. They didn't exist in my mind.

Logan, my sweet, sweet Logan, my own blood. My brother was murdered because of me. That wretched female Carly had only done it for the attention from her mate even though she had rejected him and did not want him. She wanted to get rid of me. She wanted me dead when it was actually her fault. I would never get my brother back, and I had myself to blame. Had I not been too naïve and told him about the experiments, he would have been alive.

Due to the experiments, I had lost everything. My blonde hair was turned to white, a color I had always seen as boring and plain. Zaire had turned my gold eyes violet and made my eyelashes darker and thicker. My tanned skin turned milky with all the silver pumped into me and my unhealthy environment. My cherry red lips came from the suffering I had every time a needle was injected into them. I was stick-thin and was beaten badly. The main reason why I became infertile was because of the damage done to my body by the liquid silver.

My infertility was the only reason I made that deal.

Now, I lost my one and only daughter. I may never be able to see her slightly tanned skin, copper red hair, and violet eyes. She had been a perfect mix between Cooper and me, something I may never get again. Penelope made everyone smile just at the sight of her because she resembled me so much. Her smile was infectious, and her laugh was the most adorable thing I had ever heard. Who knew how long it would take us to find her.

It's all because of me.

"Celia!" Cooper called, taking my elbow and dragging me back. "Please just listen to me."

I didn't speak but allowed him to hold me. At that moment, I cried in my mate's arms in front of everyone. It was silent; no hoots from an owl were heard, or pattering of animals' feet on the snow. Everyone heard my shattering heart as I howled in pain. Their luna was hurting, yet they could do nothing to stop it. Or to comfort me.

The stars above were shining with sadness, and I thought I even saw a lone tear-drop-looking comet fly by across the sky. It must've been late, at least two in the morning, judging by how a few were yawning. Not a cloud was in the sky, giving a full view of the crescent moon above.

"Hear my voice. Only listen to it." Cooper soothed me, rubbing his hand up and down my back. "We will find her. I promise. I love you way too much to lose you. I hate seeing you like this. Please, baby, please stop crying." He sounded so pained by my weeping, but I was still unable to stop them.

Emilia's voice was heard behind me, a soft whisper. "Moon Goddess, hear our prayers. Keep Penelope safe for us."

Epilogue

11 months later

    I stood up from the bed emotionlessly and slipped on a pair of slippers. My feet carried me to the bathroom where I did my business and brushed my overgrown hair. Pushing my hair to the side, I let it hang from my shoulder and turned to look at the calendar. A single tear fell from my eye as I realized what day it was. Written in bold letters was 'Thanksgiving' and below it 'Our pups' first birthday!'

    My head turned to face the bed where Cooper had slept in last night. I remembered hearing him get up earlier than usual and took Clayton and Rylan with him. It was hard to believe he would leave me on this day, but he obviously knew I wanted to be alone. He'd be back when I was asleep and leave before I awoke.

    That's how we'd been living ever since the night Penelope was taken away from us. I hadn't spoken or uttered even a word to anyone. I felt empty inside. Cooper and I hadn't even mated, and when my heat came, he had himself locked away. I knew how badly his wolf wanted us, but I just couldn't feel anything anymore. I felt nothing ever since that dreadful day.

We never got the chance to get married. The engagement ring was still on my ring finger, but nothing else had happened. Cooper and I didn't even kiss or hug anymore. He knew I was hurting, and I knew he was just trying to be strong for our sons' sake. I knew he didn't want either of them to grow up without a parent.

The cabin down south was once again unused, like it had been when I fell pregnant. I didn't know if I'd ever use it. I'd considered giving the key back to Emilia, or maybe hand it over to Paige and her growing family.

Paige and Adam had a private wedding. I knew both wanted to have a big wedding, but if I wasn't going to show up or even look happy, they didn't want a big celebration. They claimed I had been through too much. The wedding went on with close family and friends. It was romantic, I guess, but I really didn't see anything happy anymore. It felt like my heart had been ripped out of its chest.

Trixie gave birth to a girl about a month before Lucian's birthday. When she found out it was a girl, she tried telling me without making me burst into tears. It didn't work, and she wobbled away from me as fast as she could. A few months later, Jacqueline was born. She looked a lot like Jeremy with Trixie's eyes.

I was inconsolable to everyone; even Sage couldn't make me feel a flicker of emotion.

Alyssa, the pregnant sixteen-year-old that had been surrounded by silver a year ago, had killed herself only a few days after the boy was born. The baby was brought back to Bermuda without a name. The pack there had crumbled, but someone came and managed to help it.

That someone was Jeremy. After his honeymoon with Trixie, they decided to buy a summer home there and visited every year. During the first time they went to visit, they recruited a lot of new pack members and eventually came across a boy. His name was Kory, and he officially became a pack member a few weeks ago although he remained living in Bermuda. He was Alyssa's child. They adopted him for a brief period but could not take care of him due to their growing family. However, they did visit him every month in an orphanage.

I sat down at Cooper's desk and scanned the area. Slowly, I took a pen and paper and stared blankly at it. It was time to do this, for her, for my baby girl, Penelope.

***

My dearest Penelope,

It's hard to believe you would have been one year old today. My heart aches at just the thought of you. I have blamed myself even though your father tells me it was never my fault. I know he just doesn't want me to blame myself for what happened by telling me that it was just a cruel piece in our messed-up puzzle of a life. But I blame myself. I blame myself every single day.

I hope one day you can forgive me, my darling. I love you, and I pray every day for the time to come when I can finally say those three words to you in person.

My intention was never to leave you, and maybe someday, when you read this, you will forgive me for everything. When we find you, I hope I'll be able to look at you, no matter what age, and hold you close to me like I did when you were born. Your father and I tried so hard to find you, but a witch was born to keep balance between the supernatural world and the human one. She destroyed this family.

I think about you every day, every hour, and every minute. My heart breaks all over again when I see your empty crib close to where I sleep at night. I wonder if I'll be able to see you say your first word, take your first step, and lose your first tooth. It pains me to think that, right now, you would've been able to pick your head up without needing support from me, or have crawled around just about every inch of this house.

  Before I go to sleep, you are the only person on my mind. My broken heart cries and weeps, but my brain tells me I have to stay strong for your brothers. You and your brothers represent the significant things in my life that I am proud of or endeavor to achieve. Your older brother, Clayton, represents clarity to remind me whenever I get stuck in a situation or get confused and don't know what to do, all I have to do is understand what is more important to me—my aim and purpose—and redirect my focus with a clear mind. Your second oldest brother, Rylan, represents romance to remind me that it is more than stolen glances, sweet smiles, offering your coat when you see that your partner's cold, and surprise dinner dates on a frozen lake. It's that meaningful and pivotal force that propels you to bond with someone in a more significant, deeper way. And you…my darling, you represent so many things. You mean peace, something I have always wished for in this world. You show power—that woman can be in control and stand head on with the same confidence and strength as a man. Finally, you represent hope, making me pray every day that we will see you again.

  When you were taken from me, from us, you were only a month old. It was at that time when you learned to wrap your tiny hand around my finger and give it a powerful squeeze. During that time, you reacted instantly to my voice and face. Whenever you saw see me, you cried out in joy and kicked your feet up in the air. I laughed at you and took your cute body in my arms and held you close.

  After the night you were taken away from me, I haven't spoken. My voice can never be found, and it's like you took that from me that morning you were gone. I didn't sleep at all. It's like my body was waiting, waiting for my daughter to magically appear unharmed as if nothing happened.

  I hope when I see you again, you will be absolutely beautiful. In all hopes, I wish to see you today, tomorrow, and the days after that until I die. I miss you, and I want to be near you. It's been almost a year since I held you close, and I feel empty just looking at the blank spot between Clayton and Rylan. You always slept in between them as if they were protecting you.

It's like they knew about the deal I had made and wanted to keep you. The stupid deal I had made in order to get pregnant. My darling, please understand that I was young, naïve, and a stupid girl when I made that deal. I was desperate to make my true and only love happy. My mind played tricks on me, and I let you slip away just like that.

I've heard your father talk about me to your grandmother, completely unaware my hearing is still working. He goes on about how I'm like a ghost, walking yet not responding to my surroundings. At one point, he had cried on his own mother, frustrated that he couldn't do anything to bring my old slightly-happy-self back. When he looked up to me watching him with no reaction, he just turned around and kept his strong grip on his mother.

Baby, my sweet darling, Penelope, I will always want you as my daughter. For the rest of my life, I will mourn you. I pray to the Moon Goddess that one day, I will see your bright smile again, this time with teeth maybe. I will always be your mother, ready to greet you at the front door if you ever manage to find us. I'll be your best friend and guardian. I am someone who loves you more than anyone else could.

I miss you, Penelope. Love you with all my heart.

—Mom

THE END

Can't get enough of Celia and Cooper? Make sure you sign up for the author's blog to find out more about them!

Get these two bonus chapters and more freebies when you sign up at pamela-addato.awesomeauthors.org!

Here is a sample from another story you may enjoy:

FIGHTING BLIND

E. MARIE

Chapter 1

Kei Valancia

I stood there bored, waiting for the man to unknot his panties.

"How do we know we can trust you? You're just a filthy rogue," the man before me said with a snarl, and I simply sighed. Looking closer, the colors swirling around the man were red and blue, meaning anger and uncertainty. To be honest, I was sick of seeing those two colors. Of course, I couldn't see the man himself, but I imagined him to be a straight-laced kind of guy.

"First off, I'm not a rogue. There's a complicated process for that, and I really don't want to get into it. So, can you just *please* take me to your alpha? I kinda really want to talk to him." I sounded bored even to my own ears. He only growled in response, and I sighed. "For the love of Goddess, just take me to your freaking alpha. What can a girl like me do anyway with a pack full of wolves? *Probably, annihilate all of you without breaking a sweat, but that's just evil and totally not me.*

The man was silent before I heard him let out one more low growl.

"Fine, but if I see you do anything suspicious, then I will—"

"Yeah, yeah, you'll kill me without a second thought. Been there, done that. Now, let's go." I waved my hand in a dismissive manner just to annoy him a little more, and it worked. I was suddenly lifted up into the air by my neck, his grip tightening with his anger.

"I would watch your attitude if I were you, rogue." He spat at me. I rolled my eyes and gripped his wrist.

"Sorry but no thanks. That's just not my style." Lifting my leg and folding my body in a lawn chair sort of way, I planted one foot on his chest and kicked off. He let out a grunt in surprise while I flipped back and landed neatly on my feet. Dusting my pants, I looked in his direction, making sure it looked as if I could actually see him.

"Come on, the night is still young, and I actually have a schedule to stay on. Now, let's go."

"Cocky little—" I growled loudly, and he shut up real quick.

"I dare you to finish that sentence," I smirked smugly when he was silent and began walking away. His loud stomps with my own silent ones were the only sounds in the woods.

I was currently in the Red Moon territory, and I'd been hearing stories about how rogues have attacked this place five times in the last three weeks. To be honest, I was surprised they weren't all dead yet.

As we continued to walk in silence, I began to observe my surroundings a little more. I smiled a little in content as the familiar presence of colors swirled around me like a colorful blizzard.

What I actually "see" was something sort of like energy or, in a simpler term, auras. Every living thing emanates an aura. Whether it's dim or bright, it still has energy. Of course, energy may be transferred to an object if the owner of that object has strong enough feelings towards it. It's like giving a piece of oneself to an object.

But I love plants the most; every single one seemed to have a unique color all on its own. Same goes for humans, vampires, and so on. Usually, though, each species have their own mark. Let's say if I touch a rose or look in the general direction of it, I would know it was a rose because I would see a light pink glow coming from the object.

Of course, a plant's energy is dimmer than a person's, but it's still there, nonetheless. It's almost as if walking through pitch darkness with the occasional flashes of colors but maybe ten times more intense.

Kind of the same concept goes for someone's aura. A person emits very bright colors, and each color tells a type of feeling someone has at the moment. And as for a person's soul, let's just say they are the most beautiful things I have ever seen, but I usually have to look a little harder if I want a little peek into someone's innermost person. So, I usually don't for privacy reasons.

It's true that I love what I can see, the energy of the things around me, but I also miss how I can't see what the auras actually look like in the real world. But I don't usually like to dwell on such things when I know I can't fix it.

Sounds weird, but I'm the epitome of weird, so it only makes sense.

I stiffened when I began to hear other sounds, like children's laughter in the distance becoming louder along with the chatter of stressed conversations. Listening closer, I could even hear parts of the conversations going on.

"How will we keep the rogues back? We can't take another attack without being destroyed." The voice was strained, and I felt a pang of pity for this pack.

"I don't know. However, I heard that another rogue was sighted on the west border and was being brought in." I smirked slightly when I heard this. It's about show time.

I knew we were spotted, as everything went silent, and I tilted my head up with confidence. I knew they were tense; I could see it in their auras; plus, I could even smell the tension in the air. It was like a salty sea breeze filling my nostrils, and I really couldn't blame them.

I wore a long cloak with a thick hood over my head covering most of my features with the help of dark sunglasses covering my eyes. I pulled the cloak closer, the fabric soft against my skin. I darted my eyes around, catching glimpses of all kinds of colors. Dark brown mostly as it represents tension, and I even caught a glimpse of yellow for curiosity.

Judging by all the auras, I could tell that there were twenty adults along with ten kids in what seemed like a large yard.

Cocking my head to the side, I stared at my guide when he stopped and turned to me.

"You will wait here while I get the alpha," he ordered, not giving me time to reply before he was gone. I shrugged and simply continued to "look" around.

I manipulated my powers outward, the blackness of my sight taking shape as I could now see distinct outlines of objects. I couldn't see the details but, more or less, the shape. As I did this, I noticed a large structure emanating a feeling of grief and anger. The feelings of the people living here were influencing the energy of the house, which can happen. The atmosphere says it all, and I knew that inside it would hold a certain heaviness in the air that would sit on your shoulders until it felt like you would be crushed.

I could hear all the whispers, but I decided to ignore them. I was so used to this treatment; it didn't have an effect on me anymore. Instead, I tapped my foot with impatience and kept my face an emotionless mask. Finally, after what seemed like ages, I saw a swirl of power finally enter my vision.

I made a noise of approval as the alpha stepped in front of me, his power quite impressive as I watched it surround him and his pack in a protective cocoon. Each alpha I have met seems to always have a unique color in their power. This alpha had beautiful swirls of dark red and glittering purples.

"Alpha," I said respectfully.

"Rogue," he replied in a dark tone. I rolled my eyes knowing he couldn't see.

"Sorry, Alpha, but I'm not a rogue, just an innocent passerby," I said.

"You look like a rogue to me," he replied in an even tone, and I shrugged in return.

"I may look like one, but do I smell it?" This made him pause before answering.

"No," he said shortly. I smirked and nodded.

"I know it's not going to fully convince you, but I don't necessarily care at the moment."

"Then what is your purpose here?" he demanded. I noticed at the corner of my eye sparks of browns and other colors identifying their owners with their uniqueness.

"Well, first off, I'm not going to attack you or cause any of you harm. Secondly, I actually want to help you." I imagined him raising an eyebrow at this.

"And how would you help?" He sounded skeptical as he asked this. I smiled, and it may have come off as frightening, but it was supposed to come off as more friendly.

"I want to train your warriors into some of the best fighters in the world." I made my voice sound self-assured, which I was. I couldn't help it. I was just a very confident person in general. This caught everybody's attention, as I knew it would. I smirked and waited for his response.

"Who are you?" My smile widened, and I spread my hands out, palms facing forward.

"I'm just here to help," I replied, shrugging and trying to look as innocent as I could, which may not have been much. He was silent. The only noises were the distinct sounds of nightlife, and a faraway hoot of an owl pierced the tense air around us. Two minutes of silence passed, and he finally came to a decision.

"Fine. To prove your skills, why don't you fight one of my best warriors?" I stood there for a moment. He must have mistaken this as hesitance, as when he spoke, I could hear the smugness in his tone. "Unless you're all talk. Instead, I can have you escorted off of my land with your tail between your legs." I laughed.

"I wasn't hesitating but more like debating whether how much I wanted your poor warrior to be hurt." I would admit. I did sound rather cocky, and when I saw his power flared with annoyance, I knew I had pushed his buttons. I couldn't help but grin a little. Pushing buttons was one of my specialties, and it was one of my favorite pastimes.

"Fine." He growled. "Mark."

Almost instantly, a man appeared by his side. Electric green surrounded him completely, and I found it surprising. He was just full of excitement.

"Mark, I'll let you have full rein with this one,"

"Yes, Alpha." I could hear the grin in the man's voice or Mark, I then knew, and I couldn't help but let my own smile grow also.

"All right, pup, better get ready 'cause you're going to get your butt whooped," I taunted him, and in return, he didn't say anything but scoff. I stood still and watched as his colors swirled around him, a mixture of steely gray of concentration and the same bright green of his excitement. I cocked my head to the side and waited for him to make the first move.

I could hear the quiet crunch of grass beneath his feet, smell the salty sweat coming from the other nervous wolves around us, and taste the bitter-sweetness of the alpha's confidence. It was intoxicating.

I inhaled deeply and felt myself relax even further, a knowing smile on my lips as the wolf charged at me. I kept still, waiting it out until the last second had almost passed too late. When I did move, it was when I could feel his warm breath on my cheek as he snarled, the heat of his body searing onto mine.

With reflexes that never ceases to surprise even me, I sidestepped while subtly sticking my foot out as he whizzed past me. A second later, I heard his body thump against the ground. I chuckled as I heard gasps surround us. Their reactions were pretty predictable at this point. I'd visited many packs, and I could practically play out all of their reactions by now. The wolf before me snarled loudly, probably flashing his canines at me. I rolled my eyes. Too bad it wouldn't intimidate me.

"Come on, I don't have all day." I huffed with impatience. That seemed to spur him on as he jumped and changed in midair. I watched as the air rippled around the colorful mass, and I mean ripple. I could see how it seemed to shimmer before the mass in front of me became larger. Judging by the way the air rippling around him, I could see he was a decent-sized wolf but nothing I couldn't handle.

Letting out one loud growl, he charged once more. I quickly went into a defensive position and prepared for the impact. He was a lot heavier than I had predicted as he slammed into me with full force. Letting out a grunt, I wrapped my arms around his neck tightly while I was pushed back several feet. I heard the snap of his teeth as he tried to bite my face off while his body trembled violently with his growls.

"Dear Goddess, you need to lose weight." I gritted out before falling down onto my back, using this momentum to kick the wolf over my head. He whined from the impact, but I didn't give him a chance to recover as I stood and kicked him in the stomach. He yelped, and I knew just from the sound of a crack, I had broken a couple of his ribs. I jumped back to let him recover for a few seconds, his heavy pants filling the silent air around us.

He snarled viciously, and I yawned in return before shooting him a wide grin. He circled me all the while snapping towards me every few seconds; testing the waters, I presumed.

I almost ended it, as I was starting to get incredibly bored, but he decided to kick the excitement up a notch. As he jumped towards me a second time, he surprised me by changing back into his human form and tackled me to the ground. He elbowed me in the gut, knocking the air out of my lungs.

He straddled my waist as he threw a punch to my right cheek. My head whipped sharply to the side, and I felt my sunglasses fly off somewhere. Pain flared on my face but instantly dimmed and went away. I laughed once I was hit again. I felt his body freeze above me, and the sharp intake of his breath told me he caught sight of my eyes. I stared straight up at him, a grin once again on my face.

"Good job, pup. Not only did you land one but two punches. You even managed to surprise me. I gotta say I'm impressed." I grinned wickedly. "But sadly, I must end the fun."

"What are you—" He was cut off by his own grunt as I threw my own punch, a solid right hook might I add. His weight was lifted off me, and I jumped to my feet without a moment to spare, crouching low. He let out a groan before I noticed his outline showing him stumbling to his feet.

I attacked him one last time, running at him and jumping, my feet landing on his chest with a solid thump. His body flew back several feet, hitting what sounded like a tree. I noticed his colors dim, meaning he was unconscious. If he were dead, there would be a lifeless, dull gray, and the smell of death would reek throughout the air. Nodding in satisfaction, I brushed my hands together as if dusting them off and turned to look at the silent crowd. Gasps and soft curses surrounded me, and the color orange of surprise zinging around me. The bright color held my attention until a booming voice brought me out of my reverie.

"Take him to the pack doctor."

"Yes, Alpha," a couple men responded instantly. I saw their colorful figures picking him up and hurrying him away. I turned to face the alpha and noticed the color orange mix in with his power. I smirked once I saw it. I guess even the big, bad alpha could be surprised.

"What are you?" he demanded. I lifted my hand to run through my hair but was surprised to see my hood was still up. Wow, that was magic all on its own.

"I'm a werewolf," was my short reply.

"But what else?" I shrugged and made the show of darting my eyes around before landing back onto him.

"I think it's best told in private." He was quietly debating my answer, and I was waiting once again.

"How about you pull off that hood to show your face more clearly?" He rumbled, and I shrugged.

"Fine, not like I'm hiding my identity, anyway." Reaching up, I pushed my hood back to reveal my face. I felt my hair roll over my shoulders and down my back. More orange colored my vision, my appearance surprising everyone around me, unsurprisingly. I felt my hair spill over my shoulders and down my back. I've asked many people about my appearance; as I became blind when I was young, my memories too faded for me to remember what I looked like. From what they described, I had shifting eyes that would change between the colors bright emerald and ruby red, with a head of silver hair that looked as if the moon poured its silvery light onto the strands itself. Of course, I also joked that they were implying that I was the Moon Goddess, which is sort of a religious figure in werewolf standards. However, she is not an all-powerful being like the one the humans have with their God. The Moon Goddess is simply the first female werewolf to ever be created, along with her mate. But that's a story for another day.

"You are not only werewolf." His voice brought me out of my thoughts, and I gave him a wolfish smile.

"Like I said, let's talk in private." And with confident strides, I walked passed him and everybody else. Displaying a sure step and a cocky smirk, I knew he would follow. And he did.

If you enjoyed this sample then look for **Fighting Blind.**

Other books you might enjoy:

Dear Diary, I Have A Mate
Abbie Lynn

Fangs Vs Claws
Rua Hasan

Introducing the Characters Magazine App

Download the app to get the free issues of interviews from famous fiction characters and find your next favorite book!

iTunes: bit.ly/CharactersApple
Google Play: bit.ly/CharactersAndroid

Acknowledgements

I would like to thank my mother, father, sister, and brother for guiding me and my writing. I would like to thank my best friend, Maya, for allowing me to talk to her about organizing this book and the others that follow. I would like to thank my family and friends for molding me into the person
I am now.

Author's Note

Hey there!

Thank you so much for reading Run, Omega, Run! I can't express how grateful I am for reading something that was once just a thought inside my head.

I'd love to hear from you! Please feel free to email me at pamela_addato@awesomeauthors.org and sign up at pamela-addato.awesomeauthors.org for freebies!

One last thing: I'd love to hear your thoughts on the book. Please leave a review on Amazon or Goodreads because I just love reading your comments and getting to know YOU!

Whether that review is good or bad, I'd still love to hear it!

Can't wait to hear from you!

Pamela R. D'Addato

About the Author

Pamela D'Addato is a young author who attends college, pursuing a degree for Elementary Education and English literature. At a young age, she started writing and has loved it continuously while growing up. She is a loving sister and acknowledges her parents for encouraging her success.

Made in the USA
Middletown, DE
26 August 2018